# "Ashley, does he have to kill someone before you'll accept the fact that he has some damned difficult questions to answer?"

Jeremy's words were angry. "I've known you just a few days and lied to you out of concern for your safety and the safety of a good friend of mine—and you're ready to damn me to hell and back. Your precious Barky's probably been lying to you for years!"

She didn't want to hear the truth in his words. "You lied to me because you believe in MacGregor Stevens just as blindly as I believe in Bartholomew Wakefield. And who the hell says Stevens hasn't been deceiving you for years?"

The anger went out of Jeremy—Ashley could see the muscles in his face relax and his eyes warm with honesty and sympathy. Now, unexpectedly, she wished the anger had stayed. She didn't want him to care. She didn't want his pity. He was getting too close.

# Acknowledgments

My deepest appreciation goes to the following people:

Kati Bocsi and her family and friends, and Robert Nemeth of the *Worcester Telegram,* who helped bring to life for me the fascinating culture and history of their native Hungary.

Arthur Gudikunst, Ph.D., of Babson College, and Jeff Martin, who know about money.

Pat Fiorelli of the New England Aquarium, who knows about dolphin and whale strandings and who permitted me to use the aquarium's library.

Judy Sullivan and John Vance, who know about planes and lots of other things.

Joseph Guccione, who knows how to jump out of planes and has actually done it.

My writer friends: Linda Barlow, Elaine Raco Chase, Mary Curtis, Leslie Davis Guccione, Nancy Herman, Nancy Martin, M. J. Territo.

Denise Marcil, my agent, and Kate Duffy, my editor, for their enthusiasm, faith, patience and know-how.

And, of course, always, Joe Jewell, my husband and Kate, our daughter…for everything.

# CARLA NEGGERS

## CLAIM THE CROWN

**MIRA BOOKS**

**MIRA**

ISBN 1-55166-266-3

CLAIM THE CROWN

Copyright © 1987 by Carla Neggers.

All rights reserved. Except for use in any review, the reproduction or
utilization of this work in whole or in part in any form by any electronic,
mechanical or other means, now known or hereafter invented, including
xerography, photocopying and recording, or in any information storage or
retrieval system, is forbidden without the written permission of the publisher,
MIRA Books, 225 Duncan Mill Road, Don Mills, Ontario, Canada M3B 3K9.

All characters in this book have no existence outside the imagination of the
author and have no relation whatsoever to anyone bearing the same name
or names. They are not even distantly inspired by any individual known or
unknown to the author, and all incidents are pure invention.

MIRA and the star colophon are trademarks of MIRA Books.

**Printed in U.S.A.**

To my brothers: Jacob, Mark, Jeffrey
To my sisters: Bonnie, Hilda, Gretchen
And to our parents, Leo and Florine,
who chased the bats for us when we were little.

# PROLOGUE

*Budapest, 1956*

The young American covered her mouth as she hurried past another pile of smoldering rubble. Her turquoise eyes, usually so clear and alert, were watery, stinging from the acrid smoke, and her lungs burned. She wanted desperately to run, to be gone. But she restricted her pace to a brisk walk. She couldn't call attention to herself now. She couldn't panic.

She focused her thoughts on the people huddled in the shadowed buildings around her. Most of them wouldn't be leaving, not tonight, not ever, but they had survived centuries of this. She wondered how. Why didn't they just give up? Only eleven years ago, in the last gasps of World War II, the Germans and the Russians had waged a bloody confrontation with Budapest as the battlefield. Most of the old city on the Danube had been reduced to ruins. The Germans had left; the Russians stayed.

Now once again, here were the tanks, the shelling, the destruction, the death.

And yet as she moved through the gray, shattered streets, she, a stranger, could sense the underlying tenacity of the people. *Magyars*, the Hungarians call themselves. Over the centuries, they had outlasted the Mongols, the Turks, the Austrians. Now they would outlast the Russians.

Down a quiet, narrow alley, she found the tiny stone church. It was cold inside, and dark. She kept her hood pulled over her auburn curls. Old men and women hunched their shoulders, praying. Wide-eyed, children looked up at the echo of her footsteps.

She remembered the woman she had seen in the park, not a week ago, crying as she rushed her two small children past the bloated corpses hanging from the trees. The men had been lynched, their bodies left to rot, a testament to the depth of anger of the Hungarian people. They had been members of the hated state secret police, the Államvédelmi Hivatal, known simply, always with a shudder, as the ÁVH. Through the ÁVH, the Soviet Union and its hard-line Stalinist allies in Hungary had carried out a decade of terror against the very people they claimed to have liberated. They were responsible for thousands of tortures, deportations, forced relocations, imprison- ments, executions. During their brief moment of power, when the revolution against the Russians looked as if it might succeed, some had seized the chance to wreak vengeance against the murderers of the ÁVH.

*"Szemét gyilkosok,"* the woman in the park had said. Filthy murderers. Was she speaking of the ÁVH men rotting in the sun? Or the lynch mob? Perhaps it didn't matter. There was pain in her gaunt face, and she tried to cover the eyes of her children.

The fat priest came forward in the stillness of the church. He spoke little English, and he was arrogant. He didn't like the auburn-haired, troublesome American. She didn't like him. She'd met him during her

first days in Budapest, when the ancient city—the
Paris of the East—was filled with hope and energy,
and Hungarians still believed they could oust the Soviets from their country.

How far they'd all plunged in just two weeks!

What had begun spontaneously—without any real
plan, without any real leaders—was ending in tragedy, violence and broken dreams. Thousands had
died, and now many thousands were being arrested
and tens of thousands were fleeing their homeland. It
was all so pathetically clear now. There would be no
help from the West. There would be no formation of a
multiparty coalition government that would lead
Hungary into the future. No withdrawal of Hungary
from the Warsaw Pact. No declaration of Hungarian
neutrality.

Hungary was back in the Soviet bloc: a satellite.

Lithe and unconventionally beautiful, the American
smiled nervously at the red-faced priest, and suddenly she had to choke back her guilt, for she knew he
had been right about her, after all. He had told the others she was silly and dangerous, and she was. She had
come to Budapest as a lark.

Now she was in danger of losing everything.

Dipping into the pocket of her grimy cashmere coat,
she withdrew the tiny replica of an ornate gold crown.
She didn't know what kind of crown it was, or what it
meant, only that she had been told not to lose it. "It's
your path to freedom...." That had sounded so melodramatic.

She handed the crown to the priest, and spoke in a
whisper. "I wish to see *orült szerzetes.*" The mad monk.
She had fancied him as a latter-day Scarlet Pimpernel,

a romantic hero. Oh, Lord, how naive could she have been!

The priest nodded reluctantly toward the confessional. She mumbled her thanks and slipped behind the faded velvet curtain.

She felt weak. Slowly she knelt.

The screen slid back. Behind it, she could only see shadows. But he was there. She felt his presence.

A voice said in quiet, careful English, "You shouldn't have come."

"I had to."

She hated the quaver in her voice. She had been afraid—*was* afraid, now—but exhilarated, too. She thrived on challenge, adventure, excitement. Having babies, redecorating houses, devoting herself to the right charities, the right friends, the right man—that was all right for other women, but not for her. *This* was for her.

Licking her lips, she rushed on. "They said you won't be coming with us. It's not true, is it?"

There was no hesitation. "Yes. It's true."

"But you have to come! If you stay here you'll be killed!"

"I must stay."

Her heart pounded and she began to shiver uncontrollably, her hands twisting together in a mockery of prayer. She stared through the screen and tried to distinguish the outline of his face among the shadows.

"You must be brave," he said. She could feel his warm smile. "One day, perhaps."

And that was all.

Unable to speak, she watched the screen slide shut. There was fear in her eyes, she knew. And no hope.

# ONE

With a flagrant disregard for the sweltering heat, Ashley Wakefield dashed down the six steps of her regal brick building on the flats of Beacon Hill. She had shut her cream-colored door with a firm pull and now moved quickly, her two-inch heels clicking on the brick sidewalk. There had been a time when anything more glamorous than a pair of old sneakers had defeated her. But that had changed. So much had.

She fished her keys from an outer pocket of her Hermes leather handbag, singled out the one she wanted, and stuck it in the lock of the maroon Jaguar XJS parked unceremoniously on the curb. She paid dearly for space in a parking garage—more than what her rent used to be—but if she found a spot on lower Chestnut Street, she grabbed it. She didn't worry about car thieves. If someone stole the Jag, she'd buy another. It was only a car.

As she bent slightly to open the door, a few strands of her long, very dark hair loosened from her French twist, her only concession to the sticky weather, and dropped into her face. She brushed them impatiently away.

To her left, just beyond the hood of the car, there was a clicking noise. Then, "Got it!"

She looked around and sighed. Him again. The

skinny photographer with the high-water jeans. He'd been wearing the same outfit when she'd first encountered him in Newport a few weeks ago. One of the infuriating paparazzi following the Newport set, he'd popped out from nowhere and snapped a picture of her in a batik sarong skirt and bandeau. She'd decided it was just one of those unfortunate things and promptly forgotten the incident.

Then, a week later, he'd turned up at a gala event at Tanglewood in the Berkshires and, she supposed, got any number of shots of her in an elegant, understated Bill Blass evening gown. She'd wondered if it were just a coincidence, but somehow doubted that.

The following week he was there, in New York, when she headed into the gargantuan building on Central Park South where she had a pied-à-terre, and he'd caught her laden with bags and boxes from Bergdorf Goodman. It was obviously no damned coincidence. But as she rarely shopped, it was as if he were photographing someone else. Was *she* that slender blue-eyed woman in the white sundress?

It was now clear she was a special target for him. As they went into the dog days of August, he'd turned up at Touchstone Communications, the Boston consulting firm of which Ashley was founder and president. He hadn't ventured inside. He'd merely lurked in the main lobby of the building until she'd emerged with one of the firm's more famous clients. And then he'd pounced, clicking off a half dozen shots while Ashley had fumed.

She did *not* like having her picture taken.

Now he was on her doorstep. She supposed she wouldn't get much sympathy from her friends: they'd warned her about being so damned egalitarian and having her name, address and phone number listed in the Boston white pages. You're rich, they told her. You have to *act* rich.

But that wasn't Ashley's style.

The little worm was grinning at her. "Next time you could smile, you know."

She opened the car door wide. Dressed in a raw silk suit and a tissue linen shell, she looked the model female executive—except for her eyes, which were too large and too bright and too vivid a shade of blue. Her face had strong angular features, and she was slim through the hips, and at five six, not tall. People said she had a striking personality: once met, she wasn't easily forgotten.

"Next time," she said, "I could smash your camera over your head."

"I could write that down."

"Go ahead." Since his photographs of her had yet to appear in any periodical she knew of, she had decided he was little more than a desperate pest, looking for his first big break. Well, it wouldn't be her.

He shifted his weight onto one leg. "Quite the ice princess, huh?"

"I'm not a princess, Mr.—" She wished she could get his name.

But he didn't introduce himself. "Then what are you? You know, you had a photographer from the *Post* believing you discovered treasure on a sunken Spanish galleon."

So he knew about that. Ashley was surprised. That had been one of her many indiscretions, long regretted, but preferable to the truth. People always wanted to know where she came from. What *difference* did it make? "I'm just a hardworking woman."

"Yeah. Right."

She climbed into the car, tucked her loose hairs back into her twist and turned the key in the ignition. The photographer patted the hood. "Don't drive too fast," he said.

It was her pleasure to screech out into Chestnut Street and watch him scamper back onto the sidewalk, out of her way.

After Ashley Wakefiled buzzed off in her sporty Jaguar, Rob Gazelle walked on back to his hotel at Copley Place, one of the new high-class urban malls sprouting up in city after city. He immediately called Sybil Morgenstern. It was almost six o'clock on a sweaty Tuesday, but he knew Sybil would be in her sleek Madison Avenue office, puffing away on one of the skinny brown cigarettes she smoked by the dozen. Rob never touched the things. Sybil was the editor in chief of *You* magazine, and scores of Rob's ill-gotten photographs had graced her covers. It was a glossy national weekly that catered to the public's insatiable curiosity about celebrities. No one topped Sybil for being able to ferret out the latest juicy tidbits about the rich and the famous, but she wasn't satisfied with stopping there.

Sybil Morgenstern had to *create* celebrities.

She answered the phone herself. Rob stretched out on his bed. "Hey, Syb, how you doing?"

"What is it, Gazelle?"

No small talk for Sybil. She had a loud, demanding voice and a cutting wit, and as far as Rob knew, he was the only one who ever got away with calling her Syb. That was because he was the best in the business.

But when he could no longer produce, she'd squash him like the cockroach she kept telling him he was.

Going after Ashley Wakefield had been Sybil's idea.

"I've got some new shots of our mystery lady."

"Any info?"

"Getting there."

Sybil hissed with impatience. "For Christ's sake, Rob, how long am I going to have to wait? All I need is *one* goddamned thing I can use to pin her down."

"She's a stunner, Syb."

"I *know* that."

"But she's skittish. She doesn't like having her picture taken. If we move too fast, we'll lose her."

"Shit."

"Trust me, Syb. Look, next Saturday she's going to be at the opening of this new wing at the New England Oceanographic Institute. She's introducing the governor, and fat asses from all over New England are going to be there. I know fish aren't your thing, Syb, but this place is supposed to have the biggest exhibit tank in the world and all our Ashley's fish buddies ought to be there. I should be able to get something. Can you wrangle me a press pass?"

Sybil didn't even hesitate. "Done."


Ashley made Amherst, a college town and farming community in west central Massachusetts, in less than two hours. She drove along the back roads she knew so well to the Wakefield Farm, which occupied a hundred acres in the fertile Connecticut River Valley. In spite of soaring land values in the area, it was still a working farm, producing vegetables for market, a few eggs, lambs, wool, just getting by, as it always had, as far back as she could remember.

The farmhouse itself was old, white with red shutters, but not a classic antique. Giant maple trees shaded the front yard, which needed mowing. Close to the side of the house was a small red shed, and beyond it a kitchen garden and a dozen fruit trees. The land rose gently behind the house, where there were a red barn, a chicken coop, pigpen, sheep pen and, farther up, fields and woods.

Ashley parked her Jaguar in the horseshoe-shaped dirt driveway, behind the battered yellow pickup her uncle had driven for years. It was one of two trucks he'd owned since coming to the farm thirty years ago. The first he had driven up from Tennessee, with his infant niece and nephew strapped into the front seat beside him, now his to raise. His name was Bartholomew Wakefield, but Ashley and her twin brother, David, had found Uncle Bartholomew an impossibility, and they'd always called him Barky. Now everyone did, except bill collectors and the IRS.

The grass was yellowing in the late summer sun, and the air was still and filled with the smells of the farm. Vegetables were piled on and around the flat wooden trailer that stood on the edge of the driveway. People could just stop and serve themselves, weighing their produce on the old rusted scale, leaving their money in the three-pound Maxwell House coffee can.

With her high heels sinking slightly in the soft grass, Ashley walked up behind the shed, where Barky was hanging threadbare sheets on his handmade clothesline. She pulled off her jacket and hung it by one finger over her shoulder. She should have changed, she thought. Her businesslike, urban clothes just seemed to emphasize the differences between them, Barky the farmer, Ashley the...the what? Executive, jet setter, city girl, philanthropist? Sometimes she didn't know.

"Hi, Barky."

He shook out a sheet. She could remember hanging that very same sheet back when she was a teenager. She didn't know why it hadn't fallen apart by now, given her uncle's penchant for hanging wash in any manner of weather. He didn't believe in clothes dryers.

Ashley herself owned Porthault linens and replaced them nearly every year. Barky had refused her discards, or even to let her buy him new ones. The old ones, he insisted, still had plenty of wear in them.

"Yaa, hello," he said in his distinctive accent. He had been born in Poland, son of a Polish woman, and emigrated to his father's native England before World War II, and then, after the war, to the United States. His accent reflected the different places he'd lived.

He snapped two clothespins onto the sheet and smoothed it out as it hung limp in the hot, still air. He didn't seem surprised to see his niece on a Tuesday afternoon—didn't, in fact, seem surprised to see her at all. She could come and go as she pleased, and that was fine with him. Tumultuous as her life might be, fraught with questions and complexities, the world of Bartholomew Wakefield never changed. He tended his gardens, his animals, his wood stoves, and life went on. He was a stump of a man, with a fringe of golden brown hair and warm golden brown eyes and weather-beaten skin. He had a long prominent nose that might have been ugly on anyone else, but on him was a source of strength and character in his face. As always, he wore baggy denim work pants, a dark-colored BVD T-shirt—today's was navy blue—and sneakers. He had on a Red Sox cap.

"Is David around?" Ashley asked. "I need to talk to you guys."

"He's making iced tea."

"Where's his Rover?"

Barky nodded toward the back of the barn, where the fifteen-year-old Land Rover was parked with its hood up. Although he was nearly as rich as his twin sister and also owned a black Ferrari, David Wakefield was still partial to, and identified by, the Land Rover he'd bought to commute to the University of Massachusetts as a forestry student.

Ashley helped Barky with the last of the sheets and pillowcases, and they walked down to the house together. The kitchen was big and airy, its floor worn linoleum, its shelves open and simple, its appliances outdated but functional. Everything was spotless. There was a glass of black-eyed Susans on the middle of the big pine table, across from the cold wood cook stove.

David gave his sister a lopsided grin. "Hey, Ash, just in time for some burgers and iced tea. Hungry?"

"Sure. Why not?"

At twenty-nine, her brother was strong and sinewy with the tanned, healthy good looks of a man who spent most of his day outdoors. He had deep blue eyes, much darker than Ashley's, but his hair was exactly the same dark shade as hers. He was working sporadically on his master's in forestry, and he had no steady job—not that he needed one. He helped out at the farm, helped out his buddies, helped out owners of small woodlots and farmers struggling to hang on to their land. Mostly, though, he liked physical work.

He had built a house high on a hill in a small town north of Amherst.

He poured three tall glasses of iced tea, and they all three—the last of the Wakefields—sat at the big pine table and drank up.

Finally, Ashley said, "I came by to let you both know that I've arranged to have the jewels brought here—to Boston, I mean. They should arrive via bonded courier tomorrow."

"What the hell for?" David demanded.

Barky said nothing.

Ashley shrugged, not looking at her brother or uncle. "I want to wear them."

"I thought you said they were gaudy."

There was a note of accusation in David's voice. She understood: four years ago, she *had* said the jewels in the safe-deposit box in the vaults of Piccard Cie in Geneva, Switzerland, were indeed gaudy. And they had agreed to leave them there, untouched, hidden. "I changed my mind."

"Ash, jeez."

She bit into an ice cube, feeling the sweat drip down the middle of her back. "It's just the tiara and the choker. The rest will remain in the vault. I...wanted something different to wear to the opening of the institute's new wing next Saturday." She forced herself to brighten. "Why don't you two come?"

David pushed back his chair and stood up. "I'd have to wear a tux."

"Barky?"

"It's not a good time to leave the farm."

It never was, Ashley thought. He had come to Boston, once, to see her duplex overlooking Charles River and her offices on the Boston waterfront. He had never been to the New England Oceanographic Institute, although it consumed her every bit as much as her work. She was a director, trustee and major donor. But she had quit expecting her uncle would take an interest in that part of her life. When she was on the farm, they generally discussed canning and freezing and weather and animals—never the jewels, the money, the questions that had gone unanswered for four years. He was getting old now, into his sixties. Was that why she had taken the radical step of deciding to wear the tiara and the choker? Was she afraid he would die before he had given them answers? She wasn't sure. She had awakened one morning, at a friend's beach house on Cape Cod, and decided she had to do something. She couldn't go on like this, not knowing, not even *trying* to know. She had never been good at maintaining the status quo. Now she desperately wanted to know: what would happen if she wore the jewels in public, just for one night?

Probably nothing, she'd told herself again and again. But she had to find out.

She looked at her uncle as he downed half his tea in a single swallow. "I won't wear them," she said, "if you don't want me to."

David leaned against the cold wood stove and, too, watched their uncle intently. "Yeah, Barky. Now's the time to come clean."

But Barky got up and rotated his thick shoulders a bit, stretching, and announced he had to slop the pigs. When he reached the screen door, he pulled off his baseball cap, put it on again and turned to the niece and nephew he had raised from infancy. His expres-

sion was gentle, but there was an intensity to his gaze
Ashley had rarely seen in him. "I have faith in you,"
he said. "Now have faith in yourselves."

# TWO

The tiara and chocker, two stunning pieces of diamonds and pearls, arrived from Switzerland late the following afternoon, and Ashley promptly shoved the black velvet-bound cases into her lingerie drawer, under her silk camisoles and tap pants. The prospect of her wearing them in public hadn't sufficiently unnerved her uncle. She didn't know why she'd expected it would. In more than four years, he'd calmly maintained he knew nothing whatever about the jewels in the Swiss vault, the money, any of it.

Except Ashley and David had never believed him. They had decided that somewhere in his deep dark past, in the years before he'd been saddled with two infants, Bartholomew Wakefield must have been a jewel thief. Or known a jewel thief. Or *something*.

How else could his niece and nephew come into an anonymous fortune in jewels and cash?

But he wouldn't talk, wouldn't take a penny from them, wouldn't even *look* guilty. And that was strange. It just didn't add up.

It was also something she and David were trying to accept. As their long-suffering attorney had told them, "Ashley, David, whoever made you both millionaires went to a great deal of trouble to remain anonymous to you. Perhaps that's something you should respect."

Perhaps. But Ashley didn't really think so.

On Labor Day weekend, Ashley got the news that some hundred white-sided dolphins had stranded themselves on the tidal flats of Cape Cod Bay. An experienced and avid pilot, she bowed out of a yacht party on Cape May and flew her Cessna 172 down to Wellfleet. Once there, she bummed a ride to the beach with a couple of reporters. The New England Oceanographic Institute was coordinating the rescue efforts. An institute volunteer since college, Ashley had helped out at countless strandings, but the mystery and the tragedy of the scene never ceased to affect her.

With a jolt, she saw her skinny photographer. He had on an orange flight suit and pretended to be taking pictures of the dolphins, but Ashley knew what he was after. Her. She ignored him. In overalls and a sweatshirt, she checked in with the director of the institute's marine mammal stranding program, who was in charge on the beach, and was asked to instruct volunteers on how best to help the stranded mammals.

The New England Oceanographic Institute followed a policy of responding to any stranding in a humanitarian manner. Teams of volunteers rescued, reoriented and returned to deep water those animals they believed could survive. They brought back to the institute's outdoor tanks those they could reasonably be assured of restoring to good health, usually the smaller, younger animals. Those without hope they euthanized on the beach and studied carefully for any clues as to how and why they had ended up there.

Through the morning and afternoon, Ashley instructed volunteers, rescued dolphins and did whatever she was told to do. In the midst of a stranding, the director of the institute's marine mammal stranding program was in charge, and she tolerated no arguing, bickering or interference—even from million-dollar benefactresses.

By evening, Ashley was exhausted, muddy and bedraggled, a sorry sight for her sleazy photographer's camera. She didn't care. The institute team had decided to spend the night on the Cape, but Ashley had to get to New York for a charity fashion show the following afternoon. She had learned that if she took an interest in other people's favorite charities, they were more inclined to take an interest in hers.

Right now, all she wanted were a bath, food and rest.

Tired as she was, she performed the preflight walk-around check of the Cessna herself, refusing to delegate that responsibility to anyone, not even the most trusted of mechanics. It was her plane; she was the pilot. She was the one who'd end up in the drink if she screwed up.

In her muddy gum shoes, drenched overalls and messy braid, she ducked under the left wing.

Her nemesis photographer jumped out from behind another plane and clicked off a shot. "Hey, Girl Wonder, smile."

She groaned. "Oh, *shit.*"

And the camera clicked again.

He wouldn't leave, and she was too exhausted to argue. As she continued with her visual inspection of her plane, she could hear him jumping around, switching angles, snapping pictures. It was strange, she thought, that adept as she was at handling the media for her clients, and helping them learn the art of professional communications, she was painfully awkward at dealing with the media when *she* was the focus of attention. For four years, she had been very, very good at eluding the press. It was easier that way. Safer. She wouldn't have to answer questions to which she had no answers.

She sighed. Whoever he was, her skinny photographer had quite a spread on her now. In a bathing suit at Newport, an evening gown in the Berkshires, a sundress in New York, a business suit in Boston. Now in drenched overalls on the Cape. But who would be interested in pictures of a dolphin-rescuing Boston businesswoman?

Everyone, she thought, if they found out she was also a mystery heiress.

Devoted to oceanographic research, conservation and education, the prestigious New England Oceanographic Institute occupied an entire wharf on the Boston waterfront. The institute flag—a deep blue graphic of a dolphin against a vibrant orange background—billowed above the new wing, whose starkly graceful modern lines complemented the classic style of the old building. Out front was a wide cobblestone-and-brick plaza, with aquatic sculptures, fountains and benches. The institute's research ships were docked to the side, and the outdoor tanks were in the rear.

Inside the new wing, indirect lighting gave the feeling of being underwater, a part of the oceanic environment recreated for public exhibition. A stairless spiral encircled the giant fish tank, where predators swam among prey, content because they were fed regularly from the outside.

Lillian Parker, longtime newswoman and producer of a network news feature program, sipped a glass of champagne. She was impressed. She liked the sense of the place. And it was one hell of an accomplishment for Ashley Wakefield, whom everyone knew had been the impetus for the project.

With her practiced eye, Lillian could tell the institute people, with their beards and lack of makeup and unselfconscious style of dressing, from the guests, all so stylish and polished and very aware of themselves and the impact they were having—or weren't. She noted two United States senators, the mayor of Boston, prominent New Englanders, media people who were there as celebrities, not journalists.

Lillian herself had not been on the official guest list. A friend of hers, an anchorman for one of the Boston stations, was, and she'd seduced his invitation from him, even getting him to promise he wouldn't ask her why she had suddenly taken an interest in fish.

Of course she hadn't. It was Ashley Wakefield who interested her, whose name in a brief article announcing the opening of the wing in the *New York Times* had sent Lillian for her brandy decanter.

But Ashley Wakefield hadn't yet made her entrance, and Lillian contented herself with champagne and small talk. She knew the two senators, of course. They made sure they came over and said hello. At fifty-two, Lillian Parker was one of the most successful women in broadcasting in the nation, a trailblazer. With her deep auburn hair and cool turquoise eyes, she was attractive, although she'd never given a damn about her looks. She smoked too much, drank too much, and she was bored to distraction when her friends started talking about fanny tucks and facelifts. She was a journalist. A newshound. She always had been.

It was her greatest virtue, she thought, and her worst flaw.

There was a hushed silence. Lillian polished off her champagne and looked toward the temporary podium, erected in front of a beautiful exhibit of seashells. She expected to see the familiar figure of the governor of the Commonwealth of Massachusetts.

Instead her gaze fell on the slender, dazzling figure of a dark-haired woman in a simple black evening gown that had probably cost upward of ten thousand dollars, and glittering jewels. Her eyes were a vibrant, startling blue, and her smile left people breathless. Lillian was no exception. She found herself spellbound as she moved through the crowd toward the podium.

Ashley Wakefield. She could be no one else.

The notes on her in the program were wholly inadequate. She was a trustee and director of the institute, a longtime volunteer who had "adopted" a moray eel as a sophomore in college and now was publisher of the highly respected *Currents*, the institute's bimonthly magazine, as well as president of her own private firm. There was nothing about *her*. Her family, her friends, her background, her love life. Those were the details Lillian Parker craved.

Ashley Wakefield was stepping up to the podium now. Some of the crowd had recovered enough from the entrance of this outrageous beauty to resume whispered conversations, but Lillian was still breathless, standing just yards from the enigmatic woman who, it was said, had donated a million dollars to the institute.

"Good evening," Ashley said into the microphone. "I'm glad you all came."

But Lillian Parker didn't hear what else Ashley had

to say. The newswoman who had interviewed heads
of state and covered the major stories of the past three
decades had begun to shake uncontrollably. Her
knuckles turned white on the stem of the champagne
glass. Her heart pounded. She couldn't breathe.

Around her neck, Ashley wore a choker of diamonds and pearls. On her head, woven into her hair, a
matching tiara. In the center of the choker was a large
deep red stone. A "pigeon's blood" ruby, perfect.

In an agonized gasp, the air expelled from Lillian's
lungs. "Oh, Christ in heaven. Oh, Christ *Almighty*."

Lillian Parker managed to stagger out of the
crowded exhibit center before she collapsed.

Rob Gazelle used up three rolls of film at the gala
opening. Nearly every shot had Ashley Wakefield in
it, and he'd even caught her smiling, many times.
Dancing, laughing, toasting with champagne, showing off her fish, she dazzled everyone.

And yet as he focused shot after shot, he perceived
a melancholy about her, too, that he hoped would
come out on film. He couldn't put his finger on it: it
was as if, in a way, tonight was an end for her, a completion, and she was putting her all into looking
happy and excited, when what she was was a little bit
sad and a whole lot uncertain—as if she didn't know
what tomorrow would bring.

Rob grinned. *He* knew what tomorrow would bring
to pretty Ashley Wakefield: Sybil Morgenstern. And
this time, he thought, ol' Syb would not be denied.

# THREE

On Monday morning, Ashley and Caroline Kent, vice president of Touchstone Communications, huddled in Ashley's office overlooking Boston Harbor. They were going over a redesigned internal communications system for a corporate client. The work was decidedly dull. Ashley had slung her gray silk shantung jacket over the back of her leather chair and kicked off her Charles Jourdan open-toed pumps. Her hair was up, her face highlighted with soft-hued cosmetics, and she was feeling very brisk and businesslike...and strangely impatient. With the opening done with, the jewels worn and safely back in her lingerie drawer, there seemed to be nothing else to look forward to. No excitement, no adventure. She made a living out of telling people how to talk to other people. This morning she was sick of it.

"Ash?" Caroline looked at her with concern. Always impeccably dressed, Caroline was big boned, yet lean, and had close-cropped hair and glowing ebony skin. She had joined the company six months after its founding, and she was hard-nosed and brilliant and a good friend—despite her oft-stated opinion that fish were best served broiled with butter and a touch of lemon. "You okay?"

"Just bored, I guess." Ashley smiled. "Maybe I

should take up a new hobby. Ballooning or jumping off cliffs or skydiving—something with a little risk in it."

Caroline grunted. "*I* think you're just disappointed nobody took you by the throat Saturday night and said, 'Those're my jewels, honey.'"

"I don't know. No—maybe."

"You thought something would happen and nothing did."

Ashley shrugged. "I suppose I should be grateful."

"But gratitude won't get you answers, will it?"

Answers. For the past four years, Ashley had talked herself into believing there never would be any answers—just questions, dozens of them, locked up inside her, not even asked. Caroline Kent was one of the handful of people who knew the truth about how the Wakefield twins had suddenly and mysteriously become millionaires at age twenty-five. The others were Barky and Nick Duval, the executive director of the institute, and Evan Parrington, the Park Avenue lawyer who, just over four years ago, had driven out to the farm and informed them they were the beneficiaries of a Liechtenstein trust.

"I don't need answers," Ashley said, upper lip stiff.

Caroline snorted. "Horseshit."

"I'm going to return the jewels to Switzerland."

"Why not have them appraised by some expert? Maybe they're famous or something. Then—"

"I can't do that."

"Why the hell not?"

"What if Barky's a jewel thief?"

"For Christ's sake, the old guy hasn't taken a damned cent from you. He won't even let you buy new linoleum for his kitchen!"

"But that doesn't mean—"

"If he were a jewel thief, Ash, he'd *act* like a jewel thief. He wouldn't be out in the country slopping pigs and chopping wood."

Ashley sighed. It was a point she'd considered a thousand times over the years. "Maybe my parents were."

"They're dead, Ash. You never even knew them."

"But maybe Barky's protecting them."

"You going to keep asking yourself questions, or are you going to get off your ass and get some answers?"

Patti Morgan, Ashley's indispensable twenty-year-old secretary, poked her head into the sleek bone-and-mauve office. "A Sybil Morgenstern on the line for you, Ashley. Says she's editor in chief of *You* magazine and wants to talk to you. Won't take no for an answer."

"Thanks, Patti. I'll take the call."

Caroline looked at Ashley in consternation. "You know what you're getting yourself into?"

Ashley shrugged. "Not really. But I have a feeling I'll find out." She pressed the flashing button on her phone and said, "Ashley Wakefield."

"Ahh...the elusive mystery lady of Boston." The voice was throaty, the tone casual. "Sybil Morgenstern here. We'd like to do your story, Ashley."

"I'm flattered, but I'm afraid I don't give personal interviews."

"Don't you? Well, we can always run what we have and let the chips fall where they may."

Ashley glanced at Caroline, who shook her head in commiseration. She had always supported Ashley's decision to keep the tantalizing story of her sudden wealth to herself—although not to the point of letting it interfere with her romantic life, which it did. For Ashley, men tended to fall into two categories: those she might consider telling the truth about herself, and those she would never consider telling the truth about herself. She saw both kinds, but "might" had never translated itself into action. There had been no middle-of-the-night confessions about Liechtenstein trusts, mysterious jewels, farmer uncles, weekends spent making maple syrup and planting peas and chasing chickens. It was impossible to get close to a man and still remain an enigma, a woman who had seemingly sprung full-grown at age twenty-five from the head of Zeus.

Maybe she was tired of being mysterious.

"We have some damned intriguing photographs of you, Ashley," Sybil Morgenstern went on. "Partying in Newport and the Berkshires, shopping in New York, playing female exec in Boston, rescuing dolphins on the Cape, stomping around under your plane—"

"It's called 'preflighting,'" Ashley interrupted. "It's the pilot's manual and visual check of the aircraft before—"

"Whatever."

Ashley sighed. She was in a daze. "So the skinny photographer with the jeans works for you."

"He works for himself. Best damned paparazzo in town—but a germ. Rob Gazelle. He also has the most stunning shots of you the other night at the New England Oceanographic Institute. The dress was a Givenchy, wasn't it? Maybe fifteen grand? And the jewels. Christ, they're something."

"Damn."

"Mmm. We can just run the photos, Ashley. They'll make a hell of a spread. But look." Her tone changed, becoming conspiratorial, maternal, affectionate. "Look, Ashley, we don't want to do a hatchet job on you. We just want to know who you are."

"I'm founder and president of Touchstone Communications, publisher of *Currents*, a director and trustee for the New England Oceanographic Institute. That's me, Ms. Morgenstern. Thanks for your interest—"

"It's not enough and you know it."

"I'm afraid it'll have to be."

"Rob did some digging. We know all about your rustic roots, Ashley. The farm, the pigs, the cows."

Ashley winced as if in pain. "We never had cows."

"No matter. That little tidbit will go into our piece, and you know us: we'll draw our own conclusions. I should think you'd want to tell the story yourself."

Licking her lips, Ashley wondered what would happen if the tiara and the choker were plastered all across the country in a national magazine. But there seemed nothing at all she could do about it. And maybe, she thought, she didn't *want* to do anything.

"I'll agree to an interview," she said abruptly, "but on one condition."

"No conditions."

"Then no interview. All I want is for you to promise to leave my family out of this. I respect their privacy. If you don't agree, you can just go with what you have."

Sybil was silent for a moment. "All right. Your condition is accepted. I'll have my reporter in your office in the morning."

When Ashley hung up, Caroline looked at her and

groaned. "Good Lord, Ashley, I hope to hell you know what you're doing."

Ashley exhaled, her shoulders sagging. "So do I, Caroline. So do I."

"Are you going to warn the folks at home?"

"Not on your life."


Late Monday morning, Lillian Parker turned in to the horseshoe-shaped driveway of the Wakefield farm and parked behind a disreputable-looking Land Rover. It was a gorgeous day: high blue sky, utterly cloudless and crisp. Summer was finally over.

The farm was everything she had imagined.

By last night, she had recovered enough from the shock of seeing Ashley Wakefield to remember that Rob Gazelle owed her a favor, and to work up the courage to call him. He hadn't wanted to tell her anything: he was on Sybil Morgenstern's payroll. But he was persuaded, and finally he told her what she wanted to know.

There was an uncle, he'd said, and a brother. Bartholomew and David. And there was a farm in Amherst, Massachusetts.

"You screw up this story for me," Rob warned, "and I'll haunt you forever."

"You'll have to stand in line, Rob."

"What's your interest?"

"Curiosity."

As she climbed out of her Cadillac, she was greeted by the sounds of pigs and sheep. The air smelled fresh and clean. She just wanted to stand there, breathing.

There seemed to be no one about. Her heart pounding, Lillian walked over to a trailer at the exit of the driveway, where pumpkins, winter squash, gourds,

Brussels sprouts and Indian corn were piled high. She chose a small pumpkin and slipped two quarters into the coffee can with the price list pasted on it.

This must have been a nice place to have grown up, she thought. And felt better for having come.

Up the slope rising behind the house, a stocky man came out of the barn. His shoulders were stooped slightly against the weight of two buckets, and he wore baggy jeans and a blue plaid flannel shirt. On his head was a Red Sox cap. His face was lost in the shadows, but Lillian watched him. She couldn't breathe. Her fingers turned white as they clutched the pumpkin.

*"You should hate him."*

*"I can't!"*

*"He betrayed us. He betrayed even you."*

*"I don't believe it. I won't!"*

*"He's a murderer and a traitor."*

*"No!"*

A screen door banged. Startled, Lillian dropped the pumpkin. It didn't break open, but she could feel the tears welling in her eyes, and she was suddenly furious with herself for having come. She stooped to pick up the pumpkin.

"Hi, there," a friendly male voice said. "Can I help you with anything?"

Lillian rose, attempting to smile despite her embarrassment, fury and pain.

Then she froze. "Oh, God."

"Huh? Something wrong?"

She reeled with the shock of seeing him. Again she dropped the pumpkin. This time he picked it up, handing it to her, his dark blue eyes filled with concern. "You okay? Hey—aren't you Lillian Parker?"

"Yes, I—" She held the pumpkin close to her chest. For her excursion to the country, she had worn slacks and a cotton sweater, casual attire, but she felt so formal, so stiff, so afraid. She pushed absently at her windblown hair. "Yes, I am."

His grin was endearingly lopsided. "You sure you're okay?"

"Yes, I'm fine. I'm sorry. I... Hunger, I guess."

"Want something to eat?"

"No, no, that's all right."

"You sure?"

She nodded. He was a damned good-looking young man. Very tall and sinewy, with dark hair, eyebrows, eyes. He wore tight jeans and a navy blue chamois shirt.

"I'm surprised you recognized me," she said, hoping he would forget her ridiculous behavior. "I haven't been on camera in quite some time."

"Used to watch you every morning. My uncle's a big fan of yours—want to meet him?"

"No! No, thank you, I have to be going."

"Nice meeting you."

She managed a smile. "Nice meeting you, too."

"Name's David, by the way. David Wakefield."

"I'll remember that." Was there any chance of forgetting it, ever? "Thanks for the pumpkin."

The *You* reporter appeared in Ashley's office promptly at ten o'clock the following morning. She was fair skinned, attractive, smartly dressed, obviously tenacious and aggressive. Determined not to get too cozy, Ashley sat at her desk and offered the reporter the chair in front of her. Ashley had worn black for the occasion. Intimidating. But the reporter didn't look intimidated. In fact, as she arranged her tape recorder and flipped open her notepad and settled herself in for the millenium, she looked as if she'd eat Ashley alive, given the opportunity.

Ashley didn't intend to give her the opportunity.

"My name's Pat Oberlin." She smiled. "And you're Sybil's mystery lady."

"I'm Ashley Wakefield." She folded her hands on her desk and recited the instructions she'd given numerous clients when facing the press: "Keep smiling...don't criticize...don't be defensive...be clear and concise..." She could think of a dozen different clients who'd be snorting now with glee, seeing the shoe on the other foot.

The interview proceeded smoothly. Ashley told of her work at Touchstone, with the institute, impersonal things she didn't mind discussing.

Then Pat Oberlin asked about "romantic interests." Ashley said, "None at the moment." It was, she thought, the distressing truth.

"Do you consider yourself a jet setter?"

"No."

"But you lead an active social life?"

"I try to."

"I see." Oberlin switched tactics. "What about your childhood?"

"Very happy."

"You grew up on a farm?"

"Yes." How much more clear and concise could she be?

"Tell me about it. What was it like?"

"A mixture of hard work and fun."

"What about your family?"

"My parents died when my twin brother and I were

a few months old. Our uncle, my father's brother, raised us. And that's all I'm going to say about them. It's the condition for this interview, remember?"

"Right, right. So you went from the farm to Boston University, where you majored in communications. You were a scholarship student."

Ashley shifted in her chair: Pat Oberlin had definitely done her homework.

"Your first job was in the public relations department of a Boston management consulting group. According to former co-workers, you made *maybe* seventeen, eighteen thousand a year. You quit in 1982, and a few months later started up this outfit, revamped *Currents* with your own money into a slick, expensive magazine that still doesn't pay for itself, and, rumor has it, donated a sweet million to the New England Oceanographic Institute. You also started turning up at high-class parties all over New England and Manhattan, bought a condo here in Boston, land on Cape Cod, a co-op in New York. You took up flying, bought your own plane. You wear dresses that cost just about what you used to make in a year. So. As you can see, it just doesn't add up."

Ashley shrugged. "No, it doesn't."

"You're secretive about where you got your money. Why?"

"I was raised not to discuss such things in public." Which was a lot of nonsense. Barky would discuss money with anyone.

"You win the lottery?"

"No."

"Come on, Ashley. What do you think this interview's all about? People are going to want to know where you got your millions."

Ashley breathed heavily.

"Hey. Better to tell me right up front than have me speculate in print."

"I suppose you have a point. All right, but it's complicated—and not really very exciting. My brother and I are the beneficiaries of a Liechtenstein trust."

"What's that?"

Naturally she would ask. Ashley said, "It's complicated."

"I'm a smart person."

Pat Oberlin could find out what a Liechtenstein trust was if she put her mind to it—and Ashley had no doubt she would. Perhaps it was better this way, she thought. Perhaps, in a way, she had been gearing up for this moment for the past four years and, especially, for the past couple of months. She could have guessed Rob Gazelle would be at the opening Saturday night. She could have found out who he was if she'd really wanted to...needed to. But she hadn't. And there had to be a reason for that: she wanted the proverbial cat out of the bag.

*I think...* "Oh, hell."

"Just spit it out," Pat Oberlin suggested.

"A Liechtenstein trust is a device created by the Swiss banking system to ensure anonymity and used, most often, in cases presenting inheritance difficulties."

"Like what?"

"Annoying spouses, unpleasant children, that sort of thing. I'm not an expert. I'm just repeating what my attorney told me." Ashley put her hands in her lap so Oberlin couldn't see her twisting her fingers together. "Basically, the donor—the person setting up the trust—goes to the bank in person with the funds to be deposited, satisfies the bank the account won't infringe on any laws and signs a 'declaration of honorable intent.' This protects the bank."

Pat Oberlin rattled her pen in the crook between her thumb and forefinger but didn't interrupt.

"Then the donor assigns power of attorney to a group of Liechtenstein lawyers who will serve as the fund's trustees. They ensure the terms of the trust will be carried out precisely according to the wishes of the donor—and within the realm of the law. The beauty of a Liechtenstein trust is that this arrangement can continue even after the death of the donor."

"Now we're getting down to the grit," the *You* reporter said with a hopeful grin. "You mean your donor could be dead?"

"Theoretically, yes."

"*You don't know?*"

Shit, Ashley thought. "Let me finish. Together, the donor and the lawyers set up a portfolio management agreement, which gives the Swiss bank the authority to manage the funds in the trust. The donor may set up guidelines, but all actual buying and selling is performed by the bank."

"Who's your bank?"

"Piccard Cie in Geneva, Switzerland." There was no harm in telling Oberlin that much: no one at Piccard would discuss the terms of the trust with anyone but Ashley, David and their attorneys.

"Whoopee. Go on."

"In a Liechtenstein trust, the donor may dictate precisely when, to whom and how the trust funds will be distributed to the named beneficiaries. By law, the trustees must abide by the terms of the trust. They are permitted to tell the beneficiaries *only* what the donor has instructed them to tell, and nothing else."

Pat Oberlin leaned back in her chair and gave Ashley an astute look. "You're telling me this for a reason, aren't you?"

Ashley smiled coolly. "Because you asked."

"Right."

"Well, that's it. Basically, that's what a Liechtenstein trust is."

"Tell me about *your* Liechtenstein trust."

"Oh. Well, it's pretty straightforward. Piccard Cie retained the services of Parrington, Parrington and Smith, a Park Avenue law firm, and through a private investigator they located my brother and me shortly before our twenty-fifth birthday, when we were to be notified of the existence of the trust."

"Didn't they *know* where the hell you were?"

"Uh-uh."

"The bank didn't have your address?"

Piccard Cie only had the names, birth dates and foot and hand prints of the Wakefield twins, nothing else. But Ashley didn't think *You* magazine needed to know that. "It's a common occurrence," she said, guessing.

"How much money are we talking here?"

"A significant amount."

"Yeah, right."

In 1982, Ashley recalled, the principal of the trust was worth approximately thirty-four million U.S. dollars. According to the wishes of their particular donor, she and David were to receive annual payments, consisting of the investment income of the principal, beginning on their twenty-fifth birthday and continuing to them and their heirs in perpetuity. They would never have access to the principal itself, which would continue to be managed by Piccard Cie. Evan Parrington had said that was a clever arrangement, considering U.S. tax laws.

His figures had proven to be conservative, and had fluctuated over the years. But annual payments had never fallen below four million dollars. In general, they were higher.

More details, Ashley decided, that Pat Oberlin didn't need to know—although, certainly, she would want to.

"This is wild," the reporter said. "So who set this thing up?"

Ashley hesitated for a moment, choosing her words carefully. "You see, Ms. Oberlin, that's one of the beauties of the Liechtenstein trust—from the donor's point of view. He or she may remain anonymous to the beneficiaries. The trustees will abide by this."

"You're saying you don't know who made you and your brother millionaires." Pat Oberlin was obviously just barely containing her excitement.

Ashley smiled, also maintaining her composure. "I'm saying that information is between God and the Swiss banking system."

The reporter grinned broadly. "Fucking wow."

Ten minutes after the interview ended, a shaking Ashley Wakefield staggered into Caroline's cluttered, very functional office. "I think I'm going to throw up."

Caroline glanced up from her work. "That bad?"

"I must be out of my mind."

"Shit." With a heavy sigh, Caroline laid down her pen. "You told that reporter everything, didn't you?"

Ashley nodded grimly. "Just about."

"Oh, Ash."

"Not about the jewels...I didn't—well, she never even asked. If she had, I don't know. I'd probably have gone ahead and told her."

But Pat Oberlin hadn't questioned her about the tiara and choker. In addition to the hefty annual payments, the trust specified that Ashley and David were to be given access to a safe-deposit box at Piccard Cie. Two days after their twenty-fifth birthday, they'd flown to Geneva, found the bank on Georges-Favon Boulevard and presented themselves to their bank officer. He'd opened the box. In a private, secured room, they'd examined the contents: the tiara and choker, a diamond-and-emerald bracelet, a ring of one giant emerald surrounded by diamonds and an emerald necklace, each large perfect stone set in gold.

It had been an astounding day. And, in their shock, Ashley and David had agreed to leave the jewels in the vault. They were just too much for them to handle. They were more tangible than money. Someone had put them into the safe-deposit box, touched them the way they were now touching them. Had they been handled by human hands months ago? Years? Decades? They didn't even have a clue as to *when* the trust had been set up.

But looking at the jewels, feeling the coolness of the genuine stones, they had concluded that, despite all his protestations of ignorance, their uncle had to know more than he was admitting. Barky had insisted he knew nothing whatever about Liechtenstein trusts, certainly nothing about theirs, and that they should look to their own lives for clues, not his. But that seemed impossible. There was no one—*no one!*—who could or would leave them such an enormous amount of money in their circle of friends and acquaintances.

Barky had to be protecting someone, they'd decided on that warm day in Switzerland. Himself, their parents, a friend. Them. They had no idea. And obviously Barky didn't want them to get any ideas, and neither did the person who had set up the trust.

And so for four years, they had left well enough alone.

"Christ A'mighty, Ashley," Caroline muttered. "Feel better?"

"Actually—" Ashley paced across the cluttered office of her tireless partner in business. "Actually, I think I do. Maybe it's better this way."

"How? Yesterday you wouldn't tell a soul about your money. Today you've told the whole world. Don't you believe in *easing* into this kind of thing?"

Ashley stopped shaking and stood up straight, shoulders back. "I did ease into it. It's been four years, Caroline. I've been working up to today. And anyway, it's not all that interesting a story. Maybe we've been making too much of this anonymous trust thing and it really is no big goddamned deal. Maybe Pat Oberlin and Sybil Morgenstern will put their heads together and decide no one will give a hot damn how Ashley Wakefield got her money."

"Bull," Caroline said.

"Probably *You* will stick this story in the back pages with the hair tonics and sexy underwear. If not—" Ashley paused. "Well, I'll just cross that bridge when I come to it."

Caroline grunted dubiously. "If there is one. You might just find your ass bumping down the rapids, with nothing to grab on to."

# FOUR

On a bright, clear, gorgeous Friday morning, more than two weeks after her interview with *You*, Ashley walked up Charles Street and through the Common, joining scores of other Bostonians who had decided it was too damned nice a day to drive. There weren't that many pleasant days left. The weather had begun to cool noticeably, and even in Boston, the brightest colors of autumn were sparkling in the trees. Vibrant reds, iridescent oranges.

It was a difficult day to nurse a bad mood, and Ashley noticed the bounce in her step. She had bought a half dozen apricot-filled croissants for her and her Touchstone staff. Work had been proceeding with all too much haste and efficiency of late; they needed to relax a bit, make up an extra pot of coffee, consume some extra calories. It would be invigorating and perhaps forestall premature burnout.

"Life as you know it," Ashley mumbled to herself, "is beginning to return to normal."

She had finally immersed herself, once again, in her routines. Today she would work on her column for the winter issue of *Currents*, to be devoted entirely to new trends in marine archaeological research and exploration; meet a client for lunch; lead a staff meeting;

perform all the other varied duties the president of a small company was required, by default, to perform.

Wasn't life good? she asked herself as she grinned up at the gold dome atop the Massachusetts State House.

She wasn't thinking anymore about mysterious jewels or sleazy photographers or unnamed benefactors. It was time to be serious. Time to get down to work and forget about questions she would never get answered.

Tonight, after work, she was having her hair done and then going to dinner and the theater with a man who was very good-looking and successful, but also dull and traditional and sometimes annoying. But it was preferable to staying home and staring at a diamond-and-pearl tiara and choker, wondering who had crafted them, owned them and put them in the vaults of Piccard Cie of Geneva, Switzerland.

And preferable, she thought, to wondering just how uninteresting Sybil Morgenstern had decided Ashley Wakefield was after hearing the report from Pat Oberlin. Ashley wasn't sure whether to be relieved or insulted that she hadn't been in either of the next two issues of *You* magazine.

But she was in the third.

She was passing the Park Street station on the Common, and there she was, stacked twelve deep at the newsstand. She was smiling. Her eyes were ridiculously blue, her teeth impossibly white. She had the glittering tiara on her head, the choker around her neck.

In big bold letters were the words "ASHLEY WAKEFIELD, MYSTERY HEIRESS AND DOLPHIN RESCUER."

They'd put her on the damned cover.

MacGregor Stevens peered through the open door of Jeremy Carruthers's eggshell-colored office and noted his younger colleague's look of profound relaxation. Thirty-six, green-eyed and a good-looking devil, Jeremy had his feet up on his desk, his ankles crossed, and was reading a magazine. Mac expected nothing less. It was a warm, sunny Friday morning in San Diego, not yet eight o'clock. Jeremy rarely got going before eleven.

"Busy day today?" Mac asked.

"What? Oh." Jeremy grinned as he glanced up from his magazine. Mac got a glimpse of the cover: it was that rag, *You*. "Morning, Mac. No, today shouldn't be too busy. Just an early meeting with a client."

Not something Jeremy would plan for himself, Mac realized, but occasionally such compromises were unavoidable. Despite his casual attitude toward life and work, Jeremy was, in Mac's opinion, a damned fine attorney. His father, Allan Carruthers, was prone to think otherwise, but that was a father's prerogative— and God only knew Allan, good friend that he was, was a hard man to please. Mac had known him for thirty years. Together, he and Allan had founded Carruthers and Stevens, and today it was a prominent Southern California law firm. They made an interesting team—diligent, solid. Allan was a native Californian, educated on the G.I. Bill, a compulsive worker. Mac came from Philadelphia money. He had attended Choate and Yale, but the sun and opportunities of the West Coast had lured him to San Diego...and the possibility, the slim hope, that there he would be able to forget.

At fifty-seven, he was straight backed and gray eyed, a tall man, his hair gone completely gray. He retained much of the formality and reserve of his Main Line upbringing, though he hadn't been back home in years. If his family wanted to see him, they had to travel to San Diego.

"You look engrossed," he said with a wry smile. "Anything interesting?"

Jeremy grinned. "Beautiful and crazy mystery heiress."

"Sounds like your type."

"Not a chance, Mac. The lady's completely nuts. I couldn't keep up with her."

"All the better. She wouldn't bore you."

It was Mac's opinion, shared by the other cofounder of Carruthers and Stevens, that Jeremy had set his sights on a woman who simply didn't exist. He'd been married, once, to one of the La Jolla heiresses he often fancied, usually with disastrous results. The marriage had ended five years ago. Susie had remarried and now had two toddlers, whom she was suffocating with attention and affection the same way she had Jeremy. There was no *not* pleasing the woman, and that had been a problem. At the very least, Jeremy needed a woman who'd go head-to-head with him.

"Here," Jeremy said, shoving the magazine across his desk. "Have a look."

Putting on his reading glasses, Mac walked over and examined the cover photo. "Very pretty, I must say."

Jeremy laughed. "Hell of an understatement, Mac. Do you think anyone has eyes that blue?"

"They can work miracles with photography these days," Mac agreed. "She rescues dolphins?"

"And flies her own plane. Quite the hot shit, apparently."

"What makes her a mystery heiress?"

"She and her brother were named beneficiaries of a Liechtenstein trust."

"My, my." Intrigued, Mac flipped open to the brief article and photographs splashed across three inside pages.

"I like the one in Newport myself," Jeremy said.

Mac's eyebrows arched. "I can see why."

Ashley Wakefield was dripping wet and staring straight into the camera with that dazzling smile. Her batik top was slightly askew, revealing the edge of her light tan. The effect was far more enticing, far sexier, than if she had been standing there naked—at least in Mac's opinion. He wasn't sure about Jeremy. But there was something about the way she held herself—perhaps it was in the devil-may-care look in those bright eyes—that suggested to Mac that the young woman would be very annoyed indeed if she knew she were being scrutinized like a *Playboy* centerfold.

The other photographs suggested the unpredictability of the woman and the wildly eclectic life-style she seemed to have. She was regal in the Berkshires. Competent and businesslike at her Boston offices. Free spirited in Manhattan, with all her bags and boxes. Muddy and drenched and exhausted on Cape Cod, rescuing dolphins and inspecting her plane.

And very beautiful and strangely haunted at the gala opening at the New England Oceanographic Institute.

Mac could understand why Jeremy had been so engrossed in what was ordinarily a very shallow and uninteresting little magazine. "Dolphin rescuer and mystery heiress," the headline said. Ashley Wakefield was clearly much more complicated than that.

Then, in the lower corner of the third page, he saw the picture of the farmer. He was sitting on a red tractor in front of a sheep pen. The caption read, "Ashley credits her uncle, a farmer in Amherst, Massachusetts, with instilling in her a commitment to hard work."

Mac felt the blood pouring out of his face. His hands shook violently. He gasped for air, but managed to let the magazine fall back onto the desk.

Jeremy was on his feet. "Mac?"

"My God." The words came out in a choked whisper. He ran one hand through his hair and looked around the office, for what he didn't know. An escape? No. There wasn't one. There never had been. The face of the farmer was etched in his mind for all time. "I can't... Christ in heaven."

"The trust, you mean?" Jeremy sounded worried. "Come on, Mac, you've been a lawyer for thirty years. You know as well as I do people do some damned strange things with their money. Mac...Mac, for Christ's sake, do you *know* this woman?"

Mac shook his head, grabbing his hair, fighting to regain his composure. Don't say anything! It was none of Jeremy's affair—not a part of Mac's life in San Diego, or the past thirty years.

"Jesus, Mac. You want me to call someone?"

"No...no. I'm all right." He attempted a smile but knew it fell short. Jeremy didn't look encouraged. "I'm sorry. I must...not be feeling well. I suppose I'm seeing things."

"You sure? Anything I can do?"

"No. Thank you."

Leaving Jeremy looking concerned and unsatisfied with his explanation, Mac stumbled back to his office. For a long time he stood staring out his window, remembering. He saw the faces he'd banished from his thoughts years and years ago. He heard the old cries and felt the anguish and the desperation and the pain. And the hatred. And the horror.

There were questions he should have asked then. Answers he should have demanded. And hadn't.

He had his secretary cancel all his appointments for the day and left the office early. He drove to a drugstore and bought his own copy of *You* magazine, his first ever. And he sat in his car and studied the man in the Red Sox cap. Bartholomew Wakefield. A farmer. A man committed to frugality and hard work.

A murderer, Mac thought. A torturer and a traitor and a man Mac would hate for as long as he lived. Thirty years ago, he had left well enough alone. He'd thought it best for all concerned.

But now, he thought, everything had changed.

Ashley had bought all twelve copies of *You* at the Park Street station newsstand and had resisted the impulse to buy up every available copy in metropolitan Boston. She had locked herself in her office, checked all twelve copies out of some insane hope that maybe they wouldn't all be the same.

She felt awful. She didn't *like* having her picture on the cover of a national magazine. Good Lord, she thought, was that her? In one picture she had half a boob showing. In another she looked like shit warmed over. In another as if she ate nails for breakfast. In another like a goddamned yuppie.

But the picture of Barky was too much. *That* made her feel like a damned snake in the grass.

She picked up the phone and dialed Sybil Morgenstern's New York number herself.

Sybil was obnoxiously ebullient. "Ashley, how are you?"

"Furious. Fit to be tied."

"Oh?"

"I know there isn't a damned thing I can do about it now, but you can tell your sleazy reporter to send me back my picture of Barky."

"Barky? Ashley, what are you talking about?"

"My uncle. Your damned Pat Oberlin swiped the picture you printed of him out of my office—*without* my permission. I want it back."

"Oh, how awful. I had no idea."

Not for a second did Ashley believe that. "Just send me the picture."

"Of course."

"And, Sybil, no more interviews."

Lillian Parker laid her copy of *You* on the parson's table in her surprisingly small office high above the Avenue of the Americas. Her people subscribed to all the magazines and tabloids, including *You*. Lillian had nearly gagged when she'd seen this week's cover.

Ashley Wakefield. Smiling and beautiful. And wearing the tiara and the choker.

Good God, was there ever going to be an end to this? Her head aching, Lillian walked over to her window and looked down at the street, crowded as always. Her window was covered with a film of fine ubiquitous soot that filtered the sunlight. Life was like that, she thought. After a half century of mistakes, you just hope the sun'll be bright enough once in a while and your life not so crudded up with misery that a few rays of sunlight and joy can still get through.

She wondered at her mood. She was Lillian Parker, for God's sake. The legend. The trailblazer. The daughter of the unforgettable anchorman Addison Parker and the utilities heiress Margaret Parker.

She was rich and successful and fulfilled in countless different ways. She had no right to be miserable.

She thought of the young brats coming along today. Some of them accused her of having succeeded because she was rich and beautiful—Jesus, what did they know about beauty!—and had had "connections" because of her father, and because of her mother's wealth.

But then, too, some of the young ones said Lillian Parker had given up too much. As if they knew. They pointed out she had never married, never borne children. They could have it all. What the hell was the matter with her? Why couldn't she have had it all, too?

But they knew nothing, not about her. About her sacrifices. About her joys. They all *thought* they knew. But they didn't. No one did, she thought.

She sighed, suddenly tired. Maybe it wasn't what they knew, but what they feared. Maybe they were just plain goddamned scared they were going to hit their fifties with everything and nothing. She felt sorry for them. She wished she could impart some words of wisdom—or at least of comfort. But they'd have to find their own way, decide for themselves what was worth sacrificing and what wasn't, and learn to understand that there were always regrets.

Turning back to her desk, she saw again the incredible smile and blue eyes of Ashley Wakefield. And the glittering jewels.

I should have guessed this would happen, she thought.

In block letters, she printed "J. Land Crockett" on a label, and then a post office box in Southwest Harbor, Maine. She clipped one of her crisp business cards to the magazine and put them into a large manila envelope. She sealed it and added plenty of stamps. With a red pen, she printed "first class mail" diagonally across the lower corners.

Then she took the elevator downstairs and put the package into a mailbox on the street. Few knew she had access to J. Land Crockett. She wanted to keep it that way.

Bartholomew Wakefield pushed his grocery cart up to the express register at the supermarket on busy Route 9 between Amherst and Northampton. He had sugar, cinnamon, allspice, self-sealing canning jar lids. The apples were ready. He would pick them over the weekend and make applesauce, maybe some apple butter. It used to be that Ashley and David took care of the apples. But that had changed. Sometimes Ashley came out to the farm and helped with the canning and freezing, but only when she felt like it. It was a hobby now, not a duty. And David was busy, too, with his own house, his own land. When he was at the farm, he concentrated on the things that had to be done. Apple butter they could do without. But there was only so much one old man could do alone.

He liked them, Ashley and David. They were good people. He had done well. And the money hadn't spoiled them.

Then, looking up, he saw the smile he'd watched transform over the years, from a toothless, drooling grin of a baby to the impish smile of a child to the awkward smile of a gangly adolescent, and now to this, the sparkling smile of a confident woman.

And the jewels. He saw the tiara and the choker, glittering atop her head and around the glowing skin of her slender neck.

They looked as if they belonged on Ashley. But Barky had always known they would.

He picked up the magazine and with steady, callused hands opened to the inside article.

"Achh," he muttered in disgust when he saw the picture of himself. He'd never liked having his picture taken, for this very reason.

For thirty years, he'd dreaded this moment. Known, one day, it would come.

Others would see Ashley. The jewels. Himself. And they would have to act. Like him, they now had no choice.

# FIVE

The phones at Touchstone Communications had begun to ring. Reporters called. Photographers, magazine editors, advertisers, single men, quacks—they wanted Ashley for everything from endorsing a new line of eye makeup to modeling swimsuits in Bermuda to having dinner on Saturday night. She finally gave up on trying to get any work done and went home.

Nothing, she thought, ever seemed to penetrate the quietly regal streets of Beacon Hill. Even the flats, closer to Storrow Drive and the river, gave off the air of being wholly immune to the goings-on in the rest of Boston—or, for that matter, the world. Ashley had always loved this part of the city. When she'd been a student at Boston University, she used to like to wander the narrow streets of Beacon Hill, especially in the evening, when she could peek into the brightly lit windows. She had never been jealous of how the people lived inside the understated town houses. She hadn't desperately wanted to have what they had. She had simply been curious.

She groaned when she saw the group of reporters gathered on her steps. Cameras began clicking, and they fired a flurry of questions at her.

"Ms. Wakefield, a few minutes...."

"Tell us how you feel about being a mystery heiress. Haven't you wondered who made you rich?"

"Were those jewels real?"

"Any ideas who your secret benefactor is?"

"What about your family? What do they think?"

Pasting a smile on her face, Ashley dug out her keys and waltzed past them with apologies and assurances that anything she'd had to say was already in the pages of *You*.

She gave them a dazzling smile as she unlocked her door. "And if you all aren't off my steps in five minutes, I'll be forced to call the police. Have a pleasant evening."

Grumbling, she trudged upstairs.

In keeping with the period of the house, the furnishings of her duplex were generally high style, many of them English as well as American antiques. She had recently begun to collect art: a Winslow Homer seascape hung above the marble fireplace. Ever since she'd bought it at her first art auction, Evan Parrington had been harassing Ashley to invest in a security system for her apartment. So far she had resisted.

She wondered if all this publicity would change that. Would she have to get an unlisted number? Invest in alarms, new and tougher locks? Maybe even move?

She decided she wouldn't think about all that right now and, fixing herself a cup of tea, headed up to her rooftop deck to try to get some work done. She'd always had an enviable ability to concentrate; she'd call on it now.

But soon the telephone was ringing, and she dashed down the steep stairs to her study to answer it.

"May I speak with Ashley Wakefield, please?"

The voice was female, the accent distinctively Texas. Hurriedly, Ashley said, "Speaking."

"My name's Sarah Balaton. I...I'm from Houston. Miss Wakefield, I'm not one to beat around the bush. I saw the piece in *You* today, and I'm afraid...I'm afraid the tiara and choker you were wearing can't possibly belong to you. They're Balaton family pieces."

Ashley sank into a chair. "What?"

"I'm not accusing you of anything," Sarah Balaton went on quickly. "Please don't misunderstand me. I'm not trying to cause a fuss. The jewels disappeared before you were even born. They're of tremendous sentimental value to my family, and—well, I'd just like to investigate possible means of getting them back. Would you be interested in selling them?"

Ashley's head began to throb. This was her worst nightmare come true. I have to talk to Barky and David, she thought. "You can imagine this has come as a great surprise." She tried to keep her tone even. "I had no idea the tiara and choker had been stolen—"

"I didn't say stolen, Ms. Wakefield. I don't know what happened to them. I just know my family would never have sold them or given them away."

"Then what are the other possibilities?"

"I don't know, and it doesn't matter." Sarah Balaton was getting flustered. "As I said, I'm not interested in making any accusations. Antique jewelry of imprecise origins appears on the market all the time; usually it's impossible to prove anything. Do you think I could see the pieces?"

"I'll have to discuss this with my attorney—"

"I was hoping we could avoid lawyers. Ms. Wakefield, you strike me as a fair and generous person, one who would right an injustice if you could. I think I can prove to your satisfaction that whoever sold you the tiara and the choker had no right to. Could we start there and go on from that point?"

Ashley hesitated, choosing her words carefully. "I'll need some time to think this over. Can you come to Boston?"

"Of course—I'd be happy to."

"Give me the weekend. I'll call you Monday."

"If you don't mind, I'd prefer to call you."

"All right." Ashley suddenly found herself gulping for air. She needed to end the conversation...quickly. And to think. Lord, she needed to think! "You understand I'm not making any promises."

"I understand. And I'll be in touch."

Houston was hot and oppressively humid, no hint of winter in the sticky air, but inside the Crockett Industries mirrored-glass headquarters high above Greenway Plaza, it was a comfortable seventy-two degrees. On the thirty-fourth floor, Sarah Balaton, vice president of finance, unlocked the bottom right-hand drawer of her rosewood desk. She withdrew a burgundy leather scrapbook and laid it on her slate blotter, next to that week's edition of *You*.

Her hands were trembling. Every breath was painful. What had she expected Ashley Wakefield to say? Here, take the jewels. No. Nothing was ever that simple.

She opened the scrapbook. Pasted on the first page was a black-and-white publicity glossy of a legend. The cheekbones were prominent, stunning, the eyes heavy lashed and intense, the smile at once elegant, innocent, mischievous.

When people remembered Judith Land, they remembered her smile.

The photograph had been taken when the actress was just twenty-one and already famous, a woman with the wit of Katharine Hepburn, the ice of Grace Kelly, the fire of Marilyn Monroe.

Stiffening her hands to still their incessant trembling, Sarah flipped several pages, to the center of the scrapbook, then back a page. At the top left corner was a small clipping from a short-lived Paris gossip magazine. It was a photograph, in black-and-white, of two women at a Christmas ball in Vienna, two friends, two heiresses, one a famous actress, the other a neophyte journalist.

Judith Land and Lillian Parker.

They were dressed in the most expensive, the most stylish gowns of the day, and they were smiling, not gay smiles, not carefree smiles, but the smiles of two young women who had suddenly found themselves launched into adulthood. Poised, certain, not so innocent.

In what the caption said, in French, was a stroke of sheer audacity, Judith Land was wearing a tiara, her shining dark hair woven into the complicated pattern of diamonds and pearls. On her alabaster neck was a matching choker, its center a large, perfect ruby.

Sarah positioned the cover of *You* next to the rare Paris photograph.

The pieces were the same. She would stake her life on it.

She shut the scrapbook in her desk and took the elevator three flights up, to the offices of the president and chief executive officer of Crockett Industries. Andrew Balaton. Her father. His position with the company should have been an asset for his only child, but it wasn't. Andrew Balaton believed a woman born to wealth, beauty and social status—such as his daughter—shouldn't involve herself in the messy world of corporate empires.

But Sarah was determined to prove him wrong and to dispel his stubborn prejudice. She sensed that, deep down, her father *wanted* her to succeed in business and was secretly pleased with all she had accomplished while he had stood back, observing, offering no help. What Sarah Balaton had done, she had done on her own merits. One day she hoped her father would congratulate her on her hard work, dedication and honesty.

Nothing, she thought, was going to stop her from reaching that day, when her father would notice her for her abilities. Nothing. Not her love life, not the prejudices toward her looks and sex, not the gossip about her relationship with Andrew Balaton, not even her disgust with the waste, mismanagement and corruption she saw every day in business. She believed a principled, intelligent and committed person could excel.

Throughout Texas, however, Sarah was known more for being a beautiful and seductive heiress than a savvy businesswoman. Golden haired and golden eyed, she had a tiny waist and full, heavy breasts that she rarely showed off to any perceived advantage. She wore high collars and buttoned all but the top button of her crisp shirts. In business, big breasts were not an asset.

Andrew Balaton greeted his daughter warmly and invited her to sit on the long black leather couch facing the length of his large office. Darker in skin tone, hair and eyes than Sarah, he had her flawless skin that, despite his sixty-five years, was virtually without wrinkles. He was wiry, physically fit from daily exercise sessions, never overweight. His fine hands were manicured every week. Since he'd divorced his third wife twelve years ago, he'd had many women. Some were younger than his daughter.

Sarah tucked her ankles to one side, in an attempt to appear demure. Her father sat in a matching chair. "You work very hard, Sarah," he said. His deep voice was quiet, emotionless. Thirty years ago, when he'd fled his native Hungary as a dispossessed count, he'd anglicized his name from András, and now he retained his aristocratic formality, but little of his Hungarian accent. He smiled. "Too hard."

She lowered her eyes. They'd had this conversation before—too many times. She did work hard. She *wanted* to. And, as she pointed out ceaselessly, she worked no harder than he did. She was following in her father's footsteps. But Andrew Balaton refused to see it that way, at least not yet. Now he could see his daughter only as violating the precise code of ethics under which he operated. He was an aristocratic man, bound by form and duty, and all the pain he had witnessed, all he himself had experienced, had not shaken him free from the external rules that guided him. He never lost his temper, he never cursed, he never cried. And he no longer loved.

"Why did you want to see me?" he asked.

She handed him her copy of *You.* "I wondered if you'd seen this."

He looked at the smiling face of Ashley Wakefield and shrugged. "Is she a friend of yours?"

"No—we've never met." She leaned forward

slightly. "Father, don't you recognize the jewels she's wearing?"

"I don't, no." He handed the magazine back to her. "Do you?"

She uncrossed her ankles and pushed back her hair. Fidgety moves. She was annoyed with herself, but maintained direct eye contact with her father. "I'm positive they're the tiara and choker from the Balaton collection."

Andrew Balaton rubbed one finger across his mouth, then sighed, as he always did when he was disappointed in her. "Oh, Sarah, I've told you: the Balaton jewels are a myth."

"Are you sure?"

"Of course. I am the last Count András Balaton. If anyone would know, it's I."

She looked away. "I see."

Her words were barely audible. In 1956, following the failed Hungarian uprising against the Soviet Union's domination of its national affairs, her father had fled the country of his birth. He was a handsome, educated aristocrat, but utterly penniless. He had escaped with nothing but his not inconsiderable pride.

Now, thirty years later, he was one of the most powerful men in the country.

Last winter, the last remaining Balatons—Sarah and her father—had received a letter from a Hungarian historian. The Communist government was restoring Balaton Castle as a center for tourism, and the historian wanted to know if the surviving Balatons might know the whereabouts of the famed collection of Balaton jewels. The government was interested in securing them for a museum at the castle. The historian had enclosed a photograph of an eighteenth-century portrait of a Balaton countess wearing the tiara and choker and said he was collecting detailed descriptions of the rest of the missing collection.

Andrew had not bothered to write back. As he told Sarah, the Communists had stolen the Balaton Castle and lands, and even if he knew the whereabouts of the jewels, he wouldn't tell them. But he had never seen the so-called Balaton collection, and he didn't believe it existed. His ancestor, he maintained, had borrowed the tiara and choker from a friend.

For her part, Sarah hadn't mentioned the scrapbook—or her opinion that the jewels Judith Land had worn at the Christmas ball in Vienna in 1956 were the same jewels worn by the countess in the 1798 portrait.

She didn't want her father to know about her obsession with his first wife. Judith Land had been the love of his life, and she had destroyed any chance for his personal happiness. As a teenager, Sarah had begun the scrapbook. If she understood Judith Land, she felt, she might understand her father, and learn how to win his approval.

"Sarah."

She looked up at the unexpected sad, melodic note in her father's quiet voice. But his face was rigid, and he didn't smile.

"Sarah, where you're treading, you will find only pain. I have put the past behind me. I suggest you respect and believe that."

They were the gentlest words her father had ever spoken to her. "It might be too late."

"What do you mean?" he asked sharply.

She didn't hesitate. "I've already talked to Ashley Wakefield."

* * *

Andrew Balaton stood looking out at the Houston skyline, in his opinion the most beautiful of any in the world. With tremendous effort, he had dismissed his daughter with an affectionate kiss on the cheek. He wanted to flog her. Such a fool she was! But so tender-hearted, so devoted to him. He loved her in a thousand ways, but he had difficulty articulating any of them. She was his daughter—his flesh. He had watched her grow into a woman, and now he wanted her to be happy, a woman of strength and compassion. He admired her for her achievements. And yet every day he fought the urge to protect her from the agonies of life. In his mind, he accepted that she had to experience pain in order to grow. In his heart, he wanted nothing of cruelty ever to touch her—especially, he thought, the cruelty and pain and horror of his own past. That part of him, that agony, was his alone. She had no right to it.

Behind him, his door opened softly, and he turned to acknowledge with a nod the presence of the blond man who had entered his office. His name was Giles Smith. Not tall, he was bulky, muscular, surprisingly quick—a professional at providing security for people in such sensitive, lucrative positions as Andrew Balaton. He stood at attention, like a Marine.

"Good evening, Giles."

"Sir."

"Thank you for coming. I would like you to fly up to Massachusetts this evening and perform a little service for me."

"Sir?"

Andrew pushed his own copy of *You* across his desk. Giles picked it up and glanced at Ashley Wakefield. Andrew smiled. "She's quite attractive, isn't she?"

Giles said nothing. Andrew had known he wouldn't. In addition to being very good at what he did, Giles knew and accepted his place.

"The tiara and choker she's wearing don't belong to her, and they could cause a great deal of unnecessary anguish for myself and my daughter."

"I understand, sir."

Andrew turned back to the window. "I want them."

# SIX

Jeremy Carruthers rang the doorbell of Elaine and MacGregor Stevens's house tucked into the terraced hills of elite Point Loma, just minutes from downtown San Diego. It was late Friday afternoon, and still warm. Jeremy had been fidgety all day, ever since Mac had nearly collapsed in his office and then left early. It wasn't like Mac. It just didn't fit. And Jeremy was worried...or at least curious.

Elaine Stevens opened the door a crack. When she saw Jeremy, she pulled the door open wide and smiled. "Jeremy! What a lovely surprise. Come in."

"Thanks." He stepped into the small foyer, where Elaine always had a vase of fresh flowers. Today's were roses. "Mac home?"

"Why, no." She looked surprised, but continued to rub a pink cream into her hands. She was a tall woman with ash-blond hair and strong, chiseled features—the rock in Mac's life. As always, she was neatly but casually dressed; she loathed uncomfortable clothes. "Didn't he tell you? He left for Honolulu this afternoon."

Jeremy shook his head. Mac had said nothing of the kind, not even to his secretary. And that wasn't like the cofounder of Carruthers and Stevens and the man

Jeremy had known and admired since he was six years old.

"Not on business," Elaine said. "We have land in Hawaii. You know we plan to retire there. Mac said he'd heard rumors the adjoining property was going to be rezoned for business. He went out there to see what he could do."

"Was this planned? He never mentioned—"

"Well, no, it came up very suddenly." Concern reached her warm hazel eyes. "Why?"

"I'm just surprised." He smiled, forcing the look of skepticism from his face. "Guess I've been preoccupied with my own work.... I see you didn't go with him?"

"I have too much to do here. Do you need to get in touch with Mac? Is it important?"

"Just business."

"Well, I can have him call you. He's staying with a friend—an old buddy of his from Yale, I think he said. He didn't leave a number, but I'm sure he'll call tonight. He always does when he's away. Would you like me to have him call you?"

"Please."

Jeremy drove back to Coronado, where he lived, and went for a long run on the beach. He tried to blot out the recurring image of Mac's stricken face as he had looked through the pages of photographs of Ashley Wakefield.

Hawaii. My ass Hawaii, he thought. It was just one more element that didn't fit.

But Mac hadn't reacted until the third page of photographs. The cover hadn't bothered him, and neither had the views of beautiful Ashley Wakefield in her batik bandeau, Bill Blass gown or brass-tacks business suit. So it wasn't her. Which meant, Jeremy thought, that it had to be the grainy photograph of the man on the red tractor that had sent Mac into such a tailspin. The uncle. Bartholomew Wakefield.

With sweat pouring off him, Jeremy did a cool-down walk and listened to the rhythm of the waves pounding the beach. "Hell," he muttered to himself, "I'm probably just imagining things."

But later that evening, Elaine Stevens called: Mac *hadn't* been in touch. "I called our realtor in Honolulu," she said. "As far as she knows, there's no problem with the property and Mac isn't even in Hawaii."

Jeremy set his beer on his deck table and sank into a canvas chair. "Elaine, I didn't mean to worry you."

"Don't—please. But there's something you know or at least suspect, isn't there?"

"Elaine—" He broke off, silently cursing himself. If Mac had wanted his wife to know what the hell he was up to, he'd have told her. And me, too. "I don't know anything, Elaine."

He could hear her sharp intake of breath. She was a tough, intelligent and compassionate woman, and in Jeremy's opinion, Mac would be a damned fool to play tricks on her—without good reason. But that was the problem. He might have good reason.

"I wouldn't want you to break any confidences you might have with Mac," she said, "but if you can tell me I have no reason to worry about him—physically, I mean. If there's someone else..."

"Oh, Jesus, Elaine. No, I can't believe Mac's having an affair."

"Then *what*? Jeremy, you know Mac. He doesn't just go off like this and...and disappear! He doesn't lie to me! What if something's happened to him?"

Jeremy felt the tug of loyalty to Mac—and to Elaine. He could see clearly in his mind the vivid, unreal eyes of Ashley Wakefield, and then Mac's white face, and the desperation and the hate there.

"I think Mac's told you something and you don't feel it's right to tell me," Elaine said, without accusation. "I can understand that, Jeremy—even respect it. But if you do have some idea of where Mac is...maybe you can get him to call me. Please. It's all I ask."

Jeremy sighed heavily. "All right, Elaine. Give me the weekend. I'll see what I can do. But you know— maybe he *is* in Hawaii."

"I understand. Thank you, Jeremy."

"For God's sake, don't thank me. I probably should have kept my damned mouth shut."

He could almost see her smile. "Why start now?" Then she was serious again. "Call me with anything, Jeremy. Anything. It's better than not knowing."

After they'd hung up, Jeremy packed a carry-on bag and grabbed a seat on a night flight out of San Diego for Boston, Massachusetts. Maybe he was wrong and Ashley Wakefield didn't have a damned thing to do with Mac's strange behavior.

Then again, maybe he wasn't and she did.

First thing Saturday morning. Ashley took the tiara and choker to her bank and opened a safe-deposit box. The bank officer flirted with her and asked her if she were free for dinner that evening. Thank you, she said, but she had plans—which she did, more or less, although not with another man. Tomorrow night? he asked. No. In fact, she lamented, she was busy indefinitely. He shrugged off his defeat: what the hell, she's rich; it was worth a shot. She could read his mind.

As she entered the Touchstone offices, Ashley felt a pang of guilt. Between the ringing phones and reporters stalking the place, Caroline hadn't gotten any work done yesterday, either. "I'm sorry about all the bedlam around here, Caroline."

She waved away the apology. "What's up?"

Ashley sighed. "I'm going out to the farm. I don't know for how long, but I've got to see David and Barky. If you would, have Patti clear my calendar—business and social."

"Done." She smiled at Ashley. "Don't look so relieved, Ash. It's not a damned crime to need some help. Now what else can I do?"

"I hate to ask..."

"Never mind what you hate. What do you *need*?"

She hesitated. "Everything you can get me on Sarah Balaton of Houston, Texas."

Caroline twisted her mouth to one side. "No questions?"

"She wants the tiara and choker."

"Holy shit."

Ashley quickly related the strange call of last night.

"Well, well, well," Caroline said. "I'll start sniffing right away."

"I don't know how to thank you—"

The vice president of Touchstone Communications scowled. "I don't want to be thanked, dammit! I'd expect the same treatment from you—and I know I'd get it."

"That's right. If there's ever a time—"

"I'll let you know."

"Thanks, Caroline."

"Jerk." She grinned. "Now go on and make peace with the folks at home. Bring me back some apples."

* * *

David had the hood up on his Land Rover, parked in the driveway next to Barky's truck, and was tinkering with the carburetor. It was a perfect autumn morning, and he had a million things he wanted to get done today. But nothing could beat messing around with his Rover. He could have afforded a fleet of new ones, but it wouldn't be the same. He knew every idiosyncrasy of this one, and working on it allowed him to grease up his hands, to crawl up inside himself and sort out his problems.

He figured now that his goddamned sister had her picture in a national magazine, the shit was going to hit the fan and some of it was going to smack them both right in the face. Someone would recognize the jewels. Barky would be accused of being a jewel thief. There'd be all sorts of crap about statute of limitations, but they'd still think of some reason to haul their uncle's ass in and throw him in the slammer till his dying days.

Of course, Ashley wouldn't think any of that would happen. She was an optimist. She believed she could handle the idiots of the world, that the people she knew and admired all lived up to her high standards—especially Barky. David wasn't so sure. He figured their uncle had to have done *something* before being saddled at age thirty-four with two infants. Maybe that something was stealing jewels. Who the hell knew?

One thing was for sure: David had never believed his uncle's declarations of ignorance about the Liechtenstein trust and the collection of jewels. But he'd had nearly five years to talk—thirty if the trust had been set up when David and Ashley were born. If Barky hadn't talked by now, he wasn't going to. He was nothing if not muleheaded.

And Ashley. David had never been so pissed off at his sister. She was just plain reckless.

He heard a car turn into the driveway, but didn't bother to look up. More people than usual had been stopping by to buy pumpkins, squash, whatever happened to be on the trailer. At first David figured it was just the nice weather. Then he realized it was that goddamned magazine. The locals had recognized Ashley and Barky in *You* and come out to the farm to gawk. David didn't object particularly. He just kept emptying the money out of the coffee can. Barky was keeping to the fields, working hard, more uncommunicative than usual.

"Hey."

Sighing, David pulled his head out from under the hood. A big blond guy had snuck up behind him. He was wearing a T-shirt too tight for his broad chest and arms and stretch jeans that left no doubt about the muscles in his legs. David reached for a dirty rag and began wiping his hands. "What can I do for you?"

"You David Wakefield?"

"Uh-huh."

"Sister Ashley?"

"Uh-huh. Why?" Couldn't be Ashley's latest romantic interest, he thought; too meaty.

"You know she's put the jewels in a safe-deposit box?"

David thought, well, hell, and wiped his fingers one by one. "What jewels?"

"Don't be a smartass. The tiara and the necklace."

"Choker," David corrected. "And it's *tee*-ara. Not long *i*."

"You want me to fucking bust your head open?"

"Not especially." He wasn't lying. Although several inches taller and no slouch himself, David was beginning to realize the guy was a pro. *Definitely* not Ash's type. "So what if Ash has put them in a safe-deposit box? As far as I'm concerned, that's the first smart thing she's done this month."

"You're her brother. I'll bet you can get them out."

"Wrong."

"Then you can get her to get them out."

"Now why would I want to do that?"

"I've got a party interested in having them, that's why. Says they don't belong to you."

"Anyone I know?"

"None of your fucking business."

"Does said party want to buy them or just take them?"

"Don't make no difference to me."

David now realized he was in an untenable situation. Goddamn Ashley. Then, at the thought of her, his heart began to pound. "Have you talked to my sister?"

"Nope." He gave an apelike grin. "Just missed her. Anyway, too many hounds on her tail right now— don't need my picture in the paper. Figured you'd be able to help. But I'll track her down if I have to. You know?"

David knew. "I wish I could help." He spread his hands as if he were utterly helpless and gave an exaggerated shrug. "But you know how it is."

The guy balled up his powerful hands into fists, but David, a participant in more than his share of barroom brawls, edged sideways along the Rover's front fender and felt his muscles tightening. If he hadn't gotten himself sandwiched between the Rover and his would-be assailant, he would have made a swift and calculated retreat.

But such was not the case. He tried out a smile. "How 'bout some coffee? Tea? No need for us to get violent, you know."

"I don't trust you, Wakefield."

One of the powerful fists started up. David swore to himself, knowing he was caught, and quickly lunged toward him, trying to get inside the blow and push him away. It was his only real hope. And a slim one.

But the guy was a pro, and he slammed his fist into David's ribs, preventing him from pushing back and beating a hasty path to hell out of there. Even with the stunning pain of the blow, David's momentum carried him into the other man, who responded instantly by shoving David back hard, separating them to give him room to throw more punches.

Caught off balance, David instinctively tried to protect himself, but a sudden left jab snapped his head back. He tucked his arms in and ducked, expecting the right hook aimed for his solar plexus. The blow ended up glancing off his arms.

Swearing, gulping in air past the pain in his ribs and head, David slammed at him with a left jab and a right cross, but the blows missed, and the guy came at him again, hammering his head with a left, nailing him hard with a right cross.

Somewhere David heard Barky's voice. "What goes on here?"

And then his insides were being ripped out and he was spinning, sinking, tumbling, and finally he hit something hard and unyielding. The damned driveway. He was breathing dirt. He couldn't move.

Far away Barky was yelling, "You son of a beetch," and there was a car starting and the screech of tires. David curled up into a fetal position. The pain pulsed through him, and he decided he was just going to lie there and never move again.

Barky got him inside and onto the tattered living room couch, next to the warmth of the potbelly wood stove. His old uncle sighed irritably and brought him ice. "Shit," David said, "my head hurts."

"That's your headache, not mine."

"Thanks a lot."

"Stupid to take on a man like that."

"Think I had a frigging choice?"

"Language."

Barky stumped out of the room and returned in a few minutes with two cold wet cloths. David dabbed his bloody nose and gravel-scraped cheek. When he coughed, it was as if he were being carved for dinner.

"Your ribs aren't broken," Barky said. "Cracked, maybe. I will tape them."

"Don't fucking touch me."

But Barky was already thumping upstairs. He brought down a shoebox of ace bandages from Ashley's days playing high school field hockey and David's playing soccer. He made David remove his shirt and told him not to simper.

"Did you get the bastard's license plate?" David asked.

"No."

"Shit."

"What did he want?"

"The tiara and the choker."

"Ahh."

"Don't fucking 'ahh' me, Barky. What's going on?"

"The egg is broken."

It was one of Barky's favorite sayings. Once an egg was broken, there was no putting it back together again—and no use trying. Ashley and David called this their uncle's Humpty Dumpty philosophy.

But David wasn't in the mood for it. "Don't give me that shit."

"My basket was full," Barky said patiently. "An egg was bound to drop out sooner or later."

"Jesus Christ. What the hell are you talking about?"

"You shouldn't excite yourself."

"That fucker was going after Ashley!"

"If necessary, I will see to your sister."

Barky wrapped the bandages tight and pinned them with thirty-year-old diaper pins. When he was finished, he nodded, satisfied. "Clear liquids for today, tomorrow you will hurt, and then you will be angry and bruised. Probably you won't want to do heavy work for a few days, but there is much else to be done here. You and Ashley can make applesauce together. It's been a long time since you two worked together on the farm. Yes, that's a good idea." He handed David his shirt. "Make applesauce while I'm gone."

"What do you mean while you're gone? Where the hell are you going?"

Barky removed his Red Sox cap, revealing a balding head and a fringe of gray-streaked golden brown hair, his warm brown eyes fastened on his nephew. "I go fishing," he said.

"Fishing? You haven't been fishing in years!" The yelling prompted another stab of pain, and David lay back with a moan, taking quick, shallow breaths. "Dammit, Barky, are you in some kind of trouble?"

Wiping his brow with the back of his wrist, Barky put on his cap and patted David on the shoulder. "Trust me, David."

"*Barky!*"

His uncle didn't flinch, didn't turn, didn't glance back as he walked into the kitchen. David heard him sticking another log on the fire in the cook stove.

"Are you a goddamned jewel thief?"

The screen door creaked open and shut with a soft thud. David rolled off the couch, spun dizzily and fell to his knees, gasping in agony. He swore and tried to call his uncle, but his voice wasn't much more than a whisper. Finally he collapsed onto his side.

He lay there until the roaring in his ears stopped and the nausea subsided, and then he moved slowly, holding on to the couch as he dragged himself to his feet. He walked into the kitchen, then outside. Standing in the driveway, he listened to the wind and the animals. Barky was gone.

# SEVEN

**J.** Land Crockett sat in an overstuffed chair on the windblown sun porch of his isolated Maine summer house, on his island in Blue Hill Bay. All around him, he could smell and hear the sea. It was cold and damp out on the porch, but he was bundled up in a heavy sweater and thick blankets. He was an old man with fierce deep blue eyes and sagging, wrinkled skin. He liked the cold. It reminded him he was still alive, even if he didn't particularly care. Sometimes he'd sit out on the porch all night. He found comfort in the shadows there.

And he liked Maine in the fall. The lobsters were more plentiful, the ocean quieter, the tourists gone. He was a billionaire and a recluse, the nominal head of a diversified corporate giant. Crockett Industries. The company would carry the family name long after he was gone. It had begun as Crockett Oil on Spindletop in 1901, when for the first time in his life Johnny Crockett had been in the right place at the right time. Not one to stand on ceremony, the soft-spoken, unpredictable Texan was Johnny to everyone—rich, poor, educated, illiterate, it made no difference to him. Nor was he one to give a damn about money. He always said if he didn't have so much of it, he'd probably have gone broke.

When Johnny died in 1941, control of the Crockett fortune and the Crockett Oil Corporation went to his son, a tougher, harder man than his father. Crockett to everyone, never Johnny and rarely Land, he was just as unpredictable as his father, but he was also impatient, gruff, often remote. In the late 1950s, he'd turned the day-to-day running of the company over to his son-in-law and retired to his ranch northwest of Houston and his island off the coast of Maine. As his fortune had grown into the billions, he'd removed himself further and further from human contact.

Which, Crockett thought, was the way he liked it. He had his memories. They were all he needed.

And last night, the memories had been particularly vivid. Crockett had felt as if Judith were there on the island with him, laughing with her mother.

*"Daddy, won't you go on our picnic with us?"*

*"Another time, sweetheart."*

*"Judith, you know Daddy needs to rest. He works so hard. We'll go, just the two of us. Maybe we'll see some porpoises today."*

*"Whales, Mama! I want to see whales!"*

He had loved them both more than he could ever love himself. He would have died for them, gladly. Instead they were the ones who had died, first Judith, the mother, then Judith, the daughter.

He choked back the tears, but he couldn't stop the images from coming.

Judith had been so beautiful the night of the Christmas ball in Vienna. Her hair was shining, her eyes never so blue, her face never so happy. She had chosen an off-the-shoulder silver gown startling for its simplicity. There was nothing to distract the eye from the glittering natural beauty of Judith Land.

At first her father hadn't even noticed the tiara and the choker: they seemed a part of her. Judith rarely bought her own jewelry, and never without first consulting him. He wondered where these exquisite pieces had come from, not that it mattered. On his daughter, they were perfect.

*"Are you happy, Judith?"*

*"Daddy...I've never been happier."*

In truth, she had never looked happier. The troubled sighs and temperament of the past weeks had gone. Now she seemed to glow with health and contentment.

Reluctantly, Crockett gave the credit to Count András Balaton. Ever since Judith had rescued him from the refugee camps and brought him to their hotel in Vienna, Crockett had been trying to find out who the dashing young Hungarian really was. Count, my blue butt, he'd thought, absolutely certain the title was a wishful fabrication. But he wouldn't be the first refugee to think up an interesting past for himself.

The news coming out of Hungary was contradictory and damned frightening, Crockett had thought. The revolution—if it could be called that—had lasted a matter of days, and had been fiercely and brutally crushed. No one was surprised, least of all J. Land Crockett, who considered himself a proud cynic when it came to human nature. Not all the tens of thousands who had crossed the borders into the West proved to be so-called freedom fighters. There were whores and delinquents and opportunists among them—and good people, honest people. He couldn't deny that. They'd left behind dead brothers, fathers, mothers, sisters, and they'd fled their homeland because the hope for the future had been sucked out of them.

But Crockett didn't give a damn about them. Budapest, Belgrade, Bucharest—hell, they were all the same to him. He only wanted to know about the clever, handsome young man who had so effortlessly captured the heart of Judith Land. That was all.

*"Don't look so worried, Daddy. Everything will be wonderful."*

*"You'll let me know if it's not? You'd tell me if you're unhappy? Judith, there's nothing I wouldn't do for you. Nothing. Remember that."*

*"I will, Daddy. But please don't worry. I have every intention of being very, very happy."*

They were the last words he had ever spoken face-to-face with his daughter. The next time he saw her, she was lying twisted and broken and still in the dusty dirt of his Texas ranch.

The light of his life was dead.

Shortly after lunch, Ashley burst into the farmhouse kitchen. "David? Barky? Hey, you guys!"

A feeble voice answered, "Ash."

She found David wrapped in a ratty afghan in the living room and gasped at his bruised and bloody face. His eyes and lips were swollen, and blood had coagulated around his nose. But he attempted a grin. "Hey, Ash." He coughed a little and winced in pain, holding his abdomen. "Rotten day. How's everything in Boston?"

"David. What happened?"

Haltingly, he told her. "Don't worry, okay? I've been in bar fights worse than this—'cept I usually win."

Ashley grabbed another afghan and sat on the floor in front of the couch. She was shaking. The fire in the wood stove had died out. It felt cold. "Barky didn't say where he was going?"

"Uh-uh."

"But fishing..."

"Ash, has Barky *ever* gone fishing off his own land?"

"No," she said unnecessarily. "It's the piece in *You*."

"Of course it's the goddamned piece in *You*! Frigging millions of people are going to see those stupid jewels. What the fuck do we do if someone recognizes them?"

Ashley thought of Sarah Balaton. "Give them back."

"Shit."

"I should have left them in Switzerland."

"You should have kept your goddamned face out of that stupid-ass magazine!"

"I know."

David hissed, his energy suddenly gone. "Hell, Ash, I'm sorry. You know what Barky says." He gave a tight smile. "The egg is broken."

She hugged the afghan to her. It smelled of her uncle's stale pipe and smoke from the wood stove. "David, maybe we should call the police."

"And tell them what? That Barky's gone fishing and some goon who's probably long gone beat me up? Big goddamned deal. Ash, we can't lay out the whole story for them. They'll put us in the damned loony bin. For God's sake, Barky may be a jewel thief! Our dad may have been a jewel thief—our own *mother*."

Ashley nodded reluctantly. "I suppose you're right. The man who nailed you—what did he look like?"

"Big bastard—couple of inches shorter than me, but built like a damned bull, blond, a pro... Ash?"

She had shut her eyes. "David, I'm sorry. I tried to keep you and Barky out of this mess—"

"Forget it. It's our mess, too. What now? Any ideas?"

She looked at him and tried to smile. "I guess we could pick apples. Barky would like that."

Ashley dumped a bucket of sour-smelling slop into the trough and watched the grunting, snorting pigs shove one another to get to it. How like people, she thought, and set down the bucket. She checked the water. It was late afternoon, still sunny and gorgeous, but there was a sharpness to the breeze that foreshadowed the coming of winter. David was confined to the living room couch but had drunk a cup of chicken broth. There was no sign of Barky. She had looked everywhere, calling across the fields, hearing nothing but her own echo and the angry cry of the birds.

Barky was gone. Fishing, she thought.

Except his fishing pole was hanging in the shed, covered with cobwebs, and his truck was standing in the driveway, as always.

She tried to sweat off her frustrations with work, but as she trudged around the farm, she noticed how empty it seemed, how different, without Barky stumping around in his Red Sox cap and his dirty old sneakers.

"Dammit!"

She kicked the slop bucket. It somersaulted down the hill toward the house and landed upside down.

Then she noticed the tall man standing next to the trailer. He was examining a pumpkin. I should be looking for Barky and instead I'm selling goddamned pumpkins!

But he wasn't really looking at the pumpkin. He was looking at her.

She regretted kicking the slop bucket.

From her position in front of the pigpen, with her hair trailing down her back in a messy ponytail and the legs of her blue corduroys rolled up, she saw he had sun-streaked dark hair and wore a suit. Tan. It looked expensive. He had broad shoulders and long legs.

Not, she thought, your average pumpkin buyer.

He was probably just another vulture—another Pat Oberlin or Rob Gazelle looking for a new angle on the Ashley Wakefield story. "Mystery heiress slops pigs." Blowing stray hairs out of her face, she decided it would be wise just to ignore him.

With long strides, aware of the visitor's eyes on her, she headed over to the chicken coop. None of the dozen or so hens appeared to appreciate her self-sacrifice as she crept around in the dried hay and manure—"shet," Barky would say—and located their eggs. They were warm and brown and speckled with dried, and sometimes not so dry, manure. She held out the hem of her shirt and made a hammock for the eggs. There were eight. Not bad.

As she ducked back outside, the sun blinded her momentarily, and she sneezed. Then all at once there was a body in front of her, and a very deep voice said, "Ashley Wakefield?"

She yelled, "Jesus!" and jumped up, and the eggs went flying. They crashed with utterly final *splats* in the grass, on her sneakers, on his polished loafers. Before she'd recovered fully from the start, she glared at him and said, "Jackass."

He had green eyes, very, very pale. And the suit was silk. "Sorry. I didn't mean to startle you."

"Well, you did."

He paused—not hesitated, she noted, just paused, as if to regroup, reassess. Perhaps the *You* piece hadn't prepared him for a testy egg collector. "So I see."

She shook egg goo off her foot. "Is there something I can do for you?" It was a demand, not a polite request.

"Yes, as a matter of fact."

Wasn't there always? He turned his foot sideways and wiped egg yolk and runny albumen off his shoe onto the grass. He grimaced. With its hard lines, his face was striking. He was tanned and solid and didn't look at all like any of the reporters who had been stalking her.

He gave up on his shoe. "I was wondering if you might have seen a friend of mine. Mac—MacGregor Stevens."

"A reporter?"

"No. An attorney."

She wiped her hands on the hips of her pants. "I have an attorney."

"Parrington, Parrington and Smith of New York. Yes, I know."

So he had read the *You* piece. Naturally. A couple of barnyard cats showed up and started lapping up the eggs. Ashley left them to it. She headed down toward the apple trees in the side yard, near the trailer and the driveway. The friend of Mac Stevens followed. Glancing back, she noted his easy stride.

"He's tall," he said, coming up beside her. "Late fifties. Gray hair, gray eyes, proper sort of man. You haven't seen him?"

She shook her head. "Not that I know of."

"Has he contacted you or your uncle or brother?"

"I don't think so." She stopped and said suddenly, "You're at the farm."

His look was dry, and he didn't smile. "So it would appear."

"Then you believe your friend was headed here?"

"Actually, I'm not sure."

"But why would he want to contact my brother or my uncle?"

"I don't know that he does."

Ashley was confused. "Then why are you here?"

"I checked with Touchstone and the institute, and I stopped by your house on Chestnut Street. When I didn't find you, I guessed you'd come here—a lucky guess, as it turns out."

She didn't know why, but she didn't think he was telling her everything, and she chose not to press him. Given what had happened to David, she opted for caution.

"If you haven't seen Mac," he went on smoothly, "there's a good chance I'm on a wild-goose chase." He smiled. "Mac and I probably just have our signals crossed. My name's Carruthers, by the way." He slipped a hand inside his jacket and withdrew a slim billfold. "Jeremy Carruthers. If you do hear from Mac, I'd appreciate it if you'd leave a message with my office."

He handed her a business card. His office, she observed, was in San Diego; hardly across town. He was with a law firm called Carruthers and Stevens. "You flew all the way out here to find this friend of yours?"

"Oh, no, not exactly. It's just a lucky guess. Is your

uncle around, by any chance? Perhaps I could ask him."

Ashley felt herself stiffening, but combated it, unwilling to let Jeremy Carruthers see the effect of his simple question. So that was it. Barky. Mac Stevens was after Bartholomew Wakefield, not Ashley. She shrugged. "'Fraid not."

"I see. Well, perhaps Mac stopped by when you weren't here."

"I doubt it, but when Barky comes back, I'll ask him."

"Barky?"

"My uncle."

"Of course. Well, thank you."

The pale eyes were fixed on her, and she wondered if he guessed she was holding back. "Are you heading back to California?"

"Not just yet."

"Then perhaps I could call you at your hotel if Mr. Stevens does turn up. Where are you staying?"

He moved out ahead of her. "Just call the office."

"It's the weekend," she pointed out.

"I'm sure someone will be there to take a message." He glanced back at her, and squinted in the sun as he walked over to a black Pontiac. Ashley memorized the license number and noted the rental sticker. Jeremy Carruthers gave her a spine-tingling smile. "Thanks for your time. And sorry about the eggs."

"Lawyers, my ass," Ashley complained as she went into the kitchen, the screen door slamming behind her.

David was hunched over the big pine table, looking miserable. New, ugly colors had blossomed in his face, and he held his middle, obviously in pain. "What's up?"

She told him as she put on the kettle for tea.

"Why didn't you come get me?"

"So you could spit blood on him? Come off it, David." She reached up and pulled the Yellow Pages off the top of the refrigerator. "I think this whole thing's strange. Guys coming out from San Diego looking us up. Really."

David twisted slowly around in his chair. "If this Stevens guy is in his fifties, maybe he knew Barky back before we were born."

Ashley nodded grimly. "That's what I'm afraid of."

"Yeah."

"Anyway, I sincerely doubt they're lawyers."

"How come?"

"Paranoia, maybe. I don't know. I got the license number of Carruthers's car."

"For Christ's sake, you know his name, and he gave you his business address—"

"Could be fakes."

"You really are paranoid."

"Looking at you, David, it's hard not to be."

Using the old black phone next to the refrigerator, Ashley dialed the car rental agency advertised on the bumper of the black Pontiac Jeremy Carruthers had parked in the dirt driveway.

A polite woman answered, and Ashley asked if there was any way she could trace one of their cars through the license plate number. "Guy ran over my dog," she said.

"I'm sorry, miss, but that information is confidential. Incidentally, it would take us days to locate the lessor through the car's license plate. Is your dog all right?"

"He's at the vet's right now. Thanks, anyway."

David shook his head, battered though it was. "Hell of a detective you'd make, Ash."

"I'm calling San Diego."

"It's Saturday."

"Carruthers said someone'd be there."

Nevertheless, she was surprised when, after four rings, a male voice said, "Carruthers and Stevens."

"Well, what do you know."

"I beg your pardon? May I help you?"

She leaned against the refrigerator. "I'd like to speak with Jeremy Carruthers, please."

"He isn't in. This is Saturday—"

"But he works there?"

"Yes, of course."

She still didn't believe it. "Tall guy? Dark hair, green eyes—"

"May I ask who this is?"

"Oh, just a friend. Is Mr. Carruthers in San Diego this weekend?"

Silence.

"Sir?"

His voice was very grave. "Just what's this all about?"

"He's a lawyer, isn't he?"

"Yes, and he's also my son. If you don't mind, I would like an explanation for this phone call."

His son. *Ouch.* Ashley tugged the rubber band out of her hair, which was mostly tangles now. "Is Mac-Gregor Stevens the Stevens in Carruthers and Stevens?"

"I have no intention of continuing this conversation without an adequate explanation."

"Is that a yes?"

"Dammit, woman—"

Ashley hung up.

David rose stiffly from the table. His face went white and he grabbed his chair, but he didn't complain. "Carruthers checks?"

"So far."

"Should have asked if either of them has a client named Sarah Balaton or hired a blond goon to come after us. As far as I can see, they're our best leads."

Ashley sighed and nodded. "You're right. I'll call Caroline and see if she found out anything."

But there was no answer at Touchstone Communications. At Caroline Kent's condominium in Back Bay, Ashley got her machine and left a message for Caroline to please call the farm as soon as possible.

# EIGHT

Jeremy checked into the Lord Jeffrey Inn on the quaint town common in the center of Amherst and immediately went down to the bar and ordered himself a bourbon, straight. There were points to consider about his meeting with Ashley Wakefield. First, her eyes were as bright a shade of blue as on the cover of *You*. Second, she was holding back on something. Third, she was a god-awful pain in the ass.

But he didn't think she was lying about not having seen Mac. Somehow Jeremy felt he would have guessed that much.

Then Mac was sliding onto the chair across from Jeremy and smiling wanly as he motioned to the waitress. "A bourbon would go down well about now."

"Mac, for Christ's sake—"

"Easy, Jeremy."

For some reason, Jeremy had expected Mac to look haggard and disheveled, but he was as trim as ever, dressed neatly in tan putter pants and a pullover. His hair was combed and he was shaved. Only in his eyes could Jeremy detect any sign of fatigue or uneasiness.

"How did you find me?" Jeremy asked.

"I've been watching the Wakefield farm."

"Jesus."

Mac's bourbon arrived, and he took a big gulp,

holding it in his mouth before swallowing. He placed his forearms on the table and leaned over his glass, then ran one finger along the rim. "The uncle's not there, is he?"

"No, but I understood he'd be back."

"I doubt that." Mac smiled bitterly. "I shouldn't be surprised. I knew this wasn't going to be easy."

Checking an impulse to throttle Mac for information, Jeremy took a large swallow of his own bourbon and welcomed the path of fire down to his stomach. "Do you want to talk about it?"

Mac sighed heavily. "No."

"Mac."

"Don't push me, Jeremy."

"Elaine—"

"This has nothing to do with her—or you."

"She's worried."

"I suppose she has a right to be. Tell her—" He looked away. "Tell her whatever she needs to hear to give her peace of mind."

"She needs to hear you're all right, Mac—not having an affair, not crazy, but safe and normal and doing the kinds of things Mac Stevens does. Chasing after old farmers isn't what you do, Mac."

"It's what I should have done a long time ago." He lifted his glass, looked at it for a moment as if it possessed answers he didn't and then drank. "Tell Elaine I'll call her as soon as I can, all right? When this thing's finished, we'll go away. We'll talk, and I'll tell her everything—things I should have told her long before now. That's the best I can do, Jeremy."

"What about Ashley Wakefield?"

Mac shrugged, setting his glass back down. "This needn't involve her."

"I have a feeling she won't see it that way."

"It won't matter. I just—" He shut his eyes briefly, as if in pain. "I just hope to hell I'm not too late."

Jeremy felt his throat tighten. "Is there anything I can do?"

Mac smiled sadly. "You can convince my wife her husband isn't getting senile."

"All right." It was the least he could do, Jeremy thought. "I'll head back in the morning."

"Thanks, Jeremy. Stay out of this. Please."

"Mac, you're not in any danger, are you? I saw your face yesterday morning..."

This time the smile had a touch of the old humor, the wry wit for which MacGregor Stevens was known. "Good heavens, have you ever known me to step in front of traffic? I'm too old for that sort of thing, Jeremy. I'm merely settling an old score—getting answers to some questions that have been nagging me over the years. It's intensely personal, but not dangerous. And it has nothing whatsoever to do with Elaine or you or the firm."

"Do you know anything about this Liechtenstein trust, Mac?"

"No, nothing." He pushed his glass to the center of the table and rose, for the first time ever looking older than his years. "Have another drink on me, Jeremy— and a good flight home. Trust me."

"I always have."

The old alarm clock in Ashley's girlhood bedroom blared at five o'clock the next morning, and she sat bolt upright in the lumpy bed, banging her head on the slanted ceiling. The blue-flowered wallpaper had yellowed and was starting to peel, a tangible reminder of the passage of time. She had bought the paper when she was thirteen, with money she'd made selling sweet corn off the trailer, and hung it herself. The seams hadn't matched very well.

Feeling old and grown up, she shut off the alarm. She remembered sitting in this room and wondering what she would be like at thirty. She was almost there now. She liked the kind of kid she'd been. Hardworking and smart-assed. Hell, she was like that now, too. But different. The money had changed her, she supposed. And time. But she liked her life now. She didn't want to go back to the past. Back to this, as much as she loved it.

It was chilly and damp, and the wide pine-board floor was cold on her bare feet. She yawned and stretched, still feeling fuzzy. In Boston, she would be asleep under her hand-stitched throw, sprawled in silk pajamas on her queen-size bed. The chords of classical music on public radio would awaken her, not a cheap alarm clock and a goddamned rooster.

She pulled on some old clothes—patched corduroys and a red-and-white Boston University sweatshirt, heavy socks, beat-up sneakers—and tied her hair back. Yawned again and went to work.

Leaving David sleeping soundly in his old room, Ashley, rather virtuously she thought, did the morning chores alone. She started a fire in the cook stove in the kitchen. Then she moved outside and fed the chickens, the pigs, the sheep, the cats. She collected eggs. She hauled wood. She checked the vegetables on the trailer and emptied the change out of the coffee can. Pumpkins were selling like crazy. Finally, she looked up at all the ripe apples hanging in the two trees in the side yard. Barky would have her and David out picking them to make applesauce and apple butter, maybe some jam.

"Goddamn him," she said aloud.

Where was he? Why didn't he call? He never went anywhere. He was the original stick-in-the-mud. Hated traveling to Northampton, for God's sake.

Fishing. Jesus!

She couldn't hang around the farm all day, she decided. She'd go nuts.

Back inside, she fixed herself a breakfast of fresh eggs cooked on the wood stove, toast and coffee. Barky always bought whatever coffee was on sale. She had argued with him about acidity, caffeine levels and soil quality, but he remained unimpressed. She had gotten in the habit of buying fresh beans at a shop on Charles Street and keeping them in her freezer, grinding just enough for her two cups in the morning.

But after the fresh air and all her work, she was delighted at how good the cheap coffee tasted. Its strong, bitter flavor reminded her of her uncle, and she realized how much she missed him. She had never been to the farm when he wasn't there.

"Good God," she mumbled to herself in the quiet kitchen. "What if he never comes back?"

It was unthinkable.

A little while later, the telephone rang. She pounced on it, praying it was Barky, but instead Caroline Kent said, "Up with the crows this morning, Ash?"

"The roosters. Hi."

"You sound awful. What's wrong?"

Leave it to Caroline to sense despair, Ashley thought, and told her what she'd found since coming to the farm. "But we're doing okay. What did you get on Sarah Balaton—anything?"

"Of course. You want just the facts?"

"Please."

"Okay. Sarah Balaton is in her late twenties, lives in a high rise near Galleria in Houston. She's a vice president of finance for Crockett Industries."

Ashley began loosening her braid with her fingers. "So she's no slouch."

"No way. Got her M.B.A. from the University of Texas."

Ashley couldn't resist. "How did you find all this out?"

"Two former clients from Texas," Caroline said proudly. "But to continue. Sarah Balaton isn't just any hardworking female exec. She's Texas money and high society. Her daddy's Andrew Balaton, president and CEO of Crockett Industries, and Sarah's his only kid. He and her mama are long divorced. Sarah grew up all over the place, but she's known as a Texas honey."

"Who's her mother?"

"Frances Balaton DiDomenico. Lives in San Antonio."

"Great. Anything else?"

"Daddy's first wife was Judith Land."

Ashley blinked in surprise. "The actress?"

"As far as I know, there was only one Judith Land. She and Balaton were married shortly after Christmas in 1956 in Vienna; he's a Hungarian refugee. She met him in the camps after the Hungarian Revolution. It's all common knowledge, Ash. She died the following August. I mention it because not everyone married the legendary Judith Land—in fact, he was her only husband—*and* because she was the only child of J. Land

Crockett, reclusive oil billionaire and chairman of Crockett Industries."

"Daddy and Sarah's boss," Ashley said, ruthlessly untangling a snarl. Her eyes watered.

"You got it."

"Thanks, Caroline."

"Shall I stay on the case?"

"I'll let you know."


Sarah Balaton sat on the monstrous pale pink couch in her ultramodern condominium in a high rise near Galleria. For the first time since her adolescence, she was biting her nails. She should never, never, *never* have called Ashley Wakefield. How could she have been so emotional? So impulsive? So *stupid*?

Her father wasn't speaking to her. He had left for New York last night—on business, his personal secretary had said. Crockett Industries had a corporate condominium in Manhattan, and her father went there frequently, both on business and for pleasure. But this trip seemed too sudden. Too coincidental.

She sobbed silently to herself. What have I done?

Perhaps her misjudgment had come in contacting her father, not Ashley Wakefield. Sarah realized she should have known he would refuse to acknowledge the similarities between the jewels on the cover of *You* and the jewels in the photograph of the Countess Balaton's portrait. "The Balaton jewels are a myth." Well, they weren't.

She had debated showing him the photograph of Judith Land wearing them at the Christmas ball in Vienna. They must have been smuggled out of Hungary—by her father? No, it didn't make sense—and ended up with Judith.

Maybe her father had blotted out that night. Maybe it was too painful to remember.

But how had Ashley Wakefield ended up with them?

Sarah's thumb throbbed. She pulled it out of her mouth and surveyed the damage. It amazed her that she was still this vulnerable where her father was concerned. Was she still the little girl who adored her absent father and chewed her fingernails to shreds every time she did something to disappoint him?

She jumped up. A walk would do her good. A "blue norther" had come down and pushed out the humidity that had gripped South Texas in an oppressive, smelly haze and sticky heat for two weeks. The air was clear now, and delightfully warm, the sky high and cloudless. A perfect Sunday morning.

She took the mirrored elevator down to the show-case lobby. Her building was filled with people who were like herself—at least on the surface. They were wealthy, educated, upwardly mobile professionals. They were the doers and the risk takers.

And yet Sarah didn't think there was anyone like herself. Wherever she went, she felt like an alien. She didn't belong.

Suddenly, fervently, she wished there was someone in her life she could trust, wholly and without question, someone she could turn to, *knowing* he would be there. Then, perhaps, she could begin to feel she belonged somewhere.

She snorted in self-disgust. "Don't be such a simp."

But was it so wrong to want to love and be loved? What was she betraying?

As she moved to the double doors, a man in a navy

blue suit fell in beside her. "Good morning, Ms. Balaton," he said smoothly.

Her eyes widened as she looked up, but she said nothing. There was no need. He was a security guard for her father—a competent, loyal bodyguard.

Clearly Andrew Balaton was having his daughter watched. To protect her, she wondered, or to stop her?

And she thought, from what?

It was almost noon when Jeremy drove back out to the Wakefield farm. He stood next to an old rag mop at the side entrance and knocked at the door, but no one answered. The maroon Jaguar was still in the driveway. From the article in *You*, he knew Ashley Wakefield drove one. She was here.

He followed a *thwacking* sound around behind the red shed to a woodpile, where a tall dark-haired man was swinging an ax. Sweat poured down his face, turning the dirt and dust there to mud. His swing was slow and uneven—painful, it seemed.

David Wakefield. The twin brother and cobeneficiary of the Liechtenstein trust.

As Jeremy moved closer, he noticed the purples and yellows of fresh bruises, the places that had swelled, the places that were scabbed over. "Jeremy, there's no danger..." For whom, Mac?

He put out a hand as he introduced himself, and they shook. "I met your sister yesterday afternoon," Jeremy said pleasantly.

"Right." David winced in pain, holding his abdomen. "She told me."

"Are you all right?"

"Yeah, just trying to chase away some ghosts and goblins with a little physical labor."

Jeremy could see David Wakefield was used to physical work, probably relished it. "You look as if you're in pain."

He grimaced, stretching a bit. "Yeah."

"What happened?" Jeremy asked casually.

"I smart-assed the wrong guy. Come on inside, I'll fix some iced tea—"

"I'm sorry, I can't."

"Something up?"

Jeremy hesitated as he quickly reexamined his decision to leave Massachusetts. Seeing David Wakefield added a new element—or did it? They were wealthy people—extraordinarily, mysteriously wealthy—and they'd just had their names plastered across the entire country. Mac didn't have to be the only one pestering them.

"I'm leaving this afternoon," Jeremy said. "I stopped by to tell your sister I've talked to Mac Stevens. He's fine. He's planning to conclude some business in New York, then fly back to San Diego." The lie slipped out of his mouth, but whatever Mac was doing didn't need to involve the Wakefield twins. "It was a case of mistaken identity. Your uncle reminded Mac of an old friend. The picture in the magazine wasn't that clear."

David leaned against the ax, letting it support his weight. "You sure?"

"I'm convinced. David, I've known Mac a long time, and I don't see how he could know a Massachusetts farmer."

"Ashley checked you out, you know."

He smiled. "I'm not surprised. I imagine all this publicity has brought the crazies out of the woodwork."

"She doesn't believe you and Stevens are lawyers," David said gravely, studying Jeremy.

"Tell her I'll send her a copy of my diploma—or I'll tell her myself. Is she around?"

"Up wandering the fields."

"I see." He felt an odd disappointment. "Tell her I missed her. It's been nice meeting you both. If you're ever in San Diego, look me up."

# NINE

Ashley leaned over the wire-mesh fence and talked to the chickens. The temperature was dropping fast, and it was almost dark. She had put on her uncle's red-and-black plaid jacket to do the evening chores. David had aggravated his injuries with his wood chopping, and she'd banished him to his room with bowls of cream of carrot soup and homemade applesauce. They had passed a very frustrating afternoon.

There had been no word from Barky. No sign of the blond thug. Nothing more from Jeremy Carruthers. Nothing at all from his friend MacGregor Stevens. Tomorrow, Ashley thought, she would get in touch with Sarah Balaton—even if Sarah didn't call, as promised. Perhaps that would lead to something. If not, at least she'd feel better for having acted.

Then she might consider talking to the police. She wasn't sure. David was against it, but...she just didn't know.

The chickens clucked aimlessly in their yard. They were Rhode Island Reds, the most beautiful of chickens, but she didn't know them. When she was a girl, she would have names for all of them. Cartwright... Lefty...Mary...Flo. If they died of natural causes, she'd bury them in the field above the barn. Vividly, she could remember carting a dead chicken up on a shovel and dumping it in a hole; she'd even made little tomb-stones.

Most of the time, however, they didn't die of natural causes. When their laying days were over, Barky would butcher them. By then they'd be tough, stringy old birds and he'd have to stew them for hours. Ashley could remember sitting up in her room doing her algebra to the smell of Lefty stewing on the cook stove. Barky had never had any patience with her sniffles at the dinner table. She should be glad to have food to eat, he'd say. He didn't believe in being sentimental over a chicken.

Could such a man have stolen diamonds, pearls and emeralds? It didn't seem feasible.

Turning from the chicken coop, Ashley looked out across the road and the fields to the hills beyond. The sun was disappearing in a glow of orange and red, and the air was fresh and brisk. God, she thought, she loved this place.

Someone—something—made a noise. It sounded like a groan.

Ashley spun around. "David?"

The wind blew sharply in her face. She tried to blot out the normal sounds of the farm. Standing very still, she looked all around her.

There was an unfamiliar dark shape down by the trailer, alongside the driveway. It was lying prone next to the pumpkins piled at the base of the trailer. Ashley's knees buckled. She ran, tripping down the slope, her heart thudding.

"*David!*"

The kitchen door slammed, and David was leaping out of the house, yelling to her in a panic. "What's wrong? Ash, you okay?"

"There's someone at the trailer."

They arrived there together.

Ashley saw the gray hair, the tall figure.

"Oh, my God. It must be MacGregor Stevens."

"Is he dead?" David croaked.

She knelt beside him. He was lying on his back, and the half of his face visible in the dusk light was ghastly pale. Then he groaned, half conscious. Ashley went rigid to keep herself from shaking.

"We've got to get him inside," she said to David.

Her brother nodded grimly, kneeling beside her in the cool grass. There was a huge swelling on the side and back of Stevens's neck. "Looks like he's been hit pretty good," David muttered. "Shit."

He slipped his hand under the older man's armpits and winced as he began to ease him gently off the ground. "Fucking ribs."

Ashley put her arm around Stevens's waist and took as much of his weight from her brother as she could. The lawyer's head lolled to one side, and he lapsed into unconsciousness. She eased to his side, letting his long arm drape over her, her arm still supporting his waist. He was very tall and she felt herself sinking under the weight. David took the other side.

"Can you make it?" she asked.

"Yeah."

His voice was laced with pain. Ashley said, "We could always call an ambulance—"

"Let's just go."

Half dragging, half carrying MacGregor Stevens, they got him into the kitchen, propped him against the refrigerator and caught their breath.

"He's a big son of a bitch, isn't he?" David said.

"Tall. Jesus, I feel crushed."

"I guess Carruthers lied."

"I guess he did."

They resumed their positions and got Stevens into the living room, where they laid him on the couch, covered him with afghans and went for ice. Ashley wrapped the ice in plastic wrap and, kneeling on the floor next to the couch, placed it on the still-colorless swelling.

Stevens opened his eyes. "I can manage." His voice was less than a whisper, and the hand that took the ice from her was trembling. "I'm all right. Thank you."

"That's a matter of opinion, Mr. Stevens," Ashley said tartly. "I'm calling an ambulance."

His hand shot out, and he dropped the ice. A dozen cubes clattered to the floor. *"No."*

She collected the ice. Behind her, David paced, holding his tender ribs. Ashley pointed out gently, "Mr. Stevens, you could have a concussion."

Again the gray eyes focused on her. She thought that must be a good sign. Were they supposed to be dilated? Or not? She didn't know much about head injuries.

"I'll be fine." He was making an effort to sound fine, she realized, but it cost him. He sank into the frayed couch cushion and seemed to lose more color, although Ashley couldn't imagine that was possible. "Fine," he repeated, shutting his eyes.

Ashley held the ice to the wound. "I don't know what to do," she said to no one in particular, staving off her own incipient panic. "Oh, Lord."

"I was hit." The gray eyes didn't open; the lips barely moved. "From behind. Your uncle."

"Barky?" Her throat hurt. "But that's impossible! He's...fishing."

David came and stood next to her. "Your friend Carruthers said you didn't know Barky—you mistook him for someone else."

There was the barest shake of the head. Dark circles around Stevens's eyes made them appear sunken in his pallid face. "I need rest," he murmured. "Please. No...doctor."

He drifted off. Ashley rose up beside her brother. "Maybe we shouldn't let him sleep. God, David, what if he's really hurt? What if he dies—"

"He'll be okay, Ash. The wound's not that bad."

"What do you know about wounds? We should call the police."

"You want Barky arrested?"

She shot him a look and pushed past him to the kitchen, where she dumped out the kettle on the wood stove and refilled it with fresh water. She checked the fire, crossed her arms and paced.

David put his hand on the doorjamb. "This guy doesn't want a doctor, either. He must have a reason."

"Damn."

"I've been thinking, Ash. Maybe you're right— maybe this Stevens and Carruthers are jewel thieves or something. Barky stiffed Stevens somehow thirty years ago and now he wants revenge."

"I know, I know," she said impatiently. "But it doesn't make any sense! How could Barky be a jewel thief?"

"He's something, Ash."

She dropped her arms to her sides; her hands felt cold. "He's our uncle, dammit. He's a farmer. He—"

"Maybe he *became* those things. Ash, what do we really know about Barky's life before he came to Massachusetts? Not a goddamned thing."

"If Barky was a jewel thief before we were born, David, and Stevens does actually have a bone to pick with him—Jesus! What'll he stoop to to protect himself? My God, he could have killed Stevens!"

"But he didn't," David pointed out reasonably.

"I know. I just...I just wish the hell I knew what he was doing, why...where he is. David, what are we going to do?"

They went back to the living room and stood over MacGregor Stevens. The ice was melting, dripping down his neck. Ashley shuddered. "He looks awful."

"It's a nasty bump, but he's not hurt anywhere else." David gave a weak smile. "Unlike some of us. Ash, think you can watch him on your own?"

"Yes, but why?"

"I'm going out and have a look around. If Barky's skulking around out there, maybe I can get him to tell us what the fuck's going on, to quit the bullshit. I don't know—it's something to do."

She nodded. "Be careful. I mean—" Catching herself, she tried to smile. "It's all right. Barky would never hurt you."

*In places, they had to walk in near-freezing water that was up to their thighs. It would have been better if the swamp were frozen, but they couldn't wait. They'd had to leave now, tonight. Often, the reeds and rushes grew tall, above their heads, and were so thick they couldn't see one another. Speaking was forbidden. It was a pitch-dark night, cold. He could sense the fear in all of them. That was all right, he thought. Only an imbecile would not have been afraid.*

*As promised, they came to a spot of high ground. They stamped their feet, but it was useless. Silently, he told him-*

self there was no cause for worry. There was only a short distance more. In a little while, they could all relax and shout for joy. He thought of Viennese coffee, and his body quaked with the pain of wanting, of being cold and afraid.

Never before had he trusted another person with so much. He'd had no choice. Orült szerzetes knew the swamp better than anyone alive, and only he could get this motley, dangerous group out of Budapest, away from the Russians and their hard-line cronies. Or so went the legend of the "mad monk." Like so much during these difficult weeks, it went unconfirmed.

He didn't like to trust legends.

Making little noise, the rest of the group started back into the water, knee-deep now, ever so close to freedom. His instructions were precise. He forced himself to wait, and then he would follow. It was his job to get the others to safety; his job to accept the position of greatest risk.

A bright light flashed, blinding him.

Guns cocked.

Somewhere behind the painful light a voice commanded, in Russian, "Halt!"

"You were dreaming," Ashley said. She handed Stevens a fresh ice pack. "Feeling better?"

He tried to smile. "Some."

"You talked in your sleep—in another language. You kept saying, over and over, 'orült' and then something that sounds like a sneeze. What does it mean?"

"It means crazy monk or friar." His voice seemed stronger, and his color had improved. But his look was distant. "The mad monk."

"Oh."

"Thank you for the ice."

"No problem."

"Your brother—"

"He's outside trying to find Barky. You haven't changed your mind? It was our uncle who hit you?"

"I was hit from behind, but I know it was he."

"You're enemies, aren't you?"

He said nothing.

When David came in, they agreed to take shifts watching MacGregor Stevens. If he seemed to be worsening in any way, they'd call an ambulance and to hell with his protests. In the morning, if all went well and he improved, they would grill him. It was all they could hope to do: David had found no sign of Barky outside.

Ashley took the first shift. She stoked the fire in the potbelly wood stove and turned off most of the lights. Sitting in Barky's chair, next to his pipes and ashtray, she covered her legs with an afghan and yawned.

MacGregor Stevens slept. This time he didn't talk in his sleep.

In two hours, Ashley dragged herself upstairs. David was snoring, and she hated to wake him, but she'd been on her feet since dawn. It had been one hell of a long day. She needed rest.

She shook him. "David, come on. David—"

Downstairs the screen door banged.

"Oh, no!" She smacked her brother hard. "David, get up! Stevens is leaving."

"Huh? What?"

She ran out of the room and took the stairs two at a time and bounded through the house. The kitchen door stood open. A cold gust of air blew in. She raced outside.

The headlights of her Jaguar blinded her. The engine purred to a start. She leaped toward the light. "Wait!"

The car skidded backward, turned sharply to the right and kicked up gravel as it careered to the end of the horseshoe. Without stopping, it screeched out onto the road.

"You bastard!" she yelled. "That's my damned car you're stealing!"

David burst out in his bare feet and jeans. The situation needed no explanation. "Shit," he said, immediately leaping toward his Land Rover.

"It's useless, David. That piece of shit Rover isn't going to keep up with a Jaguar. Where's your damned Ferrari when we need it?"

"I can fucking try, can't I?"

He had his keys in his jeans pocket. She hopped in beside him. After a few huffs and puffs, the Rover rattled to a start. They drove out the backroad to Route 9. Went into town. Drove around. Asked at a few places.

But no one had seen a maroon Jaguar or an injured middle-aged man.

"The police?" David asked. They were stopped at a red light in the center of Amherst. "Your decision, Ash. It's your car."

She shook her head. "Not yet. The Jaguar's replaceable, but Barky's not. Shit. Think I'd know not to trust a damned jewel thief."

"Water over the dam, Ash."

She smiled halfheartedly. "The egg is broken."

"Yeah. What next?"

She took a deep breath and let it out in a cathartic huff. "I'm flying out to San Diego."

The light changed. David ground the gears going into first. "Sounds good to me."

"David, I think you should stay here in case Barky needs one of us or anything else happens. Or maybe Stevens will show up again."

David was silent.

"I'm not shutting you out," she said quickly. "This could be a wasted trip—maybe Carruthers didn't lie; maybe he was lied *to*. At this point, it wouldn't surprise me if I got to San Diego and found out there was no such thing as a law firm by the name of Carruthers and Stevens—or not one that has heard of *our* Mac-Gregor Stevens and Jeremy Carruthers. I don't know. Hell." Her jaw tightened. "But I damned well intend to find out."

"You're right," her brother finally agreed. "Carruthers might still be on the East Coast. We have only his word that he left—and we've already gotten a taste of how good that is. I'll stay. But if you see him, Ash, you can tell him I don't like being played for a fool."

She called up an image of the green-eyed man in the light shade of the apple tree. "If I see him," she said ominously, "I intend to make that very clear."

# TEN

Lillian Parker moved quickly through the city streets, rushing, hurrying away from the fears and doubts she hoped she'd left behind, in her Park Avenue apartment.

Dammit, this time she was going to mind her own business!

Thirty years ago, she'd stuck her nose where it didn't belong. She'd blamed her budding journalist's instincts, but now she knew that was just self-delusion. She'd been spoiled, headstrong and dangerously naive.

But she wasn't twenty-two anymore. She could make a case for forgiving herself for the terrible mistakes of the past, but now she should know better. If nothing else, life should have taught her when the hell to butt out.

She was still catching her breath when her secretary thrust the telephone at her. "He's been calling since nine," she said, exasperated. "He won't give his name."

"I'll take it in my office." Lillian closed the door and grimaced at the flashing white light. Then, inhaling deeply, she picked up the receiver. "Lillian Parker."

"Lil."

She shut her eyes at the sound of the familiar gruff

voice. "Crockett." She tried to add buoyancy to her tone, as if she were glad to hear from him. "How are you?"

"Alive. Got the magazine, Lil. You want to tell me why you sent it?"

She pictured the old man on his windswept island off the coast of Maine, on his sun porch, the screens still on, as the brisk, cutting wind swirled around him. Lillian had told him often enough he'd catch pneumonia one of these days, but she knew he didn't care. In so many ways, J. Land Crockett had died a long time ago.

"Just spur of the moment, I guess," she said.

"No note. No explanation. Lil, I know you better than that."

Her head had begun to throb. She'd known Crockett since she was twelve. A long time, she thought—for both of them. But never had she willingly done anything to hurt him. She rubbed her forehead with two fingers. "Crockett, please—"

"I laid the past to rest, Lil."

So he knew. "I shouldn't have upset you, Crockett. I apologize."

"Too late to be sorry—and no need. Never asked for anyone's pity, don't want it now. What I want, Lil, is your help."

Oh, Jesus. "I don't think we should interfere," she said, hearing the plea in her words. "Crockett, there's no point. I've been thinking, and maybe it's best just to let this ride. I shouldn't have sent you that magazine."

"But you did, Lil. And I saw it, anyway, before you sent it. I wondered if you would. You want answers just as much as I do. Don't try to deny it: I know you too well. Look, all I want is to meet this girl."

"Ashley Wakefield? Oh, Crockett. She's under tremendous media attention right now, and if they find out you want to meet her—"

"You let me worry about that, Lil."

"I don't want to get involved with this."

But her voice quavered, and she could hear the old man's sharp intake of breath. "Something you haven't told me, Lil? If there is, spit it out now."

She tensed: Crockett had known her far too long and far too well. He was a quick, accurate, nasty judge of character. "No, of course there isn't."

He chuckled. "You never could lie. But you'll talk to me when you're ready, Lil." The chuckle grew smug. "You always do."

"I don't know what your game is, Crockett."

"Hell, this isn't a game. Isn't a damned thing fun about it."

She sighed. "You know what I mean."

"I do, indeed. And it's simple, Lil: I want to know who in hell that girl is."

Jeremy groaned and rolled over in his king-size bed when the telephone rang. He glanced at his watch: seven. Hell. He'd gotten in late last night and stayed up drinking Scotch on his deck and wondering what the hell he was going to tell Elaine Stevens, how he was going to get the flash of Ashley Wakefield's eyes out of his mind. For starters, he'd get a good night's sleep.

So much for that. He fumbled for the telephone and yawned a hello into the receiver.

"It's Mac."

Jeremy was instantly awake and sitting up. "Where are you?"

"Listen to me. I don't have much time."

"Mac, what's wrong?"

"*Dammit, just listen!* I've picked up Bartholomew Wakefield's trail. He's searched Ashley's place in New York and this morning he went to see Evan Parrington, the twins' attorney."

"You *saw* him?"

"Actually, no. I spoke with Parrington myself, and he mentioned that the uncle had stopped by. Look, it doesn't matter. The point is I believe now that Wakefield wants the tiara and the choker Ashley was wearing in the *You* photographs. Apparently they're a part of the trust and—dammit, I don't *know* their significance. I have to find out, and I have to stop him. I do know that."

Jeremy reached for his terry-cloth robe. "Mac, Jesus. The guy's been planting peas and pumpkins for the past thirty years. He's a farmer—"

"Don't let him fool you, Jeremy." Mac sounded tired and bitter. "Wakefield isn't anything he says he is and never has been. He wants the jewels, and it's clear to me he'll do whatever he has to in order to get them."

"Why tell me?"

"Because Ashley Wakefield is on her way to San Diego."

"*What?*"

"I imagine she wants a word with you." Jeremy could almost see Mac's wry smile. "It's a long story, but I'm sure she'll give you all the particulars. Jeremy, I don't want to involve you in this—I told you that— but it's possible I've underestimated the gravity of this situation. I can handle things on my end. But you can help."

Jeremy was sitting on the edge of his bed now. "How?"

"Keep Ashley Wakefield from either contacting or being contacted by her uncle. He must *not* get his hands on those jewels."

Good Christ!

"If you can, Jeremy, keep her in San Diego."

"What about the brother?"

"He's safe. He doesn't have access to the jewels."

"And you, Mac?"

There was a short silence. "I know how Wakefield thinks. I can handle him."

*Click.*

Ashley had gotten some sleep on the plane. It was a night flight, crowded but quiet. She had driven Barky's truck to Boston, showered and changed at her duplex, packed an overnight bag and driven the truck out to Logan Airport. By then, nothing could keep her awake.

With the three-hour time difference, it was just before seven when she landed in Southern California. San Diego was enveloped in a cool mist. She found a pay phone inside the old east terminal and looked up Carruthers and Stevens in the San Diego telephone book.

The number and address matched those on the business card Jeremy Carruthers had given her. So that much wasn't a con. Maybe. She looked under Stevens: MacGregor and Elaine Stevens were listed in Point Loma.

Jeremy Carruthers, she discovered, lived on San Luis Rey in Coronado. She jotted down the number and address, hailed a cab and told the driver, "Coronado, please."

A small exclusive town and resort area, Coronado is only minutes from the center of San Diego by way of the two-mile modern arch of the San Diego-Coronado Bay Bridge. The only other access from the mainland to Coronado is the narrow strip of land that originally supplied railroad transportation to the famous Victorian Hotel del Coronado, still in operation. The strip forms the seaward division between San Diego and the Pacific.

San Luis Rey is on the southern end of Coronado, on the bay side. The cab deposited Ashley in front of a yellow stucco house. She asked the driver to wait.

She rang the doorbell and, while she waited, glanced at her watch: it was seven-fifteen. What would she do if the man who'd startled her into dropping eight eggs had only claimed to be Jeremy Carruthers of San Diego?

Apologize and retreat. That's what you're here to find out, remember?

The door opened.

She instantly recognized the sun-streaked hair and pale green eyes. She had the right Jeremy Carruthers. He was wearing a white terry-cloth robe that came to his knees, and his feet were bare. She noted the dark hairs on his legs and chest.

"You're not the paperboy," he said.

She gave him a cool look. "Another of my faults. May I come in?"

"Of course."

He stepped aside as she walked past him, her shoulders squared. The long flight and erratic night of sleep had left her looking rumpled and feeling tired and irritable. She wore an ice-blue silk suit, very polished, with her hair up and her face lightly highlighted with cosmetics. In the cab, she'd taken a few seconds to refresh her lipstick, but could do nothing about the red lines in her eyes.

She wondered if Jeremy Carruthers would consider her intimidating. She hoped so.

His house was airy and uncluttered, and he led her through a living room and well-equipped kitchen out onto a deck. She could smell roses and the ocean. He offered orange juice, which she gratefully accepted, and they sat on cheerful yellow canvas deck chairs. Jeremy seemed unconcerned with his lack of proper clothing. Probably entertains women like this all the time, she reflected with distaste.

"So," he said, "what can I do for you?"

She gave him a clear, unfettered look. "You're a liar, Jeremy Carruthers."

"You came all the way to San Diego to tell me that?"

"Why not?"

"Not your style."

"In public relations," she said crisply, "I often tell my clients to focus on the positive—since they're decent and reputable people, I have no qualms with this. But sometimes you just have to grit your teeth and call a liar a liar. You *lied*, Mr. Carruthers."

He folded his hands in his lap. "Jeremy."

Jackass. With difficulty, she maintained her composure. "You knew Mac Stevens had no intention of returning to San Diego, didn't you?"

Jeremy leaned forward, and he looked genuinely surprised. "You've seen Mac?"

"Yes." She glared at him. "He was at the farm last night. He stole my car."

"Jesus Christ." He flopped back in his chair and huffed loudly.

"I didn't call the police," she said.

"Why not?"

She shrugged. "I think you know why."

"Here we go playing guessing games again," he said sharply. Then he leaned forward, placing his elbows on his knees, and looked at her with an intensity and gravity that made her catch her breath. "Ashley, I'm not your enemy—and neither is Mac. Please believe that. I've known Mac and trusted him all my life. He has nothing against you."

"But he has plenty against my uncle, hasn't he?"

"I'm afraid I wouldn't know."

She sniffed. "Liar."

"You're becoming repetitious," he said mildly. "Would you like to talk about last night?"

"I'm very tired." Indeed, she thought, that was no lie on her part. It was warm on the deck; she wished she hadn't gulped down her juice so quickly. She wanted another glass. Keep your mind on business, she admonished herself. "If you don't mind," she went on, "I'd prefer to ask the questions. It's my *uncle* your MacGregor Stevens seems hell-bent on harassing. There's no mistaken identity. Your Mac knows damned well who he's after. Either he lied to you or you lied to me."

Jeremy sighed impatiently. "For God's sake, Mac and my father have been law partners for nearly thirty years—"

"Ahh. When did they start the firm?"

"What the hell difference does that make? Oh, I see. You're looking for a connection between Mac and your uncle. Fine. The firm was founded in 1958."

A year after Ashley and David had been born. "What did Mac do before then?"

"He lived on the East Coast."

"Was he ever in Tennessee?"

"I don't know. That's the truth, Ashley."

She smiled nastily. "Of course. How could I ever doubt you?"

"Ashley." Despite his scanty attire, Jeremy adopted a lawyer's demeanor. "Listen to me. MacGregor Stevens is a well-known and highly respected attorney in this town. Yes, I lied to your brother. When I saw Mac, he asked me to butt out. Because I trust him, I did."

Suddenly furious, Ashley jumped to her feet. "And now he's damned well nearly gotten himself killed and stolen a car and probably would like to murder my uncle and God knows what the hell else he's up to!"

"Wait." Jeremy rose slowly. "What do you mean Mac nearly got himself killed?"

Ashley groaned to herself. She hadn't intended to tell Carruthers about Mac's injury. Her vision was fuzzy, and she wanted to go for a jog, walk on the beach, think and be alone. "I found him last night," she said wearily. "Outside among the pumpkins. He'd been hit on the head—from behind. He didn't see his assailant, but he insists it was my uncle. He wouldn't let us call an ambulance. My brother and I did what we could to help him. We gave him ice, we offered him a place to rest, we watched over him. He repaid us by sneaking off with my car."

Jeremy Carruthers ran a hand through his wild hair and sighed heavily. "What about your uncle?"

"No sign of him."

"Damn."

Ashley slipped the strap of her handbag over her shoulder. "Strange behavior, if you ask me, for a pillar of the San Diego community. Thanks for the orange juice, Mr. Carruthers. If you feel like talking, contact my office in Boston. Meanwhile, I have a cab waiting."

"It can damned well wait! I want to know every damned word Mac said!"

Ignoring him, she found her own way through the house. The mist was slowly burning off, and the house was filling with a soft light. The mood of the decor was cheerful and energetic, but gentle somehow.

Jeremy Carruthers tramped after her, bellowing.

"Let me get dressed," he suggested as she reached for the front door. "I'll go with you. Maybe we can figure this thing out together. Look, we don't have to be enemies. You trust your uncle, I trust Mac. Maybe together we can keep them from killing each other. Goddammit, you're not even listening!"

She spun around. "As far as I'm concerned, Mr. Carruthers, you've already told me your full quota of lies. I don't give liars a second chance. Good day."

She left him standing in his entryway, cursing her soundly. Knowing he was watching, she opened the cab door with a haughty toss of the head and climbed in. She told the driver, "Point Loma, please."

And then she turned and smiled regally toward the yellow stucco house. But Jeremy Carruthers had already slammed the door.

The sanctimonious bitch, Jeremy thought, livid, as he pulled on a pair of jeans. What kind of superman did Mac think he was to stop her? He grabbed a pullover, slipped on a pair of topsiders, and dashed outside. Dammit, he had to try. He owed Mac that much. Keep her in San Diego. Fat chance.

To get back to the city, Ashley would have to cross the bay bridge. She was in a cab. He was in a Porsche. It was his only hope of catching up with her.

He shot up San Luis Rey to Glorietta and hit the bridge, swinging immediately into the left lane. He had two-plus miles of bridge to make up for lost time.

As the bridge curved downward toward San Diego, his Porsche slid in two cars behind her cab. Chuckling with satisfaction, Jeremy took a few seconds as he followed her onto I-5 to put on his shirt.

# ELEVEN

"Mrs. Stevens?" Ashley smiled politely at the attractive woman standing in the doorway of the Stevens house. She wore elastic-waist khaki pants and a shirt with the sleeves rolled up, and Ashley could smell the soil on her. A gardener. Feeling calmer, Ashley went on, introducing herself, then adding, "I'd like to talk with you about your husband, if I may."

Elaine Stevens nervously pushed back her hair and ended up smudging her cheek with dirt. She seemed surprised to see the dirt on her hands, as if she'd forgotten what she'd been doing before Ashley had rung her doorbell. She brushed them off slowly and finally looked at Ashley. "About Mac?"

"Yes, Mrs. Stevens. May I come in?"

A dark green Porsche careened into the driveway, and Jeremy jumped out and bounded across the lush front lawn. "Wakefield, what the *hell* are you doing?"

Elaine Stevens looked stunned. "You know Jeremy?"

"We've only just met," Ashley said quickly. "If we could—"

Puffing angrily, Jeremy landed on the doorstep. His hair was flying. "I'm sorry, Elaine. You don't have to talk to her. She has no right to disturb you."

"I don't understand." Elaine glanced uncertainly at

Jeremy. "If there's something about Mac I should know—"

Jeremy opened his mouth to speak, but Ashley cut in smoothly, "There is, Mrs. Stevens. Your husband was at my family's farm in Massachusetts last night."

"Hell," Jeremy said.

Elaine opened the door wide. "Why don't you both come in?"

With a deadly look, Jeremy stepped past Ashley and went inside. She caught up with him, and he muttered furiously at her, "You just had to bring Elaine into this, didn't you?"

"She's a big girl, Jeremy."

"Mac doesn't want to involve her. In fact, he doesn't want to involve *you*, which is why I was stupid enough to lie to you in the first place."

She tossed her head airily. "I don't give a damn what Mac Stevens wants."

Elaine Stevens led them to a cozy oak kitchen at the back of the house. A double window looked out onto a deck and to the bay beyond, down the terraced hill. Ashley could see rooftops of other houses. There were lemon and avocado trees in the yard, and a vibrant flower garden at the border. Elaine invited them to sit at the round oak table. There was a vase of freshly cut pink roses in the middle on a handwoven mat.

"Stop it!" Elaine said sharply as she grabbed a sponge and began wiping the spotless counter top. Her tone softened. "Both of you—please."

Jeremy adopted a conciliatory look, but turned with it to his colleague's wife. "I was going to call you this morning, Elaine. I've seen Mac. He's okay."

Ashley was surprised by the quiet and depth of his tone, and she wondered if perhaps she'd misjudged him. Then he glared at her, and any sympathy she might have been developing for his position vanished. She said briskly, "Mrs. Stevens, as far as I know your husband *is* all right. Perhaps I should explain."

"Perhaps you shouldn't," Jeremy said under his breath.

"No, Jeremy," Elaine argued. "I want to hear."

Ashley turned her attention to Elaine Stevens. "By any chance, have you seen this week's *You*?"

"Oh." Elaine stopped, the sponge suspended in midair. "You're the girl on the cover. Yes, that's right. Ashley Wakefield. You'll have to excuse me—I'm not usually so scattered."

Jeremy went and stood beside her. "It's all right, Elaine."

She shut her eyes. "Oh, Jeremy."

"Mrs. Stevens," Ashley interrupted, her tone businesslike. "I think you'll feel much better if you just hear me out. Sometimes what we imagine can be worse than the reality. In the *You* article was a snapshot of my uncle, Bartholomew Wakefield. Apparently your husband recognized him."

"What?" She was appalled. "But that's ridiculous!"

"One would think," Ashley remarked dryly.

"But we don't know anyone by that name! I'm sure of it. Miss Wakefield, there must be a terrible mistake—"

"I hope so," Ashley said gravely. "Mrs. Stevens, last night my brother, David, and I found your husband back on the farm. He had been slightly injured—"

"Oh, no." She slumped against the counter. "Oh, God, what's he doing?"

"He wasn't seriously hurt, Mrs. Stevens, I assure you."

Nodding that she understood, she gripped the sides of the counter. "Go on. Please."

"He left a little while later—we'd given him some ice, let him rest up." Tact not being her long suit, Ashley thought she was doing well. "He didn't want a doctor."

"Where was he hurt?"

"On the back of the neck." That sounded much less ominous than the head. "Mrs. Stevens, my uncle wasn't home at the time. At the moment, I don't know where either of them is—or what their business with each other might be. I was wondering if perhaps you could help me figure out just how a San Diego attorney and a Massachusetts farmer might know each other."

Jeremy touched Elaine's rigid arm. "Mac said he'd call, Elaine. Maybe we should wait to hear from him."

Her voice choked. "He's crazy, isn't he?"

"No, Elaine." His tone was gentle, his anger apparent only in his eyes, which fastened stonily on Ashley.

She sighed. "Mrs. Stevens, your husband struck me as being remarkably sane." I'll bet most jewel thieves are—ex or otherwise, she thought. "You've never heard him mention a Bartholomew Wakefield?"

"No."

"Before he came to Massachusetts, my uncle lived in Tennessee, in the Nashville area. When my parents died, he took us up to the farm and raised us. That was in 1957. Was your husband in Tennessee then or before?"

"I don't think so."

"All right. My uncle is half English and half Polish. He and my parents left England in 1947. Could your husband have known him in England?"

"No. Mac didn't go to England until after we'd met—the early sixties. We were already married."

Jeremy put his arm over Elaine's shoulder. Ashley sat at the edge of her chair, feeling unreasonably alone. She noted Jeremy's untucked shirt, his sockless ankles, his close-fitting jeans. Maybe he was a decent man after all. It was MacGregor Stevens who had the mysterious past, the unexplained connections. Maybe Jeremy hadn't lied about their relationship; they were colleagues, friends.

"Mrs. Stevens," Ashley went on, focusing on what she'd come here for. "What did your husband do before he and Jeremy's father founded their law firm?"

"Ashley, for God's sake," Jeremy spat.

Elaine patted his arm. "It's all right, Jeremy. Really. If this will help make any sense of what's going on..." She attempted an encouraging smile. "Mac and I met in late 1957—here in San Diego, in fact. Before that he did legal work with the State Department."

"In Washington?"

"Yes."

"What kind of legal work, Mrs. Stevens?"

"The usual dull, detailed diplomatic stuff, he always said."

"He speaks other languages?"

Jeremy looked surprised. "Why do you ask?"

Ashley hesitated. "He was slightly disoriented when we found him." That, she thought, wasn't being tactful, it was lying. And lying glibly. She was suddenly disgusted with herself. What was this affair doing to her? "He...he said something in another language. I asked him later what it meant, and he said 'mad monk' or 'crazy friar.' I wondered if that means anything to you."

Tucking one arm around her own waist and rubbing her mouth, Elaine began to pace across the gleaming tile floor. She looked increasingly shaken. *"Orült szerzetes."*

"That's it!"

Jeremy moved away from the counter. "What the hell are you two talking about?"

"Mac's been mumbling those words in his sleep for years," Elaine said. "They're Hungarian. I think they're the only Hungarian he knows."

From what Ashley had heard while Mac Stevens had dreamed under the tattered afghans, she didn't think so. But she said nothing.

"He told me what they meant," Elaine said. "A literal translation, at least. He's never told me what they *mean*—to him personally, why he breaks out in a sweat sometimes and says those words over and over, until I wake him up and...and tell him it's all right, he's not crazy. Oh, God!"

Jeremy grabbed her and spun her around to him. "It's all right, Elaine. Mac was hurt. Maybe this doesn't have anything to do with a mad monk or whatever the hell he was mumbling about." He dug his fingers into her shoulders in an obvious attempt to force her to regain her composure. "It was an old nightmare, Elaine. That's all."

She sank her head onto Jeremy's chest. "Please don't let my husband be crazy. Oh, God, let him come home to me! Doesn't he know what he's doing? Doesn't he care about me? About the kids?"

Jeremy put his arms around her and let her cry, and Ashley felt terrible for having badgered the woman. But now she had to think. She had let the cab go—not very bright. Now she was stuck up in the hills of Point

Loma with a near-hysterical woman and a man who probably would like to stuff tacos with her. Both would want further words with her. More specifics, more explanations. But she felt they'd already told her all they were going to—perhaps even all they knew about Mac Stevens and Bartholomew Wakefield.

She had one chance. While the other two were preoccupied, neither looking in her direction, Ashley rose and tiptoed silently out of the kitchen. In the living room she picked up her pace, moving noiselessly over the thick slate-blue carpet.

Then she was running through the foyer and damn the noise. She pushed open the door, leaped down the steps and across the lawn.

In his hurry to get to her, Jeremy Carruthers had left his keys in his car. Mac was his friend, Ashley reasoned, and had stolen her Jaguar and—what the hell, turnabout is fair play. She hopped in.

The Porsche started easily.

Jeremy burst out the front door and yelled, "Goddammit!" as she backed out of the driveway. She rolled down the window and waved.

At the airport, she called Carruthers and Stevens and told the receptionist where she had parked the Porsche. The first flight to the East Coast left in ten minutes, but it was to New York. Close enough, she thought, and bought a ticket.

*Orült szerzetes*, she repeated to herself at thirty thousand feet, when she was safe in her seat, alone. The mad monk. **What an** alias for a jewel thief!

But was the **thief** Mac Stevens?

Or Bartholomew Wakefield?

Or, somehow, both?

* * *

Allan Carruthers calmly pinched dried leaves off the Swedish ivy that hung in the floor-to-ceiling window of his sparsely furnished office while his son paced, cursing. Allan was fairer in coloring than Jeremy, not as tall, and his eyes were an even lighter shade of green. At home in La Jolla, he and his wife were avid gardeners, and they often exchanged cuttings with Elaine Stevens. They had two sons. The younger, Matthew, had no interest in law and worked at a ski resort in Aspen. Sometimes Allan thought his elder son should have made a similar career choice.

Without turning from his plant, Allan said, "Would you care to explain what the hell's going on around here?"

"I'm not sure I can." Jeremy tried not to snap at his father, not to blame him because Ashley Wakefield had stolen his car and snuck off to God knew where and he had failed Mac. Nor to blame Allan Carruthers because he, Jeremy, had impulsively promised Elaine Stevens he would find her husband, no matter what.

A goddamned knight on a white horse I'm not, he thought irritably.

"Meaning?" his father asked.

"Meaning I've made a lot of promises."

"It's Mac, isn't it?" Allan brushed a handful of dried leaves into his wastebasket. "Jeremy, Mac called me this morning."

"What? Jesus, you too? You know what's going on?"

"Hardly. He said he'd be in touch with me periodically to find out how you were doing with Ashley Wakefield, if her uncle's tried to contact her. He wants you both out. It's good advice." Allan straightened up, his expression grave. "That's all he said. Jeremy, he knew I wouldn't ask any questions, and I didn't."

Jeremy stood very still. "What are you saying?"

"I'm saying there's something I know about Mac his own wife doesn't even know. I've known it for years, and I have no right to tell you, even now." He paused, and Jeremy could see he had already come to a decision. "But I will. Jeremy, before Mac and I founded this firm, he worked for the State Department."

"Legal work," Jeremy said, his voice hollow. "In Washington."

Allan shook his head, turning back to his plant. "Mac was in Eastern Europe, not Washington."

"In the fifties? Good God. Do you know what you're saying?"

"Of course I do. I'm saying MacGregor Stevens turned to private practice after he'd done intelligence work in one of the most sensitive areas in the world—and I'd damned well keep that in mind, if I were you."

Jeremy tried to absorb this latest twist. "You mean he was a spy?"

"I mean whatever he told me to do, I'd damned well do it."

Chilled by his father's words, Jeremy went rigid. And yet all he could think of was Ashley Wakefield. She was energetic, stubborn, intelligent. And absolutely relentless. She would go after Mac *and* her uncle, and she wouldn't believe her uncle was anything but the salt of the earth unless she had tangible, irrevocable proof.

Bartholomew Wakefield isn't anything he says he is and never has been.

Mac was right. Someone had to stop Ashley.

* * *

As she pushed open the door to her co-op on Central Park South, Ashley could feel her eyes burning and the muscles in her neck and shoulders aching with fatigue and tension. She wanted to call David, take a long bubble bath and go to bed. She would tackle jewel thieves and such in the morning.

She closed the door behind her and yawned. Ashley started and straightened up, alert once more, adrenaline rushing through her veins.

The air smelled strange. Like stale pipe smoke, except she didn't smoke.

Someone had been there. Could still be here now.

No. She wouldn't get paranoid. She might simply have left something in the trash.

She put down her suitcase and handbag, sniffing. It was definitely pipe, not cigarettes.

She whirled around and quickly checked the locks for any sign of tampering. There was none. She tried to think. Who had keys? David. But he didn't smoke. Barky.

Her heart jumped.

Barky smoked a pipe.

Licking her lips with her dry tongue, she grabbed a Waterford vase off a table in the foyer and moved into the living room. The drapes were drawn. It was dark, silent. Her knees quaked, her head throbbed.

*"Barky?"*

She felt her hands grow clammy on the vase as she remembered the blond man who had brutalized her brother. She edged into the kitchen and flipped on a light.

Again, nothing.

She checked the bedroom, dining room, study, bathrooms. The stale air was strongest in her bedroom, and she stood in the middle of the floor, smelling. She looked under the bed, in the closets, in the dressing room.

Whoever had been there had gone.

She went around and opened all the drapes. Then she grabbed the phone and, sitting on her white couch and peering down at Central Park, she called her brother. "David? I'm in New York. I made it back alive. Thought you'd want to know."

"Good." She could hear the relief in his voice. She thought she'd sounded lighthearted, carefree. "Your Jag showed up, Ash."

"It did? Are you all right—"

"Yeah, yeah. Found it this afternoon in the turn-around down the road. I figure Stevens must have parked his own car around there somewhere, but because he was hurt he couldn't get to it fast enough, so he stole yours. Borrowed, I guess. Anyway, it's in good condition. What happened in San Diego?"

He listened quietly, without interruption, while she told him.

"Carruthers must be so pissed off at you," he commented when she'd finished.

"I don't give a damn. David, someone's been here, in my apartment. There's no sign of a forced entry and nothing's missing, but I can smell pipe smoke."

She sighed; it sounded so ridiculous now.

But David took her seriously. Too much had happened already for him to accuse her of paranoia. "Missing any keys?"

"I don't know. David, could you check if the keys I gave Barky are still there? They should be hanging inside the closet in the kitchen. On a penguin key chain, I think."

"I'll have a look." In a few seconds he was back, and there was an undertone of near panic in his voice. "Ash, they're gone."

"Then he was here, David." She closed her eyes. "Barky was here."

# TWELVE

Ashley slept late the next morning—sheer exhaustion had overcome her—and took the noon shuttle back to Boston. It was a gray, drizzly day, but the forecasters promised clearing by nightfall. She didn't mind the weather: the dankness fit her mood. To hell with it, she thought forcefully. I'm not going to let this get to me.

But it was, in insidious ways. She'd had trouble falling asleep, and when she had, she'd had nightmares. When she was awake, she couldn't call on her enormous ability to concentrate; her mind kept wandering to her conversations with Barky, MacGregor Stevens, Jeremy Carruthers, Elaine Stevens.

She needed answers. An end to this.

At Logan Airport, she made her way out to the garage, her stomach lurching when she saw her uncle's truck. Barky had always been there. Ashley could go to college, work in the city, buy expensive clothes, go to fancy parties, watch her investments make her richer by the hour. She could try on new identities, and she could change with the wind. But she could always count on Barky: he would never change.

Now she'd been compelled to wonder if her uncle had *ever* been the man she'd thought he was. She didn't know Bartholomew Wakefield.

She didn't know if she could still believe in him.

The heavy door of the old truck creaked when she pulled it open and climbed inside. It smelled of greasy tools and grain and stale manure. Suddenly she felt overwhelmed. There was so much she didn't know! So many options! And yet none at all, none that made sense.

If only she had left the damned jewels in the vaults of Piccard Cie...had smashed Rob Gazelle's camera into the dust...had caught Sybil Morgenstern's reporter stealing the snapshot of Barky.

But she hadn't.

As she fished the key out of her bag, she noticed a slip of paper tucked into the torn seat. It had almost disappeared into the stuffing, never to be seen again. Something she had missed earlier?

Probably a grocery list, she told herself as she unfolded the paper.

Her uncle's precise handwriting was unmistakable.

Ashley: I must have the jewels. Leave them behind the rock where you and David played pirates. I will find them. No one must see you, Ashley, and you must not see me. Tell only David what you are doing. I will ask nothing else of you. I wish I didn't have to ask this. Trust me.

B.

So it is the jewels, she thought.

How had Barky found his truck in the airport parking lot? Was he watching her?

"Where the hell are you?"

She shut the door. Locked it. Looked around the silent garage. "Trust me." Hell. She read the note again.

When had he written it? Had he already been to the rock, not found the jewels, decided she didn't trust him?

He wasn't fishing. He had lied to David.

Had he hit MacGregor Stevens on the head?

She stomped on the clutch and turned the key. The truck roared to a start. She gunned the engine. Her head hurt, and her knuckles were turning white as she gripped the steering wheel.

"Trust me."

"Oh, God," she breathed, and let out the clutch, backing out of the narrow parking space. It clattered over grates. She was going too fast and took the downward curve too sharply. She slammed on the brakes, narrowly missing the rear end of a BMW.

She had to keep a clear head.

Why did Barky need the jewels?

She paid her parking fee and headed out onto the highway, taking Sumner Tunnel under Boston Harbor, then making her way onto Storrow Drive, along the Charles River to the Cambridge Street exit. She turned up Charles Street and found a parking space a block from her building. No reporters. Thank God.

Digging out her keys, she trotted up the front steps. A voice from behind her said, "Afternoon, Ashley."

She didn't even need to turn around. "Carruthers."

He took the steps two at a time. Even in the drizzle, the highlights in his hair stood out, and she annoyed herself by staring at his eyes. They were truly magnificent eyes; she had to admit that much. He wore jeans that emphasized the slimness of his hips and the length of his legs. Or was she just suddenly attuned to these things? Shock, she supposed.

"I hope you didn't fly all the way out here just to see me," she said.

He crossed his arms and sat on the wrought-iron rail. "Now I see why you adopted an eel. You must get along famously."

She stuck her key in the door. "They remind me of most men I know, actually. If you'll excuse me—"

"Don't you even want to know why I'm here?"

"Tell only David what you are doing." The question was, was she doing it? Was she going to get the tiara and the choker from her safe-deposit box and leave them for Barky? Even as her mind raced, she was remembering that the safe-deposit key was in the bottom of her handbag. She'd refused to go anywhere without it. Melodramatics, she'd told herself. Well, maybe not.

She wondered what Jeremy Carruthers would do if he knew about the note—and the key. Did he want the jewels, too?

"I wish I didn't have to ask this," Barky had written. How much trouble was he in? Had he written the note of his own free will? Had someone already gotten to him? Who? Why?

"Trust me."

Of course. She had to. If she couldn't trust the man who had raised her from infancy, she couldn't trust herself.

She had to trust him. And she had to help him.

Which meant getting rid of Jeremy Carruthers.

"All right," she said. "Go ahead and tell me why you're here."

"Over a cup of coffee?"

She relented and took him upstairs. Again she noticed the faint smell of stale pipe smoke, but she made no comment and didn't bother searching. Her uncle had been here, looking for the jewels.

"Quaint," Jeremy said as he walked through her living room. She saw him eyeing the Homer.

"I guess it's not bad for a city place." She went into the kitchen and got a bag of Kenyan AA beans from her freezer.

"Do you have a country house, too?"

"I have land on the Cape, but I haven't built on it yet. I go camping down there sometimes. Sleep in a pup tent, cook on a Sterno. Helps reduce life to the essentials."

He leaned against the doorway. "Takes you back to your youth?"

"I suppose."

"What does your uncle think of this place?"

She dumped three scoops into her electric coffee grinder. "He says I have too many appliances. Maybe he's right. I hardly ever use them. It's quicker to chop an onion with a paring knife than to dig out the Cuisinart." She smiled. "The legacy of Bartholomew Wakefield."

"He likes being self-sufficient?"

"Either that or he's just cheap. He's condescended to own a washing machine and an electric mixer—the most inexpensive models, of course—but that's it."

"No clothes dryer?"

"God forbid. I grew up hanging out laundry in thirty-degree weather. The towels would come in feeling like plywood, but you never could change Barky."

She turned abruptly and pressed the black button on the coffee grinder. The blade whirred noisily, the beans jumping and clattering as they were quickly reduced to a strong-smelling fine grind. She put a fresh filter in the coffee maker.

"So." She filled the clear glass pot with water and poured the water into the coffee maker; positioned the filter under the drip spout; pressed the button so the little red light came on. "What brings you back to Boston?"

"Mac called."

"Ahh. And what extraordinary tale did you two fabricate this time?"

"You know," he said mildly, "you can be annoying as hell."

She grinned at him. "Didn't say that in the *You* article, did it? 'Ashley Wakefield, dolphin rescuer, mystery heiress and pain in the ass.'"

He sighed. "Mac thinks your uncle's going to contact you."

"Does he now?" She was damned proud of herself for not falling on her face. "Isn't that funny. The man who raised me might want to talk to me. That's enough for you to fly back out here, huh?"

"Has he?" Jeremy pressed.

"No. He's fishing."

Straightening, Jeremy walked into the kitchen and stood very close to her. "I think you're in over your head, Ashley."

"I can swim." She moved quickly past him and got down two mugs. "What else did your buddy Mac have to say?"

"He doesn't want to see you hurt."

"Which, I'm sure, is why he stole my Jaguar and is deeply worried about my own uncle getting in touch with me. What's Barky supposed to do? Suddenly grab all my money when for the past four years he wouldn't even take a cent to buy new linoleum? You don't seem to understand, Jeremy Carruthers. My uncle doesn't *like* money."

His face was expressionless, but Ashley sensed an underlying determination, even fear. "Mac says he'll want the tiara and the choker."

"So? He can have them."

"I don't think that would be wise," he said cautiously. "Mac says—"

"*I don't give a damn what Mac says!*" She slammed the cabinet door and thrust the mug at him, but she was more annoyed with herself for losing control than with him for being so tenacious. "Look," she began reasonably, "it's pretty obvious where your loyalties lie. That's fine: Mac Stevens is your friend. Well, Barky's my uncle."

His pale eyes shut briefly, and when they opened, the fire went out altogether in Ashley. He looked tired, honest, concerned. "Trust me," Barky had said. She had to. But that didn't mean Jeremy Carruthers was *un*trustworthy. Nevertheless, just because Stevens had no qualms about involving Jeremy didn't mean that she could do the same. Or should. Whatever was going on between the lawyer and the farmer, it had nothing to do with Jeremy. She recalled how he'd looked yesterday morning answering his door. She could see again his tanned muscular calves. How strange, she thought.

"I'm sorry," she said suddenly. "I'm a jerk."

The corners of his mouth twitched slightly. "It's all right—so am I." But the good humor didn't last, and in another second he was serious again, and he said quietly, "Tell me what happened to your brother."

"He's a klutz. He fell—"

"Don't lie to me." Jeremy didn't raise his voice.

She rested back against the counter. "Why not?"

"Good Jesus. Are you always this trying?"

"Frankly, no. I sympathize with your frustration, Jeremy, but if David had wanted you to know, he'd have told you himself. Now. Coffee's ready. Make yourself at home. Cream's in the fridge and you're welcome to go up to the deck. I have a few things to do at the office."

He looked at her in surprise. "You trust me enough to leave me here alone?"

"Are you a Winslow Homer fan?"

"I can take or leave him."

She grinned. "Well, I hope you leave him. Anyway, reporters are probably staked out all over the neighborhood and will have good sharp photographs of anyone leaving or entering my building. If you walk off with the silver, Carruthers, I'll have you arrested." She wriggled her fingers under his nose in farewell. "Enjoy."

# THIRTEEN

Jeremy felt like a sleazw, but when Ashley dashed off to Touchstone, he took his mug of coffee and wandered around her duplex. He wanted to get a sense of the woman...and maybe find some indication of whether her uncle had contacted her.

The first floor consisted of a living room, study and small foyer in the front, and a kitchen, dining room and half bathroom in the back. The rooms were all small, coolly elegant. Upstairs there were two bedrooms, two full bathrooms and a messy den. A narrow, steep staircase in the den led to a rooftop deck with a spectacular view of the Charles River and Cambridge to the west and to the southwest the skyline of Back Bay.

He began with the living room. In minutes, he discovered the house was as filled with as many intriguing contradictions as the woman who lived there. Ashley Wakefield was unpredictable, sharp, sexy and beautiful, but also, as far as he could see, damned peculiar.

She had an original Homer seascape, pricey Kosta Boda glassware, Persian rugs, antiques mixed in with expensive contemporary pieces, a stunning collection of aquatic photography. But she also had a ragged bathrobe hanging in her closet, an array of dirty sneakers, a cupboard in her kitchen crammed with old mayonnaise and peanut butter jars, a pickle jar filled with buttons and a freezer stuffed with plastic bags of home-frozen vegetables.

She saved plastic bags from the supermarket and washed used pieces of aluminum foil.

In her study, he found stubby pencils, notes scrawled on used envelopes, outdated stationery torn up for scrap paper, a vase of dead flowers and no computer. There were pictures of eels, dolphins, whales and penguins on her bulletin board.

A waste-not, want-not heiress. Jeremy didn't know many of those.

He thought of Susie and their failed marriage. She was definitely not waste-not, want-not, although very rich, beautiful and intelligent. But Susie was intense, tenacious. He had been drawn to that aura of toughness about her, only to discover, too late, that it was just an outer shell, a persona she liked to present to the world. Inside, Susie was vulnerable and insecure. Her current husband liked that: it made him feel needed, secure, masculine. Jeremy had felt only guilt: he could never have loved Susie as much as she had pretended, even to herself, that she loved him.

No, not love, he thought. Obsession. It was a different beast altogether.

Finding nothing of interest in the apartment except Ashley Wakefield herself, Jeremy called a cab. Outside on her front stoop, he smiled big for any cameras, and when the cab arrived, he said loudly, "Touchstone Communications."

Just in case Ashley threw him out on his ass, he'd have witnesses—and a bit of revenge. He could see the gossip columns in the morning: "Mystery man visits mystery heiress."

Ashley studied the aquatic photographs arranged on a plain white wall of her office. They reminded her of peace and tranquillity and, at the same time, the unpredictability of the sea, and of life.

She turned to Caroline Kent, who sat cross-legged on the bone-colored couch near the outer door. Dressed in wool gabardine, Caroline looked every inch the top-notch professional she was. She had already given Ashley the notes on Sarah Balaton.

*Örült szerzetes*, Ashley thought, was a Hungarian phrase. Andrew Balaton, Sarah's father, was a Hungarian refugee. Was there a connection?

"Caroline," she said, "what do you know about Hungary?"

She shrugged. "Damned little. It's in eastern Europe and it's Communist. What else is there to know?"

"Good question. Think you could pull together a little history report for me?"

Caroline uncrossed her legs, her only indication of surprise. "I'd be glad to, Ash. You want to talk?"

"I can't." She sighed heavily, hating the confusion that raged inside her; if only she could be more certain she was doing the right thing. "If I had more facts…"

"I'll hit the library and see what I can find out. Will that help?"

Ashley nodded, grateful for Caroline's friendship. "Thanks."

The door to the outer office opened, and both Caroline and Ashley looked up as Patti Morgan poked her head through. The young secretary looked distressed. "Ashley, you've got company. He won't—"

Jeremy Carruthers squeezed between her and the doorjamb, thrusting the door wider open, and waltzed into the office. Patti sighed and finished, "He won't take no for an answer and he won't give me his name."

From her position on the couch, Caroline scrutinized Jeremy, and Ashley could see her putting pieces together in her own peculiar way. She climbed to her feet and stood alongside her business partner. "Lovin' Jesus, Ash, what kind of hot water have you got your butt in this time?"

Ashley muttered back, "It's boiling oil, Caroline, and I'm up to my neck." Then she glared at Jeremy. "What do you want?"

He ambled over to her desk and looked around, as if he didn't expect the air of cheerfulness and efficiency. Ashley supposed, after the episode with the eggs, Touchstone Communications would come as a surprise. "You don't seem to have much time for anything in your life but work and fish," he said. "Don't you do anything for fun?"

She looked at him in annoyance. "I do *everything* for fun."

He grinned. "A point to remember."

Caroline nudged Ashley with her elbow. "Shall I call security?"

"No, it's all right. I can handle Mr. Carruthers. How soon can you get me that report?"

Caroline promised to get on it right away. She eyed Jeremy curiously and, as she left, widened her alert brown eyes at Ashley. Caroline was definitely no dummy, Ashley thought.

She snatched her handbag off the desk as Jeremy

came and stood beside her. "You're getting to be a pest, Carruthers."

"Going somewhere?" he asked mildly.

"Just to the institute." She could get rid of him there more easily, she thought, and scoot over to the bank. "I suppose you want to come, too?"

"Sure, what the hell."

She squared her shoulders. "Mac Stevens ask you to follow me around?"

He gave her a mock look of surprise. "You don't trust me."

"Right now, I don't trust anyone." Including Barky? In a way, she supposed. She tucked her handbag under her arm. "Come on, let's go."

They headed down Atlantic Avenue toward the wharf occupied by the New England Oceanographic Institute. The rain had stopped and the sun had come out; it was fairly warm. The plaza was crowded with people.

"I come here often and eat my lunch," Ashley said, hoping to keep the conversation casual and Jeremy's suspicions at bay. "It's a great place to watch people."

"And be watched," he added.

"I'm better at watching. Frankly, I'm not the type to hang out at bars and all the 'in' places just to be seen."

He studied her for a moment, his expression enigmatic, unreadable. "I suppose dates wouldn't be a problem for you."

"Not especially."

That was the truth, she thought. She did have lots of dates—but not many lasting relationships. Somehow, she'd just never met a man she'd consider bringing home to the farm and Barky, a man who'd understand them and the Liechtenstein trust and what they meant to her—and didn't mean. She'd never met a man who'd go out collecting maple sap with her in the dead of March and who'd brave the briars and the red ants to pick wild blueberries and who understood why, despite her millions, she continued to save old jars and eat Barky's pole beans. She'd never met a man who didn't want her to be just Ashley Wakefield the mystery heiress. Or just Ashley Wakefield the dolphin rescuer. Or just Ashley Wakefield the business-woman.

She was all those Ashley Wakefields. And none of them.

A reporter jumped out from behind a fountain and snapped their picture together. "Where you been hiding, Ashley?"

He sounded as if he'd known her for years. She responded with a tight smile.

"Who's the guy? Latest love interest?"

Ashley tugged on Jeremy's sleeve, but he didn't budge. "Name's Carruthers," he said. "Two r's. Jeremy Carruthers."

"Got it. From Boston?"

"San Diego."

Ashley groaned. *"Carruthers!"*

He glanced at her. "And you advise people on how to deal with the media?"

"I like operating behind the scenes, not being a scene. If I wanted my picture in the paper every day, I assure you, I could arrange it."

He laughed and slung his arm over her shoulder and smiled for the camera. Ashley knew she looked mortified. "Must you be so obnoxious?" she complained.

"It comes naturally—to both of us, I fear."

"For that, you can pay to get into the institute."

"Fine with me." Then he saw the entrance fee. "Five bucks to look at fish?"

"You can always pay more. The institute would be delighted to accept your tax-deductible contribution."

He paid precisely five dollars.

There was a lecture in ten minutes on sharks of the North Atlantic, but before she could suggest, in jest, that they attend, Jeremy shook his head. "Forget it." Instead she introduced him to the moray eel.

"Snopes," she said to the huge green slimy creature behind glass, "I'd like you to meet Carruthers. Carruthers, Snopes."

"Snopes?"

"What would *you* name an eel?"

Jeremy looked at the eel in distaste. "I'd shake his hand, but I gather he doesn't have one. My God, does he even have a head? Ugly bastard, isn't he?"

She laughed. "I wouldn't say that in front of him. Morays are the largest eel known in existence, you know."

"One would hope. Is it a snake?"

"Actually, no, it's a fish. They can be quite deadly."

She felt a stab of guilt. Jeremy Carruthers was pleasant to be around and maybe wasn't spying on her for Mac—and probably he didn't deserve what she was going to do to him. But what choice did she have? Barky needed her.

"Ashley?"

She shot away from the eel exhibit and, refusing to look at him, began to yell for security. "Security! Security—quickly!"

With remarkable speed, two beefy security guards

swooped down on Jeremy and grabbed him unmercifully by the elbows.

"What the hell is this?" Jeremy demanded, outraged. "Ashley, dammit—"

She addressed the guards, who knew her and, she suspected, had been briefed by their chief about the *You* coverage. "He won't leave me alone. Must be crazy or something. I can't seem to shake him on my own. Would you mind?"

"Not at all," one said.

"*Ashley!*" Jeremy roared. "It's the jewels, isn't it? You're getting them for your uncle. *Don't do it!*"

The other guard asked, "What would you like us to do with him, Miss Wakefield?"

She shrugged. "Feed him to the sharks."

# FOURTEEN

*Her feet were frozen, numb. Each step hurt more than the last. She kept moving because if she didn't the others would stop, and then they would have to die, too. She thought of Vienna and warmth, and of what lay behind them, in shattered Budapest. It was dangerous to cross the border tonight, because of the cold, the dark, the Russians. The mad monk had said that was good: then they wouldn't be expected.*

*"What will the Russians do if they catch us?" Judith Land whispered. It was too dark; Lillian couldn't see her. But she knew how Judith would look—incomparably beautiful, terrified.*

*"Call our fathers, probably. They wouldn't dare shoot us."*

*"But András?"*

*"They'd have to shoot him."*

*"Mac?"*

*Lillian made no reply. The water was past her knees. The effort to talk was too great as the freezing water soaked through her. Her cashmere coat would be ruined. Her mother would want to know what happened to it. "I gave it to a poor Hungarian refugee, Mother...."*

*Suddenly, behind them, there was a flash of light.*

*Judith screamed. Lillian grabbed her, clamping her*

*hand over her best friend's mouth, then her own. They both
shook violently.*

*"Come!" a voice whispered to them from the pitch-dark
in front of them. "Quickly. The border is very near."*

*"But Mac—"*

*"He's lost."*

*"Oh, God, no!"*

*A firm arm gripped her, pulled her away from the light at
her back, toward the darkness and the shadows. She clung to
Judith, stumbling with her, staying together. They had to.
There was nothing else now, only each other.*

*In the cold, clear, dark night, a shot rang out.*

In Manhattan, in the spacious master suite of Lillian
Parker's Park Avenue apartment, the telephone rang.
She sat on the edge of her king-size bed and picked up
the receiver. She was shaking, hoarse from tightening
her throat, fighting the urge to cry.

"Hello."

"Hello, Lil."

"Crockett."

"How are you, Lil?"

She tucked a leg under her. "Busy. The past few
days have been really hectic."

"You haven't returned my calls."

J. Land Crockett had been cluttering up her answering machines with messages to call him. He never left
his name. He knew she'd recognize his voice. But she
hadn't called him back. "I know. I'm sorry."

"You're afraid, Lil."

"No—"

"It's all right. You'd be a fool if you weren't. Have
you talked to Ashley Wakefield yet?"

"No—I've tried. But she hasn't returned any of my calls, either. I guess she's busy, too. Crockett, maybe it's just as well."

He chuckled softly. "Have I ever changed my mind, Lil? I want to see this woman. I have to. I thought I'd laid the past to rest, but now I know I haven't. Maybe I never will."

Good Lord, she thought, had he actually believed he'd let go of the past? He *lived* in the past! He was a bitter old man, more dead than alive, and he let no one share his pain. He believed he was the only one in the world who had a right to suffer. But Lillian couldn't criticize him. A long time ago, she had learned to deny her own pain, even to herself. No one could share her suffering because she let no one know it even existed.

"Don't give me excuses, Lil," Crockett went on gruffly. "Be afraid, but don't let your fear stop you from doing what you have to do."

"Crockett, for God's sake. Why don't you call Ashley yourself?"

"You know I can't do that. But I have to see her, Lil. You know that, too."

She rested back against the pillows. "I do know, Crockett," she said in a near whisper. "I can't make any promises, but I'll do what I can."

Ashley made the bank just before closing. Again asking her to dinner, the bank officer, George Chambers, led her to her safe-deposit box, which, with his key and hers, he opened. She removed the black velvet-bound cases, thanked him for the invitation, which unfortunately she couldn't accept, and headed back to the lobby. He was really an attractive man: tawny haired, well dressed, intelligent and probably a great deal of fun. But he also knew all about Liechtenstein trusts and he obviously was fond of money.

Picky, picky. Well, she couldn't help it. He wasn't her type. Who is? Her traitorous mind conjured up an image of Jeremy Carruthers, his pale eyes crinkled as he squinted at the bright sun.

In the lobby, a muscular blond man in a too-tight T-shirt fell in behind her.

She remembered: "built like a goddamned bull, blond, a pro."

Thinking quickly, she snapped her fingers as though she'd just remembered she'd forgotten something. "Damn." She spun around. Smiling slightly as she passed the thug—am I getting paranoid?—she walked briskly back to George's office. "I think there's a guy out there after my jewels," she said breathlessly.

"What?" George dropped his pen. "Are you sure?"

She shook her head. "No, but I have good reason to be suspicious."

He jumped to his feet. "Let's get security."

"George, I have no proof. Nothing. It might not even be the right guy. I wouldn't want the bank to get into trouble for pestering an innocent man."

"Then we'll delay him while you make your exit," he said smoothly.

But when they got back out to the lobby, the big blond man was gone. If he were a professional at assault and intimidation, Ashley thought, he'd know when someone had made him. She started to apologize to George, but he wouldn't hear of it. He was nothing if not cautious. He insisted on calling a cab and having a guard escort her and the tiara and choker out to it. He said he was free anytime for dinner with her; she promised she'd think about it and thanked him.

She didn't dare stop at her apartment. If the blond meat wasn't there, Jeremy Carruthers just might be. And she didn't want to run into either of them. She had the cab drop her at Barky's truck and asked the driver to wait until she'd gotten in, started it up and pulled out into the street. She tipped him heavily. He waited.

When she was out on Storrow Drive, she cranked the old truck up—it rattled ominously—and made Amherst in less than two hours.

Jeremy cursed Ashley all the way back to Chestnut Street. The security guards had nothing to hold him on—he'd spouted off like a lawyer—and had dumped him outside in the plaza. He'd promptly hailed a cab.

The front door was locked, and she didn't answer his buzz on the intercom. He sat down on the front stoop and cursed her some more.

"If it isn't Jeremy with two *r*'s Carruthers." The photographer who'd caught them at the institute joined him on the stoop. "Just missed our mystery heiress."

His heart thumped. "Did you see where she went?"

"Maybe. What rag you with?"

"None—"

"Free-lance? You know, if you're on to something, I can get you good money. You do the copy, I provide the photos."

"What about your partner?"

"We're not married, for Christ's sake. Here's my card."

It was mass produced and dog-eared. Jeremy

tucked it into his pocket. "I'll think about it. But if I don't find her, my story's stillborn."

"Got in some old truck parked on Mount Vernon and lit out of here like a goddamned bat out of hell. Storrow Drive West. My asshole partner's trying to follow her, but she got a pretty good head start and was really cooking. The jerk'll lose her. Hey— where're you going?"

Jeremy was bounding down the stairs to his rented car. "Following a hunch."

"Call me, okay? I'm staying at the Parker House."

"Right."

The rock where Ashley and David had played pirates as children stood just beyond a stone wall that divided field and woods. It was a large, solitary boulder, left by the glaciers of long ago, and the twins had liked to play there because it was near a shallow brook and not too deep into the woods. The possibilities for imaginative play had been endless.

Ashley laid the velvet jewel cases in the princess pine and freshly fallen leaves at the southern base of the boulder, which was taller than she or her brother. David, of course, had come with her.

She asked him, "Did you ever believe in the bogeyman?"

"Uh-uh."

"I did. When I was out here alone, I sometimes felt it watching me."

David didn't make fun of her. Instead he admitted, "I believed we had lions and tigers and bears in the woods, and I used to think I was going to be eaten alive any second."

"We all have our fears." She smiled. David's bruises

were healing nicely, but he still moved slowly, and his ribs, especially, seemed to give him some pain. She went on, talking quietly, "And we've hardly even seen a measly old fox out here."

"I know it."

"David, are we doing the right thing?"

"We're doing the only thing we can do."

He crept through the ferns and layers of dead leaves and crouched behind a smaller boulder, about ten yards south of the pirate's rock. From his vantage point, he could see anyone approach the jewels. Ashley climbed an oak near him; she was on lookout. Just like when they were kids, she thought, guarding their treasure from other marauding pirates.

The temperature had fallen, and the clouds rolled in once again, true to the changeable nature of the New England climate. It began to rain. The dampness brought out the smells of the woods, of rotting leaves and wet bark and muddy stream. Ashley wasn't prepared for the sudden afternoon shower, or even for skulking about in the woods and climbing trees. The rain pelted her silk suit and soaked her nylon stockings. In a matter of minutes, she was drenched and shivering. She had, at least, put on a pair of sneakers; they were squishy now.

The wind and rain brought down bright red leaves from the young maples. Even in the rain, the woods glittered with the brightest colors of fall. Ashley looked out across the fields, where cornstalks yellowed in the cool autumn air.

A rustling sound came from below. Twigs, leaves, the wind—it could be anything. She looked all around her.

A stout figure was moving toward them from

deeper within the woods. It was a male figure and was dressed totally in black: black turtleneck, black trousers, black socks, black shoes. He jumped lightly across the muddy stream, and Ashley saw the fringe of brown hair.

"It's Barky," she whispered down to David.

She had rarely seen him in anything but worn jeans and T-shirts. He carried a thick walking stick.

David bounced to his feet. As planned, Ashley would not immediately announce her presence. "Jesus, Barky," David said. "Where the *fuck* have you been? What kind of getup is that?"

"Ach." Barky shook his head in disgust. "You and Ashley are mosquitoes on my back. Leave me *alone*."

"Let you fish?"

"Yes!"

It was all Ashley could do to remain silent in the tree.

"Barky, what do you want with the jewels?"

He sighed heavily. "You should have done what I said in the note. You should have trusted me."

"It's not a question of trust. Barky, for Christ's sake. I want some answers. Who the hell's MacGregor Stevens? What's he got against you? And the son of a bitch who beat me up—"

"David, you must stop." Barky didn't yell. Ashley had never seen such a graveness and depth of emotion in their uncle.

"Listen, old man, I don't care if I have to goddamn knock you over the head and drag you home, we're having some words. I want to know what the hell's going on."

Barky shook his head, impatient, adamant. "I have no *time*. You and Ashley must let me do what I must do. *Trust me!* Go away. Go spend your money and have fun. Find a place and lie in the sun. *Leave me to this!*"

"No."

"Ach." The man in black regarded his nephew in despair. "Then you leave me no choice. David, I want you always to remember that I love you and Ashley as my son and my daughter. I love you more than I do myself. But you *must* stay away from this. I have kept you alive all these years; I don't intend for you to be killed now."

Talk of love and death from a man always so stoic and taciturn drew Ashley off her guard. She dug her fingers into the branch above her to steady herself.

"David, what I do, I do only for you and your sister. I have nothing left in my heart for anyone else."

"Jesus. Barky—"

"You must listen carefully. The pain will be intense, but the break will be clean. And it doesn't matter if you ever forgive me. It only matters that you live and leave me to what I must do."

"What the hell—"

Barky's face twisted in anguish and the thick cane raised up, and David yelled out in horror, and then Ashley did. *"No!"*

She leaped out of the tree and came down hard in the wet, slippery leaves. She scrambled to her feet.

The blow came—firmly, quickly, sharply. Ashley heard the snap of her brother's shinbone. Too late, she wildly jerked the walking stick from her uncle's hand and threw it as far as she could. "You goddamned maniac!" she screamed.

David cried out in agony; he had collapsed on the cold, wet ground.

Ashley was crying. "Barky, no, don't do this to us. *Barky!*"

"I must."

With a horrible deftness, he raised his big callused fist and smashed it down on the back of her neck. Disbelief and the stunning strength of the blow dropped her to her knees; pain stabbed through her.

*Barky...don't do this to me...*

She didn't know if she moaned aloud. The leaves soaked through her knees and a twig stuck in her shoe.

There was a sound. What? Where?

She tried to get up. Her head ached.

She heard the thud of another blow, and her head dropped forward as the shaft of pain sliced through her. She went down next to her brother. *Get up...you have to get up. You have to follow him!*

The rain stopped. All around her she could smell the musty dankness of the woods.

She picked herself up and looked around, but there was nothing, just her brother, her twin, writhing in pain as he moaned into the ground.

"Oh, God. What have I done?"

# FIFTEEN

The screen door banged behind him as Jeremy walked out of the farmhouse and stood on the flat step, next to the dried-up, tangled rag mop. The air smelled faintly of wet chicken manure. It was dusk and no one seemed to be around, although the Jaguar, Land Rover and truck were all parked in the horse-shoe driveway.

He cut between the red shed and the house and headed up the slope to the outbuildings. He glanced in the chicken yard. Hens clucked at him. He checked the barn, the pigpen, the sheep pen.

Where the hell were Ashley and David?

Impatient, he tucked his thumbs in his jeans pockets and looked out behind the barn, across the fields.

Two figures were moving slowly down the edge of the nearest field. One in jeans, one in silk. One male, one female. The Wakefield twins. Soaked. Clinging to each other. Bedraggled and worth millions. David was practically swamping his sister, who seemed to be holding him up entirely on her own.

Then Ashley dropped her brother and sank to her knees.

Jeremy flew. He slid in the wet grass, and the cold wind sliced through him. Neither slackened his pace.

When he reached Ashley, she was trying to get her

brother back up. David's face was ashen. Hers was flushed with pain and exertion.

Jeremy stifled a rush of panic when he noticed the unnatural angle of David's leg and the angry bruise on the back of Ashley's neck. His throat tightened. "Ashley, it's all right. Take it easy."

She couldn't speak. He tore off his shirt and threw it over her shoulders. She made a move to give it to her brother, but Jeremy stopped her. "I'll get David to my car," he told her. "Then I'll come back for you. It'll be okay."

He hoisted the taller David onto his back and shoulders caveman style and felt himself sinking into the wet ground. David was no lightweight. Grateful for the downward slope, Jeremy moved as rapidly as he could; his calves screamed in protest and his back ached.

David didn't make a sound.

As he approached his car, Ashley jumped in front of him. Naturally she hadn't waited for him. She opened the door and helped him get David into the back seat. Then she reeled, and Jeremy caught her by her waist. She was slender, but strong and fit. She smiled through her pain and anguish. "I'm all right."

"I'm glad you think so." He opened the passenger door for her and shoved her in. "Don't look in the mirror. Is there a hospital nearby?"

"Northampton."

He got in the driver's seat and turned the key in the ignition. He was sweating and his heart was thumping painfully in his chest. Adrenaline and overexertion. He glanced in the back seat.

David managed a wink and a single, vicious curse.

That seemed to hearten Ashley. She told Jeremy to

go out to Bay Road to Route 9 and follow it over the Connecticut River to Northampton. "There'll be signs."

He resisted asking questions until he hit the highway. Ashley had thrown off his shirt and, leaning over the seat, arranged it over David. Now she sat with her arms crossed, shivering violently, lips blue. He guessed there wasn't a millimeter of her that was dry.

"What happened?" he asked.

She wouldn't look at him. "It was Barky."

At Fifty-Sixth and Fifth Avenue, Trump Tower is a fashionable high rise, built by wunderkind Donald Trump, and in an area of high prices and luxury, it offers some of New York's priciest and most luxurious shops and condominiums. In the upper stories, overlooking Central Park, the Crockett Industries condominium was decorated lavishly in black lacquer and gold, more for effect than for comfort. It was a place to entertain and impress, not to live and love.

Andrew Balaton, in a velvet smoking jacket, greeted his not unexpected guest. There had been no telegram, no telephone call, no note that he was coming, but Andrew knew.

The president of Crockett Industries poured two glasses of Courvoisier brandy, and the two men sat opposite each other, each looking through the floor-to-ceiling windows to Manhattan glittering beneath them. It was after midnight.

The man who called himself Bartholomew Wakefield looked benevolent, even in his solidly black attire, a simple man out of place in the sumptuousness of the Manhattan apartment. Andrew knew better.

"So," the executive said, "it's been a long time."

"Nearly thirty years."

"Don't misunderstand me, but I assumed I'd never see you again." Andrew measured his words carefully. "Perhaps I should say I *hoped* I never would."

The farmer's expression of placidness and sympathy didn't change. "Necessity brings me here."

Andrew smiled into his brandy. "I shouldn't think you were pleased to have your picture in a national magazine. Did you know I would recognize you?"

"The picture means only that I must act now rather than later—or perhaps not at all. We shall see." The man in black spoke in a mild tone, as if he were discussing the fate of the chickens he'd been raising the past decades. "I helped you when no one else could, Andrew Balaton."

"You didn't help me."

"That's a matter of opinion, but it makes no difference now."

The farmer reached into his trouser pockets and withdrew a tiny glittering gold crown. He handed it across to Balaton.

The color had gone from Andrew's face, and his hands began to tremble. He refused to touch the crown of his nightmares. He swallowed with difficulty; shock had constricted his throat.

The man who called himself Bartholomew Wakefield smiled. "I see you recognize this little crown. Such a simple piece. Do you know it's a replica of the Crown of St. Stephen? The first king of Hungary. Pope Sylvester II sent him the crown and an apostolic cross in the year 1000. St. Stephen christianized Hungary, bringing it firmly and irrevocably into alliance with Western culture. His realm extended Hungarian influence and borders far beyond what they are today, and because of him his country became the 'shield of Christianity' for centuries, a bulwark against expansionism of the Mongols, the Turks and the Russians. Of course, in many ways St. Stephen was a brutal man, but history forgives the weaknesses of its heroes. Some say the Crown of St. Stephen *is* Hungary, even today. The Communists, naturally, would say that is counterrevolutionary propaganda. What do you say, Balaton András?"

He gave the Hungarian pronunciation of his name, with the surname first, according to custom. Andrew gripped the sides of his chair. "I am Hungarian," he said stiffly. "I know the history of my country."

"But do you know the significance of this tiny crown?" The man in black held it up between his thumb and forefinger.

Andrew looked away. "It's the sign of the mad monk."

"*Orült szerzetes.* A 'hero' of the '56 revolution."

"A myth. He never existed!"

"Anything's possible, I suppose." The farmer pocketed the crown.

Andrew cleared his throat. "Where did you get it?"

"It was left for me. You see, Balaton András—"

"Don't call me that! My name is Andrew. Andrew Balaton. I haven't been back to Hungary since the revolution. I'm an American citizen. *This* is my country."

The farmer shrugged impassively. "As you wish. But Andrew Balaton, legend or not, the 'mad monk' has returned. And he's watching us. You, Andrew. And me."

"*No!*" Balaton sprang from his chair. "It's *you* who wants to destroy me!"

"How could I destroy you? I'm a farmer. All day I

plant, I hoe, I work. You are the head of a giant corporation. I can't destroy you."

Balaton's hair was wild, his eyes blazing with anger and confusion. What was this man doing to him? What did he want? He wiped his brow with the back of his hand; only on the squash court did he sweat like this. "Why are you here?" His voice was hoarse. *"What do you want?"*

The man in black remained silent.

*"Tell me!"*

"I have the Balaton jewels."

Balaton collapsed back into his chair. "You can't."

"I wouldn't have come to you unless I did," the man in black continued calmly. "I know you want them. I know you *must* have them. However, to get them, you will have to help me."

"What is it you want me to do?"

He smiled, smug. "You're the president of Crockett Industries. I'm sure together we can come up with something that would make it worth my while to return the Balaton jewels to you. An exchange, perhaps? Information for jewels." His smile deepened. "Let us use our imaginations."

Ashley wrapped herself in a ratty afghan and settled down on the couch next to the wood stove. Jeremy was putting another log on the fire. They'd come back from the hospital, where they'd been forced to leave David. The break wasn't as clean as Barky had promised it would be. David had had to go into surgery for an open reduction; the doctors put on a fiberglass cast and hooked him up to an intravenous solution to pump some antibiotics into him. He'd have to remain in the hospital overnight, possibly longer.

Ashley had a nasty bruise; the doctor gave her a prescription for some painkillers, which Jeremy insisted they stop and have filled.

He sat next to her. "How do you feel?"

"Fine."

She could appreciate his discomfort. She had lied to the doctors about how she and her brother had been injured. She had refused to call the police. And she was beginning to resent Jeremy because the evidence was mounting against Bartholomew Wakefield instead of MacGregor Stevens.

None of it was Jeremy's fault; she knew that. And despite all the anger she directed toward him, anger that was at once as unreasonable as it was inevitable, she didn't want him to leave. She couldn't bear to be in the house alone.

It occurred to her that she never had. Barky or David had always been there.

Now they were both gone.

"When we were kids, David and I, we used to get bats upstairs at night." She spoke softly as the fire crackled and filled the air with warmth and the distinctive smell of burning oak, and nostalgia for her girlhood overcame her. "We'd wake up and hear a bat flapping its wings somewhere. We could never tell right away where it was. So we'd lie on our beds, under our blankets, and be very still and listen, and try to figure out if it was in my room or his. I can remember times when the bat would suddenly land on my bed. It would crawl on me, and I'd have to lie there, not moving, until it flew away. When we were really young, we'd scream for Barky."

"He slept downstairs?" Jeremy asked.

"Yes." She smiled. "He'd come stomping up the

stairs in his underwear, and he'd have a mop or a broom or something. He'd beat the living shit out of those poor bats. Eventually we got old enough so we could deal with them ourselves."

"I can't imagine you killing a bat with a broom."

She picked a wood chip off the pilled afghan. "We tried killing them at first, but we were never very good at it—the stupid thing would fly in our faces and we'd get mad at each other and go into a panic about getting rabies. Then we figured out it was easier just to throw a blanket over the little bastard, gather it up and toss it and the blanket out the window."

Jeremy moved closer to her. "Did the bat suffocate?"

"Never. In the morning, we'd go outside and just the blanket would be there—no bat. We'd never know how it got into the house, how it got out of the blanket, where it went. Lots of times it would come back the next night, and the next. Then it would just stop coming."

"I've never understood bats."

She looked at him. "Right now, Jeremy, I can feel the bats crawling on me. And all I've got is an empty blanket."

After Ashley went to bed, Jeremy stayed up for a while. He tried locking the doors: there were locks, but no keys. And he'd promised Ashley and David he would tend the animals. They seemed irate about their late feeding; he did his best to appease the disgruntled creatures and not get various varieties of manure on his shoes.

Ashley had refused to discuss the episode in the woods, and for the moment, she was in no condition to be badgered. In any case, Jeremy could draw his own conclusions.

Bartholomew Wakefield had gotten the tiara and the choker.

Jeremy wondered where the hell Mac was. Had the supposedly simple and amiable Barky disabled Mac as easily and cold-bloodedly as he had his niece and nephew?

Confusion and exhaustion overwhelming him, Jeremy trudged up the steep stairs.

He peered through an open door into the small slant-ceilinged room that faced north.

Ashley lay atop the worn covers of the twin bed. A lock of dark hair had fallen over one cheek. He went to her. As she slept, the angles of her face seemed softer. He noticed how smooth her skin looked, how full her mouth was. She had found an old flannel nightgown with buttons missing and a tear in the armpit, and its raggedness only added to her mysterious allure. Her long legs were lean and well muscled, the kind that evoked images of wild lovemaking.

The ice he had wrapped into a dish towel had melted, soaking her pillow and the ends of her dark hair, and the towel was lying on the floor. Outside, the temperature was dropping. Jeremy lifted her by the hips and drew back the covers, holding her aloft. She twisted limply in his arms, sighing softly, asleep. Her nightgown was askew, revealing the curve of a pale breast. She smiled in her sleep. One eye opened halfway.

"It's me—Jeremy," he whispered as he placed her back down.

She flopped over onto her back. "Hullo."

"Feeling better?"

She threw one arm over her head. Both eyes opened. Even in the dim light, they were bright. "Much."

She rolled against the wall, then snuggled under the warm covers. She was on her stomach now, butt pushed out toward him.

"Ashley?"

A slender hand reached out and patted the narrow spot alongside her. "Sleep."

He leaned over and peered down at her eyes. They were open—sort of. She smiled, not showing any teeth. Her eyes closed, and she gave a soft moan.

Oh, what the hell, he thought, and peeled off his clothes and settled in next to her.

# SIXTEEN

Her cheek was pressed up against a warm, hard, hairy chest. It seemed to go with a warm, hard, hairy body. How nice, she thought sleepily. I don't think I ever want to wake up from this dream. If she did, the warmth of the body next to her would disappear. It was so real, so delicious. She oozed with longing.

A large hand slipped inside her nightgown and gently stroked the warm flesh of her breasts. Her nipple hardened inside his palm.

*His* palm?

Whose damned palm?

Suddenly her head hurt and she sat bolt upright. "Bastard! What the hell are you doing in my bed?"

Jeremy gave her an unrepentant grin as his eyes roved over her. Her gown was open to her navel, her breasts soft and unconfined. His eyes flashed with amusement. "Just responding to your advances."

"I was asleep!"

She tore out of bed and landed firmly. God, her head hurt! Then it all flooded back to her. David, Barky, Stevens. The jewels. She turned to Jeremy. He'd propped himself up on one elbow. He had good muscle definition in his shoulders. She demanded, "Would you care to explain your presence in my bed?"

He shrugged. "I checked on you before I turned in. You invited me to stay."

"Bullshit."

"Mystery heiress, dolphin rescuer and prude." He laughed. "Your profile indicated you were particular about men. High standards—or cowardice?"

"*You* doesn't know a damned thing about my relationship with men, and neither do you. I don't discuss such things with strangers."

He rolled out of bed, and she bit her lip. He was wearing only a pair of stretch bikini underpants. They were dark blue. Good muscle definition in his thighs, too. Lord, she muttered to herself.

"You shouldn't have standards when it comes to falling in love," he told her matter-of-factly. "You should just do it."

"And risk getting burned?"

He smiled at her. "And risk everything."

"I'm going to feed the animals. At least the shit they give me is real."

She grabbed some clothes and stalked out to the sounds of Jeremy Carruthers's laughter.

Jeremy pulled his clothes back on and went downstairs, where the kitchen was chilly and quiet. It was just eight o'clock. He started a fire in the cook stove, not as deftly as the Wakefield twins, but it lit. It would be just five in San Diego. His father would still be asleep. But Ashley was up at the barn and Jeremy didn't know when he'd get another opportunity to make the call—cretin that he was. He didn't enjoy deceiving Ashley. But had *she* been forthright with him? Hardly.

He dialed the La Jolla number of his parents' house.

Allan Carruthers answered, yawning. "Jeremy? Where the hell are you? What's wrong—"

"Everything's fine; I'm in Massachusetts."

"Mac?"

"I haven't heard from him."

A short silence. "Neither have I."

Jeremy heard his mother waking up and demanding to know who was on the phone. Jeremy said, "I'm pressed for time. Dad, if Mac calls, tell him I blew it."

There was dread in Allan's sharp intake of breath. "What do you mean?"

"I can't talk. Jesus, this is getting complicated. Look—can you just give Mac the message?"

"What about you?"

"I need a few more days."

"Son." Allan Carruthers hesitated. "Be careful."

Jeremy hung up.

Behind him, the screen door banged.

"Bastard," Ashley said.

He swung around. "Ashley, look, let me explain. I was going to tell you—"

"You've been spying on me for Mac Stevens! You have your little network all set up, haven't you? *That's* why you came back from San Diego." She clenched her fists and stiffened her spine against anything logical and reasonable he might have to say. "Bastard, bastard, bastard!"

She snatched her handbag and slammed out the door. Stricken, Jeremy stood guiltily next to the old wall phone. *Damn* this entire stinking mess—and Ashley Wakefield along with it!

The stinging words of his ex-wife came back to him. "One day, Jeremy Carruthers, you're going to fall in love. You're going to be the one thinking of some woman night and day. You're not going to be able to get her out of your mind. You'll do anything to make her want you. You're going to be the one obsessed. And she's going to tell you to take a fucking hike."

But obsession wasn't love, and he was neither obsessed nor in love with Ashley Wakefield. She was sanctimonious, rich and crazy.

And he had thought about her all night.

A car roared to a start.

"Oh, shit, what *now*?"

He ran out to the driveway and jumped in front of the Jaguar, a foolhardy move, he thought, for one who had just duped a reckless and furious woman. She'd damned well run his ass over.

But she stomped on the brake. Then she poked her head out the window. "Get the hell out of my way."

"Ashley, let's talk."

"So you can tell me more lies? No, thanks. Now move."

"Where are you going?"

"Hospital."

Of course. David the wounded brother and sturdy ally was there. "There are no morning visiting hours."

"So they can throw me out. *Move*."

He stayed put. "You don't tiptoe around when you're pissed, do you?"

"Move, goddammit!"

She raced the engine. Not pressing his luck, he dived out of the way and watched her speed off. "Jer, you need an honest woman who'll tell you to go to hell once in a while," his friends had said too damned often.

He picked himself up out of the dew-soaked grass and wondered if he should have just stayed there and slithered around for a while. If nothing else, Ashley deserved some time to cool off. Then he'd tell her everything, and hope she'd do the same.

David ached all over. "The pain will be intense, but the break will be clean." Fucking lunatic. If David in his wildest imagination had seen what was coming, he'd have bonked the old man on the head and carted him off to Northampton State Hospital. Jesus! He'd go ape shit hanging around a hospital room.

He was a man of action, always had to be doing something. Back when they'd first found out about the trust, he'd tried to explain to Evan Parrington that he couldn't just sit around and be rich; he had to act. Evan hadn't understood: he'd suggested David start a business. But David had been talking about physical work. The thought of putting on a tie every day and watching the world go by from fifty stories up gave him the goddamned creeps. He had to be outside, swinging an ax, puttering around with his Rover, plowing the fields. He wanted dirt under his fingernails and calluses on his hands. That was just the way he was.

And now he couldn't even goddamned move.

He was grateful for the company when Jeremy Carruthers walked into his private room. Despite Ashley's warning, David couldn't help but like the tough-minded Californian—and he didn't have all the sparks getting in the way of his good judgment. Ash was drawn to Carruthers; David could see that.

He and Jeremy exchanged pleasantries.

"Has Ashley left yet?" Jeremy asked.

"Well—"

"David, she's been here, hasn't she?"

Ashley had asked him to lie, but he couldn't, not with the raw worry staring at him from the face of Jeremy Carruthers. "Uh-uh. She called about an hour ago."

Jeremy lunged forward. "Where is she?"

"Asked me not to tell you."

"David, I don't want to see her hurt."

"Hell." David shifted painfully in the hospital bed. "Neither do I."

"Then tell me where she is. Look, I haven't been entirely straight with you. Apparently—" He stopped himself, but only for a moment. "Apparently Mac Stevens did some intelligence work before he turned to private practice and all this business with your uncle and the jewels is tied in somehow. I know it sounds nuts, but—"

"You mean Stevens is a goddamned spook?"

Jeremy shook his head. "He hasn't been in thirty years."

"Christ Almighty. Barky getting mixed up with jewel thieves is one thing—but *spooks.* Holy shit."

"David—Ashley, where is she?"

David looked up sharply. "You falling for her?"

Jeremy's hard features seemed to soften. "I don't know."

"Word of advice? Don't get possessive. Ash gets claustrophobic real easy."

"I understand: so do I."

"She's okay, Jeremy."

"But *where* is she? Boston, New York, the Cape—"

"Tennessee," David said impulsively.

"*What?*"

David reached over to his bedside table and poured himself a glass of water from a plastic pitcher. Christ, he felt weak. "She's checking out Barky's story of what he did between the time he left England and when we were born."

"She left for Tennessee without telling me?"

"Figured she didn't owe you anything. Ash isn't perfect, Jeremy. She can be an asshole, too."

Jeremy looked troubled and uneasy. "David, you and Ashley have never looked into your uncle's past?"

"There was never any need." David drank some of the water. Nothing tasted good. "Barky always said there was nothing in Tennessee for us. The farm where our parents lived is now under a reservoir, the people who knew them are gone, and there never were any relatives. It just didn't seem worthwhile to start nosing around."

"What about their graves?"

"We thought about it, but just have never gotten around to visiting them. I mean, they were just never that real to us, as people. I guess maybe we didn't want them to be. Seeing their graves would have made them real. Maybe now—hell. Who knows?" David sighed. "We're tired of reacting, Jeremy. It's time to act. Ash has gone to Nashville to do some digging. I don't know where it'll lead us."

"Where will I find her?"

David met those cool green eyes and saw the fear in them. No one had ever been afraid for Ashley before; David wasn't sure how she'd take to it. "Ash is pretty damned good at taking care of herself, Jeremy."

He managed a smile, nodding. "You know her well, don't you?"

David lifted his shoulders in an awkward, painful shrug. "Hell, we're twins. She's all I've got."

"Then you have to understand I'm not being patronizing or paternalistic or overprotective—or anything else Ashley might think to call me."

"An asshole," David suggested cheerfully.

"Where can I find her?"

David gave it up: Carruthers hadn't had his head bashed in by the man who'd raised him. Maybe he could help. With a cast practically up to his ass, David sure as hell wasn't going to be able to. "Try Belle Meade," he said. "Woman by the name of Nelle Milligan."

Jeremy looked relieved. "Got it."

"And if you're lying to me, Carruthers, and anything happens to my sister, there's no place you can hide. No place. Understood?"

Jeremy snatched a scrap of paper off the bedside table and jotted something down. He handed the paper to David. "Those are my father's home and office numbers in San Diego. He has access to Mac. I'm the one in danger of making a mistake in judgment, David, not you."

Then Jeremy left.

David glanced at the phone numbers. Frustration seized him, and he swung his arm and in one swipe heaved his water pitcher, glass and little box of tissues across the room. A nurse flew in. *"Mr. Wakefield!"*

"Fetch me some crutches and get this goddamned needle out of me. I'm getting the fuck outta here."

"That's out of the question. Please, just be patient."

But that wasn't his style, and never had been.

With her hair tucked under the floppy yellow rain hat and wearing the shocking pink raincoat she hadn't worn in years, Sarah Balaton didn't look like herself at all. She dragged out old cosmetics and did up her face in blue-toned colors she no longer used, and she tried not to notice how her hands shook.

The moment she stepped outside her apartment, although no one seemed to be about, she called on the techniques learned in drama classes she'd taken through college: You are not Sarah Balaton; you are someone else.

She made up a secret identity for herself. She would be Mavin Hawthorne. Mavin didn't walk with Sarah's natural brisk gait. Mavin was more sultry, more seductive, and she carried her shoulders at a slight angle, hips thrust forward.

Andrew Balaton's man in the lobby glanced up and with only his eyes followed her out the door.

Mavin, you're terrific, Sarah thought, forcing herself not to leap up in jubilation. She climbed slowly into the cab she had waiting. Her coat rode up well above the knee. Sarah would have jerked it down, but Mavin let her leg linger in full view of whoever happened to be on the street. Then she pulled it into the cab and shut the door.

"Intercontinental Airport," she told the driver. She glanced back at her building: her bodyguard was running toward her. *"Hurry!"*

The cab pulled away from the curb. Her father's man—or whatever he was supposed to be—jumped into a white Cadillac.

"There's a man following me. Can you lose him?"

The driver frowned into his rearview mirror. "How much?"

"A hundred dollars above fare."

"You got it."

He hit ninety on I-45 North. The cab rattled and

shook, and Sarah chewed her lip as she watched the Cadillac coast onto the infamous interstate, well behind them. Traffic was brutal. There was no way the cab could maintain such a high speed, and he slowed, weaving in and out of the perpetual bottleneck of cars. Sarah knew her destination was obvious; her only hope was timing. According to her calculations, she would just make the last call for the eleven o'clock flight to Atlanta. In Atlanta, she'd switch planes—and airlines—and hop a three-thirty flight to Boston.

In Boston...she'd think about what she'd do there when she'd made it.

The trip to the airport took just under forty-five minutes, and the Cadillac remained well behind them. The cab driver knew his way around the monstrous circular airport, the larger of Houston's two, and dropped her off at the Continental terminal. It was another ruse: she was flying Eastern.

She shoved the cab fare and a hundred-dollar bill at the driver and raced into the terminal, then down to the monorail, which she took to the terminal where Eastern flew. She was perspiring heavily when she picked up her ticket, and near tears when she ran to the gate and just barely made the last call for the flight.

When the seat belt light went off and the flight attendants began serving drinks, Sarah made her way to the tiny bathroom and vomited into the stainless steel toilet.

# SEVENTEEN

Ashley arrived in Nashville, Tennessee, just before noon Central Time. She'd taken a flight out of Bradlee Field, near Hartford, where she'd called her brother, presenting him with a fait accompli. She warned him to be wary of Jeremy Carruthers. Then she banished Jeremy from her thoughts. Or at least she tried. Images of waking up with him that morning kept popping up. She remembered his solid body. His warmth. His reassuring presence. She had thought he was a dream, and he wasn't.

No, she thought, he's a pernicious liar.

She rarely gave liars second chances. She never gave them third chances.

At the Nashville airport, she found a pay phone and called Evan Parrington. She was still in her hog-slopping clothes, which, she thought, weren't as bad as they could have been: a deep red cotton jumpsuit and sneakers. On the plane she'd put up her hair and did her face with the cosmetics in her handbag. A little red lipstick made her look less haunted. She'd turned up the collar on her jumpsuit to hide the swelling at the back of her neck, and took some small comfort in knowing Barky had hit Mac Stevens harder than he'd hit her.

Evan sounded relieved to hear from her. "I've been

trying to call you, but it's virtually impossible to get through."

People passed her in the busy airport; it was difficult to believe there were those who lived normal lives. "I've had the crazies after me," she told Evan.

"Are you all right?"

She hesitated. Was she? "More or less."

"Your uncle was here Monday morning—and an attorney from San Diego. They wanted to discuss the jewels and the trust, but, of course, I couldn't violate client confidentiality and provide them with any information. I've been concerned those photographs might stir up some trouble. Have they? Where are you now?"

She pretended not to hear his questions. "Evan, I need you to arrange to get the rest of the jewels from Geneva. Use a bonded courier—and warn him the assignment could be more dangerous than last time. Tell him especially to watch for a blond apelike guy, about five eleven."

Evan inhaled. "Ashley, perhaps you should come to the office and we should go over this."

"Can't, Evan. When the jewels get to New York, get an expert to have a look at them. Tell them they might be Hungarian. I'll be in touch."

She rented a car, and in the heat of middle Tennessee, she began her self-imposed mission. After nearly thirty years, she was checking out the story Barky had told her and David of their roots.

Bartholomew Wakefield and his younger brother, Richard, had been born in Warsaw, their mother Polish, their father English. When World War II was upon them, they moved to London, where they fought against the Germans. During the war, their father was killed in a bombing raid. Shortly after, their mother died of cancer. At the war's end, the two brothers decided to emigrate to the United States.

But Richard fell in love with a young English girl whose family, like millions of others throughout Europe, had been decimated during the war. Mary Winston joined the Wakefield brothers, and soon she and Richard were married.

They ended up in Tennessee, where they found work on a dairy farm near Nashville. Richard and Mary lived in a cottage on the farm, and Bartholomew rented a room in a boarding house. They worked hard and pooled their savings to buy land.

In 1957, after years of infertility problems, Mary Winston Wakefield bore twins, and she and Richard named them Ashley and David.

Four months later, they were orphans. Richard's tractor fell on him in a freak accident, and his wife ran out to help him...and she, too, was crushed while trying to extricate her husband. They died together, hours later, in a Nashville hospital. Bartholomew headed north with the infants and settled on a hundred and fifty acres in the fertile Connecticut River Valley of west central Massachusetts.

Barky had never articulated to his niece and nephew his feelings that day, but they had whispered to themselves, usually at night when they couldn't sleep, and had tried to imagine. They respected his courage and loyalty in taking on infant twins, and they knew he had made sacrifices. He worked tirelessly. He had never married. And he never, never asked for anyone's pity or thanks, especially theirs.

And, in turn, they had never questioned his version of the facts.

Now Ashley traipsed from hospital to hospital, government records office to government records office, and the evidence—or the lack of evidence—became impossible to ignore, crystallized. She sifted through every level of state, county and city bureaucracy. She badgered the system. She pleaded for information, for answers that weren't there.

Intricate and fail proof though it might be, the medical and government bureaucracies of the state of Tennessee had never heard of the Wakefield family as Ashley knew it. As she had been told it existed! There were no records of any Wakefields ever having lived, married, paid taxes, worked, owned property or given birth in the state.

No records of Richard Wakefield.

No records of Mary Winston Wakefield.

No records of Bartholomew Wakefield.

And no records of Ashley and David Wakefield, twins born on July 14, 1957, in Nashville, Tennessee. She told them she had birth certificates that had satisfied Piccard Cie, one of the oldest private banking houses in the world, but the anonymous bureaucrats shook their heads. "I'm sorry, ma'am," they said everywhere, "there's no record..."

Her life was a lie.

But Piccard Cie had their hand and footprints, their names—how? And all their lives, she and David had used the birth certificates the state of Tennessee now denied existed. Were they forged? How? Why?

"Do I exist?" she asked herself aloud, hearing the panic in her tone as she climbed into the rented car.

Of course you exist. You're here!

"But I'm not Ashley Wakefield." She studied her face in the rearview mirror. Whose eyes were hers if not Mary or Richard Wakefield's? Whose cheekbones? Whose dark hair? "Jesus."

Think of the starving children in Ethiopia, she told herself. There were worse fates than not existing.

What would she do if this meant they would take away her money? She scowled ferociously. You'll work, you ass! Just as you always have.

She drove past a cemetery. Then—abruptly— stomped on the brake, did a three-point turn and swerved back to the cemetery entrance.

Barky had never mentioned the name of the cemetery where her fictitious parents were buried. It didn't matter. Now any cemetery would do.

She parked in the shade and wandered in the heat among the gravestones, and she found herself wanting, and not wanting, to find two that said Mary Winston Wakefield and Richard Wakefield.

Of course she didn't.

Of course she had to turn back.

She pinched a daisy off a plot and tucked it in her hair. She sat in the shade of a spreading oak, on a cool stone bench, and she smelled the cedars and the freshly mown grass and felt the loneliness creeping up into her.

And at last she cried, not for who she was, not even for who she wasn't, but for the parents she had learned to know and love, and who had simply never been.

Late that afternoon, Sarah Balaton wandered around the new wing of the New England Oceanographic Institute, and she marveled at the exhibits, especially of the tiny sea creatures she'd never taken the time to notice. A plaque in front of the giant fish tank stated that there, because they were fed daily and didn't have to hunt for food, prey swam safely among predator. She wondered if humans could learn something from that.

Her interest in Ashley Wakefield as a person grew. But who was she? How had she come to have the tiara and choker Judith Land had worn the night she and Andrew Balaton had announced their engagement?

At the gift shop, Sarah bought a T-shirt and asked the young man at the cash register how she could get to see Ashley Wakefield.

"You won't find her here," he said. "Your best bet is to check at her offices down the road—Touchstone Communications. I might as well warn you, though: she isn't going to see you without an appointment, especially this week."

"Because of the *You* thing?"

"Yeah."

"Well, I think she'll see me."

Sarah got directions and walked over to Touchstone Communications. It was a cool afternoon, cloudy and windy on the waterfront. She didn't know Boston well, thought it a cramped, dirty, snobby city, but she liked the fresh colors and warmth of the Touchstone offices. She asked the receptionist, a tiny woman with fire engine red nails, if she could speak with Ashley Wakefield.

"I'm sorry, Ms. Wakefield isn't in today. If you'll leave me your name and where you can be reached, I'll see that she—"

"It's urgent I speak with her today. As soon as possible, in fact."

"That's impossible. Perhaps our vice president—"

"No, I *must* speak with Ashley Wakefield." She controlled her breathing, forcing herself not to hyperventilate, not to plead, not to collapse with nervousness. Give me a company to run, she thought miserably; that I can handle—but not this. "I understand she must be in great demand this week, but I assure you this is of the utmost importance and simply can't wait. Perhaps if you called her and told her I was here?"

The young secretary shook her head. "I'm sorry. Even I don't know where she is. I'd be happy to leave your name and number. Or perhaps you'd like to talk with our vice president, Caroline Kent?"

Sarah shook her head. "The name's Balaton. Sarah Balaton. And I'll be calling her."

Jeremy took a cab from the Nashville airport to the Greek Revival mansion in Belle Meade that was the residence of Oliver and Nelle Milligan. He was mildly surprised to see the traditional house and trim landscaping: this was old Southern money. One never knew who Ashley's friends were.

A girl about twelve answered his ring and gawked at him with her happy green eyes. "Hi," she drawled, attempting coy already.

"Is your mother home?"

The girl straightened, calling on generations of breeding. "Yes, sir, I'll be glad to get her for you. Would you care to wait in the foyer?"

Jeremy smiled his thanks, and just managed not to laugh when the girl's eyes glazed over. He'd never fancied himself as a heartthrob.

He sat in a Windsor chair in the large, elegant foyer and glanced at his wristwatch. He'd give Ashley three minutes. If she didn't come out of there, he was going in after her.

# EIGHTEEN

Ashley tucked her feet under her on the bright pink-and-yellow striped cushion of the wicker couch. She was on the sun porch drinking a tall glass of "sun" tea under Nelle Milligan's watchful eye.

Nelle was a slim woman in her late thirties with bouncy ash-blond curls and a mischievous glint in her emerald eyes. Her husband was from one of Tennessee's oldest, proudest and richest families. Oliver Milligan, Jr., was widely rumored to be considering his first bid for state office—a rumor Nelle had already confirmed privately to Ashley. He was handsome, charming, industrious and he adored his wife—as long as she understood her role in his world.

Ashley had met Nelle nearly three years ago, at a charity ball in New York. To Ashley's delighted surprise, she discovered the Tennessee homemaker, mother of two and honors graduate of Vanderbilt University, had a secret passion for oceanography. "I've always fancied myself as a frustrated marine archaeologist," she'd confided in her cultured drawl. "Perhaps that's what I'll be in my next life."

Ashley had promptly invited Nelle and her family up to the New England Oceanographic Institute for a tour and a "whale watch" trip. But Nelle had come alone. "Oliver thinks his constituents might not ap-

prove his patronizing a Yankee institution—especially
when Tennessee is a landlocked state."

She spoke with a smile, but Ashley had wondered.
Nelle Milligan was not a naive woman, but she faced
the daily and often conflicting pressures of what people around her expected her to do and be. Husband,
children, in-laws, constituents, friends, parents—they
all had their expectations. And Nelle tried very hard
to please them. But sometimes what Nelle thought
was proper and expected behavior on her part and
what they thought was proper and expected behavior
on her part didn't coordinate, and she slipped painfully, unwillingly, into the unacceptable.

Such as when her visit to the institute had sparked
more than just a passing interest. She'd thought she
was promoting interstate and interregional goodwill,
but Oliver insisted that the wife of a prospective Tennessee senator should focus her charity efforts on local
institutions, or those few national institutions dealing
with dreaded diseases and such that would improve
his visibility and image at home.

In short, Nelle Milligan had no business supporting
anything to do with *salt*water.

If it had been her, Ashley would have told the SOB
to go straight to hell. But Nelle dutifully dropped out
of a month-long summer program for laypeople interested in oceanography that the institute was sponsor-
ing on Cape Cod. Ashley assumed that would spell
the end to their friendship, but she couldn't have been
more wrong. Dipping into her personal trust fund—
willfully—Nelle Milligan sent hefty annual donations
to the institute. She was a major funder of its marine
archaeological research. In the annual report, she was
listed as "anonymous." Every year, just for a few

days, she visited Ashley, telling her husband they were just going shopping. Instead they went on whale watches together and pored over charts of sunken ships, and once Nelle had joined a group of institute volunteers on a Maine beach during a stranding of pilot whales.

Unlike Ashley, Nelle had known how to keep anyone from taking her picture against her will.

Countless times, Nelle had invited Ashley down to Nashville. Ashley, in turn, had promised that one of these days she'd take her up on the invitation. It was one that, Nelle said, was always open.

When Ashley had called from a pay phone near the cemetery, Nelle didn't hesitate. "You come right on over here, hon." She set Ashley up on the sun porch with iced tea and told her just to rest and collect herself. "Then we'll talk."

Now Nelle had waited long enough. "All right, Ashley Wakefield. I want you this minute to tell me what's wrong. I've never seen you like this. You're just not acting like yourself! Now you're going to sit here until you tell me."

"Oh, Nelle, I don't even know where to begin."

Nelle scoffed. "I've got all the time in the world. You just go on and start at the beginning—or the middle or the end and we'll just work our way around. Ashley, we're friends! I've told you things, haven't I? You can't always keep everything locked up inside you."

Nelle wanted nothing more than a chance to prove her friendship, and Ashley knew it, but she didn't know if the wife of a candidate for the Tennessee State Assembly would approve of harboring a nonexistent person. And she could just imagine what Oliver would say.

Then Blythe Milligan slipped onto the porch and excused herself for interrupting. "Mother, there's a man who wants to speak with you."

"Who?" Nelle asked impatiently.

"Oh—" Her daughter blushed. "I forgot to get his name. Oh, but Mother, he's just *awesome!*"

"Ashley, don't you ever have a twelve-year-old like mine," Nelle said, laughing over her shoulder in such a way that both Blythe and Ashley knew Nelle wouldn't trade her elder daughter—or her own mixed-up life—for anything in the world.

Nelle was back in less than two minutes. "Ashley, you devil, you didn't tell me a *man* was involved!"

Ashley jumped up. "My brother—"

"At a guess, uh-uh."

"But David's the only one... *The fink!* Is this guy tall..."

"Dark, pale-eyed, and, as my sweet little girl says, awesome. That's the one. He's also gloriously fit to be tied." Nelle was clearly thrilled with this new development.

"Hell's bells. Carruthers."

Hattie, the housekeeper, was running through the adjoining den, screeching, "Sir! Sir! You can't just go bargin' in there! Sir!"

Jeremy stormed onto the sun porch, and Ashley's heart began to pound when she saw how furious and sexy and concerned he looked. Hattie scurried in after him. "I'm sorry, Mrs. Milligan, but he just wouldn't pay me no mind."

"It's all right, Hattie." Nelle gave Jeremy a dazzling smile. "Well, I declare. If you two will excuse me a moment, I believe I'm needed in the kitchen." Avoiding Ashley's glare, Nelle followed Hattie out.

"I ought to wring your damned neck," Jeremy said.

Ashley shrugged dismissively. "You can't."

He made two fists. "The hell I can't!"

"My neck doesn't exist. If you touch me, you'll get nothing but thin air. I'm not real."

His brow furrowed, and he was instantly alert, on edge. "What the hell are you talking about?"

"Nothing." She wished she'd kept her damned mouth shut. "How's David? Obviously you've seen him."

"He should be released in the morning. He's worried about you."

"How nice." She smiled bitterly. "And Mac Stevens? How's he?"

"I don't know. He's supposed to be in touch with my father in San Diego; so far he hasn't."

"Think Barky busted his leg for him?"

"I don't know what in hell to think."

"But you believe in Mac enough to deceive me."

Jeremy looked at her without guilt. "And you're so damned pristine? You believed in your uncle enough to give him a fortune in jewels."

"Correction." She slammed down her tea glass. "Believe—not believed. Present tense. And I'd give him the jewels all over again if he asked me to."

"Dammit, Ashley, does he have to kill someone before you'll accept the fact that, at the very least, he has some damned difficult questions to answer? I've known you just a few days and lied to you out of concern for your safety and the safety of a good friend of mine—and you're ready to damn me to hell and back.

Your precious Barky's probably been lying to you for years!"

She didn't want to hear the truth in his words. "You lied to me because you believe in MacGregor Stevens just as blindly as I believe in Bartholomew Wakefield. And who the hell says Stevens hasn't been deceiving you for years?"

The anger went out of Jeremy—she could see the muscles in his face relax and his eyes warm with honesty and sympathy. Now, unexpectedly, she wished the anger had stayed. She didn't want him to care. She didn't want his pity. He was getting too close.

"Mac has been deceiving me," he said simply.

"Then he has his own deep dark secrets, hmm? Is he an ex-jewel thief?"

"No, he's an ex-American intelligence officer. He was in Eastern Europe in the mid-fifties."

Ashley felt the shock snapping her head up sharply; it hurt. "Oh, wonderful. Terrific. Fabulous. I've been chasing jewel thieves the past few days while *you've* been chasing spies! Why tell me? No. Let me get carted off by the goddamned KGB or something and have me put in irons and have my fingernails torn off by some sadistic creep. Jesus Christ in heaven. How dare you not tell me?"

"I doubt this is a professional case," Jeremy said with equanimity. "It must be a personal thing between Mac and your uncle—"

"Barky's a farmer! He's not a goddamned spy." She couldn't listen to any more and started past him, just to get away, to think, to digest. A spy. Good God!

But Jeremy grabbed her in the doorway and spun her around. "What happened here today, Ashley?"

His look was intense; she felt his breath warm on her face. "What did you learn—"

"So you can report back to Mac? Forget it."

His eyes seemed to melt into her, and she realized, with a pang, that he was just as confused as she was. He didn't know whether to yell at her or charm her or be grave and distant with her. But nothing, she thought, would work. "Ashley—" He broke off, started again. "Ashley, I'm doing my damnedest to look at this objectively—"

"And failing."

"*Christ!*"

She gave him an icy smile and tossed her head back, aware of every line in his face, every tensed muscle in the arm encircling her waist. "I know: I'm a pain in the ass. A rich bitch. Difficult..Judgmental. Rash."

"Unforgiving," he added with a small smile.

"I don't trust you—and I won't."

"We don't have to be enemies."

"We don't have to be friends, either."

She jerked herself out of his hold and turned away.

Nelle was in the kitchen weaving an explanation of the goings-on out on the sun porch for her husband, a polished, fair-skinned man with horn-rimmed glasses and an easy drawl that belied his perpetual seriousness. Ashley had never pretended to understand or even like Oliver Milligan, Jr., but she thought she could rely on him now.

"I know I owe you both my thanks *and* an explanation," she said, holding herself as regally as she could, refusing to think. "But right now I have to get out of here. You saw this week's *You*? Well, Jeremy Carruthers is a sleazeball reporter who's after the 'real' story behind my so-called mysterious fortune. He's been harassing me since Friday. I'd appreciate it if you could get me to the airport—"

Oliver was already looking ominously toward the sun porch. "Nelle," he said, "get the car."

Nelle was looking dubious. "Ashley, are you sure there's not more to this?"

"Nelle, please—I promise I'll call you and tell you everything."

"Nelle," Oliver said imperiously. "I'll keep Mr. Carruthers occupied while you get Miss Wakefield out of here. What publication does he work for?"

Ashley named a particularly disreputable tabloid.

Oliver winced: no doubt he was seeing his own name splashed across its front pages, his reputation sullied, his candidacy for the state senate derailed. "Be assured," he said, "he won't follow you."

Ashley met Nelle out back in the family Mercedes station wagon. Nelle pursed her lips at her friend. "Honey, you are the *worst* liar."

"I'm sorry—"

"Don't you dare be sorry. I'd like to be a fly on the wall when your Jeremy Carruthers tracks you down again. Sweet cheeks, I have a feeling he's the man for you."

Ashley twitched uncomfortably in her seat. "I have a feeling after this he won't be."

"Nonsense. A man like that loves a good chase. He wouldn't want you if you weren't your own woman. Trust me, Ashley. I understand these things."

That certainly was true, Ashley thought. "I hope Oliver won't be furious. If I cause another rift between you two—"

"Oh, don't you worry about that!" Nelle laid on an exaggerated amount of Southern belle coy. "I've never

seen Oliver so...so *mean*. I just love it! This senate candidacy could be more fun than I thought. If all that energy translates itself in bed, I'll be all set."

For the first time that day, Ashley threw back her
head and laughed.

It wasn't until she was thirty thousand feet above
Virginia that she wondered if she'd been a perfect
jackass. Again. Perhaps she'd fled from Jeremy not because she didn't trust him, not because she was too
hardhearted to give him another chance, but because
she didn't trust herself. There were too many sparks
between them. She couldn't be thinking about sex and
romance now. Her head hurt and her brother was in
the hospital with a broken leg and her uncle was out
skulking around the countryside with a fortune in diamonds and pearls. And there was an ex-spy involved
now. And muttering about mad monks. And a desperate Houston socialite and executive.

Good Lord! How could she possibly think about
screwing with Jeremy Carruthers? Because you can't
help it. Well, tough. She was practical and self-
possessed. Besides which, she'd undoubtedly alien-
ated Jeremy for the last time. She sighed with regret.
There was nothing to be done about it now.

As Barky would say, the egg was broken, and
there'd be no putting it back together again.

# NINETEEN

The next morning was warm and bright in Boston. Ashley had spent the night, alone but in luxury, at the Four Seasons Hotel, in a room overlooking the Public Gardens. She registered under the name Phyllis Mysticeti, *mysticeti* being the Latin name for baleen or "whalebone" whales, the largest animals in the world and one of two suborders of *cetaceans*, i.e., dolphins, porpoises and whales. It was as good a name as any, she thought. Certainly as good as Wakefield. And the clerk didn't bat an eye.

More to the point, no one had found her—not Barky, not Mac Stevens, not reporters, not Jeremy Carruthers. She'd called David, but that was all. He'd promised, this time, to keep his mouth shut about her whereabouts.

She breakfasted in the elegant Four Seasons dining room, reminding herself that until a few days ago she had led a very different kind of life, and then she ventured over to lower Chestnut Street. Rumpled red jumpsuits weren't appropriate attire for the president of a prestigious communications firm. Stifling an unexpected pang of loneliness, she put on a jade linen suit.

Afterward, she stood outside on her steps and looked around. But there was no indication that Jeremy Carruthers was anywhere in the neighborhood. And even the interest of the gossip journalists was fading: there was nary a reporter or photographer to be seen.

She walked to the waterfront. Caroline Kent was there, and they shut themselves up in Ashley's office and began what Caroline called "Hungarian History 101." For more than an hour, she briefed Ashley on what she had learned during her intensive study at the Boston Public Library.

Like those of so many countries in central and eastern Europe, Hungary's borders had changed radically over the centuries. Historic—or Greater—Hungary is two-thirds larger than modern Hungary, which had been chopped up under the punitive measures of the Treaty of Trianon after World War I. Located in the Carpathian Basin, with the Danube River bisecting it, Hungary has traditionally been the breadbasket of the region.

"They're not Slavs," Caroline said. "In fact, Hungarians are linguistically and ethnically different from their Slavic neighbors. They first arrived in the Danubian area in the ninth century and were a nomadic people from Central Asia.

"They were your basic barbarians," Caroline went on as she consulted her steno pad filled with notes. "They became the scourge of Europe. People heard them coming, they cried, '*On ogur!*' Nice little phrase, huh?"

Ashley regarded her with a dry look. "I'll remember it."

"They marauded, pillaged, raped, took slaves—did what barbarians do, I guess. In the middle of the tenth century, they got their asses kicked by the Germans.

By the year 1001, when the first Christian king, Stephen, was crowned, Hungary was ready to usher in an era of peace. The people were forcibly Christianized and their leaders identified theirs as a Western culture. The geographical location of their lands was tempting—not only were they largely flat and difficult to defend, but also fertile, easy to get to, and smack where East meets West.

"They have a long history of being conquered," Caroline said.

"In 1241, the Mongols invaded and destroyed most of the city of Buda. Budapest was two cities then, Buda on one side of the Danube, Pest on the other."

Ashley brought her fingers together in a pyramid and placed her elbows on her desk top. "I know that much, Caroline."

She grinned. "I didn't. I thought Budapest was the capital of Yugoslavia."

"Liar," Ashley said, laughing.

"No, seriously. All the history I took in college, and we never seemed to get to Eastern Europe. I always figured we're talking fat peasants in bright-colored scarves. You know: Hungary has paprika, Poland has kielbasa, Rumania has gymnasts—unjust and inaccurate stereotypes. Hungary has produced some of the world's greatest poets, composers, painters—"

"Now I know why you went into P.R."

She resumed. "After the Mongols came the Turks and the Hapsburgs, each getting their own chunk of Hungary. Finally, in 1686, the Turks were kicked out—*again* Budapest was devastated—and the country came entirely under the rule of the Hapsburgs.

"In 1848," Caroline said dramatically, "Hungary revolted."

Ashley blinked. "I asked you to find out about 1956."

She held up a silencing hand. "Any Hungarian will tell you that 1848 and 1956 have a lot in common. Both were revolts that were nationalistic in spirit: Hungarians wanted to run their own country without foreign interference, they wanted national determination and sovereignty—the usual good-guy political stuff. In 1849, the revolution was crushed by the Hapsburgs with the help of the Russians—which the Hungarians, of course, never forgot. These guys have long memories. And the heroes of the 1848 revolution—the patriot Lajos Kossuth, the martyred poet Sándor Petofi—were widely quoted during the 1956 uprising. They're still national heroes.

"Following disaster in 1849, the Hungarians did eventually win some reforms from the Hapsburgs, and in 1867 the dual monarchy of the Austro-Hungarian Empire was formed. Thus, in World War I, the Hungarians again found themselves on the losing side. The country came out of the war one-third its original size, but in control of its own destiny.

"Or I should say," Caroline corrected herself, "the aristocrats, landed gentry and the clergy of Hungary were in control of everybody else in Hungary's destiny. The country remained pretty much a semifeudal state. A small percentage of the people owned a large percentage of the land; there were great numbers of landless peasants, though some peasants did hold small tracts of land. There were no real democratic traditions, no universal suffrage and little middle class. The aristocrats—who ruled—resisted reform. There were a few who cried out for change, but most were willing to maintain the status quo. As regimes of the interwar period go, theirs wasn't as appallingly authoritarian as some, but it certainly wasn't anything to brag about.

"When Hitler came to power in Germany, he agreed with Hungarian revisionists that their country had been robbed under the terms of Trianon, and Hungary was seduced into collaborating with him. Germany returned some of the territories Hungary considered rightfully its own. In turn, Hungary participated in the German war, but as little as possible.

"They were trying to play both sides against the middle," Caroline concluded. "The Hungarian fascists—the Arrow Cross Party—didn't come to power until Hitler finally invaded in late 1944.

"In 1945, Germany made what amounted to its last stand against the Russians, and Budapest—yet again—was largely destroyed in the bloody battle.

"And the Russians stayed.

"Between the end of World War II and the uprising in 1956, the Communists consolidated their power—viciously. Under the Stalinist-styled personal dictatorship of Mátyás Rákosi, Communist Hungary was set up precisely on the Soviet Union model. It didn't matter whether the Soviet model fit the circumstances of the country or the wishes of the people; that was the way it was going to be. There were excesses and abuses of every kind—arrests, tortures, show trials, executions, forced collectivization, forced industrialization. Even churches were made subservient to the state. Church-sponsored schools were abolished, priests were arrested, religious orders were dissolved—and, in a vastly unpopular move, the Roman Catholic cardinal was imprisoned.

"The terror against the people was carried out by

the state secret police, the Államvédelmi Hivatal, or the ÁVH.

"Then, in 1953, Josef Stalin died, and the thaw began."

Caroline said, "Rákosi, being Stalin's most devoted student, was more or less out on his ass, but nothing happened overnight. Attempts were made at reforming the system, but they were either too moderate or short-lived, and Hungarians became increasingly fed up with Soviet interference in their affairs. When, in 1956, Poland stood up to Khrushchev with some success, Hungarians began to believe they might actually be able to oust the Russians. Fat chance."

As Caroline explained, events leading up to the outbreak of violence in October were many and complicated: "Numerous books have been written on this period. From what I could gather, though, what actually happened depends in large part on who's doing the telling. If you're a Communist, you believe it was a counterrevolution inspired by revisionists, capitalists, warmongering fascists—anybody and anything but yourselves and mistakes you might have made. If you're a democratic socialist, you believe it was a revolt against the excesses of communism, but no one wanted to return to the conservative governments of the past. If you're a conservative, you believe it was a heroic struggle for freedom, a battle to oust communism and restore democracy. I don't know, Ash. It was probably all those things. What's clear is Hungarians wanted the Soviets *out*.

"On the night of October 23, 1956, at a mass demonstration for the reading of demands over Communist-controlled radio, violence erupted, and what's known as 'the thirteen days that shook the Kremlin' began. It was a spontaneous revolt of noble intent, virtually without organization or leaders—and," she added, "it damned well nearly succeeded.

"And it was a Hungarian affair. There was no help from the West.

"In those two weeks," she went on, "Hungary went from being a totalitarian state to a popular democracy back to a totalitarian state. It must have been a terrifying time to live through.

"Imre Nagy, a longtime Communist popular with the people, was placed in power. Through popular pressure and Russian intransigence, he was forced to radicalize Hungarian demands. He took steps to establish a multiparty coalition—anathema to hard-core Communists. He declared Hungarian neutrality, withdrew Hungary from the Warsaw Pact, did what he could to draw support from the West, condemnation of the Soviet Union from the United Nations, and to keep the Russians at bay.

"But he was a Communist, and the West, especially the United States, didn't trust him—or really understand Hungarian nationalism. Besides which, the Suez Crisis erupted at the same time." Caroline stretched out on the couch. "So they waffled. The Soviets said fuck this, and sent in the tanks."

Ashley grimaced. "End of revolution."

"But not an easy end. The Hungarians put up a hell of a fight, against incredible odds—and a far better-equipped enemy. Homemade gasoline bombs can disable only so many tanks. Estimates of the dead range from three thousand on up to thirty thousand and even higher, the most credible being on the higher side. Some two hundred fifty thousand fled over the borders to Austria and Yugoslavia. Thousands were arrested, and many were executed—most notably Imre Nagy himself."

"A heavy price to pay."

Caroline rose slowly from the couch. "Yeah. But some say that Hungary bought a few decades of Russia walking on eggs with the revolution and now they're even experimenting with limited free enterprise. I'd like to take a trip over there, check out the place."

Ashley smiled. "We can go together. Thanks, Caroline—you've done a terrific job."

"Hey, I wasn't no magna cum laude for nothing." She shut her steno pad. "But I know I've oversimplified. As I said, I don't know much about that period or that region."

"Neither do I. Do you recall any mention of the Balatons?"

"There's Lake Balaton, but that's it."

Having received word of Sarah Balaton's visit yesterday, Ashley was hoping the Texas heiress was still in the city. Patti was checking with hotels, hoping to track her down. Ashley desperately wanted to talk to the woman who said her family owned the Balaton jewels.

Again, she thanked Caroline.

"Forget it. Just get your life straightened out, Ash. We miss you around here."

Sarah Balaton fed the pigeons at Fanueil Hall Market Place with crumbs from her croissant. She was sitting on a bench in an open area between two of the three old market buildings that had been renovated into shops, boutiques, restaurants, vegetable stands. It had stimulated the revival of the entire Boston waterfront. She had bought fresh-squeezed orange juice and a croissant in the middle building.

She'd seen Ashley Wakefield enter the offices of Touchstone Communications and would have followed her, but then she saw something as disturbing as anything she'd yet witnessed.

Lillian Parker had pulled up to the Touchstone Communications building in a cab. Famous newswoman, heiress, best friend of actress Judith Land. Countless times Lillian Parker had been offered a fortune to tell her version of the Judith Land story. Each time she had refused. Her friendship with Judith, she said, was not for sale, at any price.

Had Lillian Parker recognized the tiara and choker?

Shocked, Sarah had retreated. She was more convinced than ever that she should have never contacted Ashley Wakefield personally. She hadn't weighed the facts, considered the consequences of what she was doing. She had simply acted. It wasn't like her.

Except, she thought unhappily, where her father was concerned.

"Hello, Sarah."

Giles Smith eased onto the bench beside her, and she looked at him in resignation, too worn out even to register surprise. He was such a hulk. He wore one of his T-shirts, dark raspberry. She had been to bed with Giles twice, six months ago, and had seen him little since. Motivated by simple sexual curiosity—would someone with his build be better than average in bed?—she had found the experience unexpectedly dull. The first time, Giles had hammered into her for three minutes—she'd had nothing better to do than time him. Then he'd collapsed and fallen asleep. Convinced that was a fluke, Sarah had gone to bed with him a second time. It was a repeat nonperformance. Meanwhile, she'd discovered Giles entertained romantic as well as sexual fantasies about her. He'd sent her awful poems, but she hadn't had the heart—or the guts—to tell him she wasn't interested. Instead, she'd simply been ignoring him.

All along, she'd known he was doggedly loyal to her father.

She squinted at him in the sun. "Hello, Giles."

"You shouldn't be here, Sarah. Your father's worried about you."

"Daddy?" She checked herself. Even when she'd been a baby, Andrew Balaton was never Daddy, but always Father or sir. "He sent you here?"

"He's the boss, Sarah."

She sank in the slat seat, defeated, and horribly, she felt like crying. "Just go away, Giles. Please."

He studied her, edging close to her, and the thick skin around his narrowed beady eyes made them seem even smaller. "It's not my decision."

"What do you mean?"

"Daddy's calling the shots. Always does, doesn't he?"

She wanted to scream. *I can't let him see me cry. I can't!* "What do you want me to do, Giles?"

"It's easy, Sar. Your father's in New York. He wants to meet David Wakefield."

"*David* Wakefield? Why?"

"You don't think he told me, do you?"

It was a rhetorical question, but she said, "No, of course not." She looked down at the pigeons pecking at the bread crumbs, always ready for more. Her eyes still lowered, she said, "What am I supposed to do?"

"Invite him to dinner."

"Why not Ashley?"

"Too recognizable, I guess. I don't ask questions."

"Does David have access to the jewels?"

Giles didn't respond immediately, and Sarah glanced up at him: so her question about the jewels hadn't come as a complete surprise. He was weighing his response. "I wouldn't know anything about that, Sarah."

"If I refuse to cooperate?"

He shrugged. "Then I'll have to bring him myself."

"Don't let the boss be denied?" she said with a bitter smile. "I guess you don't leave me much choice. I know you, Giles. I know your tactics."

"Then you'll do it?"

"I'll try. Is...is my father angry with me for skipping out on him?"

"Worried, Sarah, not angry."

"Maybe I can make amends. All right. I'll try to see David Wakefield, but I don't know him. I'm not sure he'll come to dinner just because I ask him to. When is the dinner?"

"Tomorrow night." He laughed and patted her on the cheek. "Dress pretty and don't be late."

# TWENTY

Ashley was stunned to find Lillian Parker waiting in the outer office, and immediately invited the famous newswoman in. She seemed much smaller off camera—unconventionally attractive, eyes a clear, alert turquoise, neatly dressed in a gray Dior suit, deep auburn hair in place. On air, Lillian Parker was renowned for her direct gaze and always was collected, controlled, calm. With uncanny and merciless accuracy, she could pinpoint what motivated a person and zero in on the central issues of that person's life.

Always, Lillian Parker knew what questions to ask.

"Please, Ms. Parker," Ashley said formally, "sit down."

"Thank you, no. The shuttle was delayed this morning. I hate sitting on planes, don't you? Right now it just feels good to stand."

She's fidgety, Ashley thought, and sat down herself at her immaculate desk. "What can I do for you, Ms. Parker?"

Not answering at once, Lillian Parker walked over to the wall of aquatic photographs and took note of a black-and-white shot of the surf at Schoodic Point in Maine. "I read your profile in *You*," she said, not turning. "I think Sybil tried to do a decent job on you. You're lucky."

"I don't feel very lucky," Ashley remarked dryly.

"Oh, the publicity will die down." She turned from the photograph and smiled. "It always does. The entertainment media have incredibly short attention spans. Sybil got hold of me a few years ago; I survived."

Ashley thought: I didn't. I learned I don't exist.

Lillian Parker's incisive gaze seemed to be reaching inside Ashley, and she found herself wanting to duck, or put up a shield or something. Suddenly she was grateful she'd been dealt Sybil Morgenstern instead of this hard-edged woman. She seemed totally objective, totally committed to digging down deep to get at the truth, no matter what it was, no matter whom it hurt. It was simply who the woman was, what she did.

Then her expression softened, and she said, "You don't think you will survive, do you? Well, if it helps, I know the feeling. I can just imagine all the people who've been hassling you."

Ashley wondered if indeed she could. "Not just reporters," she said. "Photographers, magazine people, advertisers, eligible men, charities, nut cases." Spies, thugs, lunatic lawyers from San Diego, Houston heiresses, New York newswomen. "It's really been a zoo around here."

"And you're not interested in any of their offers?" Lillian Parker spoke as if she'd known Ashley for years.

"That's right, I'm not."

"Why?"

"Because I'm not."

She smiled. "Don't get that hunted look, Ashley— may I call you Ashley?"

"Of course."

"And I'm Lillian. I'm not here to try to extract an interview from you. My visit is strictly personal."

Ashley picked up a pencil and held it between her forefingers, one on the tip, the other on the eraser. Now I'm fidgety.

"I'm here on behalf of J. Land Crockett."

"Good God!" Ashley dropped the pencil.

"I beg your pardon." Lillian took a few steps toward her. "Is something wrong?"

No, not at all, Ashley thought cynically. J. Land Crockett was only the chairman of the board of Crockett Industries and the father of Judith Land, who was the dead wife of Andrew Balaton, who was the father of Sarah Balaton, who was vice president of finance for Crockett Industries and, not at all incidentally, after the tiara and the choker. Which Barky had.

Why the hell should there be something wrong?

But she cleared her throat and shook her head, becoming disturbingly adept, she thought, at deceit. "I'm sorry—that's just the last thing I expected you to say. We're talking about J. Land Crockett, the billionaire?"

Again the direct gaze was in place. "Yes. I've been a personal friend of his for years—something very few people realize."

"Not even Sybil Morgenstern?"

Lillian smiled. "Especially not Sybil. It's common knowledge his daughter and I were friends, but Judith's been dead for almost thirty years. It's assumed I lost touch with Crockett. But he's an elderly, sad and troubled man; I can't abandon him. And when he asked me to talk with you, there was no way I could refuse."

"What could he possibly want with me?" Ashley

asked, but already she was guessing: the jewels, Barky, information.

"He'd like to learn more about the New England Oceanographic Institute."

Har-di-har, Ashley thought. "I don't understand."

Lillian moved back to the wall of photographs and eyed one, in color, of dawn on the tidal flats. "The general public knows J. Land Crockett as a Texas oilman and a recluse. Indeed, he does have a ranch northwest of Houston and there's no question he keeps largely to himself. But what most people don't realize—and he'd like to keep it that way—is that he spends half the year on an island off the coast of Maine. He loves the ocean."

Making no comment, Ashley listened with interest. What an incredible crock of bullshit Lillian Parker could come up with when she wanted to.

"It's my understanding," the savvy newswoman went on, "that he's considering making a contribution to the institute's work."

"Terrific." What else could she say?

Lillian stepped forward and handed a business card across the expanse of desk. On the back was a hand-printed telephone number. "He wants you to call him."

"Now?"

"As soon as you possibly can."

"Ms. Parker—"

"That's all I know, Ashley. Now, if you'll excuse me, I have to run. I need to be back in New York this afternoon for a staff meeting. Thanks for taking the time to see me."

Ashley jumped up. "Lillian, have you ever heard of the Balaton jewels?"

She tucked her handbag under one arm. "I must be going."

Ashley madly tried to think. "Have you ever met Sarah Balaton?"

"No."

"Her father?"

"I see Andrew on occasion. Goodbye, Ashley. And good luck with Crockett."

As soon as Lillian Parker was on the elevator, Ashley dialed the number printed on the back of her card. A light-voiced man answered. Ashley said, "I'd like to speak to J. Land Crockett. My name's Ashley Wakefield. I believe he's expecting my call."

"One moment, please."

In a few minutes, a deep rugged voice with an unmistakable Texas accent said, "Crockett here."

"Mr. Crockett, this is Ashley—"

"I know who you are."

She stiffened in annoyance: she hadn't expected a man who wanted her to call him to be so rude. "You wanted to speak with me?"

Crockett didn't hesitate. "I want to *meet* you."

"That would be—"

He broke in. "When can you get up here?"

"Mr. Crockett," she said, politely cautious, "I need to know exactly why you want to meet with me."

He grunted, annoyed himself. "We can discuss that when you get up here."

"This is about the institute?"

"Sure."

She had a feeling she could have suggested they were to discuss African gorillas and he would have said sure.

"When can you get here?"

"Mr. Crockett." Ashley weighed her next words: she didn't want to put him off, but even if she believed his interest in the institute were legitimate—and she didn't—she wouldn't just fly up to Maine at an old man's whim, regardless of who he was. There were procedures. And she figured she ought to be convincingly unsuspicious of his ulterior motives—whatever they might be. "If this is about the institute, I want you to know that anything we discuss will have to be presented to the executive director and the board. I can initiate a dialogue with you, but I want to be very clear—"

"You're not answering my question."

This time she let him hear her irritated sigh. "You're in Maine, is that correct?"

Crockett made a noise that sounded something like a hoarse chuckle, but Ashley couldn't be sure. It could just as easily have been a snort. "Correct."

"Where in Maine, Mr. Crockett? It's a big state."

There was derision in his laugh. "To you damned Yankees, I guess it is. You coming?"

He wasn't doing much to endear himself to her. She said coolly, "Perhaps you could tell me a little more about your sudden interest in the New England Oceanographic Institute and—"

"I don't do business over the phone."

"All right, Mr. Crockett." She decided she'd pushed him as far as she dared: she didn't want to alienate him. "When do you want me to come see you?"

"Tomorrow. Come for the day, spend the night. We'll talk. You fly, right? We've got an airstrip on the island. No lights, but it should do, especially for a daredevil like you. Roger'll give you directions."

"Tomorrow's impossible."

"Nothing's impossible."

The light-voiced man came on the line and gave Ashley directions to an island in Blue Hill Bay. It was named—appropriately, she thought—Badger Rock.

Dinner was promptly at seven, but she could be expected anytime before then.

David hobbled around the farmhouse kitchen, trying to get used to his crutches and the awkward weight of his cast. He'd just been released from the hospital. In all his years of hard work and rough play, he'd never broken any bones, but one swipe from a crazy old man and he was down. It pissed him off.

He flopped down at the kitchen table, sweating and frustrated. He'd had to call his buddy Iggy to help out with the animals. Fruit was rotting on the trees, some of the fall crops needed harvesting. There was work to be done, dammit. Where the hell was Barky?

A knock on the door roused him from his private bitch session. He swore, not feeling like any company. The screen door opened up anyway, and a beautiful golden-eyed woman stuck her head in and smiled. "May I come in?"

"Yeah—sure." He reached for the crutches.

Shutting the screen door softly behind her, she stepped into the kitchen. She was of average height and wore an ivory linen dress that accentuated the creaminess of her skin. She had round, heavy breasts and a small waist and golden hair. Everything about her exuded money. Her smile was elegant, but tentative, as if she weren't quite sure she ought to be smiling. "My name's Sarah Balaton. I—" Her eyes widened as he rose up on his crutches. "Oh, my God! What happened?"

"Dumb accident. You're the lady who called Ash about the tiara and the choker?"

Still staring at his broken leg, she nodded. "And you're David Wakefield."

"In several pieces, but, yeah, that's me."

"I...don't know what to say."

"No need to say anything—except why you're here."

She looked at him, and he was surprised to see how pale she was. Did he look that bad? She said uneasily, "It's a long story."

He grinned. "I've got nothing but time."

Reluctantly, she sat across from him at the table and, plucking a dried-up marigold out of a cheap vase, told him about seeing the cover piece on his sister, her reaction, and, finally, her decision to telephone Ashley. "It was an outrageous thing to do," she admitted. "I'm sure neither you nor your sister is responsible for whatever happened to the tiara and the choker after Judith Land wore them at the Christmas ball in Vienna."

No, David thought, but their uncle could have been. "That's the last time they were seen in public?"

She nodded. "As far as I know."

The marigold had been reduced to a little pile of bright yellow, which Sarah scooped into her palm. David noticed her nails were relatively short, but neat, a pale coral. She looked around the kitchen. He pointed out the wastebasket in the corner by the closet, and watched her as she walked over and dumped the mutilated marigold into the overflowing basket and brushed her palms together. She had yellow stains on her hands.

"Judith Land never reported the jewels stolen?" he asked.

Sarah shook her head. "Except for that rare photograph in the French magazine, there's never been any indication that Judith Land ever owned the pieces. Maybe she borrowed them—or maybe they were given to her. I don't know!"

"They weren't listed in her will?"

"No."

She fixed them both glasses of instant iced tea and smiled at the ancient ice trays and the tall cheap glasses. "It's hard to believe you're a millionaire, David," she said bluntly.

He laughed. Even at his house up in the hills, he had glasses from K-Mart. As far as he was concerned, a glass was a glass: he went by size. But that was all beside the point. "So what's this stuff about Balaton jewels?"

She handed him a glass of iced tea and sat back down, across from him. She left the marigolds alone. "My father insists there's no such thing as the Balaton jewels. I suppose he should know, but the coincidences... I just have to believe he's mistaken."

"He hasn't seen your picture of Judith Land in Vienna?"

She looked embarrassed. "He isn't aware I have it—but he was there, of course. That was the night he and Judith announced their engagement. You'd think he'd remember what she was wearing."

"It's been thirty years."

"But she was the love of his life, and if they were the Balaton jewels—" She broke off, confused, maybe even frightened.

David drank some of his tea; it tasted lousy. "Do you think he might have something to hide?"

"I don't know what to think."

"I can sympathize," he said, giving her one of his lopsided grins. Women usually told him he had a great smile, but he was never sure what to believe and what not to believe; women had a tendency to tell him anything they thought he wanted to hear—at least most of the ones he'd met since the trust. They tried to be whatever they thought he wanted them to be, instead of just themselves. "Why did you come out here, Sarah? Why not just cut your losses?"

"I came north because I wanted to see your sister...meet her, try to explain. As for out here, to the farm—" She shrugged. "I was asked to come here."

"*Asked?* By who?"

She snatched up a marigold. "By my father."

"Well, well, well."

"He...he'd like you to join him in New York for dinner tomorrow evening. He didn't tell me why. I don't understand anything of what's in his mind, what he's planning, why. I just know he's my father and I believe in him—and I'd like to help him."

"Why did he send you? Why not just invite me himself?"

"I don't know."

"Weird."

"He always has his reasons, David. Well? Will you come?"

"Busted leg and all?"

She smiled, an elusive tenderness coming into her eyes. "Absolutely."

"Okay, what the hell." He grabbed his crutches and climbed painfully to his feet.

"What are you doing?" she asked.

"Calling Ash."

After talking to David, Ashley walked up to her rooftop deck and looked west across the Charles River, toward Cambridge. She thought of her brother, battered and beaten, alone with Sarah Balaton, parts of their conversation still fresh in her mind.

"Do you believe her, David?"

"Yes."

"Do you trust her?"

"Yes."

"Please be careful. I couldn't bear to lose you."

"Ash, a couple of months from now, we'll be sitting in front of the wood stove laughing about all this while Barky soaks his feet and tells us he busted my leg and knocked you on the head for a damned good reason."

"And lied to us about who we are?"

"Yeah. That, too."

Her eyes burned with fatigue and tension, and with hot, unwanted tears. Would there be answers on Badger Rock Island, Maine? Was she making another mistake by leaving her disabled brother with a woman who was deeply, perhaps dangerously, involved with this mind-shattering mess?

"You must stop...I love you more than I do myself...I have kept you alive all these years... What I do, I do only for you..."

As she remembered her uncle's words, she shut her eyes and sobbed violently, gripping the rail of the deck. "Barky. Oh, God, what are you doing?"

The sound of footsteps whirled her around, and the tears vanished as she saw the tall, ramrod-straight figure of Jeremy Carruthers coming onto the deck. It was ridiculous, she thought, this running away and chasing, this finding and wanting, this aching inside her that wouldn't go away. The sun and the wind caught his dark hair, and the harsh afternoon light brought out the lines in his face and the darkness around those pale, pale eyes. He looked tired and unamused and not particularly glad to see her.

"How'd you get in?" she asked.

"I pocketed a key when you left me alone the other day. Thought it might come in handy." His smile was almost sad. "I can't be trusted, you know."

She felt an unwelcome sense of guilt, a feeling that was becoming all too familiar. "But you'd have made a good spy. You have the right instincts."

He joined her at the railing, standing close. The sun had begun to dip beyond the hills to the west, streaking the sky with fiery colors, and there was a slight breeze, tinged with the smell of exhaust fumes. Storrow Drive was clogged with rush-hour traffic.

"Was Oliver brutal?"

This time Jeremy laughed. "Not at all. In fact, we had a drink and shared tales of conniving women."

"That's a sexist remark."

"Oliver's a sexist man. However, I was able to persuade him that I was a victim of your female manipulations, a fool helplessly in love with a willful and impetuous woman—like Oliver himself."

Ashley glanced sideways at him. "You know you're full of shit, don't you?"

"Oliver suggested the same thing—not as baldly, of course. I had to prove to him I wasn't a sleazy reporter. My business card, he said, was inadequate as proof. Finally, I called my father and had him vouch

for me. Then, of course, I had to make due explanations to my father, who's beginning to get sick of all
this 'nonsense' and pointed out that Mac and I have
work piling up and clients wondering where the hell
we are."

"He hadn't heard from Mac?"

"I didn't ask—Oliver was right there—but I don't
think so."

"And Oliver was finally convinced of your innocence?"

"Finally. He drove me to the airport himself."

Ashley winced. "Poor Nelle. I wonder what she'll
do."

"If she's smart, she'll cross you off her list of
friends."

"If she's dutiful, obedient and boring, she will."

"She's none of those—and neither are you."

"Nor you."

"Liars never are."

"I suppose not." She didn't avert her eyes. "Am I a
jerk?"

He smiled. "No bigger one than I am."

Then he lifted her hands from the rail and placed
them on his chest, and he slipped his arms around her
waist. And when they kissed, languorously, she felt
the ache inside her slowly begin to ease.

# TWENTY-ONE

*H*e found her alone on the porch of the little house. She had been pacing, terrified, guilt ridden. Now she looked at him, and she saw that he was sweating in the humid southern heat. He was as dashing and mystifying as she remembered, but somehow frightening, too. It had been months since the panicky, disastrous escape across the Hungarian border. And yet, no one knew Lillian Parker had ever set foot in Budapest. It was their secret. It had to be.

And she had thought she would never see the orült szerzetes again. The mad monk.

"You must leave her with me," he said in his precise, excellent English.

"I can't."

"You have no choice. For her safety—and yours—you must trust me. If I knew to follow you here, so will others."

"Aren't you being melodramatic?"

"No."

He was a man who never wasted words; he seemed without emotion. She had learned that within minutes of meeting him. "Will you stay here?"

"It's too risky. We'll have to move."

She turned, looking out across the valley of cedars. It was so quiet here. "And you won't tell me where you are, will you? Where she is? What's happening to her?"

"That would endanger both of you."

*"You're so sure, aren't you?"*

He didn't hesitate. *"Yes, I am."*

*"She doesn't believe she's in any danger, you know."*

*"I know."*

A tense silence followed. She wondered what other young women her age were doing. Why did she always have to be so different? *"I suppose you're right,"* she said quietly, hoping. *"I have no choice. I have to trust you—as I did in Budapest. Tell me I was right then."* Her eyes lifted to him. *"Tell me it wasn't my fault."*

He met her look, and there was tenderness and firmness, a strange blend, in his golden brown eyes. For him, she could be strong. *"You must leave as soon as possible."*

*"If anything happens to her...I'll blame you forever."*

His expression remained the same. *"If anything happens to her, I will blame myself forever."*


Just this one last brandy, Lillian Parker thought as she curled up on the brocade sofa in her Park Avenue apartment. She was enveloped in a red silk charmeuse caftan. Somehow it was easier, more satisfying, to indulge in self-pity when wearing silk. The tears squeezed out from under her closed eyes, but she brushed them away angrily. She had never been one for self-pity. It was useless, a waste of valuable energy.

*"Damn."*

She hurled her glass at the fireplace. It hit the marble mantel and shattered, and she could suddenly see her own life among the shards. Her cowardice, her misery, her fear of the truth. She could look at other people, peer deep into their souls, but she could never look into herself, peer into her own soul. She had never been to a shrink, never gotten into any mystical religions, never taken up transcendental meditation.

Even the books she read were strictly entertainment and all had the happiest of happy endings. Real life was depressing enough, she told herself; she saw shitty endings every day.

She flew to her feet, found another glass, poured herself another brandy.

You're spoiled, she told herself in silent anger. Spoiled, headstrong, nosy and shallow.

No one could be as hard on Lillian Parker as Lillian Parker herself. She took grim pride in that.

As she made her way back to her couch, the intercom buzzed. The doorman announced she had a visitor. "Andrew Balaton, Miss Parker."

Well, hell, send in all the clowns. "Please admit Mr. Balaton, Louis."

Andrew arrived in an Italian suit, radiating, as always, good taste, good health, intelligence. He kissed her hand. She remembered the first time he'd done that, thirty years ago, in the midst of hell.

"Andrew, Andrew," she said, falsely ebullient, more than slightly drunk. "So good to see you! Come in, sit down. Can I get you something to drink? Brandy? Martini?"

"Nothing, thank you."

She sat nervously on the sofa. During the past twenty-five years, under his direction, Crockett Industries had grown, profited, and changed its reputation from a wild Texas oil company run by the last of the Crazy Crocketts to a dignified, reputable Fortune 500 giant. Andrew had managed to change the reality of the company without tarnishing its legend, but he was one of the few truly modest men Lillian knew. He asked for no credit. He simply collected his paycheck, watched the value of his own Crockett Industries stock multiply and thanked J. Land Crockett for giving him, a mere immigrant and his son-in-law for less than a year, a chance to prove himself.

He had loved Judith Land more desperately than Lillian had ever seen anyone love anything. And, with Lillian's help, Judith had betrayed him. For that, Lillian would never forgive herself. She almost laughed, bitterly: just add it to your long long list of regrets.

"Isn't this a surprise," she said, and, although not the tittering type, found herself nonetheless tittering. She sounded like a schoolgirl. But Andrew, she knew, wouldn't object. He found silly women reassuring. "It's been such a long time, hasn't it?"

He smiled politely, pretending not to notice the broken glass and splashes of brandy on the peach-colored carpet. "Too long."

She cleared her throat. She knew she was talking too loudly and trying too hard to sound cheerful. A man as perceptive as Andrew Balaton surely would notice. She tried to calm herself. "Well, Andrew." She paused, and took a sharp breath. "What brings you to New York?"

He watched her with his handsome deep brown eyes. "I think you know, Lillian."

"Ahh." She smiled her best ingenue smile. "Crockett Industries plans to make a bid for the network."

"You never were good at being coy." His words cut her off, and were all the more biting because they were delivered so quietly. That was Andrew's style. He could cut someone to ribbons without ever changing his tone of voice. Crockett was all bluster and noise, but not Andrew. No, never Andrew. "It doesn't suit you," he went on. "You have always been Eastern cool—very reserved, very polished, very direct. We are alike in this regard, are we not?"

"I never thought we were alike in any regard, Andrew." She took a huge gulp of brandy and held her glass precariously between two fingers. "Tell me why you're here. Obviously you have a reason."

"Of course—and one you know, Lillian. Of all people, you know why I'm here."

"Suppose you tell me."

He gave just the barest hint of a smile and inclined his head, evoking his arrogant, aristocratic ancestors. "Ashley Wakefield."

Lillian smiled, swinging her glass. "Mystery heiress and dolphin rescuer. What about her?"

"You tell me."

"Me? I don't even know her."

He stretched out his trim legs. "You met with her this morning in her office in Boston."

"Goddammit! You've been spying on me!"

"What did you see her about?"

"That's none of your damned business." She leaped to her feet, brandy splashing over her gown, and pointed toward the door. "Get out of here. Now, Andrew. Before I call someone and have you thrown out."

He didn't move; his expression didn't change. "Lillian, Lillian. You know I don't want to upset you. But you also must know how concerned I am. I don't want you to suffer, Lillian. I don't want Crockett Industries to suffer." He raised his shoulders slightly. "Perhaps I'm overcautious. Please sit down."

She sat in an antique Chippendale chair she'd inherited from her starchy, proper grandmother. It had a sobering effect. Her hair was lank, her hands shaking, and her caftan was wet, splattered with brandy. She felt disheveled and undesirable, but she'd never cared what Andrew Balaton thought of her. He'd been Judith's. He was untouchable.

She could feel the sobs rocking inside her, but she held them in until her stomach hurt. She wouldn't cry in front of him. She hadn't thirty years ago, when she thought they all would die in the swamp on the Austro-Hungarian border. And she hadn't a year later, at the funeral of her best friend. She had no intention of crying now.

"What did you and Ashley Wakefield talk about?" he asked dispassionately.

"It was personal business."

"For Crockett?"

She nodded. "He wants to see her."

"Why? Did he recognize the jewels?"

"I don't know. I don't think so."

"When?"

"I gave her his personal number. She was going to call him and arrange a time to get together."

"How did he know about her?"

All the energy went out of Lillian. "I sent him a copy of the magazine. He said he'd seen it, but I don't believe him."

"I see."

"I thought...I knew he'd see it sooner or later. I just hoped it would be easier coming from me. It was a stupid move, I know. He might never have thought twice about Ashley Wakefield. Andrew, I don't want to be involved in this. I can't—"

"Lillian." He walked over to her and took her hand; his felt so warm. "Lillian, it's very important that you find out for me when and if Ashley Wakefield will be seeing Crockett.''

"Why, Andrew? What difference does it make now?'' She tried to focus on him, but her vision was blurred, and she sank lower, so tired. "You should have been the reporter, Andrew.''

"Lillian. You *must* help me.''

"I can't.''

He squeezed her hand gently, then pushed back her auburn hair with a light touch of his fingers. "Poor Lillian.'' His voice was low, sympathetic. She knew he was being patronizing, but took no offense; it was all he understood. "I know how difficult this must be for you. I myself am torn apart inside. But we can't let our own misery cloud our judgment now. Pull yourself together. Don't force me into a situation that would be disastrous for us both.''

She stared up at him. "What are you saying?''

"Just that the world has never known what a foolish and dangerous thing the great, serious Lillian Parker did in Hungary thirty years ago. It would be a shame if your fans, your employers, your colleagues... history...had to find out.''

"You wouldn't.''

"Give me a choice.''

Her vision cleared. "Damn you. Damn you to hell and back, Andrew Balaton.''

His hands dropped to his sides, his shoulders drooped, and suddenly he seemed so small and sad and frail. "I have already been there.''

For the first time, Lillian felt truly sorry for him. For the first time, she knew he hurt as much as she. "Threats aren't necessary, Andrew,'' she said wearily. "I'll help you.''

* * *

She had even smiled when Andrew left.

Then, in a panic, she ran into her bedroom and dug a large suitcase out of the closet. She pinched her finger as she threw it open on her bed, but she paid no attention to the stab of pain. She had to leave. Get out. She would go to Monaco—anywhere. The network could survive without her for a week or so. She'd tell them she was on a hot story. Something. They trusted her.

God, she thought, she couldn't wait to get away from this.

"So you run."

The voice of her dreams!

She whirled around, expecting nothing. It had happened before—a vision, a vengeful act of the imagination. But this time he was there. As always, he wore black. He was older, stouter, more weather-beaten. The eyes were the same. Intense, knowing. When she'd first seen them, she'd known she'd never forget them.

"My God, it is you." Her voice was a strangled whisper; her heart thumped wildly. "How did you get in here?"

"There is always a way."

"For you," she said.

He shrugged, almost imperceptibly. "Where are you going, Lillian? Tell me. Where does a woman run to escape what she cannot escape?"

She threw a lace camisole into the suitcase. "I don't know what you're talking about. I'm due a vacation. Now's as good a time as any."

"Thirty years ago, we were both forced to run," the man in black said quietly. "To protect ourselves, perhaps to protect others, we ran from the truth. From finishing this."

"*No!*" She slammed the suitcase shut. "No, dammit. I'm already being manipulated by Crockett and Balaton. I won't be manipulated by you. I don't owe you a damned thing. If anything, you owe me. Now get out!"

His gaze was level and enigmatic, unforgettable. She noticed the deep lines in his face, the toughened skin, the calluses on his browned, blunt hands. "I am not here to force you to do anything," he said. "You are right: you owe me nothing. But what do you owe yourself, Lillian? What do you owe the memory of your friendship with Judith Land?"

"I don't deserve anything—and Judith was stubborn and reckless. She was my friend, and I loved her. But I know what she was. And she's dead."

"Sometimes we cannot choose what we must do."

"Don't get self-righteous with me. I know the lies you've told."

He nodded solemnly, his eyes never leaving her face. "You must do as your conscience dictates."

He started to leave.

Lillian put out a hand, but didn't touch him. "Wait—what about you?"

He refused to answer.

"Ashley and David—they call you Barky. It's difficult to imagine you with them. Raising them from infancy. Did you bounce them on your knee? Change their diapers? Play the tooth fairy and Santa Claus? I almost envy you, Bartholomew Wakefield." She dropped her hand. "I don't want anything to happen to them. Please. Save them."

He turned. "Then you must help me."

A pain started inside her, low, deep. She was having trouble breathing, but the man in black made no move toward her. She found the strength to stand up straight. "I could be ruined, you know."

"You could be killed."

She felt the blood draining from her face. "What can I do?"

"You can stop MacGregor Stevens. He will be on Badger Rock Island tomorrow."

# TWENTY-TWO

The bath was Jeremy's idea. He had said, blandly enough, that he was tired and stiff and, frankly, smelled. And, innocently enough, she had shown him to the bathroom adjoining her room. It was the one with the big tub, she'd said, and she pointed out her shelf of bath salts and potpourri and oils.

"Anything that produces bubbles?" he asked.

"The milk bath."

"Shall we try it?"

She met his eyes. "We?"

He smiled. "Shame to waste hot water and bubble bath on just one person. What would Barky say?"

"We never had bubble baths."

"I should have guessed."

"In the winter, we'd heat water on the wood stove and use that."

"The virtues of frugality." He was standing so close. "I suppose you feel guilty every time you fill the tub more than two inches?"

She grinned. "Unless it's for a good cause."

"And what would a good cause be?"

"My physical and mental well-being."

He kissed her softly. "Then turn on the faucet and get your clothes off."

The bathwater was still hot when they could stand it

no longer, and they fell onto the cool sheets of her huge bed. Their skin was damp and soft from the bath. She kissed him lightly, everywhere, and then he lifted her by the hips and brought her toward him, so that she was leaning over him, her hair dangling nearly in his mouth. And she realized she enjoyed him for who he was, for his argumentativeness and his unreasonableness and his pigheadedness, and for his intelligence and his sense of humor and his strength of personality—and for the way he poked fun at her faults, without ever asking her to change. And his eyes, of course. She adored his eyes.

"What are you smiling about?" he asked, holding her still.

"You."

And they made love. Ashley did things she had never done before, because she didn't want the feeling to stop, the sensations, the waves of passion that drowned the questions and the ugly presence of reality. Over and over she threw herself into him, deeper and harder, with the sort of wild reckless abandon that springs from wanting and fear and love. Finally, they were both spent, and they snuggled close together, warm and sweaty, smelling of each other.

Jeremy smiled. "I take back what I said."

"What's that?"

"You're not a prude."

It was right that they should be together, she thought. For no one else, then, could have made her smile. She buried her face in his chest, and she hoped he wouldn't be able to distinguish their perspiration from the tears that streamed down her cheeks.

She felt his breathing change as he fell asleep. A little while later, exhaustion overcame her, and she, too, slept.

Sarah let David talk her into spending the night at the farm, and, because of his leg, she cooked supper for him, on the wood stove. They ate fried apples and ham and butternut squash from the garden, and she told him about life as a Balaton, and he told her about life as a Wakefield. The Liechtenstein trust hadn't changed him, she decided. He was so tall and sinewy and wild looking, and she shuddered when she thought of what it would be like to have his brown callused hands on her breasts. He wouldn't be a three-minute bang. He would give as much pleasure as he took. But his leg—damn his leg.

"Are you going to tell me how you broke your leg?" she asked as she did the dishes. She'd banished him to a chair at the big pine table.

With a shrug, he grinned and said, "Rampaging cow."

"I don't believe that."

"Then you wouldn't believe a rampaging chicken, either."

She laughed at his irreverence: he was well aware she knew he was lying, and just didn't give a damn. "I hope it's nothing I caused."

"You were a thousand miles away in Houston when this happened. Go easy on yourself, Sarah."

"That's something I've never been able to do," she admitted wistfully.

"Too many standards to live up to."

"And nowhere I belong." She placed a plate, a supermarket special, in the rack; the water was hot and sudsy. "When I was a little girl, there were days—lots of days—when I would have traded all my parents' wealth for an obscure ranch house in a middle-class suburb, someplace where there were parents who really loved each other and neighbors you could count on to be there for twenty or thirty years and with whom you could trade recipes and whose kids you'd play with. I've never had the identity a sense of place can give you—that feeling of roots."

David nodded. "And no one sympathizes with you because you're rich."

"Most of my friends have backgrounds similar to mine, but they don't see themselves as rootless. They say I look at things the wrong way. I don't belong to a place, I belong to a group—and that's just as special. It's a different kind of community, that's all. We can afford to move around and have friends in faraway places. We don't have to rely on a geographical community."

"Not me. I'm tied to the land. Guess I always will be."

"What about people?"

"They're around."

She smiled at him. "I sensed that about you, David. It's an appealing quality. What about your sister? I don't see her as someone who'd drive a beat-up Land Rover with a 'Massachusetts grown and fresher' bumper sticker on it."

"Nah. She's got a Jeep."

They both laughed, and finally he got up on his crutches and hobbled through the living room to the stairs. "Ash's room is the one with the blue-flowered wallpaper. Mine's the one that smells like chicken crap and looks like a pigsty." He grinned. "Take your pick."

"Where will you sleep?"

"Barky's room. I'll keep the fires going so you don't freeze your ass off in the morning."

She couldn't quell the giddiness she felt at standing so close, smelling the male sweat on him. "I've never met anyone like you. You're too good to be true."

"No, I'm not. I can be just as big a jackass as the next guy. But I've learned to go on and be myself. That's what I like my friends to do, too."

"I hope we can be friends."

"We already are."

"So easily?"

"I'm a quick judge of character. Night, Sarah."

"Good night."

He was right: his room did stink of farm smells, and it was a glorious mess. She gathered up some of the clothes on the floor and took them into the bed with her, and she held them close as she snuggled down in the lumpy mattress, into the hole that had been made over the years by his long body. She stared out across the moonlit room, listening to the quiet of the night breeze rustling in the trees, and she felt the loneliness inside her.

# TWENTY-THREE

At the blare of her intercom, Ashley stumbled out of bed, grabbing her ratty bathrobe. Adrenaline rushed through her, quickening her pulse and making her hands shake. Her bruised neck ached. Funny, she thought, how it hadn't bothered her in bed. She pressed down the intercom button in the foyer. "Yes?"

"It's MacGregor Stevens."

Ashley froze.

Jeremy walked down the hall, stark naked. She told him who it was, but added, "Unless he's lying."

"Ask him his wife's name."

She did. The static-distorted voice said, "Elaine Melanie Stevens."

"It's him."

She buzzed him up. Jeremy put on his jeans and met her in the living room. When the knock at the door came, she insisted on opening it herself; it was her house.

The clear-eyed, confident man who walked in surprised her. Somewhere, MacGregor Stevens had found clean clothes, and he'd managed to bathe and shave. There was considerable discoloration at the back of his neck—although she hadn't been hit as hard, Ashley could sympathize—but the rest of his color was good. He appeared to have gotten more sleep in the past few days than she or Jeremy had.

Of course, she thought, spies could probably sleep through anything.

She offered him the wingback chair; she herself sat next to Jeremy on the camel-back sofa. She was wide awake.

"What is it, Mac?" Jeremy asked.

Mac took out a pack of cigarettes and looked at Ashley for approval. She nodded, although normally she wouldn't have permitted smoking in her apartment. There was nothing normal, however, about meeting a former intelligence officer in the dead of night.

"I want you both to get the hell out of this," he said as he patted out a cigarette.

Ashley kicked out her bare feet and stretched her toes. "At least you and my uncle agree on something. What are you going to use for persuasion, Mr. Stevens? More lies?"

Jeremy leaned forward. He was bare chested in the cool night; Mac Stevens would have to be an idiot, Ashley reflected, not to have guessed already what had been going on earlier in the evening. Jeremy said, "You know we're going to Maine tomorrow?"

"That's right. And I'm here to persuade you to change your minds." He looked at Ashley. "By telling you the truth."

"As you know it," Ashley nit-picked, watching him light his cigarette with a cheap disposable lighter.

"You're an attractive woman, Miss Wakefield, but damned difficult. I probably should have told you the truth from the beginning. I have the feeling you're a survivor. Am I right?"

She looked at him in irritation. "Suppose you just talk?"

He blew out a cloud of smoke. "I met the man who calls himself Bartholomew Wakefield thirty years ago, in Budapest, Hungary. Your 'uncle.'" His eyes were mocking. "As you've perhaps deduced, he's neither English nor Polish and he never had a brother named Richard or a sister-in-law named Mary Winston. He's Hungarian. Thirty years ago, I knew him only as *orült szerzetes*. The mad monk."

Ashley said nothing. Numbly, she got up and went into the kitchen for an ashtray, and handed it to Stevens. He looked up at her with compassion in his face, but he didn't smile. She sat back down in another chair so that they were in a triangle.

"I was in Budapest on a special mission." Mac flicked an ash into the bowl. "In the mid-fifties, I traveled between West Germany and Austria, doing legal work—intelligence gathering, I suppose you could say—for the United States. I knew languages, and I knew the situation in Hungary. Our people thought the revolution might succeed without our direct involvement—at best, wishful thinking. We were too damned intent on seeing even the Communist reformers as the enemy. But that's neither here nor there. I'll let history speak for itself on that score."

He paused, dragging deep on his cigarette, and when neither Ashley nor Jeremy interrupted, went on, his tone unchanged. "I was asked to go to Budapest to help one of our people there get out—someone who was in an untenable situation with both the Soviet Union and the revolutionaries. It was supposed to have been an easy job, but, of course, the revolution turned into a bloodbath—and I was in deep over my head. I had to act—fast, secretly, *successfully*. I couldn't screw up. I'd heard about this Hungarian, this mad monk who had been a legend during the Stalinist era. He was said to have been one of the few to escape Recsk prison alive, and for ten years had been a thorn in the side of the Hungarian secret police, sort of a modern-day Scarlet Pimpernel."

"Was he actually a monk?" Jeremy asked.

"He was—*is*—a traitor, a murderer, a torturer and a thief."

Ashley could neither move nor speak.

"Ashley."

It was Jeremy. His voice seemed to come from a distance. She wouldn't look at him. Barky was a farmer, she repeated to herself. He didn't know anything about spies and mad monks. He wouldn't know how to murder someone.

The image flashed in her mind, treacherously, of Barky's sharpened butcher knife slicing through the hen's neck. The scrawny headless body racing madly across the yard. Blood spurting. Barky grabbing the carcass, plunging it into hot water, plucking the feathers.

She grabbed her stomach, suddenly nauseated, sweating, trembling, pale.

"I went to him," Mac said. "I had no choice. I had to trust him. And he agreed to help. He made all the arrangements for the escape, and then he asked me to follow his instructions—no questions asked. On the night we left, he refused to come along. He couldn't, he said, but he wouldn't give any explanation. He's not the type to bother with such trivia. By then, it was too late to abort. We were desperate."

"How many people were involved in the escape?"
Again, it was Jeremy who thought of the question.

"Four, including myself."

"What happened?"

"We were betrayed. Just before we got to the border, a search party found us. The others had gone on ahead. I tried to buy them some time. I was shot. The soldiers left me for dead—and so did the others. To this day I don't know how they did it, but they got away."

Jeremy had paled. "And you?"

Mac patted out another cigarette. "I was found by some Hungarians making their way to Austria. They brought me to a nearby village, and I was hidden and nursed back to health by an old widow—or that's the story I was told, at least. I remember very little. I nearly died, Jeremy. There was no hospital, no medicine. If I'd been caught by the Russians...well, God only knows what they'd have done. Certainly they could have made great political hay with my presence there."

"But you weren't found."

"No."

"And you're positive this 'mad monk' is the one who betrayed you?"

"There's no other explanation."

Jeremy nodded. "But you got out."

"I was able to escape across the border the following March." He lit his cigarette, dragged deep, exhaled at the ceiling. "By then, the Soviets had mined the border and there were regular patrols—it was even more treacherous. When I returned to the West, my career was in ruins, and as far as I was concerned, my life was over. I went out to San Diego. I met Elaine, and she gave me a new life. I started over. That's it. That's the whole story."

Ashley didn't believe that for a minute and, loosening the grip on her stomach, managed to ask, "Who were the three you got out of Hungary?"

He shook his head. "Can't say."

"Jesus Christ," Jeremy exploded. "Mac, you haven't *explained* anything! If Bartholomew Wakefield is the mad monk, how did *he* get out of Hungary? When? How did he get hold of Ashley and David as infants? Who the hell are they? Why did he choose to raise them? Why has he been living the life of a simple farmer for *thirty fucking years*?"

"Thirty years ago, Jeremy, I gave up any hope of finding the man who betrayed me. I gave up the idea of revenge, of bringing him to justice. I satisfied my conscience by telling myself he was dead and I would have to forget the past and build a new life. So that's what I did. Then I saw his picture in *You* magazine."

"Mac." Jeremy regarded his friend seriously, closely. "Mac, are you sure?"

Mac smiled nastily. "You don't easily forget the face of the man who sent you into a hell that only by the grace of God and the love of a good woman you escaped."

"All right. So he's the mad monk. So he betrayed you. You must have some clue about what he wants out of this, who he is—"

"I don't."

"*Mac!*"

"All right." Angrily, he stubbed out his cigarette. "My best guess is he's KGB."

"Oh, Jesus, oh, *hell*."

Ashley simply shut her eyes. More spies, more

spooks, more ghouls and goblins. She wouldn't think. Don't think...don't think...don't think... That's what she used to say to herself, over and over, when she'd wake up obsessed with thoughts of death. It occupied her mind, and she'd go back to sleep.

"He's probably a sleeper," Mac went on, as if he were talking about someone ordinary, a butcher, a mailman, a farmer. "Or an agent in place—whatever the hell you want to call him. *Orült szerzetes* was always a lie, a tool of the Soviets. He'll stop anyone who gets in his way."

"Including you, Mac," Jeremy said softly, his voice hoarse with tension.

"That's a risk I have to take."

"Why not call in the law?"

He laughed bitterly. "What laws can I prove have been broken? I have no proof, Jeremy. And do you think any of my old colleagues would pay attention to me? No, I have to do this my way—and alone. Ashley, Jeremy, get yourselves out of this. Just do it. Now that he has the jewels, Bartholomew Wakefield is going to make his move. I wouldn't want either of you to get caught in the cross fire."

He rose and looked down at Ashley, and his face was gentle and filled with regret. "I'm sure you wouldn't be so devoted to your uncle if he hadn't been a kind and decent man to you. But he had to be, you understand, to pull this off. I wish I had more answers for you. I don't know what the jewels mean, I don't know who your parents are or why—or how—he got hold of you, or where the trust came from. I'm guessing. But the rest—what I told you here tonight, that I *know* to be true. I lived it, Ashley. I was there."

Then he turned around and walked out of the cold

apartment, and he shut the door softly behind him. The self-lock clicked.

The silence was strained after Mac had left. Ashley refused to look at Jeremy. She couldn't stand to have people feel sorry for her, but especially a man, a lover. "My best guess is he's KGB." No! How could a man who gave her piggyback rides and helped sheep give birth to tiny lambs and let her win at Monopoly possibly be a spy—an enemy?

She sprang to her feet. "This cloak-and-dagger shit has to stop."

"Ashley—" Jeremy rose awkwardly to his feet. "Oh, God, I'm so sorry."

"Poor little Ashley, raised by a Russian spy. Sybil Morgenstern would love it. 'Wakefield twins brought up by KGB.'"

He took her seriously. "Ashley, you're jumping to conclusions."

"Of course I'm jumping to conclusions! Dammit, do you think I believe Barky's KGB? I was just trying to get you to see how crazy this all sounds. But you don't see it, do you? You don't think your friend Mac is nuts. You'd rather think my uncle is a goddamned Russian spy!"

"There's more evidence against Barky than against Mac," he said, sounding like a lawyer. "And I've known Mac all my life."

*"And I've known Barky all my life!"*

She was choking with anger, unable to breathe, to think clearly. Unpleasant images kept flashing. Barky killing a bat with a broom. Shooting a woodchuck. Carving the head of a butchered pig for sausage. They were the grittier side of farm life, but now, in light of what Mac Stevens had accused her uncle of being, the images seemed filled with needless brutality.

All of a sudden it was dawn. The early morning sun brought out the rose accents in the Persian carpet and cast the room in a soft glow.

"I have to shower and pack," Ashley said abruptly.

Jeremy sighed. "You're going to Maine."

It was a statement—a fact—but Ashley nodded. "I have to make my own decisions. I can't let Mac Stevens make them for me—or you."

"I would never presume," he said with a small smile. "I'll pack my things while you're in the shower."

She was truly shocked. "Why?"

"You don't think I have any intention of letting you go up there alone, do you?"

"Crockett didn't invite you."

"I don't give a damn who Crockett invited! I'll charter my own damned plane if I have to, Ashley. I'm going with you."

She snorted. "You heard Mac—you even believe him."

"And I make my own decisions, too, dammit."

"Are you possessive?"

"Just stubborn."

"You sure you trust my flying?"

"Not in the least." His smile broadened into a grin now that he was seeing he'd won. "But I'm a risk taker."

She gave a toss of the head. "I could shove you out the door at four thousand feet."

He walked over to her and stood toe to toe. "Do you have a parachute aboard?"

"Two."

"Then I won't worry. I may not know how to fly a plane, smart ass, but I damned well know how to jump out of one."

# TWENTY-FOUR

Badger Rock Island was approximately forty acres of brush, pine and oak in Blue Hill Bay, southwest of Mt. Desert Island, the largest of the state's thirty-five hundred islands and a popular national park. There were granite cliffs, crashing surf, a guest cottage, tennis courts, a pool, boats moored at a gleaming dock, a boathouse—and no people. The sprawling main house, of sun-bleached cedar shingles, stood in a wide clearing overlooking the bay.

Flying had improved Ashley's spirits. Of course Barky wasn't KGB. It was ridiculous! If not crazy, MacGregor Stevens was at least very badly mistaken. As far as she was concerned, if Barky was the one source of danger for her, then she wasn't in any danger. There were just answers to be gotten to a series of sticky questions. Who set up the Liechtenstein trust? Why? When? Who were her parents? Who was Bartholomew Wakefield, really? Why had he lied to her and David? What did he plan to do with the tiara and the choker? How had they gone from the neck of Judith Land in Vienna, in 1956, to a vault at Piccard Cie in Geneva, in 1982?

And she continued, despite everything, to believe in her uncle. She could hardly imagine the fortitude it had taken to break David's leg and smash her on the head. He had nursed them, lectured them and loved them all their lives. He desperately wanted them to live—so he had tried to put them out of action, to incapacitate them in order to save them. That was the only conceivable explanation.

"Trust me."

Of course. There could be no question of that.

At her side, Jeremy peered down at the picturesque island. "I wonder if the old man shoots trespassers."

"I'm not that lucky," she said with a wry smile.

She noticed him holding his breath as she circled for a landing. The airstrip wasn't much, but she was confident. Jeremy had been singularly unhelpful during her preflight visual inspection of the plane. He'd said it was unnerving to put his life in the hands of someone in a bright yellow jumpsuit, scrunchy pink socks and running shoes. Plucking an indefinable stoppage—a squirrel's nest, perhaps—from behind the propeller, Ashley had told him to go ahead and throw caution to the wind. "As long," he said, "as my teeth and eyeballs don't go with it."

Her landing on the rough concrete runway was, all considered, fairly smooth, and she taxied to a stop, ordering Jeremy to remain quiet until she'd tried to explain his presence to the powers that be on the island.

"Just as long as you don't offer me up as eel bait," he said, climbing out.

They were met by a lanky, balding man in a perfectly pressed gray corduroy suit. He looked to be in his early thirties—and upset. Ashley gave him a dazzling smile, put out her hand and introduced herself. He shook briefly, not looking dazzled, and said fussily, "Roger Shellingworth. Miss Wakefield, we understood you were coming alone."

"Didn't you receive my secretary's call?" she lied. "Jeremy Carruthers is legal counsel for the New England Oceanographic Institute, Mr. Shellingworth. I'm afraid these days I can hardly breathe without him."

"It's true," Jeremy said. "It was either bring me along or not come at all." He smiled. "Institute policy, I'm afraid."

Shellingworth sighed, perturbed but resigned. "Very well, I suppose we'll have to make do. Don't worry about your things. I'll send someone for them. This way, please."

Ashley dropped back and walked with Jeremy. "Act like a lawyer," she said.

"I *am* a lawyer."

"Oh. Well, act like a proper lawyer."

"My God, you sound like my father. I've been an attorney for ten years, Ashley. I damned well know how to act."

They walked along a wide, sunlit gravel path that eventually narrowed into a neat brick path flanked by frostbitten flowers. Breezes came in great gusts and smelled of the ocean, and everywhere were the merry sounds of birds.

Shellingworth explained that J. Land Crockett wished his guests to settle in and make themselves at home. "You are to have full access. If there's anything you require, please don't hesitate to ask me or one of the servants. Mr. Crockett will see you at dinner."

"Not sooner?" Ashley asked, surprised.

"That would be unlikely."

They were installed in adjoining rooms on the second floor, with panoramic views of the island, the bay and, in the distance, the peaks of Mt. Desert Island.

The Crockett house was large and open, the furnishings and lines spare, the colors those of the sea: grays, blues, muted greens, whites. The effect was at once inviting and lonely. Ashley opened her window and listened to the ocean and the gusting wind and smelled the salty, chilly air. Quiet and colorful and gorgeous, Maine was stunning in autumn.

She changed into sweat clothes, braided her hair tightly and knocked on Jeremy's door.

"Yes?"

"I'm going for a run," she said. "I'll let you know if I bump into any spooks."

"Ashley, for Christ's sake!"

But she was off down the hall, her stab at black humor quickly vanishing as she headed outside. She followed the path to the airstrip, working up a sweat. The exercise helped to revive her after the two-hour flight and the lack of sleep, but she couldn't chase away the strange, silent sadness that seemed to permeate the island. Was it her? she wondered. Or was it the loneliness of the old man who made his home here, isolated, rude, undoubtedly embittered?

She jogged down to the guesthouse, painted white with blue shutters, but it was empty, unfurnished and unused. J. Land Crockett didn't throw large parties; he never had more guests than the main house could handle.

She sprinted back to the house and did some cooldown stretches in a patch of sunlight on the back lawn. The air and exercise felt good, and she was confident she could handle the chairman of Crockett Industries.

As she mounted the back steps, heading inside, a movement drew her eye to the screened sun porch. An old man stood in the window. He was bundled up in a heavy sweater, his hair iron gray and wispy, his face toughened with age and a bitterness that was almost tangible.

His eyes met hers.

Then, without so much as a smile or a nod, he turned from the screened window and walked away.

Roger Shellingworth met Lillian Parker at the airport in Bar Harbor and, in a lavish cabin cruiser, ferried her over to Badger Rock Island. The boat had its own captain, a taciturn islander himself, who asked nothing from the billionaire but a fair wage for an honest day's work; for his circumspectness, he was paid more than a fair wage.

Roger joined Lillian in the lounge and furnished her with a drink. Lillian found him obsequious and tired of him easily, but she had nothing particular against him. At least Crockett liked him. That was something, since Crockett liked so few people.

"Has Ashley Wakefield arrived yet?" she asked, feigning cheerfulness.

"Yes—rather early, in fact."

Lillian wrapped her hair in a scarf and smiled into the wind. "Have she and Crockett met yet?"

Roger shook his head. "She brought a friend."

"Uninvited? How cheeky!"

"Yes," Roger replied distastefully.

"Who is he—I presume it's a he?"

"She introduced him as an attorney with the New England Oceanographic Institute. Mr. Crockett had me verify his credentials."

Lillian was burning with curiosity, but the little

twerp was going to make her drag out every word. "And?"

"The institute has no attorney by the name of Jeremy Carruthers."

"Do tell."

Roger reddened. "At Mr. Crockett's request, I, er, investigated Mr. Carruthers's luggage."

Lillian stretched out on the padded bench. "Why, Roger, you snoop. And who is our Mr. Carruthers?"

"He's an attorney with Carruthers and Stevens, a law firm in San Diego."

"Jesus Christ!" Lillian spilled her drink down her front. "Oh, dammit. Roger, I'm sorry—what a mess. I haven't been on a boat in ages," she explained nervously. "Just give me a towel or something."

"Are you sure—"

"Roger, please, I'm fine."

She had hoped Bartholomew Wakefield, as he now called himself, would be wrong and she wouldn't have to face MacGregor Stevens, but if his associate were already here... God, how Mac hated her! She laughed sadly, wondering how many times self-righteous, proper, dutiful and upstanding MacGregor Stevens had shut her loathed face off his television set. She used to think of that, just before she went on air. Sometimes she'd smile, thinking, "This one's for you, Mac."

She'd wanted to hate him, too. But she couldn't. Not then, and not now.

"I'll see you in hell, Lillian Parker," he'd told her the last time they'd met.

Well, she thought, here we are.

# TWENTY-FIVE

**J.** Land Crockett sipped his hot tea with purplish lips. He had summoned Lillian to the sun porch minutes after her arrival. The wind blew sharply through the screens, but Crockett sat under layers of blankets and wore a thick sweater, buttoned all the way up, with a turtleneck underneath, the collar unrolled on his scrawny neck. He fastened his piercing black-blue eyes on her. "Our Ashley Wakefield looks to be ready to get us by the short hairs and start pulling, Lil." He sounded almost amused. "She wants answers, probably as bad as I do. Only I don't give a damn if she gets them. I *do* give a damn if I get mine. And I intend to."

Lillian put down her china cup so he wouldn't see how badly her hands were shaking. She never used to be afraid of Crockett. What was happening? "Who are you willing to destroy to get your answers, Crockett?"

He gazed at her with his notorious intransigence. "Anyone who stands in my way."

"Including me?" She hated how small her voice sounded.

"I need to know the truth." His voice was an odd mix of bitterness, pain, loneliness and love. "I'll even risk everything I believed and loved about my own daughter."

Lillian reached for a warm scone. Crockett even had

clotted cream; God only knew where it had come from. "Maybe the truth isn't as bad as you think."

"Maybe. I'll find out, won't I?"

"Don't look at me like that." She bit into the scone, knowing it was a diversionary tactic; that way, her eyes didn't have to be on him. "*I* don't know anything!"

"Don't you?" Crockett set down his teacup and folded his gnarled hands in his lap. "What about Jeremy Carruthers?"

Lillian tried to look huffy as she swallowed a piece of scone. "I've never even met the man! Crockett, I didn't come here to be grilled by you."

He ignored her protest. "Roger told you Carruthers is out of San Diego."

"And I'm sure he wouldn't have if you hadn't instructed him to tell me."

"That's right, Lil. His firm was founded in 1958 by Allan Carruthers—our Jeremy's father—and a man by the name of MacGregor Stevens."

Oh, shit, she thought miserably, shutting her eyes, not caring that she was giving herself away. She should have known Crockett, recluse that he was, could still get any information, any fact, he wanted.

"He's from Philadelphia high society, Lil—same as you. Know him?"

"Crockett..."

The old man leaned forward in his chair. "You want to tell me what he has to do with all this, Lil?"

"*I don't know!*"

"Doesn't matter." He rested back. "I'll find out. You know—" He paused, sighing contentedly, and again folded his hands. "You know, when Judith died, there was some money missing out of her estate. About five, six million—no way of tracking it down, finding out where it went. I checked it out, Lil. With the right investments, continually reinvesting the principal, it could have grown to a nice little pot by 1982, when the Wakefield twins suddenly came into their anonymous Liechtenstein trust. That's an interesting little coincidence, don't you think?"

"So what are you going to do? Try to prove it's Judith's money so you can take it away? They don't give a damn about the money, you know." She threw up her hands in desperation. "Damn you, Crockett. What's the point in dragging those two through hell?"

"Answers."

"Bullshit."

"I *have* to know what happened to Judith."

"She died, Crockett. She was trampled to death by a horse at age twenty-three. It was a horrible, tragic accident, and it happened thirty years ago."

He wasn't looking at Lillian; he was barely in the room with her. "Why was she there, Lil? Why was Judith on the ranch that day?"

"I don't know!" Lillian rubbed her forehead, trying wildly to restore some measure of self-control. She couldn't let Crockett get to her. But doesn't he have a right to know? No! I promised Judith; I promised everyone. "I don't know why Judith was on the ranch, Crockett. I hadn't seen her in months. We were moving in separate directions. I was on my way to becoming a journalist, she was an actress."

"She was your best friend."

"We were drifting apart."

"I don't believe that, Lil. Talk to me." His voice had become low, weak, tired, the voice of an old man who had known more pain than happiness, more loneliness than love. "Tell me about my daughter, Lil. Tell me who she was. I thought I knew her; I thought she loved me, *trusted* me. But she didn't come to me when she was in trouble. She went to you. Didn't she, Lil? When she was in trouble and there was nowhere to turn, she turned to you. Tell me, Lil. Tell me what my daughter was."

"She was everything you raised her to be, Crockett."

With tremendous effort, her heart thudding painfully, Lillian walked off the sun porch and into the relative warmth of the house. J. Land Crockett would put all his monumental resources into play to find out what had happened to his daughter thirty years ago. Stood up against his billions, his sheer intensity of will, Lillian didn't have a chance.

And neither did Ashley and David Wakefield and the man who called himself their uncle.

Roger Shellingworth collected the tea tray. "I've reached Andrew Balaton in New York. He's agreed to join you for dinner this evening, although it's necessitated canceling plans of his own. I made it clear it was of the utmost importance to have him here tonight."

"Good. And what have you gotten on MacGregor Stevens?"

"He hasn't been in his office since last Friday. Supposedly he's in Hawaii, but that's unconfirmed. Jeremy Carruthers left San Diego over the weekend."

Crockett nodded, acknowledging that he'd heard. "And David Wakefield?"

"His leg was broken earlier this week, and he was released from the hospital yesterday morning. Sarah

Balaton is with him on the farm; she arrived there yesterday afternoon."

"Bartholomew Wakefield?"

"There's nothing whatsoever on him, sir. As far as we know, he's fishing."

Crockett smirked. "Of course."

"Will that be all?"

"Tell Lil I'd like her to give Ashley Wakefield a tour of Jude's Paradise."

"Of course. When?"

"I'd like them to leave at once so they can be back before dusk."

It was brisk and clear on Jude's Paradise, an uninhabited, windswept island of scrub pines and oaks and low-lying bushes in Penobscot Bay, well south of Badger Island.

Ashley followed Lillian Parker onto a huge flat rock that looked out at Penobscot Bay, and she found herself holding in check the dozens of questions she wanted to ask. She would follow Lillian's lead. They were alone but for the taciturn islander who had piloted the boat. He waited for them at the dilapidated dock, the only evidence that humans had ever set foot on Jude's Paradise. It was a haven for birds, which were everywhere.

And it was an eerie place. As she watched Lillian's auburn hair blow freely in the cold wind, Ashley wasn't at all sure she should have come. But what choice did she have? She was playing an old man's game now. J. Land Crockett, the billionaire, the host she had yet even to meet.

"Judith used to love to come here," Lillian said wistfully. "She could just be herself—no cameras, no press, no prying eyes of any sort. It was her refuge. When she was a little girl and her mother was still alive, they'd come here together on picnics. Crockett never joined them. I think he understood this was a place where mother and daughter could get away alone, out of the public eye—away from him, too. He knows he's a difficult man.''

Ashley suspected that was an understatement, but said judiciously, "I wouldn't know. I haven't had the opportunity of meeting him yet."

Lillian hunched her shoulders against the stiffening wind. It was even colder here than on Badger Rock, but Ashley supposed, in the middle of summer, it could be an inviting place, a haven for two women who wanted to have some time together, alone. In her mind, Ashley could almost see them, beautiful Judith Land and her mother, who must have been strong to have been attracted to a man like J. Land Crockett.

"Oh, you'll meet Crockett," Lillian said, and smiled briefly, knowingly, adding, "when it suits him."

"What happened to Judith's mother—Crockett's wife?" Ashley asked, sensing Lillian wanted to talk.

The older woman gazed back out toward the water, and her clear eyes squinted against the glare off the bay. "She died when Judith was just twelve—of breast cancer. I didn't know her then, but it must have been devastating. Even after her mother's death, Judith would come out here—to be with her, I think. She always said she could feel her mother's presence here, talk to her. They were both named Judith, you know."

No, Ashley thought, I don't know; I don't know anything about Judith Land. She pulled her sweater more tightly around her, but she was still cold. And the eerie feeling wouldn't go away. It clung to her and seeped into her bones, like the chill. "Why did Mr. Crockett want me to come here?"

With a shrug, Lillian turned, her clear eyes focusing now on Ashley. "He's been talking about turning Jude's Paradise over to a group like the New England Oceanographic Institute for years—as a memorial to his wife and daughter."

It was horribly insufficient as an explanation, given everything else that had happened, but Lillian Parker seemed to make little attempt to make her words believable. Ashley said, "And you think that's why I'm here."

Lillian turned sharply away.

"It isn't, is it?" Ashley asked gently. Demanding answers now, she felt, would do no good.

"I don't think so." The reply was barely audible, but there was a wistfulness in Lillian Parker's expression that was impossible not to miss.

Ashley no longer knew what to feel. "Tell me more about Judith," she said suddenly. "You were friends?"

"Best friends." Lillian smiled and seemed reassured by the return to the subject of Judith Land and her memories. "We met when we were about thirteen, at a private girls' school. Judith was the rebel from Texas and I was the blue blood from Philadelphia. That's what we called each other, anyway. We were so different, and yet we got along right from the start." She smiled, lost in memory. "We were infamous for our exploits."

"What was she like?" Suddenly Ashley very much wanted to know.

Lillian's shoulders went up as she laughed up at the sky, as if she were laughing at the cloud where Judith

Land sat watching them. "Judith was incredible—beautiful, even as an adolescent, and just the biggest hot shit around. You'd have liked her, Ashley."

Ashley wasn't sure if that was a compliment. She said nothing, hoping Lillian would continue.

She did. "She was tremendously talented. But she was so much more than her public image ever allowed her to be. I suppose we all are."

"I know what you mean." And that surprised her because, after four years of eluding the press, Ashley didn't consider herself a public person. But she was. Just having to hide, wanting to, proved that.

Lillian hugged herself against the biting wind. "In so many ways, Judith was ahead of her time: one of the first of the superwomen. She was independent, stubborn, sanctimonious at times. She'd do anything on a dare—which often got us into heaps of trouble."

Despite the slicing wind, the tide lapped the rocks with a surprising gentleness, and the sea was calm, stunningly beautiful in the late afternoon sun. Lillian turned inland, and Ashley followed her through the brush into a stand of pines, where they were protected from the brunt of the wind.

"You still miss her, don't you?" Ashley asked, sensing Lillian's lingering melancholy. "Even after all these years."

Lillian turned her handsome face upward, looking into the sun, and she gave a slight nod, her eyes telling more. They were large, wide and sad. "It's just this place," she said.

Ashley could understand that. Isolated and bleak, strangely beautiful, Jude's Paradise was the sort of place that forced one to remember.

"But Judith wasn't perfect. You know that, don't you?"

There was an intensity in Lillian's look that told Ashley the question was one meant to be answered. She said, "No one is."

Lillian nodded, not so much in agreement as just satisfied that Ashley had spoken, understood. "She was only nineteen when she made her first film—six in all before she died. That's a lot for one so young. In some ways, she was terribly worldly and sophisticated, and in other ways, she was absolutely impossible. Her father had taught her she could do everything and have everything; she only had to want it."

"Was she spoiled?" Ashley asked, plucking a handful of pine needles, just to have something to do, something real to hang on to.

"I suppose it might have made someone else spoiled and unpleasant, but it seemed to add a touch of vulnerability to Judith. She had such blind faith in everyone around her—herself included. She believed that if she liked someone, he or she must therefore be a good person. She assumed that everyone around her lived up to all her high expectations. And she believed all her dreams would come true."

"She was young," Ashley reminded her, keeping her tone neutral. She had no desire to defend a dead woman. She only wanted information; she couldn't get enough of what Lillian Parker had to say.

Lillian shrugged as she ducked under a low-hanging pine branch and stood in a patch of blueberry bushes. "I suppose when you're young it's difficult to recognize and accept your own limitations—or those of the people around you. But I'm not sure Judith would ever have really changed. Grown wiser with time, perhaps, but not changed. It wasn't in her to be a cynic."

They walked back toward the dock, and Ashley sensed this was why J. Land Crockett had sent her here, to this hauntingly beautiful place. Not just to see the island, but to learn about the women for whom it was named, especially about one woman, Judith Land.

She didn't want to ask herself why.

"Was she happy?" Ashley asked. The wind had softened into a murmuring breeze, and the birds pranced and sang in the brush and trees.

"God, I hope so."

"Didn't she marry before she died?"

"Oh, yes—most definitely. She'd met her Prince Charming, except he was a dashing, penniless Hungarian count of little or no importance—except to Judith, of course."

Andrew Balaton, Ashley thought. Father of Sarah Balaton, the owner, perhaps, of the collection of jewels Ashley and David had found in a vault in Switzerland more than four years ago.

"Where did they meet?" she asked.

"In the refugee camps," Lillian said quickly. It was obviously not something she wanted to discuss.

But Ashley did. "What were they like? The camps, I mean."

"Crowded and sad and dreary, and yet somehow filled with hope and determination. Hungarians are a difficult people to understand, and I don't pretend to."

"What were you doing there?"

She sighed. "Judith and I were on a whirlwind tour of Europe. At the time, I was a would-be journalist whom no one took seriously. When the uprising in Hungary hit world headlines...well, I wanted to be where the action was. I dragged Judith out to see the camps. I found my first story there; Judith found her husband."

Somehow Ashley suspected that wasn't even close to everything, but Lillian was already beginning to pull back. "They were married soon after?" Ashley asked innocuously.

Lillian walked ahead of her; the dilapidated old dock was in view now, but Ashley wasn't ready yet to leave. "They were married the day after Christmas, just a few weeks after they met."

"And she died when?"

"The following August."

"How tragic."

For a long time, Lillian would say nothing, and they came to the dock. Taking the lead, Ashley walked out onto a cluster of jagged rocks, which radiated the warmth of the afternoon sun. She couldn't bear to get back on the boat and skid off to Badger Rock Island, to a gruff old man and more unanswered questions. She thought of Jeremy, and the image of him surprised her, not just because of its being there, unbidden, but also because of its intensity. He was a difficult man, once met, to forget. But how would she even begin to tell him all this? And how could she stand to listen to him guess what it all might mean?

"But at least she had a few months of happiness," Ashley said, hoping to egg Lillian on once more.

Lillian shook her head sadly, but there was a touch of humor, too, in her expression. "You don't keep up on the tales of Hollywood legends, do you, Ashley?"

"I'm afraid not," she admitted, climbing farther out

onto the rocks. "The latest in eel research, yes, but actors and actresses—I've just never been a gossip-monger."

"It doesn't matter." To Ashley's relief, Lillian followed her instead of turning back toward the boat. "I'm not sure how close the Hollywood version of Judith and Andrew's marriage is to the truth, anyway. Andrew...he's not an easy man to understand. He adored Judith from the beginning. There's no question of that. But he'd been denied so much in his own country for so many years. He was a member of the hated aristocracy, you see, and so although he was very well educated and energetic, the Communists didn't trust him—and therefore he had no opportunities in Hungary. So when he came to this country, he was determined to make something of himself."

"Which he did."

"Yes, but not without sacrifice. He and Judith went on a long honeymoon, and when they came back, she insisted they live in her house in Beverly Hills—which she'd tell anyone she'd bought with her own money, not her father's, and certainly not Andrew's."

Ashley shrugged. "That's nothing to be ashamed of."

"Andrew's a proud man. It bit."

"But that must have been minor—"

"It was the beginning," Lillian said. "Crockett didn't help matters. Being the dutiful father-in-law, he offered Andrew a position at what was then Crockett Oil."

"Did the company have Los Angeles offices?"

Lillian shook her head. "And Judith was to begin work on a new film that spring. I don't blame her for not wanting to give up her career and move to Hous-

ton, but neither of them was willing to make any compromises—out of love, they said. They insisted they
wanted to be around each other all the time."

Ashley tried to envision the circumstances and
found that she could. It was all so depressingly common. "So one had to win and one had to lose," she
said.

"I think they both lost."

"The film was never made, was it?"

Again Lillian shook her head, her energy for the
topic seeming to fade. But she said, "Judith went into
a blue funk and threatened to retire if the studio didn't
postpone the start of the film. Well, God knows why,
but they did. She packed up and left—to find herself,
we'd call it today. She said that while she still loved
Andrew, she needed some time to herself, to be alone
and find out who she was, who she wanted to be,
where she would go from there. It was a radical thing
for a woman to do in the fifties, but that was Judith."

"What did her husband do?"

"What could he do? He agreed to leave her alone
and give her some time. Crockett couldn't understand
Judith at all, and he talked Andrew into coming to
work for Crockett Oil while Judith was meditating on
her fate."

"What about you?" Ashley asked. "Did you see Judith during this time?"

"No." There was no hesitation.

"But you were best friends."

Lillian's expression hardened, her mouth tightening
as she said, "The last time I saw Judith was at the
Christmas ball in Vienna—unless you want to count
her funeral."

Abruptly, Lillian started out onto the narrow point

beyond the dock. It was all rock, with waves splashing up on either side of them, and the huge, loose boulders looked as if they had just been dropped there carelessly, to be picked up later.

"We scattered her ashes here," Lillian said in a voice curiously devoid of emotion. She was looking out at the water. "Crockett and I. He hasn't been here since. I come here when I can. When I'm here, I feel as though I can be close to her again—the way she was with her mother."

"I understand," Ashley mumbled, although she wasn't sure she did.

"We were good friends, and I failed her in so many ways. I don't know if she died hating me. I like to think not. I like to think of us as giggling thirteen-year-olds, plotting to put frogs in Babs Goodworth's bed."

For a while, neither woman spoke, and Ashley listened to the sounds of the sea and the birds. There were a thousand questions she wanted to ask Lillian Parker, but not here, not now. First she had to dispel this strange melancholy, the eeriness of Jude's Paradise, and sit quietly and add these new pieces to the puzzle and see how they might fit.

Lillian turned, standing close to Ashley, the bright sun emphasizing the years in her face. "When you get back to the house, go into the dining room. There's a portrait of Judith there. Look at it. Get to know her."

Ashley's heart began to pound. "Why?"

"Because it's the only image of her—portrait or photograph—that does her justice."

"But why do you want me to feel as if I know her?"

Lillian gave a small, curious smile. "Look at the portrait, Ashley. Then you tell me."

# TWENTY-SIX

David watched as Sarah wrung her hands and dug her top teeth into her lower lip, leaving a mark. They were sitting out on the trailer, among the pumpkins, looking out across the valley. The leaves were turning rapidly now. Sarah said, "I don't suppose this place has changed much since you and your sister were children."

"Barky doesn't like change."

"He must be an interesting man to have raised you."

David shrugged. He hadn't told Sarah about the call from Ashley in Maine, which had come while Sarah was out following Iggy around while he fed the animals. Iggy was gone now, with promises he'd be back later. Aside, he'd told David he wanted to know all about the Texas flower with the "bazooms." Iggy was a jerk, but reliable; David had known him since they were five. "I guess Barky has his points," he said.

"David—" Pausing, she touched his arm. "I know you weren't hurt in a farm accident—and I know it wasn't a rampaging cow or chicken. Don't joke with me please. I want to know the truth."

He looked at her. The slight breeze lifted her hair a few strands at a time, casting them into the sunlight, reminding him of childhood fairy tales. He held one of his crutches by the crosspiece and squashed a dandelion leaf. "What do you think happened?"

"I don't know. Someone beat you up?"

He grinned into the sun. "No: someone beat the shit out of me."

"But who? Why—"

"Big blond jackass. He stopped by Saturday afternoon wanting the tiara and the choker—the infamous Balaton jewels—only he didn't say that. I told him no, and we came to blows. Or, to be more accurate, I came to his blows."

"Oh, my God." It came out ohmygod.

"You know something about it? Jesus."

She pulled her fingers apart so she could rub her forehead furiously, as if she had a massive headache. "I...I think I know the name of the man who attacked you. It's Giles Smith. He's on my father's private security force...a professional at this sort of thing."

For the moment, David didn't quibble over who was responsible for what injury; he let Sarah think the worst. If Barky hadn't come along, Giles Smith might very well have broken David's leg. "Your father sent one of his meats after me?"

"I seriously doubt that," she said quickly. "More likely Giles was acting on his own—or on behalf of J. Land Crockett."

David was confused. "What?"

She waved a hand impatiently, trying to sort out this new information herself. "Crockett has spies everywhere in the organization. It's his way of convincing himself he still exerts some control. Father says he doesn't mind—he's always so damned lenient when it comes to that old man."

"So he and your father get along?"

"Father gets along with Crockett; Crockett doesn't get along with anybody. My father has always had tremendous respect for Crockett, but I've never been convinced the respect is mutual. Andrew Balaton is certainly good enough to run Crockett Industries, but I get the feeling Crockett has always thought my father wasn't good enough for Judith Land. In a way, I think he blames my father for Judith's death. But during the last months of her life, my father didn't even see her. And she hurt him terribly. He's never recovered, not emotionally."

"He remarried, didn't he?"

"Oh, yes, certainly. A year after Judith's death he met my mother and they were married almost immediately, but it was too soon. Their marriage lasted just long enough for her to become pregnant. By the time I was born, they were already divorced. My father has had many women since then and two more marriages, but there'll never be another Judith Land. For better or worse, she was his one true love."

"So there's tension between Crockett and your father over her."

"An underlying tension. Nothing that ever comes to the surface."

David batted a stone out of the grass with the rubber end of his crutch. It skidded onto the driveway. "Why would either of them have sent this Smith guy after the jewels?"

She shook her head, thinking. "If they're the Balaton jewels—although he insists they're not—my father would want them for the same reasons I did: because they can't possibly belong to you and your sister. They must have been stolen from Judith soon after the Christmas ball, and if Father knows something about it, he just doesn't want it all coming out into the open. He's a very private man, and he could have decided it wasn't worth risking the publicity. And you've seen Giles. Father could have told him to make quiet inquiries, and he took it upon himself to break your leg."

David didn't correct her. "And Crockett?"

"I don't know. Maybe he knows something, too—or did something that he now wants or needs to cover up."

"Like what?"

"I wish I knew, but your guess is as good as mine."

"How do you think the jewels got out of Hungary?"

"Father has a lot of friends. Maybe one of them brought them out."

"But not him?"

"No. He would have told me."

"But he didn't give them to Judith?"

"He says no." She was getting breathless. "He says he doesn't know where Judith got the tiara and the choker she wore that night."

"Judith?"

"It's possible she was approached by whoever smuggled the jewels out of Hungary and, not realizing they actually belonged to my father, bought them and wore them that night—as a surprise. Then the thief could have stolen them back. He would have known she was wearing them."

David thought of Barky: he was Hungarian, it seemed. Could he have stolen the Balaton jewels? Better that, he thought, than being KGB. Or was he both? KGB *and* a jewel thief? Hell. But why?

"Or Crockett could have purchased them from the thief and given them to Judith," Sarah suggested, becoming exasperated. "The possibilities are endless. Even if I'm wrong and they're not the Balaton jewels, Judith definitely wore them that night and they definitely haven't been seen in public since."

"Until Ashley hit the cover of *You*."

"Right."

"And now your father, my uncle, Crockett and God knows who else—" although I can make a few guesses, David thought guiltily "—are all either trying to get answers to what happened to the jewels thirty years ago or maybe even trying to cover up what happened. Interesting. And, as you say, the possibilities are endless."

"Maybe tonight we can lay all this out for my father and see what he says."

"Sounds good to me."

But later that afternoon, Giles Smith showed up at the farm. He found Sarah and David in the kitchen, making applesauce on the cook stove. David would cut and core the apples at the kitchen table; Sarah would put them on the stove and strain them. They had one more peck to do before they left for New York.

"Hey, Giles." David held up his paring knife. "Come back to check your handiwork?"

Giles shrugged his massive shoulders. "You weren't very helpful."

"Dummy me."

"I have no quarrel with you."

Sarah laid the long-handled wooden spoon across the bubbling cast-iron kettle. "Giles, what do you want?"

"Dinner's been canceled," Giles said, not wasting any time with preludes. "Daddy asked me to come by and tell his sweet little girl he's been called away unexpectedly."

Reddening at his sarcasm, Sarah peeled off the big towel she'd knotted around her waist. "Where to?"

"Maine."

"*Crockett.*"

"We're all at his beck and call, aren't we? Even Daddy." Giles grinned, looking even more apelike. "The plan is, I take you back to Houston."

"Whose plan?" Sarah demanded sharply.

"Daddy Balaton, of course. He pays the bills. Says he wants to protect you from any 'unpleasantness.'"

She glared at him. "Such as turning you in to the police for assault?"

"Now, Sarah. Your father just doesn't want you getting yourself into any more trouble."

"So he's banishing me to Houston! Don't you think he's overreacting? There's no need to treat me like a two-year-old." She slapped the towel down on the counter. "What if I say no?"

Giles looked at her impassively. "Corporate jet's ready and waiting. My orders are to get you on it—for your protection. And I don't see anybody here in any condition to stop me, do you?"

David grabbed his crutch and started to his feet. "Listen, fuckhead—"

"David, don't." Sarah put a hand on his arm; she was composed. "It's not worth another broken leg. I'll go with Giles."

"Dammit, Sarah, you don't even know if these orders came from your father," David argued. "Or maybe he's using you in some game of his own?"

"He isn't."

"You don't know that."

"No." She smiled sadly. "But I know my father."

She got her things together and left with Giles. David flopped back down at the table. He smelled the applesauce burning. The hell with it. He hobbled over to the stove to shove the pot off the heat and decided, come what may, he had to figure out some way to get to Maine.

The Crockett Industries Lear jet was waiting at Bradlee Field, and Sarah had to wonder at the red-carpet treatment. Was she being escorted to Houston to keep her out of trouble—or to keep her in the dark? Or both? What had happened? Why had her father changed his mind about meeting David? Why had he been called to Maine?

She realized she had to know. She would be disobeying a direct order from her father, yet again risking his disappointment and condemnation, but she couldn't be the silly, vulnerable creature he wanted her to be. She had never been and would never be. If nothing else, she thought, it was time her father acknowledged that his daughter had the same strength of will as he had. She could confront the truth. She didn't need to be protected.

"Why do you want to look at the dark side of life?" he would ask her. "You have no reason, no need, Sarah, to look at anything but sunshine and innocence."

Her dear father the romantic. He didn't understand that she was no longer a child who believed life was a fairy tale, with good on one side, always the winners, and evil on the other side, always the losers. For God's sake, she was mature enough to know the world wasn't that damned simple! Didn't he know that about her?

But it wasn't that she was fearless. As she had sat in sullen silence next to Giles on the drive to the airport, she had acknowledged just how desperately afraid she was. There was mounting evidence that her father had been lying to her about the Balaton jewels—and now wanted her to go away and not demand answers to all the difficult questions he knew she would ask. But she loved her father—totally and unconditionally. He was a good man, but not a perfect one. Who was?

If there was an unpleasant episode in his past, she could face it because she believed in him. So why wouldn't he let her? If only he believed in her!

Giles climbed out of the car. "I'll get your stuff out of the trunk."

She smiled sweetly. "Thank you, Giles."

He used the inside latch to pop open the trunk and circled around to the back of the car.

That meant he'd left the keys in the ignition.

Sarah scooted across the seat, knocked the transmission into drive and trod on the gas pedal. She could hear Giles swearing at her. But she didn't look back.

She sped out of the airport lot and onto Interstate 91 North. It would take time for Giles to rent another car and come after her. By then, she hoped she'd have enough of a head start.

In just over an hour, she was back at the Wakefield farm. David and his friend Iggy, a plain-looking, tawny-haired man, were arguing in front of a black Ferrari.

"Fuck," Iggy was fuming. "You can't drive a Ferrari with a busted leg! I'll drive you up to goddamned Maine!"

If anything, Iggy's language was more colorful than David's. Sarah jumped out of Giles's car. She was beaming. "How 'bout me? I can drive a Ferrari."

# TWENTY-SEVEN

Andrew Balaton arrived on Badger Rock Island from Bar Harbor via helicopter. He was met by Lillian Parker. As they walked together toward the house, she hurriedly, and reluctantly, told him about her visit with Ashley to Jude's Paradise. "I think Crockett just wants to make a memorial out of the island," she concluded. "That's all."

"Lillian, Lillian. Do you think I'm a fool?" His tone was only mildly critical, and he took her hand and squeezed it gently, his smile one of encouragement.

She looked away. "I'm just telling you what I know."

"And I appreciate it. But permit me to draw my own conclusions."

She tore her hand out of his and picked up her pace. It is so goddamned cold on this bloody island, she thought viciously. She had wrapped her hair in a brightly colored Hermes scarf and put on heavy socks, but the shivers wouldn't abate. Nerves, she thought. But thank God she'd seen nothing of Mac Stevens.

It annoyed her when Andrew treated her like a pouting teenager, but she realized that was his way with women—some even liked it. She didn't; she never had. But she had always been remarkably tolerant where the former Count András Balaton was concerned. She owed him that much. She said quietly, "I'm just telling you what I know."

He gave her one of his cool aristocratic smiles. "You've always been rebellious and outspoken, Lillian. They're qualities I admire in you."

"Andrew, do you know who the Wakefield twins are?"

"Lillian, please. There are things even you don't know."

And, stepping up his pace, he passed her on the path and finished the walk to the main house alone.

The large portrait of Judith Land was hung on a starkly white wall opposite paned double windows that looked out across a perennial garden and a rocky cliff. Beyond was the Atlantic Ocean, bluish green and still, fading into the swirling mist on the horizon. It was a view for a legend, a view for Judith Land.

In the portrait, she was standing in a rose garden, her dark hair streaming down her back and shining in the sunlight. She wore a simple white dress and strand of pearls. There was an air of gracefulness about her—in her fine slender hands, her long neck, in her liquid pose that the artist had captured.

Ashley held her breath as she scrutinized the angles of the legendary face and the smile that was at once elegant, mischievous, cool, worldly. Judith Land had been so talented, and so very young.

"There's a portrait of Judith there. Look at it. Get to know her."

When she'd returned to Badger Rock Island, Ashley had soaked in a long hot bath and considered everything Lillian Parker had told her on Jude's Paradise. She avoided drawing any conclusions; she simply wanted to be able to remember all that had been said. Then, unhurriedly, she had dressed for dinner in the gown she had brought of midnight blue silk and iridescent sequins and put up her hair. She wore no jewelry, nothing, not even earrings.

Then she had poured herself a glass of white wine and found her way to the dining room, and to the portrait of Judith Land.

At footsteps on the gleaming hardwood floor, she looked up, startled, but smiled when she saw Jeremy. His double-breasted suit emphasized the breadth of his shoulders and the slimness of his hips, and she could feel the air between them crackling with electricity. She thought of last night. And then she shook off the warmth of the memory and looked again to the portrait.

With her glass, she gestured. "She certainly was beautiful, wasn't she?"

"Very," Jeremy said.

"I should have been so beautiful at twenty-three."

He stood beside her; she liked the fresh tangy smell of him. "Weren't you?"

"God, no. For one thing, I didn't have the money. For another, I didn't have the bones—don't, I should say. And her smile. Stunning, isn't it?" Ashley laughed to herself. "I was working so hard when I was twenty-three, I don't know if I ever had time to smile."

"What about her eyes?"

"I didn't wear much makeup when I was that age."

Jeremy was curiously silent.

Ashley was having difficulty breathing. "And her eyes literally sparkle."

"So do yours," he said softly.

"Not like that. And mine...mine are a different shade of blue."

Jeremy shifted beside her. "A brighter version of the same shade—a rather vivid, unusual shade of blue, I'd say."

Dark hair.

Pale translucent skin.

High cheekbones.

A drop-dead smile.

Bright vivid blue eyes.

Ashley pivoted abruptly and left without a word, flying out the front door and out to the garden of perennials. Her heart was skidding, but she slackened her pace as she walked out to the cliff, where the wind was sharp and the waves battered the rocks. It was high tide. Turning to the west, she could see the peaks of Mt. Desert Island, dark and purplish against the glowing sunset. She was glad for the long sleeves and heavy silk of her dress, but still she was cold.

Ashley didn't pretend to be as beautiful as Judith Land. Her features lacked any subtlety, her eyes were more direct, her smile was wider. But her coloring, her shape—they were the same as those of the woman in the stunning portrait.

And the dates fit. And the facts—or the lies—about herself. And the jewels in the vaults of Piccard Cie. And the Liechtenstein trust.

Everything fit.

Judith Land was her mother. David's mother. *Their* mother.

It was a conclusion—a theory, a hypothesis, a *fact*—that had been hovering uneasily in the back of her mind since she had learned the last person seen wearing the tiara and the choker was Judith Land.

Now another dimension to this ungodly mess could be added. There were already spies, traitors, torturers, liars and jewel thieves. Now there were kidnappers, too. Baby stealers.

*Barky.*

Ashley flung her wineglass off the cliff and watched it shatter against the rocks. Within seconds, a wave crashed and washed away the shards.

"Don't get maudlin," she told herself. "There might be another explanation."

Of course there was: she was wrong. The similarities in shape and coloring between herself and Judith Land were a coincidence. A trick of the evening light and a mind that was too tired, too suspicious, too active. She didn't yet have all the facts.

Why in God's name would Bartholomew Wakefield steal someone else's children?

He hadn't.

She turned back to the house, stumbling on the rough ground. It was seven o'clock; time for dinner.

The dinner guests were gathered in the spacious living room: Jeremy, eyeing her closely; Lillian Parker, stunning in bittersweet red; a wiry, attractive middle-aged man in black tie; and an elderly man, tall and stooped, in a navy pin-striped suit that had to be forty years old.

J. Land Crockett walked over to her as she came through the door. "Ashley Wakefield."

She nodded and sniffled. Coming from the cold wind inside to the relative warmth had made her nose begin to run. "Yes," she said, "and you must be Mr. Crockett. Thank you for having me here. It's a lovely island."

He reached into his suit coat pocket, withdrew a

mound of crumpled white tissues and peeled one off, handing it to her. "Your nose is red."

"It's raw out there."

He grunted. Ashley was struck by the darkness of his narrow eyes. At first they had seemed black, but now, as she looked more closely at them, she saw they were a deep, deep nearly black blue.

Like David's.

His tone gruffly polite, he asked, "Did you enjoy your tour of Jude's Paradise?"

She called on years of work in communications and in a prestigious volunteer organization to produce what she hoped was an infectious smile. "Immensely. Does it have anything to do with your reasons for inviting me here?"

"Maybe."

"I don't think I've ever been subjected to so many mysteries in one day," she said, cheerful and blunt. She hoped he'd get the point. "I'm beginning to feel as though I'm having to pass a battery of tests before you'll take the plunge and tell me what you want with me."

He straightened his thin shoulders; the suit was baggy on him, she noticed. "That damned well may be true."

She would have argued with him, but he moved away from her, talking to Lillian, and she gave up in frustration. Had he noticed a resemblance between Judith Land and the woman on the cover of *You*? Had he recognized the tiara and the choker? Did he even give a damn that he might have grandchildren?

Jesus, she thought. Grandchildren. That made him her grandfather?

"Spare me," she muttered, and told herself again

that she couldn't jump to any conclusions without all the evidence in. She had to keep an open mind.

All at once she became aware of Jeremy standing at her side. "Are you all right?"

"Of course," she snapped. "Why shouldn't I be?"

"Just asking."

"Well, don't ask."

He gave her a cool look and said in a low voice, "I'll remember that next time I feel a jolt of genuine concern for you."

She sighed. "I'm sorry."

"It's all right." He smiled. "I'd rather have you jump down my throat than pretend to be happy when you're seething inside. Makes for a more honest relationship."

"And a more volatile one."

The handsome man in black tie joined them and introduced himself as Andrew Balaton. They exchanged comments on the weather and the beauty of the island scenery, and then Balaton said pleasantly, "My daughter, Sarah, has confided to me her behavior this past week. I understand she went to Amherst to see your brother." He said Am-herst, pronouncing the silent *h*. "I had invited him to join me in New York for dinner, as perhaps you know, and had intended to apologize to him for my daughter's behavior. I was required to be here this evening, and so I was forced to cancel our engagement. However, now I see I can apologize to you on her behalf."

Ashley smiled, marveling at his precise, formal manner. "That's not necessary, Mr. Balaton."

"It's my understanding she's returning to Houston. She's my daughter, Miss Wakefield. I feel responsible."

"You shouldn't," Ashley said smoothly.

Balaton grimaced, as if she had uttered a self-evident but nevertheless unpleasant truth. "My daughter has a stressful career. She is ambitious and clever, but occasionally it becomes necessary for her to...crack. It relieves the stress."

"I see."

"You understand."

No, she didn't, but she let it slide. "Tell me, Mr. Balaton, do you believe the jewels I wore in the *You* photographs belong to your family?"

He laughed. "No, of course not."

"Then your daughter made a mistake?"

"A terrible one, yes."

"Well, I suppose we all make mistakes. Do you have any idea why Mr. Crockett has lured me up here? He seems to be a man of many mysteries."

Again Balaton laughed, and his warm brown eyes crinkled at the corners, the only hint of his age. "Yes, that's our Crockett. I'm afraid, however, he hasn't shared his strategy with me, but I can only say that I am delighted to have your company. It's a pleasure, Miss Wakefield."

That, she knew, was supposed to change the subject, but she'd always been a tenacious sort. "Do you suppose *he* recognized the Balaton jewels, too?"

The Hungarian's face froze for an instant, but he recovered quickly and smiled. "That would be impossible, Miss Wakefield. As I have explained to my daughter many, many times, the Balaton jewels are a myth."

"But your wife wore the diamond-and-pearl tiara and choker the night you announced your engagement in Vienna."

He grew rigid. "*A* diamond-and-pearl tiara and

choker. There are so many, you understand. Please, if you'll excuse me?"

Her smile sparkled. "Of course."

When he'd walked off, clearly displeased with her, Jeremy touched her elbow. "Go easy."

"That *was* going easy," she muttered. "Arrogant son of a bitch. I'd like to start knocking some heads together around here and get some answers. How stupid do they think I am?"

"If they're smart, they won't think you're stupid at all." Jeremy turned to the cherry table behind them and poured her a glass of white wine from a simple crystal decanter. "They're all playing each other for answers. My guess is they've been nursing their own ideas and suspicions, and now they're trying to find out if they're right without having to commit themselves—or maybe expose themselves. I think Crockett's gotten you and Balaton and Lillian Parker here together to see what would happen."

"He's an old crank."

"But I wouldn't underestimate him."

She scoffed. "All we need now are Mac and Barky."

"I wouldn't be at all surprised if they're lurking outside in the shadows."

"Spooks that they are."

Jeremy gave her a look of surprise. "You're going to survive this, aren't you?"

She grinned. "Goddamned right."

Even, she thought, if she turned out to be the biological daughter of a legendary film actress and a Hungarian count–turned–corporate executive. The hell with them all, she thought with sudden vehemence. She was Barky's kid.

She noticed Lillian Parker standing alone in the far

corner of the big room, next to a spinet piano that looked unused. She was a woman who had interviewed heads of state, fanatical terrorists, generals and half the intellectual heavyweights of the twentieth century. She was tough minded and incisive, but tonight, Ashley thought, the hard-edged demeanor was all a facade. Deep down, Lillian Parker was unnerved and very shaken.

"Push has come to shove," Ashley said as she sipped some of her wine.

"Ashley, for God's sake, don't do anything crazy."

Jeremy sounded serious, but she shrugged off his concern. "Why change now?"

Ashley breezed across the room to Lillian Parker. She was asking Roger to fetch her something stiff to drink, and when Roger dashed off to comply, Ashley sidled up to the famous newswoman. "Maine air agrees with you, Lillian," she said cheerfully. "You look terrific."

Lillian laughed. Years of television work made it sound less forced than Ashley suspected it was. "Cosmetics can hide anything. And how are you? Besides stunning. Crockett said the *You* piece didn't do you justice. You have a taste for the right clothes for you, Ashley."

"I've got four years of mistakes hanging in my closet. A fashion consultant once told me I should try to get people to focus on my eyes, that they're my best feature."

"They are." Lillian's voice was hollow. Roger appeared with a Scotch, and she gulped it eagerly.

"At first," Ashley went on casually, "I didn't notice how similar they are to Judith Land's eyes because everything else about her portrait struck me so much. She was startlingly beautiful, wasn't she?"

Lillian made no reply, but stared at the amber liquid in her glass.

"Anyway, it took me a while to see how much her eyes are like mine. They are similar, don't you think, Lillian?"

Still staring into her Scotch, as if she were trying to spot a fruit fly that had just flown into it, Lillian said, "She had her mother's eyes."

"I see. And David has her father's eyes. Crockett's eyes."

Lillian drank some of her Scotch, then resumed staring into it. "Johnny, Crockett's father, had those same piercing black-blue eyes—except his were bloodshot half the time. He's in the history books. Look him up sometime."

"I intend to." Ashley sipped her wine, amazed that her hands weren't even shaking. "Was Judith Land my mother?"

But Lillian Parker's hands were shaking, and she finally had to set down her drink. She still wouldn't meet Ashley's eye. "Oh, please—I don't know. I..."

"You do know. Or at least you can make a damned good guess."

"Get out of this, Ashley." She turned then, her eyes intense, clear, remarkably direct. "For the love of God, Ashley, go home."

"You're afraid. Why?"

"Because I'm a coward," she said suddenly, her voice a vicious, tortured whisper. "I was a coward thirty years ago, and I'm a coward now—a pawn. Someone to be manipulated." She snatched up her glass, but her hands were shaking too violently, and she had to put it back down. "There's nothing you can do to change what happened. And what good are answers to questions that never should have been asked? You'll only get hurt. *Go home.*"

Ashley shook her head just once. "I have to know who I am."

There were tears in Lillian's eyes when she smiled. "Ashley, you've never *not* known who you are. Judith would have liked that."

"Talk to me, Lillian. Please—"

But Roger Shellingworth interrupted, announcing dinner. They gathered in the dining room, where the table was set simply, yet exquisitely, in white Wedgwood and Waterford. Ashley was instructed to sit next to Jeremy, their backs to the windows, facing the portrait of Judith Land. She suspected that was another part of J. Land Crockett's devious little plan.

Ashley caught Jeremy staring at the painting, as if mesmerized by the beauty and vivacity of the actress. And then she saw the certainty in his eyes, as he glanced down at her and smiled. So, she thought, he knows. Was he pitying her again? Striking up another black mark against Bartholomew Wakefield? Jewel thief, traitor, torturer, KGB agent, child stealer. Nice fellow, Barky was.

She shook out her napkin onto her lap, and dinner commenced with a surprising but delicious apple-and-onion soup.

A horrified gasp from the end of the table whipped Ashley around in her chair.

Andrew Balaton was already rising to his feet. His face was gray, his manicured hands trembling. Ashley thought he was having a heart attack.

To his left, Lillian Parker didn't move. She sat rigid, her face gone white.

Balaton clutched in his hand a tiny gold crown. "My God!" he cried, his voice strangled, his eyes wild. "*Orült szerzetes!*"

Ashley froze. Beside her, Jeremy gripped his spoon, his jaw tightening.

"Is this some hideous joke?" Balaton screamed, accusing everyone. "Who's responsible for this?"

No one answered.

At the end of the table, J. Land Crockett settled back in his cushioned chair and folded his hands in his lap, looking more curious than concerned. Ashley wouldn't have put it past him to have planted the crown, whatever it was. Obviously it had a terrible meaning to the dispossessed Hungarian count.

Then, kicking back his chair, Balaton ran from the room.

There was an uncomfortable silence.

"I'll see to him," Lillian said hoarsely.

When she'd gone, Crockett snorted. "Wonder what that was all about? Hate it when he starts muttering in Hungarian. Either of you speak it?"

They said no, neither Ashley nor Jeremy admitting they'd already had *orült szerzetes* translated for them. The mad monk. Bartholomew Wakefield.

He was there, Ashley thought. There on Badger Rock Island.

And Andrew Balaton didn't like it.

# TWENTY-EIGHT

Neither Andrew Balaton nor Lillian Parker returned to dinner, but Crockett blithely continued without them, and courses proceeded through a herbed salad, oatmeal-sage rolls, a light lobster casserole and, for dessert, almond torte. In order to figure out just what he knew and suspected, Ashley had determined to let the old man in the ill-fitting ancient suit take the conversational lead.

But J. Land Crockett said nothing. He merely ate and occasionally studied her, rudely staring, with his black-blue eyes. By her second piece of torte—fresh air and skulduggery built up an appetite, she reflected— she'd realized he was playing the same game with her.

She decided this particular game was the important one to win. Digging into her torte, she said, "Ms. Parker indicated to me that Jude's Paradise might be the reason you invited me to Maine—or Down East, I should say. It's a beautiful place, quite a bird sanctuary. By the way, have you been introduced to Jeremy Carruthers, legal counsel for the New England Oceanographic Institute?"

Crockett didn't so much as glance at Jeremy. "When I asked you up here, Miss Wakefield, I assumed you could circumvent the bureaucracy."

"Please call me Ashley. And I'm afraid I don't work

that way, Mr. Crockett. What was it about the *You* piece that prompted you to contact me?"

He grunted, appraising her. "Your attitude. Do you enjoy publicity, Ashley?"

"No."

"Then why did you permit yourself to be interviewed by that magazine?"

She smiled. "I had my reasons."

"It's caused you nothing but trouble, hasn't it?"

"Today was hardly trouble, Mr. Crockett." Heavens, she thought, but I can be slick when I want to be. "But surely you didn't invite me here to lecture me on how to deal with the press. That's my business, you know."

"And none of mine? You can be damned snippy, Ashley Wakefield. I could send you away empty-handed and make this entire trip a waste of your precious time."

Snippy, Ashley thought. How easily he trivialized her anger.

Jeremy, she noticed, didn't spring to her defense.

"Do you think this institute of yours could use an island like Jude's Paradise?" Crockett demanded to know.

Swallowing a piece of torte, Ashley laid down her fork and adopted her trustee demeanor. "I'm sure we'd be interested in discussing it with you."

"Nothing we say tonight could be considered binding or in any way the opinion of the entire board," Jeremy put in, playing his part.

Crockett ignored him. "I'd want the name to remain the same and the ecology or whatever you want to call it to be undisturbed. No one but me needs to know it's a memorial to my wife and daughter. That's the way they'd want it, and it's the way I want it. Interested?"

"Of course," Ashley said, "but, Mr. Crockett, I don't think you're being entirely frank with me."

"So? Where does it say I have to be frank?"

"I'm sure it doesn't say anywhere, but it would make me happier."

He snorted. "I'm not here to make you happy."

Bastard. Under the table, Jeremy brushed her knee, and she could read his mind: go easy. Hell! Why didn't she just up and ask the old buzzard if he thought he was her grandfather? If he hated her because she and David were all he had left of his daughter and they weren't at all what he wanted, well, then, so be it.

Did he think Barky was her father? Did he think the man who had raised her and David, who had lived for thirty years the hard frugal life of a farmer, had *seduced* his daughter? Gotten her to run off with him, give him her jewels, her children?

But the trust!

Judith's last, desperate attempt to free herself from a madman? Had she found out he had betrayed them on the border? That he was KGB? That he was a thief and a traitor?

No!

And she had contacted her father, fled to the Texas ranch where she'd grown up and, with the jewels and the Liechtenstein trust as her only consolation for failure, made her bid for freedom. And she had died.

No, no, no, no!

It was a terrible, awful, dreadful scenario, and it wasn't true.

Ashley lost her appetite for interrogation, and for almond torte.

Abruptly, she rose, reeling dizzily. Jeremy was beside her instantly. He grabbed her elbow, steadying her. "Ashley?"

"I'm ill. Please—excuse me."

And she fled.

After he'd extricated himself from afterdinner brandy with J. Land Crockett, Jeremy headed upstairs to the dark quiet hall and rapped on Ashley's door. He waited impatiently, but no answer came. He tried the knob: locked. "Ashley, it's me, Jeremy."

She was in there—she had to be—but she didn't answer. All day she'd been avoiding him, shutting him out. Instead of inviting him along, she'd gone off alone with Lillian Parker to Jude's Paradise. He'd spent the afternoon walking around Badger Rock Island, looking for signs of Mac or Bartholomew Wakefield—any clues as to who was right and who was dangerous and who was crazy. He'd found nothing but rocks and trees and the sea, and he'd tasted the rancidness of fear as he remembered last night, with Mac...and, especially, before, with Ashley. He didn't want to lose her.

He rattled the knob again. "Open the damned door!"

She wouldn't.

He couldn't blame her. He was a reminder of everything she didn't want to acknowledge. Even tonight, he'd seen the strong family resemblance among the Crocketts: father, daughter, granddaughter, grandson. And he knew Ashley had seen it, too. But she'd said nothing to him. Instead, she'd avoided his eye.

"Ashley, dammit...please."

But she didn't come to the door, and at last he left, defeated and exhausted. Since their rooms were adjoining, he should be able to hear her if she tried to leave, but he wasn't worried. They were on an island, and even Ashley Wakefield wasn't crazy enough to risk a takeoff in the dark.

Nevertheless, he'd be listening, just in case.

Toward dawn, three men gathered on the blustery sun porch. The entrance of MacGregor Stevens had silenced Andrew Balaton and J. Land Crockett, neither of whom he liked, nor ever had. Remaining on his feet, Mac patted out a cigarette and lit it. He exhaled a lungful of smoke rudely at the old man, daring him to say anything. He knew he'd been smoking too much. He could feel it in his lungs, and a callus was forming on his lower lip.

Back among his blankets and sweaters, Crockett waved the smoke away irritably. "Smoking isn't good for your health."

"I know." Mac took another deep drag and blew it out in the same place. "That's why I quit ten years ago. Something about you people brings back my old habits. I wonder what it is."

Andrew Balaton eased onto a wicker chair. "Fear of your own weaknesses, perhaps."

Mac smiled thinly. "Perhaps."

"What're you doing here?" Crockett asked gruffly, with more bluster than anything else. Although the old man wouldn't remember, Mac had met him once, more than thirty years ago. He hadn't been afraid of him then; he sure as hell wasn't now. Crockett reddened, his irritation deepening at Mac's obvious insolence. "How'd you get on this island?"

"It's not as impregnable as you think. I bribed a lobster man. It was really quite simple." He puffed again on his cigarette and thought briefly of Elaine. She hated cigarettes; she used to complain about his stinking up the house. Then he banished the thought of her, the vision, the reality. He couldn't afford any sentimentality. "Bartholomew Wakefield could easily do the same."

Crockett's eyes, more black than blue in the night air, bored into Mac, but Mac merely flicked ashes onto the gleaming bare floor. "Tell me about this man who calls himself Bartholomew Wakefield. Do you know him?"

Another thin smile. Another "Perhaps."

"I want the truth, Stevens," Crockett demanded, as imperious as ever. "I know you were in Vienna in '56, I know you got Balaton out of Hungary. Goddammit, I'm not some stupid old fool! I want to know who Ashley and David Wakefield are—who this uncle of theirs is. *I want to know what happened to my daughter!*" He erupted into spasmodic coughing and with a trembling hand reached for the crystal glass of water at his side. He managed to choke out, "And the jewels—I want to know what they mean. Did this Bartholomew Wakefield seduce my daughter? Did he steal from her? Goddamn you both to eternal hell if you've lied to me all these years!"

"If anyone lied to you," Mac said without emotion, "it was Judith—and yourself. Maybe these are questions you should have asked thirty years ago."

"My daughter was dead! What did I have left?"

Mac looked at him without sympathy. "Her children."

Crockett's thin gnarled hands, blue veins bulging, shot out from under the blankets and gripped the arms of the chair. Mac thought the old man would try to come after him, but instead he bellowed, "How the hell was I supposed to know she had children? She refused to see me!, She didn't *want* me to know!" He coughed loudly; or perhaps it was just a cover for his anguish. "My God, didn't she know she could have come to me?"

In the silence that followed, Mac crushed his cigarette butt under his shoe, on the polished floor. Andrew Balaton seemed to be trying to remove himself to another place, another time; he pretended to have no interest in the dialogue between MacGregor Stevens and the chairman of Crockett Industries. But Mac knew that was definitely not the case. Perhaps even more than he, Balaton was riveted to every word being said.

Through sheer force of will, J. Land Crockett regained his composure, and his eyes grew cold—endless dark pits of bitterness and anger. "If I'd let an autopsy be performed, I'd have known she'd given birth recently—and nothing would have stopped me from finding her child. Her *twins*. My God." He shut his eyes, steeling himself against another uncontrolled outburst of emotion. "I *never* would have stopped."

"We were both robbed," Andrew said unexpectedly, his voice calm and quiet, as if discussing the latest profit-and-loss figures.

Crockett stared at him. "Then they're yours?"

"They have to be."

Mac patted out another cigarette and left it, unlit,

hanging from the corner of his mouth. "Not necessarily. We only have the word of a proven liar that the twins were born in July of 1957. They might have been born in August—or earlier."

Balaton shook his head. "Not earlier. I would have noticed. As it was, I never suspected Judith was pregnant. I had no idea! If I had known..."

"We were both duped," Crockett said. "What possible reason could this man have had for taking these children, raising them on a farm, living in poverty all these years? And the trust—was that his doing? Or Judith's? Dammit, I want answers!"

"We all do," Mac pointed out, lighting his cigarette. "Unfortunately, all I have are suspicions."

Crockett pulled his hands back inside the warmth of the wool blanket. "You know, if those two—Ashley and David—if they can prove Judith Land was their mother, they'll inherit her entire estate. Andrew, you'd lose the nice pot Judith left you."

Andrew looked insulted. "Please, you should know that would make no difference to me. My own portfolio is not only sufficient, but ample. I would want them to have Judith's legacy. It would be their due."

Crockett grunted with obvious skepticism. "You wouldn't stand in their way?"

"Of course not."

Satisfied, Crockett looked up at Mac. "All right, Stevens. Tell me your suspicions."

As if you're in control of this, old man, Mac thought, surprised at the twinge of amusement he felt. Perhaps Ashley Wakefield's tenacity and incorrigible audacity had rubbed off on him—not that he didn't believe the beautiful young spitfire should be in bed anywhere in the world but here on Badger Rock Island. But he'd deal with that later. "First I want to know what Andrew knows about our Bartholomew Wakefield." He glanced down at Balaton. "Well? What's your story, Andrew?"

Balaton opened his fine hands placidly on his thighs. "He's a jewel thief."

"You know better than that."

Balaton said nothing.

"Tell me, dammit!"

He grimaced. "In private."

"No," Mac said, before Crockett could speak. "Crockett has a right to hear."

Balaton looked away from both men. "The man who now calls himself Bartholomew Wakefield is Hungarian."

"*What!*" Crockett bellowed. "You know him and you never told me?"

Balaton ignored his former father-in-law. "He came to me in January of 1957. He wanted a job. I had none to give him. He left, and I never saw him again—until this week's edition of *You* magazine. I had no idea he had taken Judith from me...stolen my children. If I had known—" He tightened his hands into fists and dug his whitened knuckles into his thighs. "I thought he was just another displaced Hungarian. There were many who came to me—because of my marriage to a famous American actress, because of my connections with the Crockett family. I had no reason to be suspicious!"

"What did you do with him?" Mac asked.

"I told him I couldn't help him. I sent him away."

"You didn't know he'd met Judith?"

"No."

"And now?" Mac exhaled smoke. "Now what do you think he is?"

"What can he be? An opportunist. A thief. Behind my back, he met with my wife, he seduced her into giving him things, he destroyed her happiness."

Mac dropped his cigarette into Crockett's water glass. "What if I told you he was the same man who arranged for us to get out of Budapest—and then betrayed us to the Russians?"

Balaton went white. "What are you saying?"

"We knew him as *orült szerzetes*. The mad monk. He was a true Hungarian hero—or so we were led to believe. In fact, it's my opinion that he was working for the Russians all along, and probably still is. Imagine the valuable information he could have provided them, posing as a hero of his enslaved countrymen. I've had thirty years to think over that night, Andrew. And now, from what's happened during the past few days, I can make a few educated guesses. One, our 'mad monk' wanted you that night, not just me. He must have found out you'd been supplying the Americans with information from your position with the ÁVH."

Crockett leaned forward. "The what? What the hell are you talking about, Stevens?"

"The Államvédelmi Hivatal," Balaton said hoarsely. "The Hungarian secret police. I was a member during the Stalinist period, but I served as an agent for the Americans."

"For the love of Jesus, why was I never told?"

Mac gave a raw smile. "State security, Crockett, or whatever bullshit you want to call it. I was sent into Budapest to get Balaton out. Our 'mad monk' did his damnedest to stop us—without exposing himself as a traitor to his people, of course. He got me, but Balaton escaped. And *orült szerzetes* came after him. I don't know what happened between him and Judith, I don't know about her children, I don't know about her death. But I *do* know Wakefield has been sitting tight for the past thirty years, waiting for his chance."

"Doesn't make sense," Crockett said, the sharp executive now. "Any damage Andrew could have done the Russians he's already done."

Mac nodded, patting out yet another cigarette. "My thought exactly—until I looked into how he could *help* the Russians. Crockett Industries has huge interests in the defense industries, companies and departments on the cutting edge of technology. The Soviets would be delighted to get their hands on some of your company's secrets, Crockett. If they could get to Andrew, blackmail him somehow, they could get themselves some damned valuable information."

Crockett nodded thoughtfully. "I see."

"And that," Mac went on, "is where the jewels come in."

"Don't be absurd." Balaton sniffed arrogantly. "What could this man have on me? I have a clear conscience. I have nothing to hide."

"What about the diamond-and-pearl tiara and choker, Andrew? Wakefield went to tremendous lengths to get them from Ashley. What kind of leverage do they give him against you? What do the jewels prove, Andrew?"

Balaton stared down at the floor. "Absolutely nothing. If he wanted them, it's because he needed them for the money."

"His so-called niece and nephew would have given him as much money as he asked for."

"Then I don't know. He's a murderer, a thief—a madman. How should I know how he thinks? If I'd realized when he came to me thirty years ago what he was, *who* he was, I'd have acted then. Now...now I don't know what his plans are."

"Whatever else he is, Andrew, Bartholomew Wakefield is not a fool." Mac was losing his patience. "What—do—the—jewels—prove? Dammit, tell me!"

"*I don't know!*" It was the first time Mac remembered Andrew Balaton ever losing his composure. He was beginning to perspire at the temples. "Maybe that I was AVH—"

"You were, Andrew."

"The world doesn't know that—and it's not something I'd care to have to explain now, thirty years later."

Mac laughed nastily. "When will you learn, Andrew? The world doesn't give a damn."

"You're so bitter, MacGregor Stevens."

"Just a realist. I pulled your ass out of the fire in '56, Andrew. I'll do it again—and I don't give a goddamn what you're hiding. You're *not* going to become a traitor, if I have anything to say about it! Now, dammit, tell me where and when you're meeting Wakefield."

Balaton threw up his hands in defeat. "We've already met." His voice was barely audible. "He came to me and said he could protect me from this mad monk—he had made my life in Budapest hell, and I never could understand what he was doing. Now I realize: he was on to me. If I had known you were going to him for help with our escape, possibly I would have made the connection sooner and stopped you. He must have known I was working for the United States. I had no idea—*none*—that the man who came to me in

Los Angeles, and then this week...I had no idea *he* was the mad monk, KGB. I...I just didn't know."

"What does he want?" Mac was relentless. "Where and when?"

Balaton licked his lips. "He said he'd contact me. The crown—tonight, in the soup...that must be his warning, his sign. It always was in Hungary."

"Then he's on the island?" Crockett said. "I'll have it searched at once."

"Save your energy," Mac said. "He's had thirty years to plan this night. You won't find him unless he wants to be found."

Balaton was breathing rapidly, a wreck of a man, terrified. "He must know now that I can't be blackmailed with the jewels—that they mean nothing to me; he was misled. But the twins... He knows they believe in him, trust him."

Crockett rose to his feet, almost as tall as Mac. "What are you saying? Goddammit, man, spit it out!"

"If I don't do as he says, he will kill them. No sooner have we found them—your grandchildren, my *children*—than they will be dead."

# TWENTY-NINE

Looking out her window at the glittering starlit ocean, Lillian Parker sat on the chaise longue, hugging her knees to her chest, glad to be alone.

*The cellar was cold and damp and smelled of gasoline, smoke and death. Huddled under the frayed woolen blanket, Judith Land was pale and sick. No longer the cool, witty American actress, she was a frightened young woman in a place where she didn't belong. "Please, Lil," she said, "let's just call the American embassy and ask them to help."*

*"We can't."*

*"Oh, Lil. They'll only call our fathers. Nothing will happen."*

*Lillian Parker, who wanted so to be taken seriously, shook her head, adamant. "You can make it, Judith."*

*"I can't! Something terrible will happen, I know it!"*

*Lillian was annoyed. "Do you want us to be the laughingstocks of the whole world?"*

*"Oh, Lil, no one will care!"*

*Shivering herself, Lillian knelt beside her friend. "Let's do it my way, Judith, please. It was your idea to come along. Look, you'll feel better in a couple of days, and everything will be fine. I promise. Thousands have already made it over the border."*

*"But how many Americans, Lil? How many heiresses*

*who are here illegally in the first place? I feel like such an id-iot!"*

*Lillian sighed. "So do I."*

Finally, although it was nearly dawn, Lillian walked downstairs and found Crockett still sitting up on the sun porch. He'd suffered from insomnia for years, but refused to take any medication for it. He wanted to die, he'd always said, wide awake.

She sat near him, on a wicker chair. He didn't look at her. "They're in danger, Lil," he said.

"Who, Crockett?"

"My grandchildren." He smirked, facing her. "You've known who they are from the beginning, haven't you?"

Lillian wished she'd worn something over her flannel caftan; it was frigid on the porch. She didn't know how Crockett stood it. "How would I?"

"You tell me."

"Crockett—"

"You knew Judith was pregnant."

*"You can't tell Daddy...you can't tell anyone! Lillian, please, you're the only one I can trust!"*

*"But Judith—how?"*

*"Oh, Lil, don't be so dumb! Now promise me, Lil. Please promise me."*

*"Of course I promise."*

"I couldn't have," she told the man who had loved and mourned his only child. "I never saw her after the Christmas ball."

He nodded to himself. "You knew."

"Please don't."

"Don't what, Lil? Don't say anything I'll regret? Don't ask questions now that I should have asked years ago? Don't open my old fool's eyes? All these years I've had something—two children growing up on a farm in Massachusetts, raised by a madman, and I didn't even know it. Damn anyone to hell who kept me from them—who put *me* in hell."

Lillian shook her head, so tired of it all. "You put yourself into hell, Crockett."

"This man—this filth who calls himself Bartholomew Wakefield—stole my children, stole Judith from me. If she hadn't tried running from him, if she hadn't been on the ranch that day..."

"But she was, Crockett. We can't change the past."

"No. But we can punish the people who caused such pain."

Lillian shuddered. You must be brave... One day, perhaps. She had been brave, and her one day had never come. She needed a brandy...oblivion. "What are you going to do?"

He scrunched lower under the covers. "Protect Ashley and David, if I can—and stop this madman. I want to see him rot in hell."

"Maybe he's already there."


Jeremy lay fully dressed atop the hand-stitched patchwork quilt. Sometimes he thought he could hear Ashley breathing, but then he'd realize it was just the waves, and he'd shut his eyes tightly and wonder if she were in bed, thinking of him.

When the knock at his door came, he sprang out of bed and instantly tore open the door, but there was Mac Stevens, looking haggard and nervous. Uninvited, he walked into the dark room. Ominous black clouds had rolled in during the night—appropriately, Jeremy thought. It promised to be a miserable day.

Mac said matter-of-factly, "I'm sorry you didn't heed my advice, Jeremy."

"I did—Ashley Wakefield didn't." He sat on the lower end of the double bed.

"You're falling for her, aren't you?"

"Fallen, Mac."

He nodded, as if he'd expected nothing else. "She's the sort of woman I've always envisioned your ending up with. I hope things work out, Jeremy, but this is going to be hell on her. She still believes in her uncle, doesn't she?"

"If it were my father, Mac, so would I."

"Despite the evidence?"

Jeremy looked at his friend, his colleague, a man he had admired since childhood. Was Mac slipping quietly over the edge? Had he lost any semblance of perspective on this bizarre situation—or had he never any to begin with? Jeremy said carefully, "There hasn't been much actual evidence, Mac."

"He'll kill her, Jeremy."

"He *raised* her."

"He's raised pigs and chickens, too. To a man like that, they're all the same."

Jeremy shook his head. "I can't convince her of that."

"I wouldn't ask you to." Mac moved toward the window and smiled grimly. "You're bigger than she is, Jeremy. You can stop her. Hog-tie her, if you must."

Jeremy had to laugh at the idea: she'd have a royal fit!

But Mac wasn't laughing. "Do whatever you have to—*anything*. But keep her away from her uncle."

"Mac, Jesus. Talk to her yourself. Tell her. She has to make her own decisions."

"Don't be so damned honorable!"

"If I collude with you again, Mac, I'm afraid I'll lose her."

"If you don't, she'll get herself killed."

With a weary sigh, Jeremy climbed to his feet. Mac had his back turned to him now, one hand outstretched on the wall, bracing him as he looked out the window. He must be exhausted, Jeremy thought. Had he slept at all last night?

"Do you know where her uncle is?" he asked.

Mac shook his head. "Not for sure, but I think he's somewhere on the island."

"*Here?*"

"Yes, dammit, here. He'll be contacting Balaton."

"Jesus—"

Then, from a distance, came the sound of a motor, for Jeremy a joltingly familiar sound. He flew to the window, swearing, but it was too late. The trim white Cessna 172 was already lifting above the treetops, flying into the cloudy pale dawn sky.

"*Son of a bitch!*" He pounded the wall.

"Maybe this once she's going to be sensible," Mac said hopefully.

"Don't count on it, Mac."

"If it's not her?"

They ran together to her room and tried the door, but it was still locked. They kicked it in together.

The room was empty.

The sound of the plane overhead brought Lillian out of her room, pounding down the stairs and running outside, through the freezing wet grass. She reached up to the sky as if she could pull Ashley Wakefield back down to earth, but she felt only the raw wind blowing through her. Where was Ashley off to now?

I shouldn't have goaded her into looking at Judith's portrait... Oh, damn. Damn and hell and just fuck it!

Why couldn't Judith have thrown those stupid jewels into the ocean thirty years ago? Then, Lillian thought as she ran breathlessly toward the cliff, none of this would be happening. The money, the Liechtenstein trust itself, was all right—innocuous enough. Money couldn't be traced or remembered the way jewels could, and the Swiss were so dependably close-mouthed. Ashley and David could have gone on being rich and feeling warmhearted toward their mysterious benefactor...their mother. Judith would have been happy with that course of events; she would have loved the drama of it all.

As she came to the cliff, the Cessna dipped to the right, as if mocking them all, and disappeared from view.

And when Lillian turned, Mac was there.

"I'd hoped I'd manage to avoid you," he said coldly.

He hadn't changed, she thought. He was still straight and tall and handsome and so goddamned self-righteous. Among the many who'd laughed at her ambitions, he'd been the worst. "How can you be a reporter, lovely Lil? You don't even know which side Hungary was on in World War II." The bastard! The problem was, she really hadn't. He'd goaded her into finding out, studying, learning, asking questions, stretching herself. Of course, that hadn't been his intention.

"Mac, I need to talk to you."

"Save your energy."

She touched his arm. "Leave him alone, Mac—please. Let him do what he has to do."

"And what's that, Lillian?" He smirked in disgust. "It's amazing to me that after all that's happened, after everything he's done to you, you can still want to protect him. My God, Lillian, don't be so pathetic."

"Mac, you're wrong. He's not what you think he is."

Mac's arms dropped to his sides, a small gesture, but it made him seem more human, more tired, and Lillian bit her lip, hoping she wasn't the one who was wrong. He sighed, the anger going out of him. "God knows I can't hate you anymore, Lillian. Did he tell you to stop me?" He smiled at her moment's discomfort, reading into it. "I thought as much. Well, tell him you tried."

He started into a stand of pines, but she couldn't let him go. Shivering in the early morning cold, she ran after him. Her toe caught a stone, but she ignored the stab of pain. "Why go after him?" she called softly. "Tell me, Mac. Is revenge worth this kind of risk?"

He stopped, his shoulders squared, and turned to her in disbelief. "Revenge? Is that what you think this is? No, Lillian—God, no. I admit when I first saw his picture I thought to myself, this man deserves to pay, and pay dearly, for what he did to me. But then I thought of Elaine, the children, the life I'd built for myself. No, revenge certainly wasn't worth the risk."

"Then what is?"

"The life of a brother and sister who were born innocent into this hell we created. It's a question of honor, Lillian. But I don't expect you to understand that."

And he disappeared into the shadows.

# THIRTY

David and Sarah arrived in Southwest Harbor, on the quiet side of Mt. Desert Island, around seven o'clock in the morning. "You look terrible," Sarah told him as she parked the Ferrari on a picturesque street near the water. "Does your leg hurt much?"

He managed a wan grin. "Yeah."

In fact, his leg hurt like hell and he was stiff and sore and irritable, but he didn't want to take any of the painkillers he'd been given. The stuff made him crazy as well as drowsy, neither of which intrigued him. He hadn't slept at all during the long ride up. Sarah was a hell of a trooper: she wouldn't have stopped at all, except David couldn't bear sitting in the cramped car for long, and they had needed gas and coffee and a bathroom. All in all, he thought they'd made good time.

David insisted on being the one to call Badger Rock Island, and with Sarah alongside him, he got up on his crutches and hobbled over to a phone booth on the sidewalk. It felt better to be upright, and he wasn't bothered by the cold damp morning air.

He dialed the unlisted number Ashley had given him. A prissy-sounding guy answered on the first ring. Shifting all his weight onto his good leg and easing the crutch out from under the arm on the side of his bad leg, David tried to arrange himself so he wouldn't fall over. It was damned awkward, he thought, having a busted leg. He said, "Tell your boss I'd like to talk to him."

Sarah winced, warning him against such a tone, but David just gave her one of his lopsided grins.

"Mr. Crockett is unavailable. How may I help you?"

"You can send someone out to fetch me," David told him. "I'm in Southwest Harbor."

A horrified silence, very brief, followed. "That's quite impossible."

"Look, buddy, you can either come out here to fetch me or I'll just get some guy around here to give me a ride out. I know where your frigging island is. Makes no difference to me how I get there."

"You're being rude and unreasonable."

"I know it. I don't care if I have to fucking swim—"

"Just who are you?"

"David Wakefield."

There was a sharp intake of breath. "One moment."

The one moment was long enough that David had to come up with more quarters, an involved process with the phone and the crutches and the cast, but Sarah came to his rescue.

The guy on Badger Rock Island came back on the line. "A boat will arrive within the hour to pick you up."

Before David could thank him, he'd hung up.

He and Sarah grabbed something to eat at a coffee shop and walked down to the pier together. "You're moving very slowly, David," she said worriedly. "Are you sure you can manage?"

"No problem."

"Such bravado." She smiled up at him. "It's not a sign of weakness to say you're in pain, you know."

He gritted his teeth as he and Sarah headed down an incline. "I'm in pain."

"The boat ride will be rough. Why don't you just take one of your painkillers?"

"Can't. They knock me out."

"Well, then," she said cheerfully, "I'll just have to see if I can find a store open that sells aspirin. You'll never make it at this rate, David. At least it will help with the swelling."

"But—"

She grinned. "No buts. I'll be back in five minutes."

Trotting up the street, she turned and blew him a kiss. In spite of everything else, David laughed.

It was Andrew Balaton who eased up to the pier, in an ultrafast Chris-Craft racer. He wore a white cap and looked tanned and fit as he jumped lightly out of the boat and introduced himself. Climbing onto his crutches, David limped out to meet him. "That was quick," he said. "I didn't expect you so soon. Sarah'll be here in a minute—"

Balaton went white. "Sarah?"

"Oh, yeah. Sorry. I forgot, you thought she'd be on her way to Houston." He gave the older man a lop-sided grin. "Well, guess she had ideas of her own."

But her father looked truly pained, shaking his head, and he said softly, "I wish none of this had to touch her."

"She just wants to help."

"Where is she now?"

"Buying aspirin."

"Then we can leave now, quickly, before she returns."

"Hey—wait just a minute. I'm not running out on her."

Balaton seemed to lose all his energy, and he looked at David with pleading eyes. "There's so much to tell you. Your sister..."

David reeled. "Ash? Nothing's happened to her—"

"She's missing."

Ash!

"Please...my daughter could be in danger, too. There's no need—I can explain everything on our way? Perhaps this time Sarah will understand that I do what I do out of love, not because I underestimate her talents or her resolve. Must she be hurt, too?"

Never mind Sarah. Tell me about my sister!

As if reading his mind, Balaton said, "I believe I know what has happened to your sister."

David leaned on his crutches. Christ, even his armpits hurt. "Okay. Let's go."

Moving quickly, Balaton helped him into the boat—although small and wiry, the Hungarian was surprisingly strong—and in minutes, they were pulling out into the bay. Sarah ran out onto the pier, and it was with a wrenching, aching guilt that David watched her drop her brown bag in anger. He couldn't hear her cry above the roar of the engine, but he could read her lips. She was yelling, "Bastards! Bastards, bastards, bastards!"

And that, thought David, about summed it up.

By nine o'clock, Ashley was at the Park Avenue law offices of Parrington, Parrington and Smith. Evan, in gray pin stripes for the blustery day, rose to greet her.

"It's good to see you, Ashley. I've been trying to get in touch with you. It seems—" His eyes widened with shock as he studied her more closely. "Ashley. Good heavens. What's happened?"

Shaking her head, assuring him she was fine, she paced in front of his massive desk. She had had no sleep, and the past days had taken their toll, obliterating the devil-may-care look about her and dulling the vibrancy of her eyes. She no longer felt young and carefree. Sneaking around the cold, dark and lonely Maine house last night, she'd overheard conversations, accusations, stories, words. The pain and horror on the faces of the people she had seen was real enough, but that Bartholomew Wakefield—*Barky*—was the source of it was beyond comprehension. Not real. Not fathomable.

"I have kept you alive all these years; I do not intend for you to be killed now."

Was that real? Was that fathomable?

Evan urged her to sit down; she couldn't. Her entire body was shaking with too little sleep and too much caffeine. She was tired, jittery, crazy with fear. After dinner, she had sat alone in her room and decided what she had to do. She had locked her bedroom door, and slipping into a black knit body suit, feeling like a spy herself, she had torn open her window. From that point on, she had never hesitated, never doubted. There were no choices left; she had to act.

The drop from the window was about twelve feet. She and David used to throw each other off the barn roof all the time when they were kids and life was innocent and simple, or had seemed so. This would be no problem.

But when she'd had one leg out the window, Jeremy had knocked.

Jeremy. Passion, light, hope, strength. He wouldn't stand for her to run from him again. This time, she had qualms about deceiving him.

But his loyalties were torn. Hers weren't.

She'd thrown out her other leg and, forcing her muscles to relax, jumped.

She'd been outside, hovering among the frostbitten marigolds, below the screens of the sun porch, when Mac Stevens had found J. Land Crockett and Andrew Balaton.

She knew she wouldn't stop, wouldn't believe them, until she had heard what Barky had to say.

Now, stopping abruptly, she turned to Evan. "Tell me about the jewels, Evan. What did you find out?"

A troubled look on his mild face, Evan nonetheless came straight to the point. "First, that we could have established their provenance in 1982 if we'd pursued the matter. As it turns out, they're relatively well-known pieces. Ashley, are you sure—if you'll pardon my saying so, you look exhausted."

She smiled, reassured by the gentle manner of this prominent lawyer, and, she thought, trusted friend. "I look like hell, Evan—imagine how I feel. But I'll be okay. Please, just go on."

"They were crafted in the mid-eighteenth century, over a period of years, it seems, by a Viennese jeweler for a wealthy land-owning family in Royal Hungary—the Balatons. They were known for their horses and Tokay wine and, from the latter years of the nineteenth century through World War II, were one of the few aristocratic families clamoring for reform of Hungary's outmoded political and economic system."

Ashley nodded as another piece fell neatly into place...further condemning her uncle. Hadn't anywhere, anytime, anyone but Barky lied?

Evan went on. "The Balatons were respected and tolerated for their reformist tendencies during the conservative regime that was in power during the interwar period, and they managed to get away with redistributing some of their own vast land holdings, with the idea that others would see that it was not only a just but a perfectly reasonable thing to do. When the regime collaborated with Nazi Germany, however, the Balatons began to have their problems."

"They were anti-Nazi?"

"Vehemently so. Then the Hungarian fascists, a small fanatical group that apparently had little popular support, were placed in power toward the end of the war—"

"When the Germans occupied Hungary in late 1944," Ashley added.

Evan was impressed. "You're familiar with this period?"

"I've had a crash course, you might say. What does this have to do with the jewels?"

"I'm getting to that. You see, with the German occupation came a virulent campaign against the thousands of Jews in Hungary. They were rounded up, marched out and slaughtered. Count István Balaton set up a network to hide Jews and smuggle them out of the country, but he was exposed and executed, along with perhaps two dozen Jews then in hiding near Balaton Castle. Apparently they were tortured in front of him, and then he was killed."

"How awful."

"The story doesn't get any prettier, I'm afraid.

When the Germans were defeated, Hungary was faced with permanent occupation by the Soviet Union. The Balatons were in favor of their country introducing long-overdue land and economic reform and becoming a neutral democratic republic, as became the case with Austria. Young Count András Balaton returned from fighting with the Resistance in Yugoslavia, and what was left of the Balaton family prepared to do their part to oust the Soviets. But in 1947, while the Communists were consolidating their power, a band of thugs broke into Balaton Castle. The count was away at the time, but his mother, his two sisters and his young brother were brutally murdered."

"Good God."

"Horrifying, isn't it?"

"How did you find all this out?"

Evan shifted some papers on his desk, an apparent attempt to dispel some of the melancholy that had invaded the room. "As it turns out, a young Hungarian historian came to see me. He's been working on the restoration of Balaton Castle for tourism. He recognized the tiara and choker and flew at once to New York." Evan gave a wry smile. "Apparently he has access to decadent Western magazines. He told me the whole horrid tale. He's a bit of an ideologue, but I don't doubt the facts of the case—only his interpretation. The jewelry expert I contacted was able to confirm that the remaining jewels from the safe-deposit box, as well as the tiara and choker, belonged to the Balaton collection."

No wonder, Ashley thought, Andrew Balaton had been willing to risk his life by passing information to the West from within the ÁVH. But would the Russians have permitted a man with such a troubled past to become a trusted member of the state secret police? It seemed unlikely, which meant Balaton had probably adopted a new identity.

And Barky had betrayed him....

She wouldn't think about that now. Stick to what you know, not what you guess. She stood at the front edge of Evan's desk, facing him. "Did the Hungarian historian know how Count Balaton and the Balaton jewels got out of Hungary?"

Evan hesitated. Then, with a heavy sigh, he handed Ashley a manila folder. "Here. See for yourself."

Twenty minutes later, in a Park Avenue coffee shop, Ashley closed the folder. She had to see David. Together, she and her brother could stop the insanity that was about to unfold. They *had* to.

She found a pay phone and tried him at the farm, but Iggy answered, telling her David had gone to Maine with a "built blond sweetie." Iggy was unreal. Ashley hung up and tried Maine. Roger answered and impatiently explained that David was on his way to Badger Rock, and yes, he would certainly tell him his sister had called.

"May I speak with Jeremy, please?"

Roger huffed. "Very well."

In a moment, Jeremy came on the line and swore at her for at least ten seconds. Amazing, she thought, how good that made her feel. "Jeremy, I'm on my way back to the island. Wait for me?"

"Forever, Ashley."

Then, with a refreshing bounce to her step, she stopped at the bank and, with the key Evan Parrington had given her, identified herself to the bank officer— this one didn't flirt with her in her unkempt state—

and opened the safe-deposit box. Tucking the velvet-bound cases into a canvas bag, she headed out. She had bummed a helicopter ride into the city from Westchester Airport. On the way back, however, she had to get her Alfa Romeo out of the garage and drive herself to the airport. She had asked a couple of mechanics to refuel her plane and give it a good going-over, and when she arrived, they were eager to show her their handiwork.

Within minutes, she was back at four thousand feet, hoping she could hold herself together a while longer. The remaining Balaton jewels were at her side; so was the folder.

# THIRTY-ONE

David concentrated on keeping himself seated as the boat skidded over the waves. With his broken leg, he couldn't anchor himself, and even the slightest bump brought waves of throbbing pain. His jaw was cramped from gritting his teeth and his eyes burned... and he was sick with worry. Ash. Jesus, what was she into now?

"So what happened to my sister?" he asked, hanging on as they bounced over a line of rolling waves.

Balaton kept his gaze on the gray ocean ahead. "We don't know, but it's my belief your uncle has her."

"Barky? What the hell for? He could have—"

"He will want the remaining jewels."

"*Jesus.*"

David recalled that single day in Geneva, more than four years ago, when he had stared dumbfounded at a queen's ransom in jewels. He'd thought them old-fashioned, but later, on the flight home, Ashley mentioned that she had kind of liked the tiara and the choker, except then she couldn't imagine where she'd wear them. To a fish-tank opening, David thought.

But there had been no mention in the *You* profile of the other jewels in the collection...or the safe-deposit box at Piccard Cie.

"How do you know there are more jewels?" David asked sharply.

Balaton hissed impatiently, his expression steely, "Because I am a Balaton."

"But you told Sarah—"

"I know what I told her!" he erupted, suddenly out of control. Despite the nonstop biting wind, beads of perspiration broke out across his forehead, but he did not turn to face David. He took off his cap and rubbed the sweat off with a swipe of his forearm, like a pitcher on the mound in August. "Please." He sounded calmer. "There's so much you don't understand. Your uncle—the man who calls himself Bartholomew Wakefield—will stop at nothing to get those jewels."

David scoffed. "That's the pot calling the kettle black, Balaton. You sent your muscle—what's his name, Smith—after the jewels..."

"Giles was overzealous," Balaton snapped. "He was not to have hurt you. I made the mistake of telling him how absolutely vital it is that your 'uncle' not get his hands on the jewels. He has only the tiara and the choker, am I right?"

"Look, I don't give a goddamn about the jewels. As far as I'm concerned, anybody wants them, they can have them. It's Ash I care about. Now what the hell's happened to her?"

"She's gone...this morning. David, listen to me." Perspiration was gleaming on his upper lip now, too. "If I can get the remaining jewels of the Balaton collection, I can expose this man Bartholomew Wakefield for the traitor and thief he is."

David made a sudden movement that nearly sent

him sprawling off his chair, but he held tight. Jewel thief he was willing to believe, but traitor? Not Barky.

Balaton put his cap back on. "Please forgive me for being so blunt." He had regained his formal manner and even managed to smile apologetically at David. "I forget what he is to you."

"It's okay." David didn't give a damn what people were calling Barky; he wanted facts. "Do you think Barky'll try to get Ash to get him the rest of the jewels?"

"I know it."

Why now? If Barky had ever asked Ashley and David for the contents of the safe-deposit box, in all likelihood they'd have given them to him. But David vividly remembered their argument over a new linoleum floor.

*"What's wrong with this floor?"*

*"It's worn out."*

*"It still has years of use left."*

*"Barky, I'll pay for a goddamned new floor!"*

*"Don't waste your money."*

That was Barky. Not this person Balaton was talking about, not the man in black who'd battered him and Ashley in the woods.

"What do you think we should do?" he asked Balaton.

"Stop him."

"Sure, but how?"

Balaton seemed clearheaded and calm now. "We must beat him to the jewels, David. You have access to them, don't you? Perhaps we can get to Switzerland before they do and—" He stopped as David shook his head.

"Won't work."

"And why not?"

"Because the jewels aren't in Switzerland."

After Ashley's call, Jeremy found Lillian Parker in the dining room, where she sat with an ashtray, a pack of cigarettes and coffee. She had dressed casually in jeans and a bright turquoise cotton sweater, but her hair was lank, and because she hadn't put on any makeup, he could see the lines of age around her mouth and eyes. Knowing she'd been worried, he told her Ashley was on her way back.

Lillian smiled. "She's irrepressible, isn't she? I wonder if she went after the rest of the jewels."

"The what?" Stunned, Jeremy sat diagonally across from her. "Lillian..."

She didn't seem to hear him as she tapped her cigarette lightly on the edge of the ashtray; a whitened ash dropped off. "Mac will be furious—probably'll blame me for her, too."

Hell, woman, talk! But he contained his impatience. "I'm sorry, Lillian, I don't understand."

"Of course not." She laughed, tired and sad and bitter, and put the cigarette back in her mouth. "You were just a little boy yourself thirty years ago. You couldn't know about all the honest but disastrous mistakes I made when I was young and oh, so stupid."

"Don't be so hard on yourself."

"Why not? Everyone else is."

Jeremy wished he could think of some way to comfort her, and yet at the same time, he only wanted to pin her down and get her to talk. At the moment, sitting under the portrait of the dead Judith Land, Lillian was just rambling and feeling sorry for herself....

And then, all at once, it became clear. His eyes widened, but ever the lawyer, he forced a note of calm into his voice. "You and Judith were in Hungary in '56. You're the other two Mac helped escape."

Lillian exhaled smoke at the ceiling. "Bingo."

*Jesus!* What a bombshell that would have been—and would be now, if it were widely known. In an effort to keep from strangling the woman for answers, Jeremy pulled the insulated coffeepot over to him and had a look. Practically full. Lillian had an extra mug; he filled it. As he did so, he tried to imagine two rich young Americans caught in the hell of Budapest during one of its revolutions.

"You lost Mac that night," he said with compassion. "It must have been frightening."

"The whole thing was frightening from start to finish—pure hell. And much, much more than either of us, Judith *or* I, had bargained for." She stubbed out her cigarette in the ashtray. "Crockett hates it when I smoke here. He says he can smell it for weeks afterward. Poor Crockett, he's been through so much. Usually I oblige him, but today...I just don't give a damn."

Jeremy steered her back to the subject. "He never knew about your foray into Hungary?"

"God, no. He'd have started another war to get us out."

"What made you go?"

"Romance, adventure. I'd wanted to be a journalist as long as I could remember, but, you see, I was young, rich, pretty and female—and no one took me seriously, especially at age twenty-two. Judith and I were in Vienna when the revolution broke out in Hungary, and I saw my chance."

"Did you know Mac was there?"

She sighed. "Dear stuffy Mac. Yes, I knew. We'd known each other since we were tots, and so naturally we looked him up when we got to Austria. When the trouble started and I'd made up my mind I was going to pursue my first big story, I decided I'd go to Mac for information. There were dozens of journalists in Vienna—colleagues of my father's—I could have bugged, but Mac was an expert. He knew Eastern Europe, he knew the language, he was a part of the story. But he'd also disappeared. Well, of course, I guessed exactly where he'd gone."

"Didn't you also guess he was on a mission?"

"Naturally. But I didn't care."

Jeremy winced.

"I'd made up my mind I was going, too. I didn't think there would be any danger. You have to understand, Jeremy, that during those first few days, after the initial uprising, there was a real euphoria in the air—people actually thought the Hungarians were going to win. Journalists were pouring into Budapest. I wanted to be there, too."

"But you weren't a journalist," Jeremy pointed out softly. "You didn't have credentials..."

"I know: but I had money. It was ridiculously simple to gain illegal entry into the country."

"What about Judith?"

"Judith—" She smiled wistfully, going after another cigarette. "Judith believed she could do anything I could do—and ought to. She insisted on coming with me. I argued, but she said she'd tell my father what I was doing if I didn't let her tag along. So I did. And there we were, two little rich girls, one with an internationally famous face, prancing about a Soviet bloc country in the midst of a revolution. By the time we reached Budapest, all hell was breaking loose."

Jeremy nodded sympathetically. "How did you hook up with Mac?"

"A Hungarian had heard about us—from the people who'd smuggled us into the country."

"Balaton?"

She shook her head. "Bartholomew Wakefield."

"Oh, Jesus."

"Mmm. It was strange. He never made fun of us, never told us what silly fools we were. He just helped us. I've never known anyone else like him. Well, I trusted him immediately—it took Judith a bit longer—and told him about Mac. But he already knew about Mac, and he brought us to him, more or less dropping us on Mac's doorstep like a couple of orphans."

"Mac must have loved that."

She laughed. "He was properly furious."

"But he agreed to help you?"

"Yes."

"And he compromised his own mission."

"That's right." With a sterling silver lighter, she finally lit the cigarette she'd been holding tightly in her palm. "He was helping a Hungarian who'd been passing information to the Americans—our dear sweet Andrew Balaton. Mac hid us out with him and told us he'd leave us to the KGB if we didn't do as he said. At first, we had no idea he was a count. We thought his name was József Major and he was a dashing freedom fighter. He told us stories, restored our confidence in ourselves, made us believe we weren't the idiots we knew we were. He made us feel brave at a time when we deserved to feel only stupid and terrified."

When she paused, blowing out smoke, Jeremy looked at her thoughtfully, trying to imagine what it must have been like. "You were in an untenable situation."

"Oh, Lord, yes. We didn't know what was worse: facing Mac, the Russians, J. Land Crockett or Addison Parker. And my mother—my mother would have skinned me alive."

"When did you learn József Major was a count?"

Lillian left her cigarette to burn on the edge of the ashtray. "The night before we were to make our escape, Judith wasn't feeling well; the cellar where we were hidden was damp, freezing, a perfect hellhole. So Andrew told us his own story, about being the last of the Balatons, hiding from the Russians all these years, right under their noses all the time, pretending to be a trusted servant. We were mesmerized."

"What was his position?"

"He wasn't permitted to say, but I imagine it was a government clerical post—one of those positions where you have no power but access to tremendous amounts of information. Given the paranoia of the regime, it's a wonder he was able to pull it off."

"Had he been exposed?"

"Apparently it was imminent. I know Mac made it very clear Balaton had to get out of the country, but with two more added to the list...well, I was worried. I snuck out one evening, and I found the Hungarian who'd helped us earlier—and I asked him to help Mac now. He was a legend, you see. A sort of Scarlet Pimpernel."

"*Orült szerzetes.*"

She sighed. "I suppose I shouldn't be surprised. Yes, the mad monk."

"You were thinking what a hell of a story you had, weren't you?"

"Oh, but of course. I'd already thought of how I'd change the names of the people involved, to protect the innocent, and all that noble stuff journalists sometimes do. I was keeping notes."

Thirty years later, in light of what Lillian Parker had become, Jeremy thought he could understand her desperation. "And Mac?"

"I sent our 'mad monk' to him. Mac reluctantly accepted his help. Originally, our monk was to escort us to the border, but that plan fell through at the last minute. We had to go alone—the four of us. There was a clearing near the border. It was a landmark, a place where we could rest. It was so cold, and Judith had taken ill. Mac was in charge." She licked her lips as her voice grew increasingly hollow. "He moved us out of the clearing as quickly as he could—we were so damned tired and just numb with the cold. But it was dangerous to waste time. Mac picked up the rear. There was a light, and we heard voices...shots. Andrew kept us moving. There was nothing we could do. We knew the Russians had Mac."

"Jesus," Jeremy breathed.

With eerie calm, Lillian picked up her cigarette. "It was obvious to everyone but me that our mad monk had betrayed us."

"Why not to you?"

"Because I believed in him. He's that sort of man, Jeremy."

He nodded, thinking of Ashley. "So I've been told. Lillian, what about the jewels?"

"They represent the second stupidest thing I've ever done. Andrew showed them to us, in the cellar, as a way of proving to us that he wasn't lying about being this Hungarian count. It was very dramatic."

Jeremy had to smile. "You took notes?"

"Of course." And she, too, smiled. "Whatever mistakes I made, at least I meant well. Anyway, Andrew insisted that he wouldn't take the jewels—the Balaton jewels, he called them—to the West with him. It was too dangerous, and he didn't want them; they belonged in his homeland. But Judith and I decided he was being absurdly heroic. So we snuck the jewels into Austria ourselves, inside our clothing. Andrew had no idea."

"Mac?"

"Lord, no. It was our secret. After the disaster on the border, we felt damned silly carrying a fortune in jewels around with us. For a long time we just didn't say anything. Then Judith and Andrew decided to marry, and she came up with her plan to wear them the night they announced their engagement, at a Christmas ball, and surprise Andrew. She was absolutely stunning. Jaws literally dropped when she walked into the ballroom in that silver gown with the choker on that long white neck of hers and her hair woven in among the diamonds and pearls of the tiara. I'd never seen her so beautiful."

Jeremy conjured up images of old Judith Land movies, the face, the smile of the legendary actress. And then he glanced up, and there she was, laughing and smiling in the oil painting. "Was Andrew surprised?"

"I suppose so. I didn't spend much time with either him or Judith. And the next time I saw the tiara and choker, Ashley Wakefield was wearing them that night at the institute."

# THIRTY-TWO

After a much longer ride than David had expected, they came to a dilapidated dock on an island enveloped in a damp cover of fog. "Weird place for a billionaire to hang out," David muttered, looking around. As far as he could see, the place was uninhabited—but, he noted, he couldn't see far. "Is the house on the other side of the island?"

Balaton had taken the crutches and tossed them onto the half-rotted dock. Now he smiled as he offered David his shoulder, "Crockett is an eccentric."

"I guess so."

As he staggered under a wave of dizziness, David gladly took the wiry little man's help in getting out of the boat, although they both damned well nearly ended up in the drink. When, breathless, they were standing together on the dock, Balaton handed David his crutches. "Come," Balaton said, "I'll show you."

At best, the dock was unsteady, teetering ominously under David's weight, and there were places where the boards had completely rotted through. As Balaton strutted ahead, David swung over a couple of missing boards. "Is Ash around here someplace?" he called. "If anything happens to her, all you assholes will pay!"

The bluster went a long way to harden his spirit, taking the edge off some of the uneasiness that nagged at him, but he knew he was in no condition to make good on his threats. As he stood in the wild untrampled grass at the end of the dock, he looked around for any sign of human life, but he saw only trees and rocks outlined in the heavy gray mist, and the only sounds that came to him were the cawing, peeping, twittering and yelping of scores of birds, hidden and unseen.

"Where the hell are we?"

Balaton inhaled deeply of the cold island air. "It's called Jude's Paradise."

"What happened to Badger Rock Island? Listen, don't I have a right to know what the hell's going on—"

"I must leave you here," the president of Crockett Industries told him bluntly.

David groaned. "Oh, *shit.*"

With a small smile, Balaton sadly shook his head. "You should have lied to me, David. You should have told me the jewels were still in Switzerland. I would have made you go with me to Geneva to get them. Perhaps then you would have bought yourself enough time, and you'd have had a chance. But there's no need to blame yourself. You've never known the kind of fear that can drive good men into doing things they'd never have done if only they'd been allowed to live in peace. Be glad, David. You've never faced the horror of having to lie. For that, I envy you."

"So you're what Barky's been trying to protect me from. You're fucking crazy."

"Not crazy, David," Balaton said mildly. "Afraid."

"*Jee-*sus Christ."

"You see, the jewels never should have left Buda-pest. I showed them to those two girls, just so that they would believe me. If I had guessed what they were planning..."

David couldn't make any sense out of what Balaton was saying and didn't care, instead readying himself. He leaned heavily on the crutch supporting his good leg and eased up the other crutch. When Balaton, lost in his own unhappy memories, turned back toward the dock, David lunged forward and swiped at him with the crutch.

But Balaton was quick. He scooted away from the blow, which missed him entirely, and jumped lightly onto the dock, springing over to the boat with the energy of a man half his age.

Gritting his teeth against the pain, David hobbled as fast as he could after the madman.

"I'm sorry, David." Balaton hopped into the boat. "Truly I am. But now you're my only leverage."

One of his crutches sank into a rotted place on the dock, sticking there, and David lost his balance, falling fast as the other crutch went flying and he twisted around so he wouldn't land on his cast. There was a terrible creaking and swaying, and he thought the whole dock would come crashing down, but miraculously it held.

Balaton had the boat's engine started.

"Sarah will figure it out!" David yelled, trying to scramble up. "She'd know what you're up to."

"No." Balaton seemed supremely confident, at least of that. "She won't. You see, Sarah believes in me. She always has. Goodbye, David."

"Balaton, for Christ's sake—nobody fucking cares what you did thirty years ago!"

"Yes, David, someone does: Bartholomew Wakefield."

"So I'll talk to him—"

But Balaton had turned his back, and he eased the boat away from the teetering dock, out into the gray ocean, picking up speed. There was a roar from its engines, and then it was bouncing over the rippling waves. Soon it disappeared. Lying on the dock, aching and utterly shaken, David listened. In the distance, he could still hear the faint sound of the racer's engine, and the *zing-zing-zing* as it skidded across the bay.

What bay?

Where the hell am I?

One crutch was hanging halfway over the edge of the dock. He slid forward on his side, reaching for it, but a board gave way beneath his elbow, and as his arms shot up and out to brace him his hand just nicked the tip of the crutch. He watched it topple into the water. A wave slammed it against a rock, and it fell back into the water, and it was slammed again and again and again.

David lay flat on his stomach and searched for the strength and the will to make himself move. He was afraid the dock would cave in...afraid he'd lose the other crutch when he went after it...afraid of the agony that came with every movement.

"Ash," he cried, his voice carried down between the treacherous boards, into the swirling sea beneath him, lost. The wind was slicing through him; he wondered idly how much exposure to the cold and the damp his leg and battered body would tolerate. *"Barky!"*

What if Balaton had already brought Ashley out to this Jude's Paradise and dumped her? She could be hurt, in pain, needing him....

He saw the other crutch. It was lying parallel to the edge of the dock. If it moved just an inch in the other direction, it would be lost. He had to swing his arm down in an arc, to shoulder level, and then maybe stretch a bit to get it. Slowly...move slowly. Wiggling his fingers, forcing the tension in his arm muscles to ease, he edged it downward.

Don't lunge, jackass!

Then his arm was straight out from his shoulder. Looking down the length of it, he could see the top of the crutch just half a foot from his fingertips. Too far to stretch. With the bulky cast, he couldn't easily roll onto his other side, which left maintaining his present position and sort of sidling his whole body in that general direction. But he had to distribute his weight carefully as he moved. If he moved too suddenly, or too heavily, the dock, the crutch and he could go crashing into the ocean.

And that, he thought, would be that.

"To hell with it."

He sidled; he grabbed the crutch; he tucked it under his arm; he got himself to his feet—or more precisely, he thought, with his gallows humor, to his foot. The going would be slow, awkward and painful with just one crutch. But you acted, goddammit.

It wasn't much, but it was something.

Hhe had come to him at dawn, the man in black, this traitor, this mad monk. Balaton had wanted to kill him then, but knew he couldn't. Not yet...he must bide his time, act only when he was assured of success. "In the morning," the farmer had said, "by the cliffs on the eastern point of the island. I will see you there; I will find you...."

As the boat sliced through the open bay, Andrew Balaton's heart thumped wildly and he watched his knuckles turn white on the wheel of the boat, but he couldn't loosen his grip. He could feel the sweat pouring down from his armpits. He stank with fear. But this time he wouldn't permit his fear to incapacitate him. He would act.

No. I will find you, *orült szerzetes*.

He could be confident now. There was no reason to worry about the old fears coming back. Why should they? He was the head of one of the world's largest companies. He was accustomed to taking risks and dealing with the consequences of failure.

But there could be no failure now! Everything was at stake. As before.

It had been an excruciatingly hot day in Texas. He remembered that most vividly. He hadn't been used to such heat. Although summers in Hungary could be brutal, he'd never experienced a summer like that one, his first in the United States. He met Judith Land out on the deserted trail where she had used to ride as a child. It was at her request. She had called him.

*"Please come, Andrew. We can discuss our future. And I'll bring the jewels. I promise."*

But she hadn't. They were her trump card.

*"I want a divorce, Andrew. Give me my freedom, and you can have the jewels. I'll even talk to Daddy. He knows you're a good executive. He'll keep you on."*

*"Do you know why I want the jewels?"*

"No. And I don't care. I just want to be left alone."

"Judith, I love you. You're the only woman I've ever truly loved. Stay with me. Give me a chance."

"It won't work, Andrew. I'm sorry."

She had been unreasonable, intransigent. She didn't love him. She never had. That, too, became clear to him. And there was nothing he could do to change her mind. She was in control, and he was lost.

"I know what you are, Andrew."

"Ah, Judith, but you don't."

"Yes: you're a coward. Deep down, you're more terrified of me than I am of you."

"No!"

And yet it was true. They both knew that.

She went pale when she saw the gun. He took some small satisfaction in that. She had backed up toward his horse; it was where he wanted her.

He fired the gun into the air. And then he walked away. Judith Land had cried out only once before she was rendered unconscious, and then died.

During the tortures, in Hungary, he used to hope—to silently pray as he waited—that the victims would talk or just go ahead and die. He never relished their cries of agony, as so many of the others did. He wasn't a sadist. He was the one they would send into the cell, after the torture, to talk to the prisoners about their stubborn refusals to admit to their crimes against the state.

"You must confess," he'd tell them.

"But I am innocent," they'd sob to him.

"Then why are you here? We don't arrest innocent people. Confess. It will be easier for you."

Of course that was a lie. Confessions resulted in

more torture, rigged trials, deportations, executions. How could they release a confessed enemy of the state?

But during the tortures, the interrogations, even the regular staff meetings, he would look around him, peer into the eyes of his comrades and wait for them to see his fear. He was always waiting for someone to call his bluff. He believed they all knew how afraid he was inside, beneath the outer shell of nervelessness. When they weren't looking, he trembled. At night, he'd vomit silently into his shirt, which he washed before morning, thus developing a reputation for manic cleanliness.

And always, always there were the unbidden, unpredictable outbreaks of sweating. It could happen anywhere, anytime, and he'd have to do something, react quickly, so the others wouldn't notice. He'd grab a prisoner and flog him. He'd drop to the floor and do push-ups—anything to explain away the flood of sweat.

After a while, his comrades understood that he was different from them: zealous, tough, superior. They didn't know he was afraid, and had been since childhood. Whoever carried the biggest stick, whoever had the vilest reputation, whoever would use violence and terror as means to an end—those were the ones with whom he allied himself. If he were their friend, they couldn't hurt him.

And then he would live in fear that they would discover his weakness.

Stop!

All that was over, Balaton told himself as Badger Rock Island came into view. He had buried that absurd, cowardly creature he'd been. There was no need to worry about him—to *be* him.

Ah, but who can stop you? Who knows you better than you know yourself?

No. He smiled to himself: the *orült szerzetes* had been trying to destroy him for decades. And had he ever succeeded? Of course not. And now he himself was strong. Confident. Without fear. Not as in the old days.

Sarah...

He shut his eyes and breathed deeply, calming himself. If he acted quickly, surely, none of this would touch Sarah. It couldn't. She was his life, and she would never, never know the terror and violence and horror he had known.

# THIRTY-THREE

J. Land Crockett had grown tired of sitting. With his
morning tea finished and Roger, after providing no
additional information, dismissed, Crockett stood
looking out the screens. The fog had abated, but a light
drizzle had started to fall; he hoped Ashley's flight
wouldn't be impeded. He wanted her here, where he
could see her, keep her safe and not fail her as he had
failed Judith. He should have guessed how desperate
she had felt during the last months. Instead he
thought she was being selfish and cruel, acting the
spoiled brat.

He had amends to make to her.

Balaton should be arriving any moment with David, the twin brother. The son. The grandson. *My
grandson,* the old man thought with a slight shudder.

And the father? Was it Balaton, whom Crockett had
liked, nurtured, treated like a son? Or was it the
farmer? The madman.

In the beginning, when he'd seen the tiara and
choker and studied the impertinent lovely face of Ashley Wakefield, seeing the eyes of his wife, his daughter, comparing the photograph with the portrait—in
the beginning, he had wanted only to hate her. She
had lived and Judith had died. He wanted to know

who she was, wanted answers, but he didn't want anything to do with this woman who called herself Ashley Wakefield.

But he had changed his mind. An old man, he thought, has that right.

There was a commotion going on behind him. Roger was saying sharply, "Miss Balaton, please be reasonable—"

"No, dammit! I want to talk to Crockett!"

She stormed onto the porch, and turning from the screens, Crockett controlled any surprise he might have felt from entering his face. She was wet and windblown, exhausted and very angry. "Sarah Balaton. Well, well. Did you come with your father and David Wakefield?"

Her face went pale, but she made an effort to retain her sense of outrage. "No, of course not. You told them to leave me behind...."

"Don't be ridiculous. I did no such thing."

"Aren't they here?" Her voice was very small.

"No."

"But they...they left about forty-five minutes before I did. I had to find a boat, and...they should be here by now! What have you done with them?"

Crockett recalled the phone call from David, that Balaton had volunteered to get him. What was his game? Had Bartholomew Wakefield intercepted them? How?

"Well, then where in the name of hell are they now?" he demanded of no one in particular. "Dammit. Roger, notify the Coast Guard at once. I want that boat found."

Sarah was beginning to hyperventilate. "Daddy..."

"There's nothing we can do, Sarah," Crockett snapped, but he regretted his gruffness. The poor girl looked so forlorn. Despite his own impatience and concern, he softened his tone. "We'll just have to wait. And Roger, bring more tea, with lots of sugar. Sarah'll be needing something in her system to keep her going."

*Even in the torture of labor, Judith Land was radiant. Her lightly tanned skin gleamed with perspiration, and her hair was matted and tangled; dark soaked tendrils hung in her face. For fourteen hours, the pains had been coming. Now it was nearly impossible to tell when they began and when they ended.*

*The man who had agreed to help her laid a fresh white sheet under her, and he softly told her she could begin to push now.*

*She shook her head. "I can't."*

*"You must. Just let the baby come...."*

*"I can't do it!"*

*Her abdomen was enormous. In the last days, her joints had swelled in the blistering summer heat and humidity, and she had moved about slowly, wishing for an end to this miserable pregnancy. She had no qualms about swearing about her discomfort. Women had babies, she said, because men could never tolerate such prolonged agony.*

*"Judith...push. Now!"*

*She reached up behind her and gripped the headboard of the simple oak bed, and, her teeth gritted and her face twisted in pain and exertion, she heaved with all her might. It wasn't enough. He told her more. "Push," he said. "Push!"*

*But she'd had enough. "Fuck you."*

*She was utterly drained. For a moment, he let her rest. Her face grew strangely placid. Then her eyes focused on him, and she smiled and whispered, "This one's for you, monk."*

*And her body found the strength to push, to force out the tiny contents of her uterus, and the man she called the monk caught the blue, wet, bloody infant as she spurted out. A girl. She looked healthy, perfect. The placenta came easily. He cut the umbilical cord with a sterile knife and cleaned off the baby, wrapping her in a fresh cotton blanket.*

*He started to hand the infant to her mother, whose arms were reaching out for her, but suddenly she grabbed her stomach and she howled with pain, swearing viciously.*

*He gently touched her abdomen, and he felt the hardness, the lump of another tiny person still inside her. He told her, "You're having twins, Judith."*

*"Oh, God—oh, shit!" But in her agony, she smiled.*

*The baby came quickly, a boy, dark haired and perfect. Holding her infants, smiling, pale and spent, Judith named them Ashley and David.*

*It was the man who delivered them, the monk, who made the foot and handprints, but it was the actress, a few days later, who thought of the fictitious surname. "Wakefield," she said. "Ashley and David Wakefield...for now."*

*He was relieved that she saw the necessity of such extreme caution.*

*But her clear vibrant eyes focused on him. "I want my babies to have a good life. If anything happens to me..."*

*"No, Judith. Let's not think of such things."*

*She smiled. "You're hardly one to talk, monk. This time, listen to me. If something does happen—and I don't for a moment believe it will, but for God's sake, I'm not a child anymore! I have to think of my children. If something hap-*

*pens, I want you to take Ashley and David away from all
this. Raise them yourself. Let them lead good, simple, honest
lives. I'll provide for their futures, monk. You just get them
into adulthood."*

He didn't know what she meant. She was always planning and plotting, this beautiful woman of the cinema, this
reckless, tireless heiress. "I will see that nothing happens to
you," he told her. "You will be able to raise your children
yourself."

"I know. But just in case." Her expression grew even
more intent. "Promise me."

She was so tired. To ease her fears, he promised.

"Of course," she said, smiling, "you'll have to have a
new name."

"Of course."

"That way the three of you can sneak away and no one
will ever find you. You can be their...their uncle. And your
name—" She paused, thinking. "It can be Bartholomew.
Bartholomew Wakefield."

And so it was.

The man who, for the past thirty years, had been
Bartholomew Wakefield, the creation of Judith Land,
watched from behind a large hemlock as Andrew Balaton tied his boat to the small dock on the eastern edge
of Badger Rock Island. The wind had picked up, and
the ocean was choppy and as gray as the sky. For the
moment, the rain had stopped.

A wiry, timid figure, Andrew Balaton walked down
the dock, and he had a hunted look as he glanced all
around him. He had always tried to hide from his own
fears, to run away from the terror that was inside him,
from who and what he was. So he had come to the

West. He had married a famous actress. He had become the head of a giant corporation.

But inside he had not changed, and Bartholomew Wakefield was the one person left in the world who could remind Andrew Balaton of who and what he was. Who could prove to him that he could never run far enough or long enough to escape from his own wretched skin.

Better than most, the man they had called *orült szer-zetes* knew the horror a frightened man could wreak. When he was threatened, this Andrew Balaton would resort to his old methods. He would strike again, viciously and wantonly.

And this time, Bartholomew Wakefield was determined not to arrive too late to stop his destruction—not as in Hungary, not as in Los Angeles, when he had found Judith Land had already challenged her husband. Already pregnant and disillusioned, she had left. She wanted an immediate divorce. She wanted to cut her losses, quickly and cleanly, and get on with her life. But she made the mistake of thinking her penniless husband would acquiesce to her wishes.

Bartholomew Wakefield knew better. Before anyone else could, he had volunteered to find the straying wife of a fellow Hungarian...only to stop Balaton from finding someone who *would* bring Judith back to him. Following Lillian Parker, he had located Judith Land in a Tennessee valley. And he had convinced her, he thought, of what she must do.

*"You must wait, Judith. Don't press your demands now."*

*"Why?"*

"He won't permit you to divorce him. For the sake of your child, you must wait."

"Balaton has nothing I want for my baby—not even a name. And no matter what happens to me, the baby will inherit everything I have over him. It's in my will."

"Trust me. If he sees his new life disintegrating before it's even had a chance to begin, he'll do anything to stop you."

"He can't stop me! I'll talk to my father—"

"It won't matter. This Andrew Balaton will ensure that you never draw another breath of happiness in your life. For now, you must give him some hope. Hide here with me, have your baby. Then we will see what must be done."

"He wouldn't...hurt my baby."

"If he perceives either you or your child as a threat, he wouldn't hesitate to kill you both."

As Balaton looked among the windswept rocks and blueberry bushes and gnarled oaks, Bartholomew Wakefield remained concealed, observing the executive's mounting terror. This time, he thought, he would let Balaton sweat.

Lillian Parker moved quickly along the grassy path, one of the many she and Judith had followed so many times on their endless summer explorations of the island, but never on such a dank, freezing day as this, never with so much at stake. Christ, she thought, they'd been as free as birds! If only they'd known— but the young never do. Nor, perhaps, should they.

After blabbing to Jeremy Carruthers, she had retreated to her room, where she locked her door and sat in the gloom, hoping for a swift and happy ending to whatever was about to unfold. She would leave the

dirty work to the others. There was no need for her to
get involved. What could she accomplish?

"*Can I trust him, Lil?*"

"*Of course. How can you even ask!*"

"*After what happened to Mac...*"

"*Oh, Jude, please let's not talk about that. It wasn't his
fault. You can trust him. I know it.*"

"*Won't you stay with me?*"

"*I can't. I have a job....*"

If she had stayed, Lillian wondered if she might
have been able to stop Judith—brave, impulsive beautiful Judith—from doing something stupid. Instead,
Lillian had run.

But not this time. Snatching an army-green rain
poncho from a pegboard at the back door, Lillian had
set off. Last night she had seen the golden crown; she
knew the man the twins called Barky was on Badger
Rock Island. And so was Mac. She felt certain neither
had left. She might be wrong and find nothing, but at
least she had to try.

"*I hate him, Lil. He's so arrogant and overprotective. I
can't breathe with him in my life!*"

"*But are you sure? Have you tried to talk to him?*"

"*Of course I've talked to him! But he won't listen. He
says I know nothing about these things; I'm too young.*"

"*But he loves you so much.*"

"*I don't care!*"

Poor wretched Andrew, Lillian thought. My God,
Judith, haven't we all suffered enough for you?

She pushed back a branch hanging low on the overgrown path, and water spilled out of it, splattering her
face. But she kept moving, resolute and, at the same
time, praying she would find nothing.

* * *

Standing in the rain, shivering and soaked and so very tired, MacGregor Stevens saw him at last. *Orült szerzetes.* Traitor, torturer, thief, kidnapper. A farmer, he called himself. It was too ridiculous for Mac even to fathom. He held up the .38 caliber Smith & Wesson he had borrowed from Crockett's gun closet and pointed it at the man in black. "Don't move." His voice was low, but the farmer heard him. Mac watched him stiffen as he faced the open sea. "Turn around... slowly."

The man who called himself Bartholomew Wakefield turned, but there was no fear in his weather-beaten face when he looked at Mac, only an irritation that bordered on disgust. "You are a fool, MacGregor Stevens. I have no quarrel with you."

It was the first time they had faced each other in thirty years. The farmer was an old man now, Mac realized, stout and still strong, but old. Human. He forced himself to recall the flash of the lights on the border, the cry in Russian, the burning pain of the bullet in his gut.

"But I have one hell of a quarrel with you," he said, his teeth clenched. "I nearly got killed saving Andrew Balaton from the Russians and his own people thirty years ago. I'll be damned to hell and back if I'm going to let you compromise him now."

"Ahh." Wakefield seemed almost amused. "So you believe I'm KGB."

"That's right."

"So with someone at least my strategy has worked." He lifted his shoulders slightly in a shrug. "Unfortunately, it has not worked with Balaton."

Mac's grip on the gun was steady, despite the pelting rain. "What do you mean?" he asked sharply, painfully aware he shouldn't, couldn't, believe a word this man said.

"You are right: I was prepared to exchange the Balaton jewels for technological secrets. But not to sell to the KGB. No, I merely wanted to flush out Balaton. And I have. But now the stakes are much greater—for me, personally. As always, Balaton is ready with a counterstrike."

Mac shook his head, denying everything the farmer claimed, everything he had been for the past thirty years. "You were KGB in '56; you're KGB now."

"No, that's not true." His accent was more American now than thirty years ago, his tone faintly superior, as if he were gently chastising a small child for a ridiculous assumption. "I did not betray you that night on the border, MacGregor Stevens."

"Then who did?" Mac sneered. "Judith Land? Lillian Parker? *Balaton?* They *all* could have been killed. You were the one who backed out at the last minute, the one who planned the whole fiasco. Don't tell me I'm wrong! Dammit, I've relived that night thousands of times in the past thirty years! I know what happened!"

The stout man in black sighed patiently, but there was despair in his warm brown eyes. "You are a good man, MacGregor Stevens, but you are very, very wrong. You don't see the truth, do you?"

"Oh, yes, my friend, I do see the truth. I'd like to shoot you here and now for what you did, but those would be your tactics. I'm taking you in. We'll let a court of law decide what and who you are." He steadied the gun. "But give me an excuse to shoot you, and I won't hesitate."

"Achh. Listen to me, while there is still time. Balaton is here—moving this way. He will stop at nothing now, do you understand? *He* betrayed you on the border."

"No."

"Yes! Because you could identify him as Major József, a trusted member of the Hungarian state secret police."

"He was working for us."

"He was working for himself." There was despair now in the voice of the mad monk. "He turned to the United States because his mission within the ÁVH was being thwarted at every turn by *orült szerzetes* and he was desperate lest his comrades somehow think he was disloyal—not the victim of the 'mad monk,' but a collaborator. A man like that cannot tolerate being afraid."

Mac shook his head and scoffed. "You're just trying to save your own skin, monk."

"No. My skin means nothing to me. I'm trying to save Ashley and David. Balaton went to your people for help in combating the mad monk; he would trade information for their help in ridding him of the monk's campaign against him. What he didn't know was that *orült szerzetes* was never controlled by the Americans. He acted on behalf of the Hungarian people—his friends and neighbors."

"It's a little late to sound so goddamned holy. But go ahead, monk. Keep trying. You won't convince me."

"Then innocents will die."

"Not if you're in custody, they won't."

"You must take Balaton with me, then. Take us both in. Let us both face a court of law! Don't you see? Once Balaton had gone to your people, he had to provide them with information or they would compromise him. But he also had to prove himself to his superiors within the ÁVH. So he renewed his campaign of terrorizing innocent Hungarians. If anything, you made him worse than he already was. He was involved in a dangerous, treacherous game of playing both sides against the middle, neither knowing what he really was, and he became increasingly desperate."

"*Christ!*" Mac yelled. He had forgotten how glib and educated this man was; he had been seduced by the *You* piece's talk of his being a simple farmer. "Just stop."

"No. It's time you heard the truth, MacGregor Stevens. When violence broke out in Budapest, Balaton saw his chance to escape everyone—his past, the ÁVH, your people. He decided to *become* Count András Balaton in all eyes."

"He is Balaton. He took on the identity of József Major to get himself inside the ÁVH." The gun was getting heavy, and fatigue had begun to cloud Mac's thinking. He knew he had to stop this. And yet he couldn't. Was the farmer beginning to make sense? But of course. He's had thirty years to work out a plausible scenario. "You're wrong, monk."

The farmer took a step toward Mac, but Mac straightened himself up, the gun pointing at the man who called himself Bartholomew Wakefield, and he stopped.

"Call him what you will, he couldn't bear to live

with the fear of having MacGregor Stevens, the only man who had actually *seen* him, identify him as József Major, not a dispossessed Hungarian count. So he decided to get rid of you. He betrayed you at the border. He told the Russians not about himself and the two women, only about you. He said an American intelligence agent would be crossing the border. He gave what details he had to."

"Bullshit." It was all Mac could think of to say.

The farmer ignored him. "The Russians didn't want to kill you, of course. There was much propaganda to be gained from exposing you. I was able to divert them, and some of my friends grabbed you and took you away. I'm sorry you were shot. But that's what happened, MacGregor Stevens. I did not betray you."

"You're grasping at straws." But Mac's voice was hoarse, his nerves raw. Could I be wrong? No! "You're KGB and I'm going to see you stand trial for what you are."

Wakefield sighed. "Balaton won't permit that. He's here, don't you understand? And he'll stop you—again. Ask yourself why I thought I could blackmail him with the Balaton jewels. Ask yourself if he will permit the jewels to be used as evidence in a trial against me. Peel back the face of Andrew Balaton and you will find the face of an officer of the ÁVH. Peel back the face of József Major and what will you find? You don't know, do you? It's something the Americans never bothered to do."

"What are you saying?"

But there was a rustling in the brush behind them, and Balaton came forward. He was wet and shaking, but he held a .38 at both men. "That's enough." He licked his lips. "No more lies."

Mac continued to level his Smith & Wesson at the farmer, but he didn't like the look of Balaton. The man was stretched tight and ready to snap. "It's all right," Mac said soothingly, ignoring his own fear. "We've got him. We'll let the courts decide his fate now."

Balaton was staring at the farmer. "I want the jewels."

The man who called himself Bartholomew Wakefield nodded slightly, but there was no defeat in his face, only renewed determination. "I knew you would."

"Forget the damned jewels!" Mac yelled. But as he swung around at Balaton, he saw the ugly terror in the Hungarian's eyes...and the determination. "Oh, bloody Jesus," Mac whispered, "how could I have been so wrong?"

There was a flicker in Balaton's expression, something there quickly and then gone, like a flash. The farmer jumped forward. "Get down, Stevens! *Now!*"

Mac hesitated in confusion. Was it a warning or a lie? Then he felt his legs go out from under him and he didn't know why and he tried to stop himself from falling but couldn't. He heard the explosion. And he felt the searing pain in his shoulder, as he had before, thirty years ago, and he sank into the blueberry bushes and the rocky soil. Groaning mindlessly, he saw only the face of Elaine...the love of my life.

# THIRTY-FOUR

Mercifully, the fog had lifted and Ashley was able to land her tired little Cessna on Badger Rock Island. She grabbed her satchel and bounded out of the plane, but it immediately began to rain. She didn't give a damn. In fact, the rain felt good—like a nice cold shower. She felt revived as she started down the wide gravel path.

She heard the pounding footsteps of someone running, and she thought of lurching off the path, but then Jeremy came into view, wild-eyed and *there*. Her arms opened and she was running, too, and then he caught her up in his arms. Thousands of dollars worth of gems bounced in the bottom of the satchel as it swung against his back.

"I thought you'd given up on me," she said as he set her down.

"You won't get rid of me that easily. Ashley—"

She saw his face had clouded, and suddenly she couldn't breathe. "Where's David?"

Quickly, Jeremy told her what had transpired since she'd left at dawn. She shook her head, trying to think clearly. "But I just saw Crockett's racer tied to a dock on the other side of the island. If Balaton has David..." She couldn't articulate the rest.

"Ashley, Balaton doesn't pose a threat to your brother."

"According to what I have in this satchel—"

Jeremy needed no more. "Jesus. Come on, let's go."

They veered off the gravel path into the woods, not caring that there wasn't a path, just moving east, toward the other side of the island, the boat...David. Ashley began to run. In just minutes, her sneakers were soaked and she was slipping and sliding in the wet leaves. They hooked up to a narrow overgrown path and followed it.

Just then, there came the loud crack of gunfire; then another.

David!

Barky!

Ashley dashed ahead of Jeremy. She had had no sleep, little food, shock after shock after shock. She had nothing left. She was without reserves, utterly drained. But somewhere she found the energy to move even faster, to run, and it was as if she wasn't touching the ground, but moved several inches above it, hurrying, pressing herself to go faster. The cold air sliced into her lungs and her hamstrings ached, her entire body pushed beyond endurance as she sprinted, faster, faster.

Jeremy stayed close behind her. She could hear the pounding of his footsteps and the steadying breathing of an experienced runner. He wouldn't leave her. Thank God. It was her only reassurance.

David had uttered every swearword he knew and had counted to a thousand to stop himself from considering the misery and gravity of his situation. What were the consequences of exposure to rain, cold, fog and wind for an individual as weakened—and as god-damned stupid!—as he? No. Jesus, Lord help him, he couldn't think about that now!

The rain had resumed, a full-fledged downpour now, and he sat propped up against a lichen-covered boulder and listened to the tide wash in all around him. He had crept off the dock and gotten this far. In a little while, he hoped to be able to creep under a tree, where he might be more sheltered from the brutal, ceaseless wind. But right now he couldn't move. Right now, he could only hope to keep his mind off the se-vere pain in his leg and the anger, the desperation and the bald, inescapable fear that were welling up inside him.

It was a small comfort that he had a fiberglass cast. An ordinary plaster cast would have disintegrated by now, but the fiberglass repelled water. A plus for modern medicine, he thought wryly. But there wasn't a damned thing he could do about the water dripping down his leg and seeping inside the cast. The doctor had said to keep his leg dry. He'd been operated on, for Christ's sake; he had stitches to mind.

Maybe they'll have to lop off my goddamned leg.

He blinked tiredly up at the sky, letting the cold rain pelt onto his face. "Maybe they won't get a chance to lop it off," he said aloud, talking to the frigging birds who did nothing all day but eat and shit. "Maybe I'll just die out here and the goddamned birds'll pick my bones clean, and one of these days some jerk-off orni-thologist'll find my skeleton and...shit! Get hold of yourself." And he began again to count: "One thou-sand one, one thousand two..."

His teeth were chattering and his hands had turned shades of purple, blue and orange, clashing, he observed idly, with the bright reds of the young maple a couple of yards off. He'd never known a body could hurt so constantly. The pain never let up. He ached and ached and it just wouldn't stop.

"I'm going to die out here with nobody to come to my funeral but the goddamned birds."

One thousand three, one thousand four...

"I'll get hypothermia and freeze to death like one of Ashley's goddamned stranded dolphins. Maybe they'll do an autopsy on me right here, like they do the dolphins. Oh, shit—Ash, where the fuck are you?"

One thousand five, one thousand six...

"Don't be such a simp." He tried to straighten up. "Sarah'll figure things out—unless she's in cahoots with her old man, the bastard." He yelled into the sky. "Fuck you, Balaton! Bastard! Son of a bitch! Asshole!"

One thousand seven, one thousand eight...

"Oh, Christ!" Lillian cried, tripping, when she heard the shots. "Please God, don't let me be too late."

The shots had been fired near her...just ahead, near the dock. She had to get there. She had to stop them from killing each other.

Then abruptly her pace slowed, and sucking in deep lungfuls of the cold air and feeling her legs wobble, she appraised the situation with the clear eye of an experienced reporter. What could a small, unarmed terrified middle-aged woman do? They had guns. Perhaps someone already lay dead.

Who?

She had to know.

In her breakneck run, the hood of her poncho had dropped back off her head, and now her hair was soaked and rain ran in streams down her back. *Good God, I'm cold.*

"And you're a coward, too," she said aloud.

She kicked a rock loose and grabbed it, brushing off some little slimy creature that clung to its bottom, and she pressed on.

The path opened up into a small clearing, and there was the dock with Crockett's Chris-Craft racer tied up to it. Looking around, alert, Lillian edged into the clearing. Just beyond the dock was a picturesque point where she and Judith, as happy-go-lucky teenagers, used to sit and talk about boys and careers and children and death. A tall hemlock stood above a bank of jagged rocks, where the surf crashed wildly. On the opposite side of the point, she knew, was a cliff with a dramatic panoramic view and a sheer, treacherous drop.

Holding her rock tightly, Lillian slipped along the perimeter of the clearing, past the dock. She hated to leave the protection of the woods, but to get onto the point, she had to cross a patch of low-lying bushes and head up a rocky, sandy slope to the hemlock.

She held her breath and walked with purpose, daring anybody to shoot her.

No one did.

The rain was tapering off as she stood at the hemlock and looked around.

And saw them.

"Oh, Jesus..."

They were on the very tip of the point, among the rocks and blueberry bushes, exposed to the bitter wind off the ocean. MacGregor Stevens and the man called Bartholomew Wakefield. Bare chested and ashen faced, the farmer was half reclining against a boulder. Mac lay in his lap.

Neither was moving.

She knelt beside them and saw the blood that had seeped into Mac's shirt and the blood all over the farmer's arm...and everywhere.

"Oh, God," Lillian croaked, kneeling. "I'm too late."

"No." The farmer's eyes opened, and she saw the warm brown eyes of the man behind the confessional screen in Budapest, the only man she had ever truly loved. They focused on her. "We're alive."

His voice was little more than a hoarse whisper, but seeing her seemed to give him strength. He started to move, but Mac was a heavy weight on him. Lillian saw now that the farmer, Barky, had taken off his own shirt and stuffed it under Mac's shirt to staunch the bleeding. She held back tears as she peeled off her poncho and covered Mac. Together they managed to get him off Barky, and laid him gently on the ground. Lillian tore off her sweater and wrapped it around his head, so just his mouth and nose were exposed.

"The bleeding has stopped," Barky said.

"I'll have to leave...call for the Coast Guard for help, paramedics."

Barky grabbed her hand. "Ashley...David... where are they?"

"A plane just landed. I assume it's Ashley. And David...David's missing. Andrew picked him up in Southwest Harbor. I see the boat..."

"David isn't with him."

"Oh, God."

Barky nodded, knowing now. "David is his leverage."

Laboriously, agonizingly, Barky climbed to his feet. Lillian offered her shoulder, but he refused. "Get your MacGregor Stevens to the hospital. He knows he has made a terrible mistake. He'll need you."

"You'll both go to the hospital," she said, her voice cracking as she fought tears. She hadn't cried thirty years ago; she wouldn't cry now.

"No."

And not looking at her, the stout old man hobbled unsteadily down to the woods.

Lillian stumbled toward him. "You'll never make it."

"I must stop József Major from killing Ashley and David."

"Killing them? But why—"

"Because that is how he thinks. For him, to be afraid is intolerable. And he's never been more afraid than now." He gave her a steely look. "You should never have listened to Judith."

"Let me go with you."

He had turned his brown, naked back to her. "Stay with Stevens. He needs you now more than I do. I'll call the Coast Guard. Wait with him. Keep him warm."

If not for Mac, she'd have gone after him, *made* him stop her. But Mac needed her. This time, she couldn't just leave him to his fate.

She knelt back down beside him, and took him into her lap—he was so damned heavy!—and held him, sheltering him from the wind and cold. "You should

never have listened to Judith." But how was she to
have known?

*The letter had come to Lillian Parker in New York, where*
*she had her first job, behind the scenes, in television. In it,*
*Judith Land explained exactly what she wanted her best*
*friend—her only friend, she wrote—to do for her. And she*
*would never, never, never ask another thing of Lillian.*

*Judith had had five million dollars in gold and stocks*
*transferred to an account in Lillian's name. She wanted her*
*friend to go to Switzerland, to Piccard Cie in Geneva, and*
*open up an account in the names of Ashley and David*
*Wakefield.*

*A Liechtenstein trust.*

*In addition, she was to go to Judith's New York attorneys*
*and they would give her access to a safe-deposit box. In the*
*box were the hand and footprints of Ashley and David*
*Wakefield and, she wrote, the Balaton jewels. Lillian was to*
*put the jewels in the vaults at Piccard Cie, with instructions*
*for the box to be opened on the same day as they were to be-*
*come beneficiaries of the Liechtenstein trust...on July 14,*
*1982.*

*It seemed such a long time off. But that was Judith—se-*
*cretive, impulsive, melodramatic. "I'm sure it will all come*
*to nothing," she wrote. "But please do it. Please, please,*
*please."*

*And Lillian had.*

*Two weeks later, when Judith Land was trampled by a*
*horse on her father's ranch and there was no mention of any*
*surviving twins, any babies, Lillian Parker told herself that*
*Judith's babies must have died.*

*There were no Ashley and David Wakefield. The Swiss*
*would do whatever they did when beneficiaries couldn't be*
*located, and that would be that.*

# THIRTY-FIVE

Jeremy spotted Lillian Parker out on the windswept point, and he shot ahead of Ashley, moving faster, yelling, "Mac!"

Tripping on the wet ground as she looked around in panic for her brother and uncle, Ashley ran after him. He had squatted beside Mac and was taking off his sweater, handing it to Lillian, who eschewed it for herself and instead covered Mac. His face was ashen, but he was breathing steadily. Lillian's lips were blue and she shivered uncontrollably as in rapid phrases she tried to tell them what had happened. They got the idea.

"David wasn't with Balaton?" Ashley repeated breathlessly, forming a question to which she already knew the answer. "Oh, Jesus! Then where the hell is he?"

Lillian closed her eyes, and Ashley could see the tears squeezing out the corners. "Your uncle said your brother was leverage."

Ashley straightened up. Coupled with everything else she now knew or suspected, it made sense. "Balaton will exchange David's life for the rest of the Balaton jewels."

Lillian gave up any attempt at stoicism and began to cry softly.

"He has a broken leg," Ashley went on, thinking out loud. "Balaton wouldn't be able to drag him along with him. He had to stick him someplace he knows David won't be able to get help or have someone stumble on him. He..."

"Jude's Paradise," Lillian was saying.

Ashley stiffened. "Of course."

Jeremy stared at both women. "In this weather? He's been out there hours already. Good Christ, what kind of madman is Balaton?"

"A frightened one," Lillian said hopelessly.

"We'll call the Coast Guard," Jeremy said.

Ashley was shaking all over. "But if he's been out there six or seven hours and it takes the Coast Guard a while to get there and... Jeremy, I could fly."

He was instantly alert. "Is there a place to land?"

She shook her head.

"But I could parachute, couldn't I?"

"I wouldn't ask you..."

His look was serious, but without fear. "I'm volunteering, Ashley."

"It's a small island. You won't have your pick of spots—"

He managed a grin. "I can parachute onto the hood of a car."

From the air, they radioed the Coast Guard for paramedics on Jude's Paradise and Badger Rock Island and warned them that there was a madman loose on the latter. Ashley thought of old J. Land Crockett and

Sarah Balaton and Barky. Would Balaton kill them all? Would he kill his own daughter?

And then she saw David out on the rocks at the edge of the dilapidated dock on Jude's Paradise and she thought, he'll kill his own son, too.

Her brother didn't respond as she circled low over the island.

"Jeremy?"

He had slipped on one of her parachutes. "Did you pack this yourself?"

"Uh-huh. It's been double-checked."

"Good. I've never used someone else's chute before—always like to pack my own." He was peering down at the small island. "Impromptu jumps aren't my thing, but what the hell."

"You don't have to—"

"I didn't see a Coast Guard boat anywhere near here, did you? David's in rough shape, Ashley. He'll need help."

She nodded. "If anything happens to you..."

"Nothing will," he said quickly. "Do you know how to spot a jump?"

"I've never done it before, but I know the procedure."

"We'll try the clearing at the end of the dock, near David. See it?"

It was more a bit of bare ground than an actual clearing, but she said, "Yes."

She maintained control of the plane as Jeremy opened the door and hung out a bright yellow streamer, which floated down with the wind. He watched it closely. It would tell him how far upwind of his target he would need to be when he jumped, providing his ideal exit spot. "Got it," he said.

Ashley circled back around, and as Jeremy leaned out the door, he gave her precise directions to exactly the point at which he wanted to exit.

"Okay. Cut the engine."

She throttled down. Standing on the tire, Jeremy pushed away from the plane and went into a free-fall. Ashley didn't have time to worry about him. She throttled up and banked the plane to the left, and turning on a point, she looked down at the island.

When she saw the multicolored canopy of the parachute, she sobbed with relief. Jeremy gently touched down, and she watched as he feverishly unstrapped the harness and dropped the pack. Even as the voluminous canopy billowed in the wind, he was running.

He knelt beside David. And he looked up at Ashley and waved furiously.

Her brother was alive.

MacGregor Stevens had regained consciousness and was nearly delirious with pain, but he insisted on telling Lillian how stupid he'd been. "I was wrong about everything."

"Just rest easy, Mac," she told him gently.

He winced, his face ghastly pale. "I loved her, you know."

Tears streamed down Lillian's face. "I know. She loved you, too."

"I...I never saw her again after that night on the border."

"Mac, don't torture yourself."

Tears streamed down his tanned temples, but she

didn't think he was even aware of them. "She fell in love with Balaton so quickly.... It never would have worked between us."

"Oh, Mac—Jesus, don't you know how much she loved you? She thought you were *dead*. She thought her life was over. We'd had to practically knock her out and drag her over the border. She wanted to die with you. We thought... We were so sure you were dead. Why didn't you try to reach her after you got out of Hungary?"

He tried to lift his head, but his face grimaced in agony, and he lay still. "She was married."

Lillian laughed softly, sadly, even as she cried. "You're always so goddamned honorable, Mac. That's one of the things Judith loved about you. I guess we were both doomed to fall in love with honorable men."

He closed his eyes. "I have Elaine now."

And I have no one. Lillian tried to sound cheerful: "I'll call her just as soon as we get you squared away. You're going to be fine, Mac. Really."

"Wakefield?"

"He's gone after Andrew. He thinks—he knows Andrew will try to get the rest of the jewels and murder the twins. Their Barky has been protecting them from him all these years and... Goddamn him, if I'd only known!"

Mac's hand slipped out from under the poncho and covered hers. He felt so damned cold. "I'm sorry, Lil. But Balaton—even he wouldn't kill his own children."

"Oh, Mac," she sobbed. "Oh, Mac, you damned fool. Ashley and David are yours. That's why Judith rushed into marrying Andrew. She was pregnant.

She—Christ in heaven, Mac, except for Crockett's eyes, David is you all over again."

Bartholomew Wakefield headed toward the western edge of the island—away from Stevens. He had heard a small plane landing and assumed it would be Ashley. If she heard the shot, she would investigate. So would the others. And Balaton couldn't be there when they arrived.

Barky had to draw him away. But there was no problem there: he knew he could. He still had the tiara and the choker. There was no question that Balaton would follow him.

He had crept among the rocks and the woods, and when he heard the plane again take off, he knew now he could act.

Barky moved quickly through the silent, isolated house and listened for sounds of any of the others. He found the old man out on the sun porch. Crockett, they called him. Given the opportunity, he would interfere—and Balaton would kill him. Barky could see both Ashley and David in the tall, scrawny figure. He was on his feet, looking impatiently out the screened windows, muttering to himself.

He turned at the sound of the footsteps behind him. "You!"

There was more hatred than fear in the black-blue eyes. So he knew the lies and believed them, Barky thought. He stepped forward. "There's no time for explanations—"

"Bastard. You killed my daughter!"

"Achh."

There could be no arguing with the man. Bartholomew Wakefield raised his powerful fist and swatted J. Land Crockett on the back of the neck. The billionaire sank to the floor in a crumpled heap of bones and dried skin.

The farmer slipped out the porch door. Now it was time to let Balaton find him.

Sarah Balaton had nearly cried out when Bartholomew Wakefield had knocked Crockett unconscious, but she held her breath as she watched from the hall. It couldn't be! He was Barky, David's uncle. She had slept in his house, made applesauce on his wood stove.

Poor David, she thought. Poor, poor David. What would she tell him?

She had to find him, talk to him...and her father. They had to know what kind of madman they were up against. But where were they? Her father must have known David was in danger from this insane uncle of his and had hidden him, helped him....

Quickly, refusing to consider the consequences of failure, she padded across the porch. Crockett was breathing steadily. Thank God he wasn't dead! She felt a passing guilt for what she had thought him capable of, but it wasn't her fault—and nothing, yet, made any sense.

She headed outside. The uncle was creeping toward the airstrip. It doesn't matter, she thought: I won't be afraid. If necessary, she would stop this Bartholomew Wakefield herself.

"So." Barky walked out to the edge of the airstrip to greet the president and chief executive officer of

Crockett Industries. "Now it's just the two of us. As it should be. Yes, József Major?"

"I want the jewels."

The farmer shrugged. "They mean nothing to me."

Balaton's entire body shook violently, but his knuckles were white on the handle of the gun. Barky refused to look at the weapon. He had seen guns before, witnessed what they could do, felt the burning pain in his own body. He wasn't afraid. He hadn't been, not for decades. It was one reason this Andrew Balaton had always hated him.

Barky pulled out the edge of his black jacket so Balaton could see there was no weapon inside. With Balaton's nod, Barky removed the black opaque plastic bag in which he had put the tiara and the choker. He handed them across to Balaton.

Balaton took them, but there was no relief in his eyes. "I want the rest."

"Those are all there are left."

"Don't lie to me!"

Barky said nothing.

"I'm not a fool. You've always thought that, haven't you? József Major, the idiot, the inferior, the low-class moron. You were always so superior."

"Only in your mind, József."

"Now you know the truth."

Barky gave a small smile. "I have always known the truth."

There came the sound of a small plane overhead. Barky looked up and swore silently. Ashley. He raised up his arms to wave her away.

"No." It was Balaton.

Barky ignored him. Go away, Ashley. Go!

"Stop it! She can get me the rest of the jewels—"

Barky ran out onto the airstrip, but Balaton grabbed him and jerked him back, heaving him to the pavement. The farmer fought, heedless of the gun. But Balaton didn't pull the trigger. Instead he slammed the butt of the gun down on the side of Barky's head. He groaned, rolling over, but it wasn't worse than any of the thousand kinds of pain he'd had inflicted on him over the years. Once, a long time ago, he had been a victim of the senseless tortures of this man who now pretended to be a rich and polished executive. The physical pain Barky could tolerate. It was the mental anguish that had nearly driven him over the edge of sanity.

As he lay on the runway, he heard the engine of the Cessna as it came lower, and then felt the vibrations beneath him when it landed. He would will himself to move. He had to. This time, he couldn't permit Balaton to kill those he, Barky, loved in order to save himself.

But the pain seared through him as he tried to roll up onto all fours. And Balaton laughed. "You've set me up beautifully, my friend," he sneered. "All this can be blamed on you."

With a loud snort, the corporate executive kicked Barky in the head.

"Barky!" Ashley screamed as she jumped out of the plane. She had watched in horror as Balaton had kicked Barky in the head. Now he was lying facedown near the fuel pump, and Balaton was moving toward her. She had left the drenched, battered satchel inside the plane. She had brought them along only in case worse came to worst. Apparently it had. But having the contents of the satchel couldn't save Balaton now. She had to make him see that. She was looking down at her uncle. "Is he alive?"

"For now." And the president and CEO of Crockett Industries pointed his monstrous gun at her. "I want the jewels, Miss Wakefield."

She had never dealt with guns before. "You can have them." Her voice quavered. And why not? She was terrified. "But they won't help you."

"Get them. Now! *Or I will kill your damned Barky!*"

Then he was alive! Fighting to retain her self-control, Ashley gestured behind her, toward the plane. "They're in the cockpit. And...and killing Barky won't change anything. It can't help you. Please, Mr. Balaton. You haven't murdered anyone yet. Mac Stevens is still alive—and David. There's no reason this can't end now."

Despite the cold, Balaton was perspiring heavily, and Ashley found no comfort in his deteriorating self-possession. She guessed he was at least as terrified as she was, although he had the gun. She could almost feel his fear. Perhaps if she could reassure him, she thought, they had a chance.

"This will end," he said. "Believe me, it will end. The jewels, Miss Wakefield."

She shrugged. "Okay. But they won't stop the truth from coming out. Even killing everyone on this damned island won't stop that."

"What do you mean?" he demanded, lunging toward her.

Involuntarily, she took a step backward. He seemed to like that; his mouth curled with satisfaction as she twisted her hands together. Did he want her to be terrified? Or soothing? Or in control of herself, if not him? She wished she knew.

Now she could only tell the truth. "You never intended the Balaton jewels to leave Hungary, did you? You couldn't have. It was too dangerous. You see, Mr. Balaton, it's known that the Balaton jewels were stolen from Balaton Castle the night Countess Balaton and her children were slaughtered at the end of World War II."

The gun wavered. *"No!"*

It was a strangled sob more than a cry, but Ashley knew she had struck a nerve: he didn't expect her to know the story of the Balaton jewels. "It was another atrocity during an era of atrocities, but the Balaton jewels—they're the link to that night. And you have them, which means you must have been there."

"Lies—all of it."

And yet he seemed mesmerized by her words, which she was choosing carefully, hoping to get him to follow her logic. "Early in the war, young András Balaton—the *real* András Balaton—left Hungary to fight with the Resistance. You befriended his family. Your real name is József Major. You came from the same village as the Balatons."

"József Major is an identity I assumed in order to pass information to the Americans."

"No," she said in a soothing voice, "it's not. You befriended the Balatons and you betrayed them and they were shot—and you stole the Balaton jewels."

*"Lies!"*

Ashley tried to ignore the raw fear in the pit of her stomach. How far did she dare push him? He seemed weakened by her words, but if she went too far... She couldn't think about consequences now. "Mr. Balaton, I'm sure those were difficult years, and impossible for Americans like myself to understand. But the truth will come out. You see, the Balaton jewels have been examined and photographed in detail by an expert in New York; his report is in the hands of my attorney."

Balaton shut his eyes and sobbed, but the gun remained pointed at Ashley.

"Also," she went on, not challenging him, but speaking reasonably, as if they were merely arguing about the weather, "I have two photographs from the 1940s. One shows a young József Major—you—with a group of his comrades. All, including you, are wearing the uniform of the Hungarian fascist party, the Arrow Cross. The other photograph—both were sent by a Hungarian historian in charge of restoring Balaton Castle, by the way—is the only known photograph of Count Istvan Balaton and his eldest child, András. That András is clearly not you."

Balaton shuddered against her accusations. "No... stop. It's not true. I'm president of a Fortune 500 company."

The bluster, the arrogance were gone, but Ashley felt no twinge of sympathy: he still had the gun. "You know the rest, don't you?" Her voice was deadly quiet. "The real András Balaton became the *orült szerzetes*, the mad monk, after his family was murdered...and then a farmer, Bartholomew Wakefield, the man who raised my brother and me."

Balaton's eyes were barely focused. "He tried to destroy me."

"I can hardly blame him. Even if you kill him—and

me—the photographs will be released and the story of the Balaton jewels told. And the others will talk. Mac Stevens, Lillian Parker, Jeremy Carruthers, my brother. You can't kill us all to save yourself."

"Can't I?" He rallied, giving a raw, pathetic smile. "It would all be blamed on your Bartholomew Wakefield."

"I doubt that. In any case, the Coast Guard will be here any second. You won't be able to escape. Why exacerbate your situation?"

The man who for thirty years had pretended to be an aristocrat, a count, shut his eyes against the rationality of her words. Ashley didn't dare move. She knew she had him...hoped, prayed.

Then a golden-haired woman was jumping from the shadows of the trees along the edge of the runway. Tears streamed down her face as she staggered toward Balaton. "It's not true," she sobbed, tearing at her hair. "Tell me it's not true...*Daddy!*"

Sarah Balaton, Ashley thought, sagging. Had she heard everything?

"Sarah..." Balaton mouthed his daughter's name and looked at her. He swallowed, visibly pained. "This...this has nothing to do with you."

Her face was blotched from crying. "It has everything to do with me! Oh, Daddy, tell me what she says isn't true. I won't believe it if you tell me...."

Ashley knew that feeling all too well. If she had been presented with the kind of incontrovertible proof she had against the president of Crockett Industries, would she have believed Barky capable of such heinous crimes? But it was an unfair question: Barky *wasn't* capable of those things. Balaton was. Somewhere, sometime, in some small way, he had to have indicated that to his daughter.

"My Sarah," he choked out. "I love you."

He was crying, too, and in his despair he lowered his gun. Ashley thought he'd given up the struggle, but she couldn't take that chance. She lunged forward.

At the same time, the prone figure on the ground leaped up, and together she and Barky knocked down the broken, dispirited man and took away his gun. They watched him roll over in the mud and cry uncontrollably, calling his daughter's name.

Sarah Balaton knelt beside him, but although he was her father, she didn't touch him. She stared at him as if he were a creature she had never seen before and didn't understand.

Breathing heavily, bruised and shaken, Barky leaned against Ashley for support. "Forty years I have waited for this moment," he said.

"I know." Suddenly she became aware of the hot tears on her own cheeks.

Barky looked down at the man who had been responsible for the murder of the Countess Balaton and her children—his mother and his brother and sisters.

"It's over," Ashley said.

"Yes. And I feel no satisfaction."

## THIRTY-SIX

MacGregor Stevens breathed in the warm mist on the terrace, and welcomed the light scent of his wife's flowers. He'd been through hell, and he was glad to be back to this heaven. Elaine came out with a tray of lemonade, and she smiled at him so damned sweetly. And, not for the first time since he'd been transferred home from the Maine hospital, he felt himself brimming with emotion as he marveled at the miracle of her. She had every right to be done with him; he'd told her that. But she had said, "Haven't you suffered enough already, my darling?"

No, he thought, not by a long shot.

"You're thinking about them, aren't you?" She handed him a glass of fresh-squeezed lemonade and sat on the chair near him, always near him. "Ashley and David."

He smiled at her and wished this damned weakness and melancholy would just disappear. He couldn't maintain a smile, even one directed at this wonderful woman, to whom he'd finally told everything, from the beginning, when, in Vienna, he'd fallen madly, passionately, stupidly in love with Judith Land. "I never knew she was pregnant," he said now, again. "It was my fault; I should have known."

His wife leaned over and grasped his thin wrist. He'd lost so much weight during the past weeks. "Everything can't be your fault, Mac. For heaven's sake, you're human. Don't be so damned hard on yourself. Judith had plenty of opportunities to call you and tell you she was pregnant. Even after the babies were born, she could have asked you for help."

"She didn't know where I was."

"She could have found out."

He looked out across the terrace, to the Pacific Ocean, lost in the mist. "I never tried contacting her. It's possible she died thinking I was already dead... that she was joining me."

"Mac," Elaine said sharply, "she died trying to make a life for herself and her babies. No matter what she and Andrew Balaton came to, she *did* marry the man. She wasn't a goddess, Mac. She made mistakes. So did you. You were young and in circumstances beyond your depth. You did your best to do what was right. Now stop punishing yourself. If you'd known about Ashley and David, you'd have gone and fetched them, and we would have raised them."

He nodded slowly, trying to accept the wisdom of her words, and to ease his own stubborn guilt. She could forgive him for never having told her about his brief, wild love affair with a legend. But could he forgive himself for not having pursued the truth sooner? For not knowing, for the love of God, that he had children? *Twins!*

"Mac." Elaine still had her hand on his wrist, and now she massaged it tenderly, her eyes so warm, so filled with love and sympathy. Would he have forgiven her? Yes—my God, I couldn't live without her.

"Mac, Ashley and David should have the chance to know their father, and their brother and sister."

Oh, Christ! He leaned forward, sinking his head into her shoulder, and he wanted to stay there forever. He thought of Ashley, bright eyed and a wise ass, and David, dark eyed and physical, both of them brave, sturdy, kind. He could thank Bartholomew Wakefield for that. András Balaton. God, how could he expect them to want to know him!

"I just don't know if they'll want that chance, Elaine."

Jeremy Carruthers had worked furiously to catch up. He brought home work at night and weekends, earning both kudos and consternation from his father. Now, as he stood at his window looking out across the mist-enshrouded city, he could see Ashley's smile, hear her laugh, feel her soft skin under his hands. Christ! He wanted her so much.

And then he saw her face, gaunt and stricken as she had waited for word from the doctors about her uncle and her brother. She couldn't talk to him or look at him, he who had accused her uncle, believed in his own colleague and nearly destroyed her faith in herself. Don't be an ass! You both knew where your loyalties lay, and you fell in love, anyway. Had they? Or had it been just a passing fling, two people who'd needed to be reminded of their humanity, their ability to love and be loved.

Susie's shrieks came to him, again and again. "You'll do anything to make her want you. You're going to be the one obsessed. And she's going to tell you to take a fucking hike."

"Enjoy your revenge, sweet Susie," he said to the mist.

Ashley, of course, hadn't been that vicious. She had simply said, "I just need some time...distance."

Dammit, how could he blame her? How could he ask her to give anything? Even now, weeks later, he felt his chest constrict as he choked back the emotion, the passion, the love. Jesus, how he wanted to see her!

If only she had said, "I want to be with you, Jeremy. I want to sort all this out *with* you, not away from you."

But she hadn't.

Now, with every day that passed, he wondered if they were drawing further, and irrevocably, apart.

On a blustery Friday afternoon the week before Christmas, Ashley and David brought a Christmas tree in from the woods. His cast finally off, David still walked with a slight limp, but that would go away in time. Otherwise, he was healthy and overflowing with energy. In her bright red parka, Ashley was the same—on the outside. On the inside, she wasn't sure about anything. Least of all herself. And yet in so many ways she knew herself better now than she ever had.

She had stayed in Maine, at an inn, eschewing J. Land Crockett's offer to stay with him on Badger Rock, and waited until both David and Barky were released from the hospital. Neither had enjoyed being cooped up and eating institutional food, and both had made their stays as short as possible. David had suffered primarily from hypothermia and an infection in his leg; Barky had been badly bruised and had a concussion from having been pistol-whipped and kicked.

J. Land Crockett had visited every day. He never mentioned being their grandfather, never was anything but gruffly polite, and he got his pictures in the papers by trying to chase off a reporter with his walking stick. Ashley had made a wry comment about remembering his lesson on dealing with the media, and to her immeasurable surprise, he'd laughed.

She wondered how long it had been since the reclusive billionaire had laughed.

The walking stick, he had reminded her, was needed because of her "ornery uncle," who had knocked the old man over the head to keep him from getting himself killed. Ashley had told him she was familiar with Barky's methods. Nevertheless, the billionaire and the farmer had become fast friends, and they sat together in the hospital, exchanging stories.

Ashley, meanwhile, had gone about assembling the facts. She had them all, except for one.

"Why did Judith Land go to the ranch the day she died?" she asked Barky bluntly.

He sighed and lifted his shoulders in a shrug. "Judith arranged to meet him, against my advice; I had no idea what she was doing or I would have stopped her. But she never believed me when I told her the measure of treachery her husband was capable of. She thought she could talk sense into him—and, I suspect, blackmail him with the Balaton jewels. She didn't know what they meant, only that her husband wanted them a great deal and had been horrified the night she'd worn them to the Christmas ball in Vienna. When she left him, she had taken the jewels."

"Did you know that?" Ashley asked.

"No, of course not. If I had, I would have thrown them into the sea and prayed they never saw the light again."

"Balaton—Major, I mean—must have been desperate when he realized the jewels were missing."

Barky had nodded grimly. "That was another reason he was so anxious to find her. He *had* to have the jewels. I'm sure she was trying to barter them for her freedom when the horse trampled her. Until you returned from Switzerland in 1982 ready to accuse me of being a jewel thief, I had always believed József Major had gotten the jewels that day. I bided my time, hoping against all hope that the jewels would remain in their safe-deposit box forever."

"Sometimes I wish they had."

"No. It's better the truth is known."

"All those years, Major must have been terrified that one day the jewels would surface...and then they did, in the worst possible way." She winced, thinking of herself on the cover of *You.* "And he saw your picture and must have known what was happening."

"Not entirely. He had never met me until I came to him in Los Angeles. He knew me neither as András Balaton nor *orült szerzetes.*"

"So he was willing to believe you were KGB and would help him—and then David and I started meddling." She smiled. "But it's just as well, you know. You'd probably have gotten yourself arrested as an enemy spy."

He looked away. "I wouldn't have cared."

"Self-sacrifice doesn't suit you, Barky. What about

Mac Stevens? Did you know he was the father?" She couldn't say "my" father.

"No. I thought József Major was your father. And I loved you, anyway."

Now the leaves had all fallen, and there was a dusting of snow, vivid against the high blue sky. The days of early autumn seemed so long ago, and yet fresh, unfinished. Every weekend, Ashley came home to work the farm with her brother. The physical labor helped with the demons, the confusion, the memories.

They leaned the tree up against the house and went inside, where the two wood stoves were furiously pumping heat through the old house. They made coffee in the dented percolator and got out fresh oatmeal muffins.

Last week, Barky had left for Hungary—to still the walking ghosts, he'd said. He didn't know when he'd be back. Yesterday, Evan Parrington had called to arrange to have them join him and J. Land Crockett's attorneys in New York the following week. Crockett, it seemed, was taking steps to make Ashley and David his legal heirs.

"It already looks as though the bulk of his daughter's estate will come to you," he'd explained. "We're discussing enormous amounts of money, I hope you realize. I want you to understand precisely what we're doing. You should have some say in this."

Ashley had been stunned. As far as she was concerned, she had enough damned money. Too much. And David agreed with her.

"It's no use, Ash," he said now, seated across from her at the big pine table. He was eating a muffin slathered with apple butter. He had made it from some of the applesauce he and Sarah Balaton had made. Sarah, shattered by what her father was, had left Badger Rock Island without speaking to anyone. From Lillian Parker, David and Ashley had learned she had quit the vice presidency of Crockett Industries and moved to Seattle. Whatever might have been between her and David was over now. Looking at his sister, David sighed. He seemed so much older. "We can't sit here and pretend everything's normal."

"I know."

"And Crockett. Jesus. I can't even spend all the money I've got—what the hell would we do with *more* millions, Ash?"

She shook her head, saying nothing.

"I've been thinking," David went on.

She smiled. "That's a switch."

"Asshole."

They grinned at each other. The wounds were healing, Ashley thought. David was still the same brother she'd always had. "Go ahead," she said. "What were you thinking?"

He leaned back. "I figure I ought to fly down to Texas and have a talk with old man Crockett."

David left the next morning. It was colder than he expected in Houston, and he was annoyed as hell when a limousine arrived to take him out to the ranch. He sat up front and asked the chauffeur if he'd be seeing any tumbleweed. The chauffeur looked at him as if he were some kind of lunatic, and hardly said a word the entire two-hour trip.

The ranch was a hell of a spread: endless fields, white fences, gardens, roads, a huge low-slung house and no tumbleweed. He found the old man out back in a stone stable with the horses. "Hey, Pops," David said.

J. Land Crockett glanced up, looking mildly offended.

David grinned. "Nice place you got here."

"Thank you."

"Land interests me."

"Does it?" The old man moved away from a stall. "My father's father had a shack on this property in the last century. When my father struck oil on Spindletop, he bought up as much land around the shack as he could." He looked at his grandson with steely black-blue eyes. "It's always saddened me to think this place would no longer be in the Crockett family when I die."

"What you need, old man, is family, not money."

Crockett looked amused, and touched. "You think so?"

"Damned right. Land and family—what the hell else is there?"

"Nothing of any meaning," J. Land Crockett said quietly. "Is that what you came here to tell me?"

"Nope. Came here to tell you to shove your billions."

Crockett looked stricken.

David went over to his grandfather and clapped him on the shoulder. He breathed in the musty smell of the barn and was suddenly glad he'd come. "But this place... Would you mind showing me around?"

Ashley set the Christmas tree in the window overlooking the front yard, away from the potbelly stove, and she got the old cloth suitcase of decorations down out of the attic and decorated the tree herself. David was in Texas with J. Land Crockett. Barky was in Hungary. She'd had a card from him, saying he'd stolen the Balaton jewels from her and David and was donating them to the new museum at Balaton Castle. Ashley had laughed. That, at least, had seemed right. Lately so little did.

Touchstone Communications was rolling merrily along, with or without her. The New England Oceanographic Institute had come out with a report stating that the new wing was a resounding, astounding success and they all, but especially Ashley, were to be congratulated. Since she'd missed the deadline, someone else had written her column for *Currents*, saying exactly what she'd wanted to say, only better.

There was a sense of completion about her life that hadn't been there before. And also of emptiness.

Outside, snow had begun to fall. She put Mitch Miller's Christmas carols on Barky's old record player and sang "Santa Claus Is Coming to Town" while she placed cheap ornaments on the fresh tree and watched the snow and cried.

Damn, you're getting sentimental....

She'd been invited to dozens of Christmas parties. There were literally hundreds of places to go, thousands of people who would love to have the dolphin-rescuing, hot-shit mystery daughter of Judith Land over to see them.

She thought of warmth. She thought of family and love and happiness. David had already called: he and J. Land Crockett were getting along famously, already plotting ways to improve the ranch.

David was in Texas. Barky was in Hungary. Mac Stevens—my father—was in San Diego.

And so was Jeremy. What was he?

The man she loved.

They were both in San Diego, and suddenly she couldn't stand the idea of not seeing them. She didn't know if either of them would want to see her. Perhaps they'd forgotten those crazy days in October...or wanted to forget.

But she had to try. She had to know.

When he got home from work on Christmas Eve and walked out onto his deck, Jeremy's heart skipped several beats, and he had to stop himself from lurching forward, grabbing her. He was afraid she would prove to be only thin air, a vision.

She was wearing one of her jumpsuits, a short one, bright fuchsia. And she was barefoot. A slender leg was thrown over one arm of the deck chair, and her hair was shining in the afternoon sun. She'd cut it to shoulder length; it made her look even sassier.

Papers, maps and charts were strewn all over his table.

"Ashley." It was just a breath.

But she turned sideways and smiled up at him. Her eyes were even brighter, more vivid than he remembered. He felt a stirring of a deep, familiar passion. She was so goddamned sexy. Christ, his life had been empty without her.

"Hello, Jeremy," she said, still smiling. "I stole some o.j. out of your fridge."

"What're you doing here?"

She shrugged. "Studying charts."

Charts. "Why?"

"I've decided to fund a research project on marine archaeology in the Pacific. There must be some interesting ships sunk around here—something. Anyway, my friend Nelle Milligan's thrilled."

He couldn't concentrate on what she was saying. Were they just friends? Didn't she know what she was doing to him? He moved toward her. "Is this an institute project?"

She shook her head. "A new outfit."

"Oh. I—"

"Based in San Diego. We're calling it the Crockett Foundation. I'm supposed to be chairman of the board and president. It'll mean relocating to the West Coast, but what the hell, I could use a change." She pulled her lips together and nodded decisively. "I'm selling Touchstone. Caroline's buying it."

He wanted to jump up and yell, but she was acting so damned funny. Why? What was on her mind? He said cautiously, "Why San Diego?"

This time when she looked at him, he saw the fear in her eyes. "Because you're here."

He grinned as the relief and joy washed over him. "That's all I need to hear."

The fear vanished in her eyes, leaving only the brightness. "Is it? Don't you want to hear that I've fallen hopelessly in love with you?"

"Not hopelessly, Ashley."

It was all he could bring himself to say. They ran to each other then and clung together in the fading sunlight. Nothing had ever felt so right to him, Jeremy thought. She was strong willed and direct and argumentative...and so was he.

"We'll make a hell of a pair," he said.

"Damned right." She laughed into his eyes. "We're both blunt and cantankerous. You don't want me for my money, do you?"

"It's the only strike against you."

"But can you live with it?"

He laughed. "I can handle it."

She held his hands and stood back from him, just looking at him and smiling. "Well. I think I'm going to like San Diego."

"I'd come to Boston."

"I know you would. But I'm looking forward to the change. It'll be good. No one really knows me here, and with the new foundation...there's so much work to be done."

There wasn't even the slightest question in her eyes that he would—or should—mind that she was a compulsive worker. He liked that. He grinned at her. "Do you suppose you can break for Christmas?"

"Oh, longer than that. It'll take months to work out all the details for the foundation. I'm just thinking and planning."

"Does that mean you're free for dinner?" he asked, pulling her toward him.

"Yes, but if you already have plans—"

"I can include you in them." His arms encircled her waist, and he smelled the light scent of her. "You're wonderful. I love you."

She kissed him lightly. "Good."

"I'm supposed to be at the annual family Christmas Eve dinner in thirty minutes. Think you can be ready?"

"Jeremy—"

"It's all right." He held her tightly and was unable to understand how he had tolerated the bleak weeks without her. "My father's dying to meet you, and you'll love my mother. I'll call and have them set an extra place."

"You're sure they won't mind?"

"Of course not."

"It'll be just family?"

"Us and the Stevenses. We get together every year." He saw the cloud come over her face. "Ashley, it's all right. Mac wants to see you."

She looked pained. "But after everything that's happened...I wouldn't want to spoil his Christmas. And Elaine—"

"Ashley—good God. Every day Mac asks if I've heard from you. Every day I see the pain in him, the longing just to know you. And Elaine—she knows you and David are a part of Mac, and she's too secure in her love for him and too damned sure of herself to be threatened by you." Jeremy sighed, wanting desperately to make her understand. "Ashley...they want to know you."

The cloud vanished, and she couldn't seem to stop smiling. "Give me a few minutes to get ready."

On Christmas morning, Mac stopped by the little house in Coronado. Ashley had put away her maps and her charts and her papers and was having a late brunch with Jeremy on the deck. They hadn't gotten much sleep last night. It was a wonderful Christmas, she thought. She had never been so happy.

When he saw Mac, Jeremy made an excuse to go inside, leaving them alone. Mac sat across from Ashley.

For a man so strong and intelligent and handsome, he seemed awkward and ill at ease.

"Good morning," she said with a smile. "Merry Christmas."

"Merry Christmas." He cleared his throat then, and from inside his jacket pocket he withdrew a small unwrapped case and handed it to her. "I want you to have this."

She opened it. Inside was a cameo brooch, simple, beautiful. She couldn't speak. Looking at MacGregor Stevens, she saw the slight but distinct tremble in his hands.

"It...it was my mother's," he said. "Your grandmother's. I had planned to give it to your mother. Somehow it seemed wrong, after she died, to give it to Elaine. I want you to have it."

Tears welled in Ashley's eyes, and she had to lay the case in her lap. Her hands were shaking. She looked up at MacGregor Stevens. "Thank you...Father."

# EPILOGUE

Bartholomew Wakefield didn't return from Hungary until late that winter. The moment he arrived, he walked up to the barn and looked out across the snow-covered fields. Hungary was a different country now. This place was home. He could tell Iggy had been minding the farm: nothing was as clean as it should be. But that would change in time. He was back now.

Soon there would be planting to do, he thought. Spring would come.

He had talked to Ashley and David from Budapest, telling them he thought it was good they had separated from the farm. They were adults now; they had their own lives to lead. His faith in them remained firm. Ashley would be marrying Jeremy Carruthers in May, in the side yard, she'd said, when the apple trees were in blossom. That was good, Barky thought. And she wanted him to stand on one side of her and MacGregor Stevens on the other. That had touched him, and for the first time in many years, he had let the tears stream down his leathery old cheeks.

And David. David had his land. In time, he would find love...and if he were smart, he would recognize it when it came. And seize it. And never let go. That was

David. He wouldn't let happiness slip through his fingers.

Not like the man who had raised him had, so long ago.

But that was all right, he thought. He had his chickens, his pigs, his sheep, his fields. There was always work to be done.

As he turned back to the house, he noticed the thin line of pale gray smoke coming from the chimney, and he swore to himself. Iggy was irresponsible; he'd gone off and left the fire in the wood stove burning. Shaking his head in disgust, Barky stumped down to the house.

But there was a woman in his kitchen. She was wearing one of his sweaters, the shoulder seams drooping halfway to her elbows, and expensive corduroy pants, but her eyes were as clear and turquoise as he remembered.

"Lillian." The door shut hard behind him and he found that he couldn't move. His voice caught. "Lil."

She was standing over the cook stove, and she turned and smiled nervously at him, as she had thirty years ago in the old stone church, only now there were lines in her face, around her eyes, but her hair was still that arresting shade of auburn. He had dreamed about it many times over the years.

"I'm baking beans," she said.

He smiled. "You are."

"Indeed. My grandmother once taught me how—it was the only thing she knew how to cook—and I've never forgotten, since it's the only thing *I* know how to cook. How do they smell?"

"Burned."

She laughed. "Well, it's all because of this damned wood stove. I'm not a pioneer, you know."

The smile left Barky's worn face. "Lillian...why are you here?"

She laid her wooden spoon on the pine table. "I'm on leave from my job," she said quietly, not looking at him. "I rode out the scandal...sort of. All these years, I thought the whole world would laugh their asses off if they knew what I'd done. As it turns out, people have been pretty understanding. But, of course, I'm part of a major story now—and I'm being stubborn and making enemies because I still refuse to discuss Judith Land. So it seemed best just to leave. I don't know what I'll tackle next. Maybe pigs and chickens?" She looked at him now. "For a while, anyway."

There was uncertainty in her eyes, he saw. And then, as he laughed and walked to her, there was hope.

# Take 3 of
## "The Best of the Best™"
## Novels FREE
### Plus get a FREE surprise gift!

## Special Limited-time Offer

**Mail to The Best of the Best™**

### 3010 Walden Avenue
### P.O. Box 1867
### Buffalo, N.Y. 14240-1867

**YES!** Please send me 3 free novels and my free surprise gift. Then send me 3 of "The Best of the Best™" novels each month. I'll receive the best books by the world's hottest romance authors. Bill me at the low price of $3.99 each plus 25¢ delivery per book and applicable sales tax, if any.* That's the complete price and a savings of over 20% off the cover prices—quite a bargain! I understand that accepting the books and gift places me under no obligation ever to buy any books. I can always return a shipment and cancel at any time. Even if I never buy another book, the 3 free books and the surprise gift are mine to keep forever.

183 BPA A4V9

| Name | (PLEASE PRINT) | |
|------|----------------|---|
| Address | | Apt. No. |
| City | State | Zip |

This offer is limited to one order per household and not valid to current subscribers.
*Terms and prices are subject to change without notice. Sales tax applicable in N.Y. All orders subject to approval.

UB08-197

©1996 MIRA BOOKS

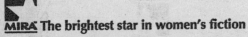

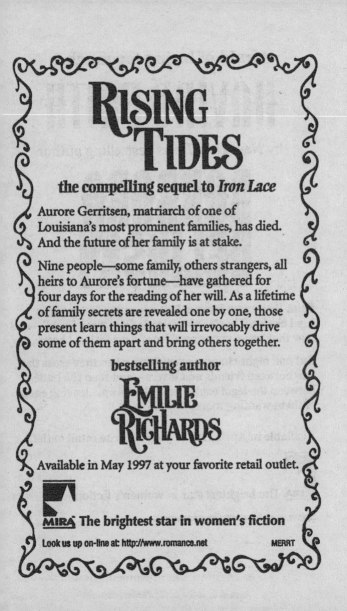

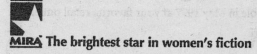

*New York Times* bestselling author

# LINDA HOWARD

*as this the man she'd married...or a total stranger?*

When Jay Granger is escorted by the FBI to the bedside
of her injured ex-husband, she is unprepared for her
own reaction—something is different about him.
Although he doesn't remember anything, his effect on
her is intense...sensual...uncontrollable. And each day
as he grows stronger, he gains back more of his life.
including Jay.

Linda Howard delivers a suspenseful and emotional
story of love and deception...

# WHITE LIES

Available in May 1997 at your favorite retail outlet.

**MIRA** The brightest star in women's fiction

Look us up on-line at: http://www.romance.net

MLH4

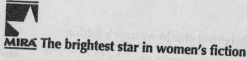